Morning Missed

Bromley Coughlan

authorHOUSE®

AuthorHouse™ UK
1663 Liberty Drive
Bloomington, IN 47403 USA
www.authorhouse.co.uk
Phone: 0800.197.4150

Published by AuthorHouse 12/05/2016

ISBN: 978-1-5246-6679-8 (sc)
ISBN: 978-1-5246-6678-1 (e)

Acknowledgements

Call it self-indulgence, or perhaps even arrogance, but I (or more correctly 'we') have been persuaded to put pen to paper once more and continue the adventures of Marcus Edge.

After *Scorpion's Tale* was (self) published, my wife and I are under no illusion that novel writing will not bring us fame and fortune. The writing was the easiest, and most enjoyable, part of the process. Selling and marketing is much more time consuming than we ever considered, and waiting for the first reviews was tortuous. Despite the various glitches, inconsistencies and split-infinitives, the book was well received and the whole journey was great fun. So, whilst there are still boxes of *Scorpion's Tale* still to be sold, after another five years here we go again.

Holidays and long plane journeys passed in a flash, and during the process only one book from the pile on my beside table was read, with the rest still gathering dust – especially as my wife now has a kindle. Halfway through the process the 'difficult second album' syndrome became apparent, and there was a period of writers block, but after no small amount of badgering and remodelling the second book is now complete. *BC*

Part 1

The Awakening

The lights coming towards us were blinding and I couldn't see the road ahead. The horn of the lorry in front was blowing continuously, getting closer every second, and now only one car's distance away. I briefly glanced forward. In that split second I realised that the lights were from the headlights of a string of powerful lights on the top of the cabin of the lorry bearing down on us. There was no way to pass the lorry on the narrow road. I slammed on the brakes, and slew the Range Rover onto the right-hand verge.

"Hang on Jimmy!" I screamed at the top of my voice over the roar of the engine as the wheels lost friction with the road.

Trees were rushing towards us, I threw the steering wheel wildly to the left and the car started to respond, but then careered broadside towards the trees. Only a few metres from the trees we hit something very solid behind the driver's door. The car turned onto its right side at the same time pointing it forward, the roof grazed a large tree as we slid past, the engine screaming as the wheels lost contact with the ground. I was powerless to be able to stop the car sliding across the ground and over an incline down a ravine. Trees were flashing past the windows, any moment we were bound to hit a tree, but instead the car turned onto the roof. The momentum increased with the car rolling back onto the passenger's side onto its wheels again, but it didn't stop; over and over again the car rolled and then nothing; I blacked-out.

All I could hear was the noise of dripping, nothing else. Was I awake or was I hallucinating? I tried opening my eyes but the lids wouldn't part. I felt sick and disorientated. I felt the blood pumping in my head. I lost consciousness again.

As soon as I woke the nausea returned, as did the sense of helplessness and disorientation, but this time something was pervading my sense of smell. It was not a wholly unpleasant odour, but my brain was registering danger, whilst the incessant 'plip-plop' of the dripping continued.

I made a renewed effort to open my eyes, but with little success, although on this occasion I knew that they were gummed together. Instinctively I realised it was blood. It was the same sensation I had felt five years earlier, after I had been beaten senseless by my father-in-law's factotum. I presumed the blood was from a wound on my head, which had dried over my eyes.

I tried bringing my hands to my face, but my arms were pinned behind my head, and something was preventing me from moving them forward. I stopped moving and tried to think where I was, but nothing came to me. 'Plip-plop' was all I could hear and it seemed that those two-toned sounds drove every other thought from my head.

"Help!" I tried shouting, but it was only a loud croak, rather than an audible cry for assistance. My tongue was resting on the roof of my saliva-less mouth, which seemed odd, and blood was pounding in my ears. I cleared my throat the best I could, and tried shouting again. "Help! For god's sake help me!" It sounded much louder at the beginning, but trailed away to a whisper, and I doubted that anyone would hear me from the confined space of the Range Rover.

The exertion had momentarily banished the 'plip-plop' from my thoughts, and when they returned the tempo and sound had changed their resonance. It was obvious that the pool of liquid had enlarged. 'What was that smell?' I said to myself. It was familiar but my head was fuzzy. Petrol!

"Shit!" I swore to myself and started to struggle again. Why wouldn't my arms move? Why was blood in my eyes? Why did I feel so sick and disorientated?

I took a deep breath through my nose to relax and think, but instead I inhaled something gooey, and it lodged in my wind-pipe. Instantly I started to choke. Whatever was blocking my wind-pipe wasn't clearing. If anything the choking had lodged it more firmly in my throat. I retched. I coughed. I coughed much harder again, and felt a massive familiar pain in the right-side of my chest.

"Ahhhhhh!" It was an animal's scream. It was also the best thing I could have done, because I had dislodged the mucus from my throat and my right eye opened.

I was coughing again, less violently than before, as though a crumb had 'gone the wrong way' as my Mother would chide me. I still could not see where I was, because it was dark outside, but there was enough luminance for me to tell that I was upside-down. The Range Rover was old, but had been specially strengthened by Overfinch for my former father-in-law, for which I was now eternally grateful. I never knew exactly all the modifications, but I did know that the cost of the modifications were as much as the original price of the car. He was paranoid about his security, which was not surprising as he was not only a very wealthy shipping magnet, and owner of a number of companies – including a successful Lloyd's Insurance Broker – but also he was planning a military coup in Zimbabwe. The irony was that he was killed by something – or rather someone – from his car. His chauffeur come man-servant stabbed him to death with an African spear, the factotum who had beaten me senseless.

With events of the past flashing through my mind, I hoped that one of the security features fitted by my former father-in-law might be an automatic fire extinguisher, because the 'plip-plop' was continuing, ever relentlessly, no faster, no slower.

I rotated my eyes upwards and could just about make out that the roof of the car had been partially crushed, and was only a couple of centimetres above my head. Somehow my arms were behind my head, and were pinned back by the roof of the car. I had been thrown up against the door pillar, and I tried leaning into it further, whilst trying to move my left hand sideways. I screamed again when it moved, and I suspected it was fractured in one or more places, but it moved. Slowly, and painfully, I brought my left hand to my face. I wiped away the vomit and blood from my eyes.

My eyes were adjusting to the darkness and my night vision was improving, and then I retched again, as I saw the lifeless body of Jimmy Black lolling in the seat beside me.

Poor Jimmy. He was always so eager to help me, even when I was *persona non grata* in Lloyd's of London. Jimmy was an insurance broker at Lloyd's Brokers Judge Palmer & Gown, which I inherited following the deaths of my former father-in-law and estranged wife. As soon as he knew I was in need of assistance he jumped to help me, and now he was dead, leaving behind a wife and young son Johnny.

"What have I done?" I wailed.

I looked down at my hands and saw I had wiped away from my eyes a mixture of dry and uncongealed blood. I reasoned that I had been unconscious for a while.

The 'plip-plop' of petrol remained unerringly constant, and I could now make out that the windscreen had cracked and it was out of its mountings on the driver's side of the car. I guessed that the flammable liquid was dripping onto the underside of the up-turned bonnet. The car was not lying solely on the roof, but was tipped forwards being supported by the front edge of the bonnet, which should mean the liquid would eventually run out of the front of the car. The electrics were off, so no petrol should be pumped from the fuel tank.

Where was I? I tried recalling what happened, but my mind was blank, and my head hurt.

Was Jimmy really dead? I needed to get out of the car and check Jimmy. My right arm was trapped by the collapsed roof, so I tried bringing my left arm across my body to open the door. As soon as I moved my arm the pain around my collar bone was excruciating and I couldn't even get close to touching the door handle.

Why had I not been found? At that moment I heard an engine, it was some distance away, and sounded like a lorry revving in low gears. I strained to see any lights.

"Low gears." I spoke to myself. Why would a lorry be revving in low gears? It could be a junction, or perhaps a hill? A sharp bend on a hill, some vague memory, was I driving too fast and misjudged a corner?

"Yes," again to myself "I came off the road and rolled down an incline." That's why no-one can see me.

Where was my mobile phone? Usually I would put it back into my right-hand jacket pocket, after enabling the 'hands-free' function. With no electrics I could not operate the 'hands-free'. I tried feeling for the phone in my left-hand pocket, just in case I had put there, but there was nothing and the pain in my shoulder was horrific every time I moved my arm.

I felt so useless. Jimmy might be dead, but he might be alive, and I felt helpless to save him. I resigned myself to having to wait until morning, and hope that I would be found by someone, unless of course the petrol ignited, when both Jimmy and I would be cremated. Rather than panic, I resigned myself to the fact that my fate was not in my hands, and this resignation meant I drifted unwillingly into a restless sleep.

Figures with no faces appeared in my dreams. They were clawing at the door of the car.

"Get away" I shouted "there's petrol leaking everywhere!" Then a sensation of falling as I lost consciousness for the third time.

I screamed in pain as I woke up. The door of the car was open. I had been released from my seat belt, and I was being manhandled out of the car. Dawn had broken, but even in the morning sun I still couldn't see the faces of my rescuers. They were wearing hoodies, with the hoods up covering a baseball cap, plus they wore scarves across their faces. All I could see were their eyes as they carried me through the woods.

"Jimmy," I shouted "please check on Jimmy."

"He's dead." Came the reply.

At that point there was an explosion, I realised that the petrol had ignited, whether by accident or deliberately I couldn't tell. I went limp with the thought of Jimmy in his fiery metal coffin.

I saw that we were coming out of the trees and were heading towards the rear of a lorry parked in a lay-by. The door of the lorry opened as we approached and I saw someone standing in the lorry with a mask around his face and a hypodermic needle in his hand.

"Let's make you more comfortable, Mr Edge."

The man pulled up my sleeve as we entered the lorry and, within seconds of him plunging the needle into my arm, I was asleep.

Two Days Earlier

The morning mist was still noticeable at eight o'clock as I edged my Range Rover out of the parking at Stansted Airport. The late March sun was trying its best to burn off the mist, which had been much thicker when I left London an hour and a half earlier. It was a day before the start of the Easter school holidays and I had brought Gerda my wife and four-year-old twins - Jack and Catherine - to the airport this Friday morning to avoid the crowds that would be thronging to the airport the following day. My family were flying to Schiphol near Amsterdam, where they would be met by Gerda's brother, and taken to Vieland for three weeks.

Gerda and the children loved their time with Uncle Paul, on Vieland, one of the West Frisian Islands (or Wadden Eilnaden to give them their native name). Paul did not have children of his own, and would spoil his niece and nephew terribly. Paul nearly died six years before, and although he recovered after being in a coma for over a year, he was never quite the same as before the accident which put him in hospital. It wasn't as though he bought the twins lavish gifts, or showered them with money or presents, he spoilt them with his time. He was a tireless entertainer, and they were never bored, on occasions it had crossed my mind that they needed a holiday to recuperate from their time with Paul. Very little time was spent off the island with lots of outdoor activity. The only rule - upon which Paul was adamant - was that they must only speak Dutch when they were on the island. Whilst this was difficult at first for the children - and nearly impossible for me - they were quick learners. I too was pleased that Paul was taking such a pastoral interest in his niece's and nephew's upbringing. Whilst I really enjoyed spending my time with them all on Vieland, I realised they needed their own space, particularly Gerda who missed not living in Holland. I would not join them on this holiday until the last week of their trip on Vieland, when I would drive over to the island spending a week with them - the children whispering conspiratorially to me in English when Paul was out of hearing - and then we would all spend a week in Center Parcs, Zandvoort, before returning home to London.

So now I would return to London on my own in the wispy mist of an early spring morning. My right foot was firmly braced on the accelerator as I increased my speed towards the M11 motorway, and in my quiet cocoon I started to think of what my day would hold for me when I arrived at my office, in less than an hour. I was startled out of my pensive thoughts by the sound of my mobile phone ringing. 'The Hall' flashed up on my hands free display.

"Hello K-P," I greeted my best friend and colleague jovially "aren't you at work yet?"

I owed my life to K-P as he literally saved my life five years earlier, when my then father-in-law's factotum tried to kill me at The Hall. After I inherited The Hall I persuaded K-P, together with Jane his fiery red-headed wife and their four children, to live as my permanent guests at The Hall. K-P totally adored Jane, and Jane kept K-P on the straight and narrow. I paid for all the running costs and maintenance for the Victorian mansion house, which was the least I could do for K-P saving my life, as well as his support when I was considered a pariah in the London Insurance Market.

"It's not K-P!" Jane's high pitched voice clearly indicated that she was not a happy person.

"Hello Jane." I replied nervously.

"Was he out with you last night?" Jane continued in an accusatory tone.

"No, I haven't seen him since lunchtime yesterday; we shared a sandwich in the office."

"You don't know where he is then?" Jane's voice sounded even more strained as though it might crack. "He didn't come home last night and his mobile phone is diverting directly to his voicemail. He always keeps in touch. He has never ever not phoned me!"

I made a late decision not to turn onto the M11 and braking I cut across the chevrons and was able to just take the turning for Bishop's Stortford. Luckily the roads were relatively empty as my manoeuvre would have earned the disapproval and no doubt a few curses of anyone driving behind me.

"Jane, I am near Stansted Airport and will be with you in fifteen minutes."

As soon as the call with Jane ended I punched in the speed dial for K-P's direct line at JPG hoping that K-P was at his desk. I was trained as an Insurance Broker at JPG, before I left to join a global broking house - Intercontinental. Whilst I was working at Intercontinental I was - unjustly - banned by Lloyd's of London, during which there was a tumultuous two-week period of my life. I was redeemed and proved innocent at the cost of several lives, including my estranged wife, her boyfriend, her father, her mother, her grandfather, her illegitimate half-brother and his mother. Upon their deaths I inherited a Lloyd's Insurance Broker (JPG), majority shareholding in my father-in-law's shipping company, The Hall near Bishop's Stortford, a flat in Docklands, a suite of offices in St. James's in London's West End, as well as a large pile of cash and tracts of land in Zimbabwe and Goa.

The land in Zimbabwe and Goa was basically worthless, but everything else made me a multi-millionaire overnight. I sold the flat in Docklands, as well as the offices in St. James's, and bought a flat in Tredegar Square near Mile End in East London. Tredegar Square had been built by the merchants of East London to ape the fine squares of West London. Unlike a lot of the fine homes Tredegar Square survived intact during the blitz of London during World War Two. I thought Tredegar Square appropriate as a marital home for myself and Gerda. I, like the merchantmen of East London, came from a humble background; coming into my fortune unexpectedly and surviving my own blitz.

I head-hunted a Chief Executive from another shipping firm to head the shipping company I now controlled, and I only attended Board Meetings, the Audit Committee and Shareholders' Meetings as the Non-Executive Chairman. I loved insurance broking and became Chief Executive at JPG, installing John Eastwood - my former mentor - as Chairman.

K-P and I met while broking in Lloyd's of London and whilst playing rugby for Lloyd's Rugby Club. We had been through thick and thin together, and often if I was uncertain about a particular issue I would turn to K-P whose analytical mind could look at most problems from a different point of view. He was - in my opinion - a great loss to Her Majesty's Royal Navy, in which he served only a short time. He was best man at both my weddings, and I was his when he married Jane. He had always worked at a rival Lloyd's Broker to me, but as soon as I took over the reins at JPG I started to woo him to join JPG.

He was fiercely loyal and tenacious, which I knew only too well when he saved my life. This quality also meant he was not going to be easily prised away from his employer, but this concerned Jane that he would be totally beholden to me, so I drew up an agreement that K-P, Jane and their family could live in The Hall for as long as they were both alive. Also I was god-father to their eldest child, so if anything were to happen to K-P and Jane, they knew that they could rely upon me to look after the children. So after months of appeasing Jane's concerns I eventually persuaded K-P to join JPG as Managing Director of our Special Risks Division. Initially he was worried that he did not know the other classes of insurance business, beyond his sole knowledge of Marine risks. He needn't have been concerned, because within weeks of joining JPG he was relishing the challenges of the weird and unusual risks that belonged to his fiefdom. By far his favourite type of risks were the Special Contingency covers including Kidnap, Ransom, Expropriation and Confiscation. K-P was unusually tall and muscular for a person whose forebears originally hailed from the Indian sub-continent via East Africa, and his mere size plus military background was reassuring for Special Contingency clients, together with his charm which he used to good effect when negotiating with both clients and underwriters alike.

He breathed life into a hitherto unprofitable division of JPG, placing facilities that would take on risks that other parts of the firm would shy away from. After only a few months a number of employees from other divisions were asking if there were any openings in K-P's area. So I wasn't surprised that if K-P didn't answer his telephone, someone else would, and that 'someone' else was often Jimmy Black.

"Hello, Jimmy Black speaking. Can I help you?" It was the voice of K-P's reliable number two. Jimmy had been my own broker at JPG, when I needed someone to purchase insurance for my unsuccessful claims investigation business, after I had been banned by Lloyd's. He was my choice to assist K-P and the two of them got along famously.

"It's Marc, what are you doing in so early?"

"Hi Marc, the baby was awake early this morning so after feeding her I came into work and I was hoping to slip away shortly after lunch."

I could swear that he was stifling a yawn. The baby's wakefulness would account for the tiredness in his voice rather than the fact he had been out on a drinking binge with K-P.

"That's of course if it's OK with K-P."

"Is K-P not in the office yet?" I asked casually.

"No," came Jimmy's reply "do you want me to pass him a message when he comes in?"

I hesitated and thought about telling him that K-P had not gone home last night. I decided not to do so and changed tack. "Do you know where K-P went yesterday evening?" Again I tried to make it seem an innocent question.

I obviously stirred a concern that all was not well because Jimmy's tone noticeably changed. "Is there a problem Marc?"

"Well it may be nothing, but Jane just rang to say K-P didn't make it home last night."

The words were hardly out of my mouth when Jimmy's voice escalated by at least two octaves. "Jane will have his guts-for-garters."

"Exactly." I concurred.

"Marc, give me a sec please?" Jimmy put the phone down and I could hear him opening drawers. "There's nothing on his desk, or in his desk drawers, but I am sure he said he was going to meet with a new prospect yesterday afternoon, and by the state of his desk he didn't come back because his computer hasn't been turned off."

"Does he usually turn it off?"

"Always," Jimmy replied "he is meticulous."

"Hmm" was my less than insightful response.

"Marc, give me twenty minutes and I will call you back."

"Thanks. I am going to see Jane now, as I have just dropped Gerda and the twins at Stansted Airport."

"Ok, speak soon." Jimmy hung up and I guessed he would be onto Gupta our IT manager (or Chief Information Officer as he liked to be called) to see if he could get access to K-P's email and calendar.

Gupta was a miracle worker when it came to IT issues, and looked about eighteen years of age. He was in fact nearly thirty and had a Batchelor and Masters' Degree from UEA in Norwich, and met my parents by chance and they suggested that he reach out to me. I met him for coffee and in less than fifteen minutes I offered him a job as Assistant IT manager. Within six months, our existing Head of IT resigned as he felt so uncomfortable about this young man challenging him at every turn and was usually right. After a couple of hours of hard negotiation, I persuaded the Head of IT to stay, and gave Gupta the Chief Information Officer role. There was an uneasy partnership between the two of them and eventually the Head of IT resigned again to move to another post. I let him go this time, learning a valuable lesson – again – that whenever someone resigned, don't try and talk them out of it.

In less than fifteen minutes after speaking to Jimmy, I was turning into the long drive that led to The Hall. It was a large and unattractive building. I reflected that if K-P and his family had not agreed to live in The Hall, I would probably have sold it for a low price, as The Hall held very few good memories for me. What few that remained, were totally obliterated by my near death experience and my former father-in-law's violent end.

The door of The Hall swung open and Jane was at my car door before the Range Rover had even stopped.

"Marc, where is he?" Jane's eyes were red and any tears were most probably due to anger and frustration.

"I don't know," I replied in all truthfulness "and Jimmy is checking to see who he was meeting yesterday afternoon. Apparently it was a potential new client."

Jane nodded and I felt sure the tears would flow freely again if she spoke, so I filled the pause by asking if the children were alright. On sounder ground she pulled herself up to her full height and said that the three older children were at school and that the youngest was being looked after by Jane's cleaner come home-help.

"Did K-P say anything about where he would be going yesterday? Or what time he would be home?" I asked.

"No, just that he had a meeting and that he would be back at his normal time. When he didn't appear I presumed the two of you had bumped into each other and, being thirsty Thursday, you had gone out on a session." Jane paused before continuing "It wouldn't have been the first time - would it?"

I smiled wanly and an uncomfortable silence descended. "Come on make me a cup of tea while we wait for Jimmy to call back."

I thought Jane was going to shout at me as her face reddened, but she obviously thought tea was the most practical solution, and she turned on her heel and walked back into The Hall.

Dominique

Jane and I were sitting in silence in the kitchen of The Hall, waiting for my phone to ring. We were both shocked when it was the house phone of The Hall which rang instead. Jane leapt to answer it.

"Hello." I could not read her face as she listened intently to whoever was speaking to her. Then without a word, she passed the phone over to me.

"Hello?" I said.

"Good morning Mar.," It was John Eastwood, the Chairman of JPG, who was in early as he was almost every Friday so that he could leave early to drive to the country for the weekend. "Jimmy told me what was going on. So I just wanted to reassure Jane that we are doing everything to find out who K-P was meeting yesterday and where."

"Thank you John. That's very considerate of you. Have you been able to open K-P's e-mail and electronic calendar yet?"

"Just now, and, before you ask, it is not very enlightening. The only entry for yesterday afternoon was *Dominique. Grange City.*"

"What time was the entry in his diary for? And for how long?" I added quickly.

"Four o'clock for an hour." John replied.

"Well, we should be able to track that quite quickly."

"I hope so" John's reply was non-committal "and I have sent Jimmy there straight away."

John Eastwood's son, Tony, had also been killed by my former father-in-law's factotum. Tony and I had not got along, which wasn't surprising as I whisked Mercédès, to whom Tony

16

felt betrothed, right from under his nose; and when Mercédès and I separated, Tony stepped back in before he was killed. I was suspect number one for Tony's death until the whole sorry episode unravelled. John Eastwood was running JPG when I started Insurance Broking and when I inherited JPG I asked him to stay on as Chairman. Although he was deeply hurt by the death of his son, he accepted it was not of my doing, and he agreed to my proposal. A very safe pair of hands in a crisis, he was the ideal Chairman for JPG - as he was proving today.

"Jimmy will call you on your mobile phone, as soon as he finds out any information, which is why I phoned Jane."

"Thanks again, John." We spoke briefly about another matter and I finished the call saying that I would stay with Jane for the rest of the morning.

As I put down the phone, Jane was boiling the kettle again.

"More tea?" Jane's complexion was paler now than before, and it was a remarkable contrast with her fiery red hair. A tall thin figure, Jane was more than a match for K-P.

"Yes please," I replied, "Jimmy is on his way to the Grange City where K-P had his appointment yesterday afternoon."

"John told me that already." Jane's voice was strained again.

"Did K-P ever mention the name Dominique?" I asked.

Jane's eyes flashed and her skin reddened again, "No, who is she?" her voice increasing in volume word by word.

"I don't know if it is a woman or a man," I quickly tried to diffuse Jane's anger "it's just a name in his diary."

Jane was not convinced and it was lucky that the mugs for the tea did not break as she slammed them down on the table, tea flying in all directions. Jane ran out of the kitchen, and I was left on my own. The kitchen of The Hall had always been the most social and friendliest room in the house, and K-P's family spent most of their time in this room. It was warm and unpretentious, unlike the rest of the house.

I sat drinking the remainder of the tea in my mug, and it was a few minutes before I realised that Jane was leaning against the doorway behind me.

"Jane." I started.

"Marc, I'm sorry" she apologised "it's just that I love K-P so much and he has never ever not phoned me to tell me where he is," she smiled "even it if means I will be furious with him when he comes home. I am worried Marc, especially with all the heightened security tension surrounding the terrorist attacks in Europe last year."

"Don't worry he is always careful. Not foolish like me." I tried to lighten the mood but it only sounded patronizing.

"Sorry." I added after a silence.

"I told K-P that I wanted him to come home early today because the children finish term at lunchtime, and we would do something to celebrate tonight." Jane was gazing past me as she was talking "Perhaps a barbecue in the kitchen garden if this warm March weather holds."

"Do you like living here?" I asked randomly.

She turned towards me and fixed me with a stare "Why do you ask?"

"No particular reason, except I didn't really give you much of a choice."

"No you didn't but you meant well, and it is fantastic for the children, so safe and clean compared to London." Jane smiled for the second time since I arrived that morning.

"Would you never want to…?" My question was interrupted by my mobile.

Jimmy's name was shown on the display "Jimmy, any news?"

"Well, not much progress at all I'm afraid" Jimmy started "I have established that there was no-one with the name of Dominique, staying at any of the Grange hotels in London this week."

"Did you check 'Dominic' as well as 'Dominique'?" I said the two names phonetically.

"Yes I did" replied Jimmy "but the Concierge who was on duty yesterday at four o'clock is not around until noon today."

"OK." My mind was whirring as to why someone would make an appointment at a hotel when they were not staying there, but then of course 'Dominique' may not have been their real name.

"What should I do now Marc?" Jimmy enquired.

"Go back to work and see if we can get a list of telephone numbers K-P rang from his office phone; also contact the mobile network to ask for details of all calls to and from his mobile over the last week. I am going to make a couple of calls from here and then I will join you at the Grange City at noon to speak to the Concierge."

"OK, see you here at noon." Jimmy hung up and I turned to Jane who knew there was no news.

"Go back to London Marc." Jane was trying to appear calm, and I think she wanted to be alone before facing her children with no K-P.

I was just leaving the kitchen when my phone rang again, it was Jimmy.

"Yes Jimmy."

"It's Mr Dominique! The Concierge came in early and remembers K-P asking him to page a Mr Dominique yesterday at quarter past four." Jimmy hardly drew breath as he gave me his news.

"Anything else?" I asked.

19

"The Concierge can't be sure but thought he saw K-P leave with a well-dressed sun-tanned man about five minutes after he paged Mr Dominique."

"I am on my way back now Jimmy, and I will see you in the office in an hour." I hung up and went back into the kitchen.

"Jane, Jane?" I called into the entrance hall as there was no sign of her in the kitchen.

"Yes Marc." Jane re-appeared at the top of the stairs.

"It is a Mr Dominique, and Jimmy has confirmed that K-P met with him after four o'clock and then left shortly afterwards."

"Where to?" She asked.

"No idea yet, but I am going to meet Jimmy at the office as soon as I am back in London."

"Find him for me Marc, please, find him." Jane looked the most vulnerable I have ever seen her.

"I promise." I hoped that I would make good that promise.

I was on the M11 in twelve minutes flying down the motorway at least ten to fifteen miles an hour over the speed limit. After thirty minutes I slowed down, for the speed camera in the lower fifty miles an hour speed limit, just before the end of the motorway and the beginning of the North Circular Road. As I slowed down I punched in 'S' and 'M' on the hands-free dial built into the dashboard of the Range Rover, and the name 'Smithson' flashed up. I pressed the call button on the hands-free.

"Hello?" The reassuring voice of Brian Smithson, a former policeman, could be heard loud and clear in the Range Rover.

"It's Marc Edge," I announced. "Brian I wondered if you could make a couple of calls for me please?"

I met Brian Smithson when I was arrested, and he was the desk sergeant at Bishopsgate Police Station. After my name was cleared, we kept in touch, and I even offered him a part time job at JPG when he retired from the City of London police, which he politely declined.

"Are you in trouble again?" Brian said in a half-mocking tone.

"Not me, but K-P did not go home last night."

"Wait another twenty-four hours," Brian interrupted me "and if he doesn't show, then report him missing."

"Brian, K-P has lived with his wife for eight years, and he has never ever not phoned - or gone home in that time. Plus, he was supposed to be home early today as their children break-up from school for the Easter holidays."

"Not enough time has elapsed to be able to do anything yet." Brian replied.

"He met with a Mr Dominique – a new prospective client – at the Grange Hotel, near Tower Hill. There was no-one with the name Dominique staying at that or any other Grange Hotel in London anytime this week." I paused before continuing "And since then he has just disappeared into thin air."

"I will ask a friend to check other police stations and the hospitals. You should wait until tomorrow morning and then report him missing. Have you tried to track his mobile phone?"

"Thank you Brian. His wife is very distraught, and the fact you're making some calls may ease her strain. Yes, we are speaking to the providers of his work and personal mobile phones."

"OK, but don't expect any news for a while." Brian hung up as I was passing the site of where the Olympic Games were held in 2012. In the sunshine, which had burnt off the early morning mist, I could clearly see the stadium bedecked in West Ham Football Club's colours.

My mobile rang and my wife's name - Gerda - was displayed on the hands-free screen.

"Hello, my darling. How was the flight and how are the twins?" I asked her.

"Fine. Paul was waiting and we are in his car on the way to Vieland. It's taken me a while to get through to you." There was a slight edge in Gerda's voice.

"K-P didn't come home last night and he has seemingly disappeared, with not even a phone call to Jane."

"Oh, my goodness, how is Jane?" Gerda and Jane got on very well, unlike my first wife – Mercédès – who did not see eye-to-eye with Jane.

"Not good I'm afraid. Would you.........?"

"Give her a call? Yes, certainly." Gerda anticipated my question before I had asked it.

"I stopped by The Hall for a while and now I am going into the office, where I will meet Jimmy and try and pick up K-P's trail."

"Where was he last seen?" Gerda enquired.

"At the Grange Hotel, near Tower Hill."

"OK, when shall we speak next?" I could tell that Gerda was planning the rest of the day.

"Unless I have more news on K-P, I will call to say good night to the twins at six o'clock tonight." I was on Bow Road heading towards Whitechapel and eager to conclude the call so I could speak to Jimmy.

"OK" Gerda replied.

"Sorry, one last thing. When you speak to Jane, can you tell her I spoke to Brian Smithson, who agreed to make a couple of calls, but we can't report K-P missing officially until tomorrow." I was passing the Royal London Hospital and hoped that K-P wasn't there, or in another hospital.

"Will do, Marc, love you."

"Love you too, my darling."

I rang Jimmy's office telephone extension.

"Hello, Jimmy Black speaking."

"Jimmy, its Marc. Can you meet me outside the office in five minutes please?"

"Sure."

"And Jimmy, can you bring some change for parking meters?"

A number of the older parking meters would only take cash, rather than allow for payment by credit card, or more often the credit card facility would not work.

Jimmy was waiting outside the offices of JPG, near Old Spitalfields Market, just a five-minute walk from Liverpool Street Station. He opened the car door as soon as I was stationary.

"Morning Jimmy, let's get over to the Grange City and start from there."

"Ok."

"How are Carla and the baby?" I asked.

"The baby is teething and woke up in the night," he looked tired but the stress of K-P probably hadn't helped his appearance "that's why I was in the office early. I was hoping to slip off early tonight to give Carla a break."

Carla I knew from experience could be a handful, as we were an item before I married Mercédès. At one stage she was with a fitness instructor come body-builder, and one theory is that she simply wore him out. In fact, the real reason that they split up was that Carla loved her job at JPG, and whilst she was less refined than other women in the Lloyd's Insurance Market, she had a good mind and an eye for detail that often saved the brokers making mistakes. People thought that Jimmy and Carla was an odd match at first, but the fact that they worked together so closely resulted in a mutual respect, which transcended into their personal life. I am sure Jimmy had suffered the wrong side of Carla's fishwife tongue, but his genial good nature would often result in him shrugging his shoulders and giving a wry smile.

"Well if we make some progress this morning, I am sure you can hold the fort from your blackberry at home this afternoon" I suggested.

"Carla told me just to help you as much as possible to find K-P" Jimmy replied.

I don't think I know a woman who met K-P who didn't like him instantly.

Ten minutes later we were parked on a side road off The Minories, next to Ibex House. I knew of the parking from when I worked in Ibex House, an unusual building in that it is the last remaining building in the City of London that was built in the style of a ship's super-structure. The Minories used to house a number of ship-brokers and insurance brokers, but now restaurants, hotels and public houses dominated this street. Ibex House was regarded by many as an ugly building, but its unusual architecture had saved it from the demolition ball. The water inside Ibex House can sometimes look brown, and this is because it draws its water from its own natural spring. The fact that Ibex House's water could not be affected by someone poisoning London's water supply, gave the property special significance when Germany were drawing up plans to invade Britain during the Second World War; it was earmarked to be a possible headquarters of the Gestapo in London given its proximity to the old prison in the Tower of London.

We took the footpath past some of the remnants of the old city wall that encased medieval London, which brought us to the back of the Grange City Hotel. Jimmy had said that he had only by-chance met with the Concierge who was on duty the previous afternoon. The Concierge would not be on duty until noon, but when he was here earlier Jimmy happened to bump into the Concierge whilst he was off-duty. We went into the reception area of the Grange City Hotel and reception confirmed that the person we wanted to talk to would not be available until noon.

The Grange City Hotel at Tower Hill quickly became a firm favourite for visitors to the Lloyd's Insurance Market, even though a number of other hotels had sprung up within a few hundred metres of it. The England Cricket Team stayed at this hotel when they regained the Ashes in 2005 and when they won them again in 2010.

"OK Jimmy, it's just after half past ten" I checked my watch "we have ninety minutes to do the rounds of all the other hotels close by to see if they had a Mr Dominique staying this week."

"We can't cover them all in that time." Jimmy ventured.

"Yes, we can if we split up. I will go to the Grange Tower Bridge then Tower Thistle as well as the Hilton and Holiday Inn across the river. You go across the road to Chamberlain's, the Novotel, the Doubletree and the Apex."

Jimmy nodded.

"We now know it is Mr Dominique, so hopefully it shouldn't take too long to ascertain whether he stayed in any of the hotels."

"What shall we say if they want to know why we are asking?" Jimmy posed a very good question.

"You can say that Mr Dominique met with our colleague yesterday and dropped his very expensive pen which we wanted to return to him personally." I added "And you can say there is a fifty-pound reward."

I cut through the back of the Grange City Hotel to collect my car from The Crescent, agreeing with Jimmy that we would meet back at the Grange City Hotel just before noon. I was in and out of the Tower Thistle before eleven o'clock but was held up over twenty minutes whilst Tower Bridge was raised to let though a cruise liner. So it was ten minutes after twelve o'clock when I walked back into the Grange City Hotel. Jimmy was sitting with his back to the entrance and when I caught his eye he shook his head. I sat down beside him.

"No luck Marc, and I even tried the Hotel bar here."

"Me neither Jimmy. Is the Concierge on duty yet?" I asked.

"Yes, he's the one behind the desk now." Jimmy cocked his head towards the desk on the far side of the reception.

"Come on let's see if he can remember anything else?" I stood up and walked across to the middle-aged man at the Concierge's desk.

"How can I help you?" The Concierge had a faint trace of a Mediterranean accent. I noticed that whilst he wore a smart uniform, it was ill-fitting, slightly too small.

Jimmy was behind me and, when I spoke to the Concierge, I noticed that he seemed nervous as soon as he saw Jimmy.

"I believe you spoke earlier today to my colleague here, about another of our colleagues who met with Mr. Dominique yesterday."

"Y-yes." The Concierge hesitated.

"Unfortunately Mr Dominique dropped his pen during this meeting with our colleague," the Concierge seemed suspicious as I told my cock-and-bull story "and we are anxious to return it to him personally."

"Why did your colleague not mention this earlier?"

"Because I told him not to. There's a fifty-pound reward if you can help us find him......"

"No, I can't." The Concierge snapped.

"Can't or won't?" I asked.

"Sorry, I don't understand." The Concierge looked confused.

I changed tack "To be honest, we have lost track of our colleague and he didn't go home to his wife and children last night. Can you help us with any information as to where they might have been going, please?"

"Ah, so that's why there's so much interest." The Concierge was nodding, with a slight smile, and obviously was more relaxed.

"Yes," I nodded in agreement, "his wife is very cross and very worried. Did you see them leave?"

The Concierge nodded.

"Did they take a taxi?" Jimmy asked.

"No, they turned left towards the river. I saw them walk past the window." The Concierge was looking uncomfortable again.

"What did Mr Dominique look like?" Trying to put the Concierge at ease by changing the question.

"Tall, well-tanned" he paused "possibly from France."

"Why France?" I was eager to know.

"Your friend asked for Mr Dominique, not Mr Dominic. I am French." I wasn't sure that made it conclusive that Mr Dominique came from France, but it was not a bad assumption to make.

I palmed a fifty pound note to the Concierge and was just about to leave when he offered another piece of information.

"You are not the only people looking for this Mr Dominique."

"How so?" I asked.

"Two men in plain suits were looking for him yesterday afternoon. After your friend left with Mr Dominique. I would guess they might be policemen." He walked away from Jimmy and I to indicate the interview was over.

"It might just have been another firm of brokers chasing Mr Dominique's business?" I felt that there was more to this than the Concierge was telling us.

"No I don't think so Jimmy. Did you see how nervous he was? He kept looking over my shoulder when he was talking to us. I am going to come back at the end of his shift and see if I can have another word with him away from the hotel." I turned and headed for the exit "Come on, let's go back to the office."

I was about to cut through to the alley behind the hotel, when a thought occurred to me.

"French?" I said under my breath to no-one in particular. I started walking towards the river and Tower Hill underground station, but before I had gone fifteen metres I descended steps that led to a wine retailer, which also was licensed as a wine bar. It was a well-kept secret in the City, where you could go and take the wines whilst having a plate of cheese or pate, accompanied by the best French bread in London.

It was a Friday before the start of the Easter school holidays, and a small number of City gents were celebrating the forthcoming weekend, but otherwise it was quieter than normal.

"Marc, why are we here?" Jimmy was confused as I had just walked off in a different direction, leaving him to catch up with me.

"Let's have a glass of wine shall we?" I suggested.

The manager approached us asking if he could help us with anything.

"Yes, can we have two glasses of your mid-priced white Burgundy please?"

"Large or small?"

"Small please because we may want to try a different one afterwards."

"Certainly. I have a bottle open which I think you may like and we are offering six cases for the price of five" the manager offered.

"Let's wait to try it first," I added "and a plate of cheese please?"

The manager was back in two seconds with a bottle and two glasses. He poured a little for me to try. It was lovely, so I nodded my head indicating that he should continue pouring.

"How much is a case?" I asked.

"One hundred and thirty pounds but I think in a year's time it could be worth twice that amount. This is the first batch by an Australian lady winemaker who is currently undiscovered, but when she is, the price will soar." He was certainly saying all the right things to stir my interest.

"It is very good and I think a friend of mine bought some from you." I was starting to fish again and Jimmy had the good grace not to stop drinking as I lied.

"And who might that be, sir?" asked the wine bar manager as he poured the wine.

"Mr Dominique."

The manager shook his head "No I haven't sold anything that I can recall to a Mr Dominique."

"That's strange because he said that he was here yesterday late afternoon, with a colleague of ours." I ploughed on despite the blank look from the manager.

"Mr Dominique is a tall, well-tanned French gentleman, and our colleague is also tall, but much fatter and was originally from India." I knew this wasn't strictly true and that K-P would have been very offended to be referred to as fat.

"Ah yes, I do recall them, but they were not drinking the white Burgundy."

"Really?" I said.

"No, they were drinking champagne and quite a bit actually." The manager seemed pleased to have joined the dots for us.

"Really?" I said again "How many bottles?"

"Three, and it was your colleague who paid."

"Did they eat here?" I tried to make it sound an innocent question.

"Only nibbles." He excused himself when two more customers came into the bar.

"How did you know they came here?" Jimmy was impressed with my decision to come into the wine bar.

"Because I know K-P and he knows that the best French wines in the City are here. It was a lucky guess when the Concierge said he saw them walking towards the river and that he thought Mr Dominique was French."

So what now?" Jimmy was keen to follow up.

"Back to the office, and we need to speak to our corporate credit card provider, and see if we can trace K-P's movements from there." I explained.

The manager returned with the bottle. "Another? Or something else?"

"No thank you."

The manager looked disappointed until I added that I would like to buy ten cases, which is twelve given the offer.

"Very good sir. The drinks and food today are obviously with my compliments."

"Thank you. Would you be able to store it for me?" I didn't have enough space to lay down a hundred and forty-four bottles of wine.

I handed over my credit card and gave my address to the manager.

"Do you know what time my colleague and Mr Dominique left last night?"

The manager hesitated before answering, and if I hadn't spent thirteen hundred pounds, I doubt he would have answered me.

"Half past seven." He replied with a shortness in his voice.

"Thank you."

"Good bye sir." The manager obviously felt used, as there was none of the warmness, which accompanied the early part of our conversation.

Into Thin Air

Jimmy and I returned to the offices of JPG. Jimmy went to look for Gupta, JPG's IT manager. I went in search of John Eastwood, when my mobile rang, and 'The Hall' was displayed.

"Hello." I answered.

"Marc any news?" Jane's voice was still tight.

"Yes and no," I replied honestly "we know that he met with Mr Dominique at four-ish, and they went for a glass of wine near Tower Hill."

I paused before continuing "It appears that they left together at half past seven."

"Where to?" Jane asked.

"No idea at the moment. I have returned back to the office and we are checking the IT records of K-P's email. Plus, we have asked for details from our mobile telephone and credit card suppliers about any calls and transactions since yesterday morning."

"Oh. Do you think I should do the same for our bank account and personal credit cards?" Jane's question was a sign of her practicality coming to the fore.

"Yes, that's probably a good idea." I thought that doing something might be cathartic for her.

"I will give them a quick call now before picking up the children from school."

"OK, speak later?" I unsubtly signalled that I wished to end the call.

"Yes please Marc."

I was just about to resume my search for John Eastwood when my mobile rang again, this time the display showed Brian Smithson.

"Hello, Brian, any joy?" I asked.

"Marc, I have checked with my network of former colleagues and K-P hasn't been arrested."

"So he hadn't ended up in hospital either?" I sounded less relieved than I should have been.

"I can't confirm that yet," Brian continued cautiously "but he has not been reported dead or in an intensive care unit. Obviously there is no news from your end?"

"Well yes and no," I replied. "We know that he met with a potential new customer late afternoon at The Grange, by Tower Hill, and then went for drinks at a wine bar close to The Grange. We are checking with our credit card company to establish whether it was used elsewhere, after they left the wine bar at about seven thirty last night. Also we have contacted our mobile phone suppliers to see if they can give us a clue to his whereabouts."

"Marc, can you give me his mobile phone network, and his number, plus the mobile phone's IMEI details, please?"

"Why?" I asked.

"I have friends who might be able to use their box of tricks." Brian would not elaborate further.

"Well, your friends might be able to help more than you realise."

"Hmm, how so?" Brian could be a man of few words when it suited him.

I explained that I had tracked down an employee of The Grange who actually saw K-P meet with the new potential customer and he believed him to be French. Also, I was not the only person interested in the rendezvous.

"Hmm" was Brian's non-committal response.

"The Grange Concierge felt sure the other two men asking about the Frenchman might have been policemen." I hoped this might produce a more positive response and I was not disappointed.

"How do you know the person was French?"

"Firstly the person K-P met was Mr Dominique and the Concierge is himself French. He thought he could tell from how he spoke to K-P." I was embarrassed that my explanation sounded very flimsy.

"I think its pure guesswork from someone you have probably bribed to get the information. He has just thrown you another bone, in the hope of earning more money."

"He didn't ask for anything." I countered.

"OK, Marc, I will ask a couple of people…."

"Thanks Brian" I interrupted.

Brian continued "Don't get your hopes up; I don't expect this to be anything at all. From the way you have described events it is probably just another business meeting."

I decided there was no point in arguing and just asked him to do anything he could, and I finished the call in order to resume my search for John Eastwood.

I found our erstwhile Chairman at the desk of Gupta our IT Manager, and he was accompanied by our Operations Manager. I stood back whilst they reviewed the information that had come back from the mobile phone and credit card suppliers, which obviously wasn't very much. The phone had not been used after the meeting with Mr Dominique, and K-P's credit card showed the last transaction as the champagne in the wine bar.

John turned to me and said "Jimmy is working through the list of calls made and received on K-P's mobile over the past week."

"What about his e-mail?" I asked.

"Jimmy has also been through everything K-P received and sent last week, nothing unusual, and no clues as to who the mysterious Mr Dominique might be."

"John, I am going back to my office, perhaps we can catch up in half an hour please."

"Certainly Marc."

I returned to my office via Jimmy's desk. He had a six-page list of telephone numbers that he was colour coding with a marker pen.

"That looks to be a laborious task." I spoke quietly to Jimmy as I approached his desk.

"Not at all, Marc. I've nearly finished now."

"And any clues?" I asked more in hope than expectation.

Jimmy shook his head as he replied "there are only six numbers I don't recognise."

"Only six!" I expressed surprise.

"Yes but that is not necessarily good." Jimmy went on to explain that any calls received to K-P's mobile, which were re-routed from his office landline would simply show 'number unknown'.

"Damn." I swore quietly to myself.

"I will start calling the six numbers I don't recognise."

"And then go home," Jimmy started to protest when I added "please?"

"What are you going to do?" Jimmy's eyes were starting to redden, showing the weariness of his broken night's sleep.

I had been thinking of my next steps ever since we had returned to the office. Our visit to The Grange and the wine bar had raised more questions in my mind.

"I am going to take a picture of K-P to The Grange at four-thirty. I am going to ask around to find out if they were there yesterday at the same time, and if they were, did they see K-P?"

Jimmy's face brightened when he heard that I would not be sitting on my hands "And will you also go back to the wine vaults?"

"Yes, but I am not sure I will be very welcome." I frowned at the thought of my next encounter with the manager of the wine bar.

"Are you sure you don't want company?" Jimmy's eagerness and good nature was showing through.

"No thanks. I prefer to do this alone – people are less intimidated by being approached by only one person."

Jimmy paused for a moment, and then replied "We were supposed to be going over to Carla's sister tomorrow for a BBQ. I will drop Carla and the baby with her sister and then come into the City."

I had already resigned myself to the fact that very few of the little jobs Gerda had asked me to do, while she and the twins were on holiday, would be started this weekend.

"Ok Jimmy lets meet back here at eleven o'clock tomorrow morning. And call me if any of those numbers turn up something, please?"

"And you too, if your visits to The Grange or the wine bar prove to be fruitful."

I returned to my office gazing at my computer screen, but I was unable to concentrate on the stream of unopened e-mails mounting in my inbox.

I called Jane.

"Hello?" I heard the hesitancy in her voice, as though she was steeling herself against any potential bad news.

"It's Marc" I replied.

"Any news?" Jane demanded.

"No, sorry nothing further to report. Did Gerda call?"

"Yes, thank you" Jane's voice relaxed slightly "she was very sweet and asked after the children and how they were feeling."

Typical of Gerda, and I asked the same question as Gerda.

"Not great – they were expecting to see their Dad and start the Easter holidays with a party at home. He is not only large, but larger than life itself, so he is sorely missed."

I felt that Jane might break down in tears, so I suggested I would go to The Hall and stay the night.

"No, you don't have to do that Marc." Jane was firm in her tone so I acquiesced.

"OK, but I'll come over tomorrow late afternoon for tea, if we have made no progress" I said.

"That's fine" Jane agreed.

"In the meantime, can you send me a recent photograph of K-P please?"

"Why?" Jane asked and I explained.

"OK I will email you one shortly. Please call me if you unearth anything at the hotel or wine bar."

I promised I would.

Jane sent an e-mail with K-P's photograph within two minutes from the end of our call. I thanked her and asked her whether there had been any transactions on their personal credit card. I opened the attachment to Jane's e-mail and gazed upon K-P's face. The ready smile which was never far from his lips, and the lack of grey hair gave K-P a peter-pan quality; only the deeper laughter lines around his eyes betrayed his aging.

"How can you disappear, my friend?" I addressed the photograph. Then another question started to form "Why would you disappear?" I could not possibly imagine that it was anything to do with his personal life. His time with the Royal

Navy was firmly behind him, I could not possibly imagine it was linked to any of the terrorist activity in Europe. It must be something to do with business. I sent the photograph to print and at the same time dialled Jimmy's mobile.

"Hello Marc."

"Jimmy, do you know what K-P was working on, in the last – say - month?"

"Pretty much," he responded positively.

"Not for tonight, but tomorrow, can we go through each new enquiry – not existing business – to see if there is anything there to help us."

"Sure."

I saw another email from Jane, saying that there had been no transactions on K-P's personal credit card for over a week. I was just about to make a start on the unread e-mails in my Inbox when John Eastwood appeared at the door of my office.

"Please come in John."

John motioned to the chair next to me rather than either of those available on the other side of my desk. I nodded and he reached down to the top of his thighs and gently raised his trousers slightly before he sat down. It was a habit that reflected the nature of a man who was always very considered in what he said, and what he did. He was my mentor and had become a good friend.

"How are you doing Marc?"

"Annoyed" I replied.

"Why?"

"Because of K-P getting himself into this situation – whatever the situation may be – and cross with myself for feeling so useless."

John merely smiled at me.

"John, I think we should be asking why has he disappeared rather than how?"

"What do you mean?"

"What has K-P got that someone would want?" I posed the question.

"Not money – possibly a brood of children?" John's attempt to lighten the mood was welcomed. It was my turn to smile.

We both sat in silence for a few moments, which was broken by the sound of my mobile ringing. I snatched to answer it when I saw it was Brian Smithson.

"Yes Brian."

"You may, I repeat may, be right about the boys in blue having an interest in Mr Dominique and K-P."

"Yes." I asked

"Nothing more than that I am afraid."

"Come on Brian, tell me why you say what you've said?"

There was a pause at the end of the phone.

"Brian…?"

"I was told in no uncertain terms to keep my nose out of it."

"By whom?" I was probing, but could tell Brian was holding something back.

"I don't know exactly," Brian continued "I spoke to a friend of mine who is still in the force and within minutes of me hanging up the phone, someone I had never heard of called me back telling me to mind my own business."

"Did he say who he was or what department he worked for?"

"No, but if I was to guess, I would think it was a special unit of some kind."

"Why?" I asked.

"He sounded young, arrogant, with a posh voice."

"What should we do? Jane is beside herself".

"I would sit tight for another twenty-four hours and hope that K-P makes contact," Brian paused "but I know you won't, will you?"

"No, of course not" I replied.

"Just be careful Marc. You know you have a penchant for getting yourself into trouble" Brian chided me.

"Hmm" I replied.

"Good luck" Brian said as he hung up.

"What was that all about?" John asked me as the call with Brian ended. I recounted the full conversation to John, as much for my own benefit to get it straight in my own head.

After I had done so, I added "Brian was rattled and hasn't told us everything so I think I might take him a bottle of wine after my visit to The Grange."

"When are you going back to The Grange?"

I checked my watch; it was already half past three. "In about forty-five minutes."

"Ok, I have told my wife that I will be late tonight," John would normally leave early on a Friday to drive back to the country "so I will be here until six if you need me Marc?"

"Thank you John."

The clock seemed to crawl around to quarter-past four. I tried reading my e-mails, but found that I couldn't concentrate. I kept looking at my watch and recalling my telephone conversation with Brian Smithson. Should I call Jane? I decided against doing so as there were more questions than answers. I printed another half-a-dozen photos of K-P and turned off my computer and left JPG for my second visit to The Grange Hotel in the same day.

I reached the hotel in less than fifteen minutes and saw that the Concierge to whom Jimmy and I spoke earlier was still on duty. He was assisting an elderly couple with their luggage as they checked in. The Grange Hotel is popular with Americans because of its proximity to Tower Bridge and the Tower of London, plus it is very close to the financial and insurance centres of the City of London.

I approached the Concierge as soon as he was free.

"Hello again, do you remember me from earlier today?"

"Mais oui, you are one of the gentlemen who asked me about your friend and his meeting with the Frenchman, Mr Dominique."

"Are you sure he was French?" I asked.

He reflected for a few seconds before answering.

"I am certain that the gentleman spoke French as a French person, although there was a very slight accent."

"Of where?" I eagerly asked him. He shrugged his shoulders in a typical French manner with a downward pursing of his lips which is reminiscent of so many French people when they don't know something.

I tried another tack "How old was he?"

"He was tall and well-tanned so it would be difficult to tell."

"Have a guess?" I pressed.

"In his forties, perhaps there was some grey hair," he pointed to his temples "he seemed to be very confident. Non, how you say? Self......"

"...... assured," I finished his sentence for him and I pulled out one of the copies of K-P's photograph that Jane had sent me "would you show it to your colleagues and if any of them have any more information about my friend, or Mr Dominique, please could you call me?" I passed the Concierge

41

one of my business cards, and was about to give him another twenty-pound note.

"Non monsieur, save your money until there is information worth paying for?" The Concierge smiled as he spoke.

"Thank you." I replied as I put my wallet away. I saw that he was looking to see if he was needed by a guest, and was about to walk away when I enquired as to whether the hotel's lobby had close circuit television."

"Bien sur, of course."

"Would I be able to look at the tapes from yesterday?"

The Concierge started slowly shaking his head.

"I will make it worth your while."

He hesitated for a moment as I held his gaze.

"Come back in one-hour monsieur."

Having already engaged the Concierge as my eyes and ears at The Grange, I thought there was no point in asking another member of the hotel staff whether they had seen K-P. I glanced at my watch it was just past five o'clock. I left The Grange Hotel and walked down towards the river to where the evening newspapers were being distributed by the entrance of Tower Hill Station and I approached the person handing out the free newspapers and showed him a picture of K-P.

"Excuse me, but did you see this gentleman last night?"

"No!" was his curt reply, and I could see that there was no point in engaging him further.

It was late Friday afternoon and London was bathed in pleasant warm sunshine; this together with the start of the school holidays meant that lots of commuters were not hanging around. Tower Hill underground station was already heaving; either people were entering the station at the lower entrance, or coming out from the higher exit and walking towards the railway station at Fenchurch Street. With the sunshine some braver souls were baring skin that had remained covered over the winter and there were plenty of smiles on peoples' faces. K-P should already be at home BBQ'ing dinner for his family. This thought urged me on in my task.

I turned back towards The Grange Hotel. I was level with the wine bar where Jimmy and I had been at lunchtime. I hadn't made the best of impressions with the manager, but now I had forty-five minutes before I should return to The Grange Hotel, so I decided to have a drink in the wine bar to see if I could glean any further information about last night's events. I descended the stairs to the wine bar and to my surprise it was very full with customers. It looked as though a large group had decided to take the afternoon off, because the volume of chatter was very loud, and I had to raise my voice to be able to make my order at the bar. The manager who I spoke to earlier wasn't to be seen. I paid for my glass of wine and retreated from the bar to look around the wines on sale in the adjacent room. There were a few other patrons seeking sanctuary from the noise in the bar and we politely nodded as we passed each other, examining the labels and the descriptions of the wine extolling their various attributes.

I checked my mobile phone for messages and emails. One was from Gerda saying that the children were tired, and that I should phone soon, if I wanted to speak to them before they were asleep. The second was another email from Jane asking me to phone at any time, as soon as I discovered any new piece of information. I decided I would call Gerda in a short while once I finished my wine and I would be walking back to The Grange, and sent an email to Jane promising I would call as soon as I heard anything. There were many unread e-mail messages on my mobile; I scanned them quickly as I sipped my wine looking for anything related to K-P. I couldn't concentrate on other matters, and I said to myself that I would look at them properly after dinner. There was nothing new other than Jimmy confirming that he would be in the office by eleven o'clock the next morning.

I finished my drink and as I climbed the stairs I dialled my brother-in-law's telephone number in Holland. Paul answered it on the second ring.

"Hello, how's everything?" I asked.

"The children are exhausted and we have only just been able to keep them awake for you to say goodnight to them." There was just a hint of recrimination in his voice. Paul had never wanted children when he was married, but with the birth of the twins, a more doting uncle you could not find. "Gerda told me about K-P. Any news?"

"We have drawn a blank so far and the police will not even consider him missing yet."

"Idiots." Paul held law enforcement officers in low esteem, largely because of the way they treated me, before I was able to clear my name.

I continued "Also, one of my contacts in the police has been told to mind his business."

"Why?" Paul asked.

"No idea, but there have been other people asking after K-P at The Grange Hotel which is where he had an appointment yesterday......" I paused in mid-sentence when a thought occurred to me.

"Marc, Marc, are you still there?"

"Y-yes." Paul's voice brought me out of my reverie.

"Are you OK?" he asked.

"Yes, fine. Please can I speak to the children and Gerda?"

"Of course, my dear brother." I was unsure if he was mocking me, because he was a very good friend of mine before he introduced me to his younger sister.

It was chaos speaking to the twins, as they both wanted to speak at once so they shared the phone. Speaking over each other, their voices excited and shouting, to tell me their news of the day. It was all over in less than a minute and I told them that I was missing them, to be good and have a good night's sleep.

"Night, night, Daddy" they chorused together and I was sure I could hear a little yawn from one of them.

"Hello." It was Gerda.

"Hello my darling." I replied.

"Paul has just told me that there is no news about K-P."

"That's right. I have a couple of leads to pursue, but I am clutching at straws."

"What?" Gerda asked, not understanding my colloquialism.

"Sorry, I meant to say that I have a couple of ideas but I don't hold out much hope."

"Ah" Gerda continued with "how is Jane coping?"

"OK, I am never sure I can read her" I admitted.

"She just puts up a defence barrage to protect herself," Gerda had been able to get on with Jane from the first moment they met - unlike my first wife. "I will call her after we have finished speaking."

"Thank you my darling. Can you remind her that I will go to The Hall tomorrow, if there is no news?"

"Of course. How are you Marc?" Typical selfless Gerda making sure all around her are in a good place, before she thinks of herself.

"Angry. Confused. Energized." I was always honest with Gerda. She was able to see beyond the surface and would rarely, if ever, be judgmental.

"Too much time behind a desk." Gerda giggled.

"Perhaps?" I admitted.

We continued to talk for another few minutes about her day with the children and Paul. We ended the call with air kisses, and Gerda saying that she would act as my alarm call for the following morning.

As I put my mobile phone away, I surveyed the area around me. The street was thinning quickly of the office workers, with the tourists making up the majority of the people in view. K-P would – should – be with his family at the beginning of school holidays. I drew myself up to my full height, pushed back my shoulders and walked purposefully toward The Grange Hotel, for the third time in a day.

The Concierge was not to be seen, so I took a seat waiting for him to return, hoping that he had not had a change of heart. As I sat in the reception I tried to see where the close circuit television cameras were sited. I was pretty certain that there were at least two and possibly a third. One was towards the back of reception, trained on the reception desk in the centre of the room, and I espied another covering the entrance to the hotel, but any other was not obvious.

Hotel receptions are a great place to people-watch and being so close to one of London's top tourist attractions – the Tower of London – the number of people passing through let alone those staying was phenomenal. The number of people attending seminars alone could easily exceed a hundred each day. I started to doubt my chances of successfully seeing anything on the close circuit television recording.

I glanced at my watch. I had been sitting unchallenged by any hotel staff for fifteen minutes, before I was asked if I wanted anything to eat or drink.

"A glass of red wine, please?" I replied to a tall blonde girl with an eastern European accent.

She began to list the red wines available by the glass.

I interrupted her by asking if they served a Chilean Cabernet Sauvignon by the glass. She replied that they did and I said that a small glass would be fine. The wine arrived within two minutes, together with a small bowl of salty Chinese crackers that were intended to keep the clients asking for more drinks.

I was nearly halfway through my wine before the Concierge came into reception. When he saw me he held up his hand in the universal gesture that he would be with me shortly. He disappeared towards the rear of the reception and then almost immediately reappeared, beckoning me to come to him. I stood up and caught the eye of the tall blonde waitress. She came to me with the bill for the glass of wine and I gave her ten pounds, saying that she could keep the change which, from her expression, wasn't very generous.

"Come quickly please," the Concierge urged "I had to wait for the duty manager to take his evening meal."

"How long do we have?" I asked.

"We are safe for at least twenty minutes," then he added "possibly thirty."

We went through an unmarked door in the corridor between the Reception and Restaurant. It was a windowless room with two television monitors, both linked to a desktop computer on a desk behind. The desk was manned by a thin spotty youth, wearing the hotel uniform, which completely drowned him.

The youth half turned towards us as we closed the door "Hi." His voice was surprisingly quite clear and assured.

"This is Joe" announced the Concierge as more of an explanation than an introduction.

"We don't have long" Joe said as his fingers furiously darted across the keyboard.

"Can we please start looking at the tapes from four o'clock yesterday?" I asked.

"Tapes, who has tapes nowadays?" Joe replied "We are at four o'clock yesterday" he pointed at the left hand-screen "I will scroll forward in two minute frames, until we see something you want to look at in more detail."

"OK," I asked "which camera is this?"

"The one situated at the back of reception" he replied without his eyes leaving the screen.

I knew this to be the case because the picture showed the activity at the reception desk in two minute intervals. Within a few minutes we were well past the time that K-P allegedly left with Mr Dominique - according to the Concierge – and there was no sign of K-P.

"Can we please look at the other camera?" I asked.

Again Joe's fingers flew across the keyboard and the image on the screen showed the entrance of the hotel and, after fifteen jerky images, K-P filled the screen.

"Stop!" I shouted. "Go back to the previous two-minute period and can you play the close circuit television forward at normal speed please?"

I saw K-P come into the hotel and he hesitated for an instant as he surveyed the room. He then walked out of shot.

"I think this is when he came to my desk" the Concierge volunteered.

The images continued in real time for a further five minutes. I looked at my watch and we were already fifteen minutes through the duty manager's meal break. I was about to ask Joe to revert to the two minute intervals when the Concierge said "Arret – stop!"

Joe stopped the images.

"Go back please?" the Concierge asked.

"What is it?" I asked.

"Those two men were the ones I talked to you about today. They were also asking about your friend".

"Interesting" I muttered under my breath. The two men were both dressed in light grey suits, non-descript individuals, but both above average height and not overweight. If I were a betting man, they had the look of officials in plain clothes.

"Let the video run please?" I stared intensely at the screen.

The time seemed to crawl by, and I was looking at my watch every few seconds. The twenty minutes had elapsed and overrun by at least two minutes when the back of K-P and another man came into view. K-P paused to let the other man exit before him. Whilst courteous, it was unfortunate because K-P blocked Mr Dominique from the lens of the camera, but even in those briefest of images of the back of Mr Dominique's head there was some familiarity buried in the recess of my mind. Just as I was about to tell Joe to turn off the recording, I saw K-P drop a piece of paper as he turned to follow Mr Dominique out of the hotel.

"Hold it, can you play that last sequence again in slow motion please?"

I watched the scene again and K-P wasn't just being polite, he was shielding his actions from Mr Dominique. K-P didn't accidentally drop the paper; it was quite deliberate.

"Let it continue at normal speed, please?" I wanted to see what happened to the piece of paper. My question was answered almost immediately. The blonde waitress who served my wine to me earlier, came into view and picked up the paper.

"I must speak to that waitress."

I was halfway out of the door when Joe turned to me and said "It might be better if I speak with her."

"Why?"

"She's my fiancée."

A vivid image of their two bean-pole bodies lying together flashed through my mind.

"Stay here please," Joe commanded "I'll be back in a minute."

Before he left, his fingers hit two buttons and the left hand screen showed the current activity within reception.

Whilst Joe was out of the room, I reached into my pocket for my wallet.

"Keep your money monsieur," the Concierge said "buy me a bottle of good champagne when you have found your friend."

I smiled "I hope that will be soon."

"Moi aussi" he replied.

Joe returned a couple of moments after the Concierge and I finished our conversation. The look on his face told its own story.

"No luck I'm afraid. My girlfriend remembers picking up the paper but she threw it away without looking at it."

"When is the waste collected?" I asked.

"This morning" both Joe and the Concierge answered in unison.

They could both see that I was crestfallen.

"Who do you think the message was intended for?" Joe posed the question.

None of us said anything for a moment.

"What about the two men we saw in the foyer who asked after your friend today?" the Concierge suggested.

"Yes indeed" I echoed.

Paper Chase

I felt a familiar sensation returning to me that I had not experienced in the last five years. Cognisant that once again when I was making progress in an investigation, I was only to be thwarted, with a break-through just beyond my reach. Knowing that K-P tried leaving a message for someone put a whole new complexion on the rendezvous with Mr Dominique, and possibly his disappearance.

I was outside the hotel pondering my next move, when a sense of rage came over me. What was K-P doing? Why had he not spoken to me, or his colleagues, or his family? Was he up to no good, trying to line his own pockets? Was he working for himself on the side; or even feeding confidential information to a competitor?

I physically shuddered at the thought. I had known K-P since I first started in Lloyd's of London, and he had never shown any of these traits in the years of our friendship. Quite the opposite, he was one of the loyalist people I know, which he exhibited on many occasions to me and others. Was he in trouble and pressured into giving information? This was more likely. Without a second thought, I dialled the number for The Hall on my mobile phone. It rang three times before Jane answered.

"Hello?" Her voice sounded strained.

"It's Marc."

"Any news?" Jane interrupted.

"Yes and no," I replied "I have a couple of questions first. Then I will tell you what I think has happened."

"Don't play games with me, Marc!" Jane's hackles were rising.

"I'm not" I said as firmly yet quietly as possible. "I need to know if K-P has been secretive recently, making phone calls out of earshot, and do you have money problems?"

"Oh my God, he's having an affair and he's run off with her!" Jane's voice almost reached a screech.

"No, it's not that Jane." I tried to reassure her "He loves you and the children too much; and he knows you would skin him alive."

"Mmmmm."

"Jane, please think has he been secretive? Have there been any strangers visiting The Hall?"

"No, he hasn't been secretive, and no-one unusual has come to The Hall."

"That's a good start. Now what about money? Is there more or less in the bank account?"

Jane hesitated "I-I-don't think so…. hang on just let me check. I had the credit card and bank statements out earlier."

I heard the phone being put down. It was less than a minute when Jane returned to our conversation.

"I have the statements for the last three months and nothing seems untoward."

"Ok" I replied trying to sound as non-committal as possible. I paused trying to make sense of what I had learned, and then to articulate it to Jane in as positive a way as I could, without offering any false hopes. "Strictly speaking K-P is not missing in the eyes of the police for another twenty-four hours, and whilst neither of us like the thought, I think this was in part planned by K-P, and may have misfired."

"What do you mean?" again the cadence in Jane's voice rising with each word she spoke.

I explained about the note in his diary confirming the meeting with *Mr Dominique,* and the fact that he was being watched during his rendezvous. I told Jane what I saw on the closed circuit television recording, that it seemed like he was trying to pass a note to someone, but it didn't reach its intended recipient. Also that the Concierge at the hotel identified the two people who were watching K-P were asking after him today at the hotel. What I didn't mention to Jane, was anything about the call I had from Brian Smithson, during which he was told to mind his own business.

"So what now?" Jane's voice had moderated only slightly, probably she was feeling the same anger as I, with the realization that K-P had not taken either of us into his confidence. Why not? I had an idea that it was linked to the warning Brian Smithson had received, and he would be the next person I should be speaking to. I replied to Jane that I would ask a few more questions tonight and then continue again tomorrow.

"Jane, I will come over tomorrow evening if I haven't turned up anything."

"OK – but let me know the instant you find anything. Promise, please?"

"Yes, I promise" I agreed, and added "try to sleep – you sound tired Jane."

"I'll try but I doubt I will get more than a few minutes. I miss him so much."

With that Jane ended the call. I thought about calling Gerda and arranging for her and the children to return to England, to keep Jane company. I decided to leave that in abeyance, in case the news did not improve. I tried calling Brian but there was no reply, so I returned to the hotel and caught the Concierge's eye. He came over to me at once.

"You have news monsieur?"

"No I don't," his face fell "but I have a question."

"Oui?" The Concierge enquired.

"Did the two men who followed my friend yesterday, and came asking about him today, have anything to drink?"

The Concierge made the same facial expression as he did earlier in the day, with the shrug of his shoulders and palms of his hands facing me. "Je ne sais pas, attend une minute, si vous plait?" He walked over to the bar and he was back in less than a minute.

"I spoke to the waitress but she did not serve them."

"Hmm. When you spoke with them, did they sound foreign?"

He replied with a smile "No-no. They were very English, they spoke as you say, the Queen's English."

I thanked him and left the hotel for the fourth time in the day.

I knew exactly where I was going next, and I reached my destination in less than fifty steps. I descended the stairs to the wine bar between the hotel and Tower Hill Station. As I entered the wine bar I could see that it was much less busy that earlier, and that the manager had returned. Upon seeing me he was not displaying the normal bon-homie which he exhibited the first time I walked in at lunchtime. Then a quizzical look came over his face when the barmaid whispered something in his ear.

As I approached the bar I held up my hand "I am sorry but I have not been entirely honest with you."

He cocked his head to one side "Really?" he replied in a very sarcastic tone.

"My colleague, whom I was asking about earlier, has disappeared and I am trying to retrace his steps."

The manager's face softened a bit, but he still looked sceptical, and replied "I told you everything earlier, and it would have been easier and cheaper for you, without going through the façade of buying those cases of wine."

"No, I really did want to buy some wine."

"Please don't patronize me, Mr Edge."

"I am not, and I am sorry we got off on the wrong foot."

"OK" he replied.

"I have a question for you, please?"

"What is it?" his voice hardened.

"Has the rubbish been collected since yesterday?"

He was puzzled and was about to ask why, but I could see him relenting. "No, I forgot to put it out this morning."

"Great. Can I search it please?"

"What are you looking for?"

"My friend left a note at the Grange where he met someone, and he may have left a clue to his whereabouts."

"You are joking?" The manager was in danger of losing his patience.

"My friend is an inveterate doodler, and often scribbles as he talks." I lied fluently.

"I am not sure?" The manager was on the verge of saying no, but had a change of heart when I said that, after I had searched for the note, I would dispose of the rubbish.

"Ok – when?"

"Tomorrow morning?" I suggested.

"As long as it's gone by mid-day" he stipulated.

"Perfect" I said before he could change his mind.

"Be here at half-past ten please?"

"Thank you, I will."

I walked back to the offices of JPG and on the way I tried Brian Smithson again. The phone rang a number of times without answer before his service provider invited me to leave a message.

"Hi, it's Marc – Edge - there's still no sign of K-P but I have discovered an interesting development, and please could you give me a call back."

I arrived back at the office and saw it was after eight o'clock. I went to my office to turn off my computer and pick up my iPad. I would check my e-mails at home. I thought about calling Gerda but decided to leave it until the morning as she would probably be exhausted with the early start and all the travelling to Holland with the twins.

I turned the ignition key as I climbed into my car, the radio broke into life, and I was tuned into my favourite sports channel. There was a panel discussion about England's chances at the next World Cup in Russia the following year. I turned the radio off and drove home in silence, thinking of K-P. Was he really missing, or had he just gone absent without leave, for two days?

I arrived home in a few minutes to an empty house. Whenever Gerda and the twins were away I struggled with the quiet, and my first instinct would be to turn on the television. Not tonight, I said to myself. Tonight, I needed to plan the following day, so as to not lurch around in typical Marc Edge haphazard fashion.

I resisted alcohol, and drank tea with my TV dinner. I fell asleep on my sofa, before I had even finished reading the day's e-mails.

It was still dark when I woke up, and initially I was disorientated by the ringing in my ears, until I realised it was the house phone that had awoken me. I reached for the phone but the ringing stopped just as I answered the call. Almost immediately my mobile vibrated, and I saw that Jane had tried to call me a number of times.

"He phoned me!"

"Er-r-r." Was my incomprehensive response.

"Marc, did you hear me?" Jane's voice was a mixture of relief and hysteria.

"What did he say?" I asked.

"Nothing! That's the point."

I was totally confused "What do you mean?"

"The phone rang three times then it stopped, then it rang twice more, and finally it rang once more." Jane was breathing hard.

"Sorry I am confused" I croaked.

"It is our code. When we first met without using minutes or texts on our mobile phones, this was our way of saying 'Hi' without necessarily speaking to each other."

I was still feeling very sluggish from falling asleep on the sofa. I peered at my watch. It was showing half-past six. K-P was always an early riser; he blamed the habit on his stint in the Royal Navy. No matter how late he went to bed, he would be awake with metronome consistency at six o'clock.

"Did you try calling back?" I eventually asked a sensible question.

"Yes, but the only response was that the caller withheld their number." Jane's voice had modulated but I detected anger just below the surface. "What the hell is he playing at, Marc?"

"I honestly don't know" I replied.

We continued to talk for another minute or so, during which I asked whether she would like Gerda to come back from Holland.

"She has already offered, Marc. I said no – thank you all the same but the kids will be more worried if things are not normal."

"What have you told them?" I asked.

"Hmm – I have said that daddy is staying with Uncle Marc."

"What?"

"Sorry, Marc, but I said that you are upset about Gerda and the twins going to Holland, and you had too much to drink."

"Thanks a bunch."

"It explains why I am on the phone so much, but it also means you can't come here – unless it is with K-P."

After the call with Jane, I undressed and went to bed, but sleep did not come to me for at least an hour. I turned over what Jane had told me about the unanswered phone call. I then slept fitfully for only an hour when I was again woken by my mobile phone vibrating under my pillow. It was Brian Smithson.

"Good morning Brian" I mumbled.

"Oh dear, it sounds like someone had a lot to drink last night."

"Not at all." I explained about what Jane had told me earlier.

"That's inconclusive" Brian said.

"Exactly," I conceded "either it is K-P telling Jane he is OK - and can't talk - or someone is making the call on his behalf, to put us off the scent."

"You do have the sense of the melodramatic Marc." Brian's sceptical reply was borne out of years in the City of London Police.

"But you must agree that something is strange?" I asked him.

"I may do" Brian said unconvinced.

I told him about what I saw on the close circuit television footage.

"Hmm," he was still not convinced. "Tell me about the two people who followed K-P into the hotel?"

I tried to describe them the best I could, but there was little to distinguish them other than they were above average height, lean and both wearing light grey suits and white shirts. "And they spoke with an English accent."

Brian sighed for the second time in as many minutes.

"Your lot?" I questioned him.

"Possibly, but since I have retired there have been so many changes, especially with the police cuts in the recession. I am unlikely to recognise them."

"Would you come to look at the close circuit television footage today if I can arrange it?"

"No way - I am going to watch the England World Cup qualification match on the tele. Mrs S is out, and a couple of mates are coming around when we will eat rubbish, talk rubbish and drink loads as we reminisce about nineteen sixty-six."

"Ok, but what about tomorrow?" I pushed him.

"If he doesn't pitch up by Monday, I will come then."

"Thanks Brian."

No sooner had I returned from the bathroom did the house phone ring. It was the twins calling Daddy before their day's excursion with Gerda and Paul. I brought Gerda up to speed with the close circuit television and Jane's phone call that never was.

"That's sweet." Gerda commented when I explained K-P and Jane's private code.

I said that I would call them late afternoon when they were back at Paul's house.

Within the hour I had changed, eaten breakfast and I was at my desk in my decorating clothes, prepared to search the refuse bins of the wine bar. I was still ploughing through my email inbox when I sensed rather than heard Jimmy in my doorway.

"Morning Jimmy, grab a coffee and then come in here. I have lots to tell you."

He was back in my office within two minutes, and then I proceeded to give him a full account of what happened since we parted the previous day. He sat quietly without interrupting me, just taking notes of what I was saying. It was making me uncomfortable because it is exactly how K-P behaves, and obviously this trait was being learned by Jimmy. By the time I had finished, it was nearly quarter to ten.

"We have to be at the wine bar in forty-five minutes" I explained.

"I am going out to buy some rubber gloves and plastic bags and will be back just after ten o'clock." Jimmy was out of the chair before he had finished his sentence.

"OK" I said to the back of Jimmy's head as he left my office.

True to his word he was back just after ten o'clock, with four pairs of rubber gloves, a roll of bin bags, two vinyl tablecloths, and a cooking pinafore for each of us to use, as well as antiseptic hand gel. I nodded my approval, closed down my desktop computer, and we made our way to where my car was parked.

We bought coffee and drank it in silence outside the wine bar waiting for the manager to arrive. The quietness inside the car was punctuated with the odd slurp, and allowed each of us to think about what we might discover. We had discussed the possible reasons for K-P's disappearance, both hoping that it was not a case of wrong-doing, and that K-P was doing something untoward. But the phone call - that never was – to Jane may cast his actions in a slightly different hue, rather than a different colour.

It was just after half past ten when the manager arrived in a casual shirt and old jeans, prepared to undertake some running repairs or maintenance, as the tool box in his hand bore testament.

"Good morning" I announced our presence as he retrieved a step-ladder from the back of his car.

"Oh, yes." He seemed surprised to see us. He looked us up and down.

"I hope you have a change of clothes?" He turned on his heel and proceeded to walk down the steps to the basement entrance to the wine bar. Once inside, he led us through the wine bar, through the kitchen to the rear door. After unlocking the door, we were outside again on a small concrete floored yard the width of the wine bar and only four feet long. The yard was some six feet below ground level and to the right of us stood two large metal bins, about five feet high and three feet in diameter. They were overflowing with a pile of black rubbish bags at their base. One of the bins was in a metal cage, sitting on a metal platform that I assumed was how the bins were raised to ground level for collection. There was a metal gate in the wall at ground level.

The manager saw me looking at the cage and gate.

"It is a blessing and a curse."

"I think it looks quite practical." I was being positive.

"Yes, when it works," the manager retorted "that's why I came in today. I am trying to repair the motorised winch."

"Ah" I replied.

"The bin on the right – in the cage – is for rubbish other than bottles, and the other bin…"

"Is for bottles perchance?"

"Yes," the manager smiled "but they are collected at different times and the first thing we need to do is get that bin out of the cage so I can try and repair the winch. I would suggest that you start sifting through the black bags first as they certainly have yesterday's rubbish and some of Thursday's but not all I am afraid. You were lucky that the winch broke, otherwise the rubbish from Thursday would have gone."

Jimmy and I looked at each other and neither of us felt 'lucky'. I also hoped it was not going to be a wild goose chase.

We helped manoeuvre the bin out of the cage, having first moved the black bags to the left hand side of the yard on top of one of the vinyl tablecloths that we had already laid out on the concrete. We opened a bag each and the stench was appalling, the mixture of food remains and alcohol. The wine bar was famed for selling cheese and pâtés, the residue of these specialties having stood in a black plastic bag for a day or so made the smell worse.

Initially my sifting through the contents of the black bag was laborious and slow going, until I saw the method employed by Jimmy. He emptied the contents on the vinyl tablecloth and then separated the food from any paper, including any paper napkins. He would then put the food back into one of the fresh bin bags we brought, after which he methodically checked anything that could be written upon.

After a half-hour he had finished two of the original bin bags and I was about half way through my second bag.

"Is this is all the rubbish from Friday?" Jimmy asked.

"I guess so" I replied.

"I think so too," as he held up a receipt "this bill shows yesterday's date and the time is early evening."

"It means that the rubbish from Thursday is probably in the big bin."

He nodded.

"But we better make sure" I said with a frown on my face.

Again he just nodded.

An hour later and we had finished examining the contents of the black bags. None of which had any rubbish from Thursday.

I looked at my watch and it was a quarter past twelve. Our work was punctuated by grunts and curses from the wine bar manager as he battled with the winch. About twenty minutes earlier he had it working, the cage lifted about a foot off the ground, and then the winch cut-out to a cascade of swearing from the wine bar manager.

We then lifted the first two bags out of the big bin, and after a few minutes it became clear that this was also from Friday. We had become much more efficient, and within twenty minutes we were both starting on our second pair of black bags, from the large bin. Initially we could tell that the contents were from earlier in the week. The smell was not necessarily worse but it was a more subtly different odour, and paid testament to the fact that smell was the body's most sensitive sense. Not only the change of smell, but also the paper napkins were disintegrating upon touch due to the moisture they had absorbed, over the past thirty-six hours - or more.

I was about to give up when I saw a JPG business card. My heart leapt.

"Jimmy, look at this!" I shouted despite him being only a few feet away from me.

I gently removed the card from the paper napkin that had been wrapped around the card. Had it not been for half the napkins disintegrating, I might not have found it so quickly.

Jimmy was beside me. "There's something written on it." His voice was no more than a hushed whisper.

'*Por->Dub. Sat*' in K-P's neat handwriting on the back of his own business card.

"Let's get cleaned up here and back to the office," I spoke quietly to Jimmy, "don't tell the manager that we have found anything."

The manager was deeply engrossed in his repairs, and I hoped he hadn't heard my cry when I found the card, which was now in my pocket. I wandered over to him and as I did so the cage leapt into life. This time it continued all the way to the street level. He then brought it back down to the level where we were standing, and only then did he notice that I was standing close to him.

"No luck then?" he asked.

"No. The contents of the rubbish bags from Thursday and earlier are too far gone."

I cocked my head towards Jimmy who was folding the vinyl tablecloth into a black bin bag.

"We are packing up now; can we use the platform to take the rubbish away?"

"Don't worry about taking it away. If you can just help me get it up to the street level, as long as it is well sealed we can pile the extra bags on top of the metal bin. The council will pick it up early Monday morning."

"Are you sure?" I asked, crossing my fingers hoping he wouldn't change his mind. It would be a long time until I next ate any pâté or cheese, as the reek was stuck in my nostrils.

Thankfully he nodded his head.

It took us another half hour before we left the wine bar and it was quarter to two when we were back in my office. On the way back to the office I asked Jimmy if he wanted anything to eat.

"I couldn't" he replied "just a cup of coffee, very strong coffee."

So we sat in my office slowing sipping our coffees, trying to decipher what K-P had written on his card.

"Well '*Sat*' is today, I would think?" was my opening gambit.

"That would be the obvious conclusion" Jimmy replied.

I raised my head and stared at him.

He responded by saying "K-P could be oblique at times."

I nodded and returned to the computer on my desk. I was waiting for it to fire up properly because I wanted to check the IATA codes for airports. We sat in silence as my computer whirred into action. Within a few seconds I was searching '*POR*'.

"Damn."

"What is it?" Jimmy asked.

"'*POR*' is the code for Pori in Finland" I answered him as I knew that '*DUB*' was the code for Dublin "and there are no flights between Pori and Dublin."

"What about searching for other airports beginning with '*POR*'?" Jimmy suggested.

As I was trying various combinations, Jimmy offered further thoughts.

"It could be a country, like Portugal."

"That's not helping." I replied as I worked through the cities beginning with '*POR*' that had airports. It was quite a short list and I was soon finished.

"Nothing flying in to Dublin today from cities beginning with '*POR*'. There is one flight from Faro and another from Lisbon, but I don't think that is what K-P was trying to tell us."

Again we sat in silence and my eyes caught a glimpse of Friday's edition of Lloyd's List. Now published by the same company which prints the Telegraph newspapers, it is in fact the oldest daily newspaper in the World; each day it was filled with news of ships, cargo and all things marine. Completely boring to anyone not involved with shipping, but a must for anyone who is involved in the shipping industry. Insurance Brokers were no exception and, being a marine broker myself, I would always glance at the contents each day.

"What about if it wasn't airports but ports?" I had already returned to the keyboard and had typed in sailings from Portsmouth to Dublin and entered today's date.

"Damn again!" There were no results.

Jimmy had stood up and walked behind me. "What about Dubai instead of Dublin?"

"Bingo!" I cried as there was one sailing listed to depart from Portsmouth later in the day. It was a Masterson Shipping vessel. I picked up the phone and dialled the number of the Chief Operations Officer of Masterson Shipping and asked him what the current status of this voyage was. He was extremely polite, given the fact that his Non-Executive Chairman had phoned him on a Saturday asking about a routine voyage with a normal cargo. He said he didn't know, but he would get back to me as soon as he found out.

"What shall we do?" Jimmy asked.

"K-P still isn't officially missing until tomorrow," I added. "Also the police will probably say that the call to Jane means that he is not missing at all."

"So we do nothing?"

"I don't know," I was looking at my computer screen. "The ship is due to sail at half past eight tonight."

"That's just under six hours from now." Then Jimmy said what I had been thinking. "It would give us plenty of time to get down to Portsmouth."

"And then what do we do? Even as Chairman of Masterson Shipping I don't think I could halt the sailing. Also, I have no idea what the message means. Is it to do with the cargo they're carrying? We do not know the context of the message."

"But I don't think we should do nothing."

Jimmy was right; we could not do nothing, but that's exactly what we did do for the next forty-five minutes other than drink more coffee. Our inaction was brought to an end when my office telephone rang and it was the Chief Operations Officer of Masterson Shipping. He confirmed that the ship was due to be departing on time and that according to the Captain it was a regular sailing taking containers to Dubai.

"Do you have the Captain's telephone number please?" I asked.

"Is there something wrong Mr Edge?" the Chief Operations Officer enquired.

"Not with the ship, no. But I have a friend who has gone *AWOL* and I think it is connected with this sailing," I replied honestly.

"Is it not a matter for the police?"

"Not yet, and by the time it is, the ship will be well away from Portsmouth." As I spoke I realised that there was no alternative but for me to go to Portsmouth.

As the call ended I turned to Jimmy "I am going to drive down to Portsmouth…"

"Good, I will come with you."

"Jimmy, you don't have to, you have given up enough of your free time today already."

"I am not going to let you go on your own, Marc. You have a habit of getting yourself into trouble, if you are left alone."

"Thanks" I retorted in mock seriousness.

"A quick shower, a change of clothes, and then we can get going."

Jimmy was already on his feet reaching for his back-pack, in which he had the foresight to bring extra clothes. I always kept a spare suit and shirt in the office.

The Devil's Punch Bowl

It was a lovely Saturday afternoon and it seemed as though most of London had taken to the roads. Added to which there was a football match in the evening, which meant that most of the male population wanted to be in front of a television by seven o'clock. So at half past three any progress through London was very slow going.

It took until five o'clock to reach Wandsworth and we were looking to head out on the A3 that would take us past Guildford and from then on to Portsmouth. We continued to crawl through the suburbs of south-west London, with tempers and driving courtesy deteriorating almost by the minute and we were tuned into in a Championship Football match as the Premier League had no games due to the internationals being played. The Travel Alerts explained that our slow progress was not just weight of traffic, but the result of a lorry colliding with traffic lights at a key junction about one mile away. Apparently the traffic was locked solid as the lorry was still slewed across the junction. Buses could not turn off the main roads and were causing bottlenecks. Drivers with local knowledge were trying to take other routes only to be prevented in their journey so the whole area became grid-locked.

Jimmy had spoken to Carla to say that he was accompanying me to Portsmouth, and that he would not be home until very late. I had tried to call Gerda earlier at Paul's house, but it had been only the briefest of calls as it was the twins' bath time, and Gerda said she would call back after dinner. The radio commentators were excited about the upcoming international match with Lithuania, pointing out a couple of key injuries, and Gareth Southgate's sixth match in charge as England Manager, after the fiasco of the short reign of Sam Allardyce.

We hadn't moved for nearly an hour and it was six o'clock when the round-up of the Championship and other matches had finished. There had been no update on the traffic for a while, and Jimmy took the opportunity to grab two coffees from a fast food store, less than fifty metres away. With little to do, my mind would flit between listening to the radio, and what we might find if we got to Portsmouth before the ship sailed. I had tried calling the ship's captain on three occasions, and each time the phone switched to his voice-mail. I left a message asking him to call me as soon as it was convenient. There was not much of a view due largely to the buses in front and behind us. The early annoyance of drivers and their passengers had turned mostly to resignation with half of the vehicles having their doors open. Most were families and I got out of the car to stretch my legs. I had to move to the centre of the road to see past the bus in front of me; nothing was moving. I turned to look behind the bus that was directly to the rear of my Range Rover. The queue was endless, and stationary, on both sides of the road. As I looked down the line of vehicles, and their drivers, something caught my eye as being out of place. About five vehicles behind us there was a Ford Mondeo, but it was not the car that was unusual, but the occupants. There were two youngish men dressed in suits, and I could have sworn that when I looked directly at them, they both turned their heads away from me. I acted nonchalantly and returned to the car.

When Jimmy returned with the coffees I said "Jimmy, I think we are being followed."

"What?" Jimmy nearly spilled his coffee in surprise.

"I said, I think we are being followed."

"Who by?" Jimmy asked.

"Two men in suits" I continued. "I couldn't see them well enough, but if I was guessing I think they were the two people I saw on the close circuit television at the Grange yesterday."

We sat without speaking; the radio programme was briefly interrupted by the traffic report explaining that the lorry which had taken out the traffic lights in South London had been recovered and that the traffic was being controlled manually.

"What shall we do?" Jimmy asked.

"I don't know" I replied. Although a number of scenarios were playing out in my mind.

Then three things happened in short succession. Firstly, the bus moved in front of us, not far, but enough to give hope that the traffic jam was starting to clear. Secondly, I espied that one of the men in suits was standing outside his car smoking a cigarette, and thirdly I decided what to do.

"Jimmy, they know who we are, but they don't know where we are going; so let's try and lose them."

The traffic started to gain more momentum, and within fifteen minutes we were almost upon the junction which was the cause of the long delay. Shortly after passing the junction Gerda and the twins phoned. The twins sounded tired and I could tell that they were ready for bed. They told me about their day through their eyes, the highlight for them was ice-cream in the afternoon. Gerda came on the phone, and I told her about our discovery at the wine bar earlier today, and that Jimmy and I were going to Portsmouth.

"Why?" Gerda asked.

"I don't honestly know, but it appears that we have company." I then explained that there was a car behind us and it could be the two people who asked about K-P in the Grange Hotel.

"So what are you going to do?" Gerda sounded apprehensive as she asked after my plans.

"Try and get them off our tails."

"How?" Gerda's voice had raised an octave or two.

I hadn't really thought it through properly, but I replied confidently that I would turn off towards Guildford, and then double-back returning to the A3.

"Call me early tomorrow please and don't do anything stupid?" Gerda said firmly but kindly to me.

"I will be sensible" I promised.

"Love you."

"Love you too" I replied.

When I had finished my call with Gerda, I turned to Jimmy.

"What do you make of the situation?" I asked him candidly.

"I think we are in danger of dancing with shadows."

"Hmm….. you're right." I continued "If those two characters are who we think they are then they have probably been following us since we were at the wine bar this morning."

"How do you think they found us?" Jimmy asked.

"I think they had lost K-P's trail at the Grange Hotel yesterday, and if they are official, then from the call to Brian Smithson they knew we were poking around. So when my car is parked less than thirty metres from the Grange Hotel, they may just have decided to follow, a hunch, and tail us."

"So why do we want to lose them? If they are official, they might be useful in Portsmouth."

"I feel that we are the ones in the dark. I want to change the dynamics and, by putting them on the back foot, they might have to reveal more about what is going on."

Jimmy paused for a moment and then suggested at the next traffic lights to let him out of the car, so he could try and puncture one of their tyres.

"No! Firstly, you would expose the fact that we are on to them, and secondly they might phone ahead to someone to prevent us from getting to Portsmouth."

By the time we were a few miles from Guildford it was dark and approaching seven o'clock. As we had left the suburbs of London I had accelerated very hard, to try and make up for lost time from the traffic jam. Also, it was to see if the Ford Mondeo was really following us, or just a figment of my imagination.

The speedometer was rarely below eighty-five miles an hour, but I tried to make sure I didn't exceed ninety-five miles an hour. So it appeared we were beetling along at a quick pace rather than trying to outrun the Ford Mondeo. Whilst we ran the risk of being stopped by the police for speeding, I was hoping they would turn a blind eye given the holdup in South London. Because of the dark it was difficult to spot the Ford Mondeo in the rear view mirror, so Jimmy turned in his seat to look out of the large tinted windows of my Range Rover.

"He's a good driver," Jimmy remarked.

"How so?" I asked.

"He is keeping almost the exact distance between us at all times, irrespective of the number of vehicles between us, and he is not allowing himself to become boxed-in."

"Let's see if we can get him a bit closer to us, shall we?"

As we approached the first of the junctions for Guildford I slowed to seventy miles an hour. I indicated as I manoeuvred into the inside lane. I slowed again, down to sixty miles an hour, and continued slowing down to forty-five miles an hour. The traffic behind was becoming impatient and was very close to my rear bumper. The Ford Mondeo had no option but to follow suit and only one car separated them from us. We were just starting to leave the A3, when I gunned the twin super chargers into life and the full thrust of the five and a half litres made the Range Rover lurch forward, as if it had been launched from a catapult. I indicated right and then slew the car to the outside lane and re-joined the A3. As I powered down the dual carriage-way, I could see lights flashing in my rear view mirror as the Ford Mondeo tried to replicate my manoeuvre, but they were surprised and did not have the same horsepower as the Range Rover. I was out of sight before the Ford Mondeo was fully back onto the A3. Now I went for broke and kept the accelerator on the floor. The speedometer was well beyond one hundred and twenty miles an hour, and in less than two minutes we reached the next junction for Guildford. We flew up the slip road in excess of ninety-five miles an hour and I only rammed on the brakes as we approached the roundabout.

"They have only just come into view and haven't reached the slip road yet," Jimmy's voice came from behind me as he watched the cars out of the rear window.

"Hold tight!" I yelled.

We flew around the roundabout heading towards the centre of Guildford, but instead of following the road into the Town Centre, I turned into the opening to a garage and drove to the left of a white van that was filling up with diesel. We were hidden from the road and I turned off the lights. About a minute later the Ford Mondeo passed the garage on its way to Guildford Town Centre. I turned the lights back on and exited the garage, retracing our steps until we reached the roundabout where we took the slip road that would take us back on the A3 towards Portsmouth.

"Do you think we have lost them Marc?"

"Only temporarily," I replied "we need to crack-on if we are going to get to Portsmouth before the ship sails."

I increased the speed back up towards ninety miles an hour.

Within fifteen minutes, the ability to continue to drive at speed had become much more difficult, as the road south of Guildford became much more twisty and hilly. In parts, it was only single carriageway, and on occasions I was overtaking very dangerously. I was relentless and kept thrashing the Range Rover through the gears, in an effort to keep its speed as high as possible, through the area south of Guildford known as the Devil's Punch Bowl.

The phone rang briefly and I was distracted for an instant.

Jimmy shouted "Watch out!"

I had drifted onto the wrong side of the road and the lorry coming toward me flashed his lights. I corrected the positioning of the Range Rover, but the lorry veered over to our side of the road, and a band of spot lights on the top of the lorry's cab came on, together with the full beam of the head-lights. I couldn't see where I was going. I put my hand to my eyes and could just about make out the lorry bearing down on us. We left the road.

"Jimmy we're going to crash!" I screamed.

Jimmy didn't say another word.

PART II

Guilt

I sensed that I was waking before I did so. It was very unpleasant. Images of the accident, alternating between Jimmy's dead body, Carla's snarling face as she cursed and shouted at me, Gerda shaking her head in disbelief. Then the whole scene played itself again and again, each time faster than before, until they all merged together. I woke with a shock and then was violently sick.

My eyes were still closed but I heard a voice in the room directed at me. "It's the medication that has caused the nausea." It was a man's voice which I recognised but could not place. "Stay still. I will call for a nurse."

I heard the door open, and then close, as I lay back in my own vomit. It seemed ages but was probably less than a minute when the door opened. Almost immediately my mouth was being wiped and another pair of hands was removing whatever was covering me. The ease and dexterity of the operation suggested that I had been dressed in a surgical gown. Two pairs of hands were now at work as I was efficiently rolled to one side of the bed and the bed linen beneath me was removed and replaced by fresh sheets. I was put into a clean surgical gown.

The whole operation took less than five minutes and I kept my eyes closed throughout, frightened that if I opened them I might throw up again. Either that, or not wanting to face the reality that would face me when I awoke properly.

The familiar male voice spoke to me again. "How are you doing Marc? Feeling like shit and sorry for yourself, I bet?"

I didn't reply.

"I will leave you alone for an hour, but I will be back for a chat with you then. Try to be ready to talk. We need to act quickly to avoid any further accidents."

He left the room and only then did I open my eyes. The room was lit naturally by the light from the windows. The windows had venetian blinds that were half open. The room was white, completely white, walls, ceiling, floor, furniture, bed, everything white, which made the whole sensation very disorientating. When I moved my head, the nausea returned. I sank back into the pillow and dropped off into a fitful sleep.

The dream returned more vivid but more controlled, without the abrupt finale, and I awoke without being sick. I opened my eyes and saw someone sitting across the room, looking at a file of papers. It was Eric Jones, ostensibly a claims manager of Neptune Re, but, as I knew from a previous episode, connected somehow to Britain's Security Services.

"So spooks-ville is involved." My voice was barely louder than a whisper.

Eric looked up and smiled, but I could feel no warmth from his grimace.

"Am I in hospital?" I asked.

"Of sorts" he replied.

"Why?"

"Well a hospital is usually where people who are critically ill are cared for?"

"Who's critically ill? Is Jimmy still alive?" I could feel my heart racing.

"No, he isn't. He was dead when we arrived at your car."

"I don't understand. Who is critically ill?" I asked again.

"You are." Eric fixed me with an icy stare.

I said nothing and obviously looked bewildered.

"Your car exploded, and you were thrown clear, with life threatening injuries. You are being kept unconscious to prevent a fatal blood clot forming on your brain." Eric returned to the file and held up a piece of paper.

"This is the press release that was sent to news agencies earlier today, which cover television, radio and newspapers."

"But..." I started.

"But the car exploded after you were in the ambulance?" Eric finished.

I nodded.

"And you are not critically ill; but that is what everyone must believe, because if some people believe you are alive and well, then you would be of no use."

"Why? And who are 'some people'?" I demanded.

"The why is for your own protection, because you're poking around following K-P's disappearance is bound to have aroused suspicion in certain quarters. Particularly your clumsy bull-in-a-china-shop approach and they may think, incorrectly, that you found a clue to K-P's whereabouts?" Eric phrased his statement as a question and cocked his eye at me.

I said nothing.

Without a response, he continued. "As regards 'some people', we don't know their true identities and that is why K-P agreed to help us, in an effort to try and flush them out."

A wave of relief washed over me as soon as I knew that K-P's disappearance was not for the wrong reasons. Then I felt ridiculously selfish as that sense of relief only served to make me feel good for doubting K-P's intentions. Little would it help to get K-P out of his present predicament, nor - I guessed - could I tell Jane the truth, if I was supposed to have critical injuries; but saddest of all, it wouldn't bring Jimmy back to life.

I wasn't prepared to tell Eric about my discovery at the wine bar just yet.

"Why do you want to flush them out? What have they done? And why use K-P as bait?"

"We have been analysing a series of crimes such as arson, large thefts, robberies, kidnappings and abductions over the last three years and we have seen a pattern emerging. We have found a common theme, that all of these crimes have been insured by Lloyd's Syndicates. Also, we think that there is a link to a new outfit whose leader is unknown to us and very secretive." Eric's legitimate job was Claims Director of one of the London Insurance Market's foremost reinsurance companies, Neptune Re. Whilst Neptune Re's roots were clearly in marine insurance, the modernisation of Lloyd's of London in the early nineteen nineties saw most insurance and reinsurance syndicates becoming corporations in some shape or form, and diversifying as they grew from mono-line business. Neptune Re was no exception and in their stable they had both a Lloyd's Syndicate and insurance companies. Neptune Re was in the premier division of worldwide reinsurers with offices in London, Bermuda, Singapore and more recently in Dubai. They were one of the most technical of reinsurers and it didn't surprise me when Eric admitted to analysing claims trends. From a previous encounter with Eric some five years previously, I knew that not only did they undertake such analysis themselves, but that they also shared it with both the police and the Security Services. I presumed that, at some stage in his past, Eric had been connected to one or other of these organisations.

"So why K-P? And why now?" I wanted more information before I shared my one and only nugget of information.

Just at that moment, a nurse came in to check on me, and as the door opened I saw that someone was standing on guard outside, and I faintly recognised him.

"Can I have a glass of water, please?" I asked the nurse.

"No – not until you have been examined by the consultant," she replied.

"When will that be?"

"Hopefully he should arrive within the hour."

"So he's not on-site then?" I asked.

I was stone walled by the nurse who left the room.

Eric had his head in the file and was making notes. It was a minute or so until he lifted his head to address any questions.

"We have tried to get someone on the inside of the group, but as we don't know who they are, let alone where they are based, it has been impossible to trace them. But their targets all seem to be well insured, and therefore we think they are being fed information from someone inside the Insurance Market."

"Why don't you just follow the money?" I asked.

Eric frowned at me for asking such a stupid question "Don't you think we would have already tried that?"

"Well?"

"What money trail? There isn't an obvious person or organisation benefiting. All the events seem to be random and fortuitous. But we are convinced they are not. And if we knew why we have a better clue as to who."

Eric paused before answering the question that was forming in my mind.

"Why K-P? Cyber-crime is their latest *modus operandi*, and we needed someone totally reliable, who handled kidnap and ransom business; also someone whom we could build a legend around" Eric answered.

"How did you do that?" I was curious as to the story they had concocted.

"It doesn't matter." Eric was very off-hand with his reply and I felt he was hiding something.

Eric looked uncomfortable and I let it become very clear that if he wanted my help he would need to tell me about the 'legend' created for K-P. "We very subtly let it be known that K-P felt uncomfortable being beholden to you."

"What? That is ridiculous."

"Is it?" Eric looked directly into my eyes.

"Yes, it is!" I spoke as loudly as my throat would allow.

"Well, look at it from the outside. He lives in your mansion in Hertfordshire, works for you and when he goes on holiday it is to your property in Goa. Also there are some people in the market who believe all your good fortune is ill-deserved."

"But K-P would not have said any of this to anyone, he just wouldn't." I believed all that I said to be absolutely true.

"Unfortunately you are correct and K-P more than once threatened to pull out of the operation when we outlined his 'legend' to him. But given the tittle-tattle nature of the London Insurance Market, all we had to do was to very discretely mention this between two people having a conversation in a packed bar or pub, and then let the market grapevine do its work."

"How long ago did you spread this 'legend'?"

"Just after Christmas."

"And was this meeting with Mr Dominique the first contact?" I asked.

"So you have learned his name," Eric looked genuinely surprised. "Yes, the only contact was a phone call to arrange the meeting. Mr Dominique was very secretive about the purpose of the meeting other than he was potentially a new client. K-P would feed me details on all his meetings and phone calls. There were no records of a legitimate businessman called Mr Dominique, but our background checks threw up a Mr Dominique who was associated with criminal activities in the Middle East, and we thought that we might be in business."

"So it was your two goons who were waiting in the Grange Hotel?"

"Yes" Eric replied "and how did you know we had anyone there?"

"The Concierge told me that two people had been asking similar questions about K-P and Mr Dominique. Then you tried warning me off with the call to Brian Smithson. The Concierge pointed them out to me on the hotel's close circuit television. The clincher is that one of them is standing right outside the door at the moment."

Eric smiled, but again the eyes showed no warmth. "Very good Marc – the money hasn't dulled your senses then?"

"And then you had them follow us yesterday?"

"That wasn't the plan. We used K-P's code to try and reassure Jane, which we hoped would mean you might get off the scene, but when you returned to the area the following morning, we just decided to follow you. We sent another team to maintain surveillance at the Grange Hotel." Again Eric paused before asking his question "So why did you spend all that time in a closed wine bar on a Saturday morning? Expanding your wine cellar?" He asked with his sly smile.

I debated to myself whether I would tell him the truth and decided that I would. I explained that I had traced K-P and Mr Dominique to the wine bar after their meeting on Thursday.

"So that's how they lost them" Eric remarked as he wrote his notes, "they went next door so when my guys came out of the hotel they were already out of sight."

When I checked the close circuit TV in the hotel I saw that K-P dropped a piece of paper on the floor. I assumed it was a message for your guys, but the efficiency of the waitress meant that it was picked up as rubbish before it could be read."

Eric nodded as he continued to write in his file.

"It was a long-shot but the wine bar had not put out their rubbish from Thursday, so we searched the bins."

"Did you find anything?" There was anxiety in Eric's voice.

"Yes."

"What was it?"

I explained about our discovery. I asked him to look in my trouser pocket, from which he retrieved K-P's business card.

"We came to the conclusion that it referred to a sailing from Portsmouth to Dubai. And a Masterson Shipping vessel at that."

"So that's where you were heading," Eric was still writing as I spoke "and what did you expect to do when you got there?"

"No idea," I admitted.

"Still charging off with no preparation, as usual."

I felt myself becoming angry. "It wouldn't have been thus if you had told me what was going on" I retaliated.

"We couldn't afford to put K-P in further danger" Eric retorted.

"But Jimmy might still be alive." I felt tears coming to my eyes.

Eric got up and left the room.

I lay back on my pillow and closed my eyes, but I could not rest as I disseminated what I had learned from Eric. The confirmation that K-P's intentions were honourable was tempered by the needless waste of Jimmy's life. Also, Eric's reference to me being of use to him, concerned me as to what he meant by that comment. I had no idea what to expect next.

After a short while the door opened and a man dressed in a suit came into the room accompanied by the nurse who refused me water earlier.

"Hello?" I greeted the visitors.

The man merely smiled and came over and took my pulse, whilst the nurse put a thermometer in my right ear. It beeped and she walked around to my left ear and took my temperature from that side. They then left the room. I tried straining to hear anything that might give a clue to my whereabouts but I could hear absolutely nothing, not even the whirring of any air-conditioning, even though the temperature in the room was uncommonly cool for a hospital. I had not heard the two people come into my room earlier, so I guessed they were wearing rubber soled footwear. The man in the suit was the only colour in an otherwise white desert. In fact, if he had been himself dressed in white, I would have seriously considered that I was dead and at St Peter's gates.

Time to investigate I decided. I tried pulling back the bed clothes, but as hard as I yanked and tugged the sheet, blanket and top cover, I could not free them. They were either tucked so far under the bed or secured somehow to the bed frame. I tried wiggling up the bed but it became clear that I was somehow attached to the bottom of the bed frame as well. The bed clothes were so tightly tucked in that I could not even slide under the bed clothes to try and release myself.

I was becoming annoyed and then moved the top half of my body to the edge of the bed and was able to lean over sufficiently to look down the side of the bed. There was no sign of how to release the bed clothes. I reached as far as I could but was unable to feel anything other than the tautly pulled top cover. I shuffled across to the other side of the bed, but it was the same story. The exertions had made me very weary. I had been very effectively immobilized, only having my hands and arms free from the covers. I reached out to the 'call' button and pushed it twice. Within a minute the nurse noiselessly opened the door and entered the room, immediately closing the door behind her.

She cocked her head to one side in an enquiring manner. A natural way to invite someone to ask a question, without uttering a sound. Perhaps she was dumb?

"I need to go to the toilet, please?" I asked.

Noiselessly she glided across the room towards my bed and she leaned down, I thought to release the bed clothes, but no, an all-white bedpan appeared in her hands. She put the bedpan on the bed, then fiddled at the end of the bed and an electric motor started, and immediately the sheets loosened. After a few seconds the nurse turned off the electric motor, turned on her heel and left the room, without a single sound. The door opened and the security guard came into the room.

"Please do not get out of bed Mr Edge" was all he said.

Whilst the toilet request was a subterfuge, I was able to relieve myself. I placed the bedpan on the bedside cabinet and, feeling exhausted probably through dehydration, I turned on my side and closed my eyes. After less than a minute, the nurse came into the room to collect the bed-pan, but did not tighten the sheets.

The guard suggested that I stay in bed and get some rest. He reassured me that he would be just outside if I needed anything. The lights in the room were extinguished as he exited. Big brother was definitely at play here, and I realised that someone had been watching my futile efforts of trying to get out of bed. I fell fast asleep.

My slumber was fitful and I re-dreamt the accident, waking with the shout of "Jimmy" on my lips, and the headlights on the lorry bearing down on us. I woke with a shock. The lights in the room were on, and it was obviously time for me to wake up. I looked around the room, and felt much less queasy than my previous reveille. What's more there was a white beaker on the bedside cabinet. A white post-it note was stuck to the side of the beaker, with the works "WATER. SIP SLOWLY" written in precise capital letters upon the paper.

I followed instructions. As I surveyed the room I saw a page of a newspaper in a white plastic sleeve, lying on the bed. I picked it up and instantly regretted doing so as I read the headline of the article *Young Father Killed in Accident*. I pulled the article from the plastic sleeve. It appeared from the type-face and style of writing that the article came from a tabloid newspaper. The Daily Mail or Daily Express was my best guess.

The article gave an account of my Range Rover being found in Surrey with no explanation as to why my car left the road.

"What about the lorry coming the other way?" I spoke aloud to my unseen watchers. "He must have seen us?"

Obviously not; the reporter had sources claiming we were exceeding the speed limit, which was absolutely true. The article named Jimmy as being a fatal casualty in the accident, and I felt a pain in my chest. If that was not enough the next sentence of the article rocked me to the very core: *Multi-millionaire Marcus Edge who was driving the car at the time of the accident is in a drug-induced coma and it is feared that he may not survive the accident..*

The Long Sleep

I tried to keep awake and think through the implications of what I had just read, but despite the wild thoughts running amok in my mind I kept drifting in and out of consciousness. When I did wake from one of these passages I was sure I was dreaming because Gerda's face was smiling down on me.

"Hello Marc, my darling." Her voice seemed so real.

I reached out my hand and touched her face. She was flesh. A tear fell from her eyes and landed on my lips. I tasted the sweet saltiness and my own eyes welled up with absolute joy. I then realised that she was not alone. Behind her was Eric Jones, gazing upon our reunion with a half-smile dancing on his lips.

"Hello Gerda, my love. How did you get here? Are the children OK?"

"They're fine with Paul, back in Vieland," she smiled and took my hands in hers. "Eric arranged for me to travel back here in a private plane."

I turned to look at Eric and his face gave nothing away.

"I suppose there is a very important reason to fly my wife here at the expense of the taxpayer?"

He said nothing.

"And by the way where is here? What day is it?"

Again no response – visibly or audibly.

"I hope it's worth it because apparently I am not long for this world." I held up the newspaper with Monday's date, which indicated that my life was in the balance.

"Marc, its Tuesday. I am sorry but I can't tell you where you are for your own, and your family's safety. Gerda was brought here in the back of a van and only knows that it is two hours from an airport in the south of the country. And what's more, all the staff at this establishment have been told not to talk to you – again for your safety."

"Can you please ask them to release me?"

Gerda looked startled. "Eric, is Marc a prisoner?"

"No he is not – but we need both of you to understand the situation and then we can all decide what happens next" Eric replied.

"That's no excuse to keep him…" Gerda searched for the right words "…strapped in bed." She started pulling at the loosened bed-clothes but they wouldn't budge.

"Hang on, I will call the nurse." Eric could see Gerda's eyes flaring with anger and knew he would have to do something. He left the room.

"Thank you my darling." I was so pleased to see Gerda.

"Is it true that Jimmy is dead?"

"Y-y-yes." I just about whispered my reply but every time I thought of Jimmy I felt sick.

"What happened?" she asked.

"I am not quite sure" I hesitated before continuing. "Initially I thought it was just an accident. A lorry was coming the other way and I swerved to avoid it. The car left the road and rolled down a hill. I was knocked unconscious and Jimmy…." my voice tailed away, unable to say the words "was killed."

"Why do you say you thought it was an accident?"

"Well the lorry must have seen us leave the road, but it was the next morning before anyone found us. Also the article in the newspaper makes no mention of the lorry."

"Perhaps the driver of the lorry has other reasons not to make himself known?" Gerda's good nature showing itself.

"Hmm," I replied non-committally.

The door opened and Eric returned not only with the nurse but also the doctor. The doctor marched up to the bed, produced a blood pressure device from one pocket and a stethoscope from the other. He took my blood pressure and pulse whilst the nurse used the digital device to take my temperature in each ear. A perfunctory nod from the doctor and the nurse went to the bottom of the bed and operated the release mechanism, because in seconds the bed-covers were completely loose. She then reached under the bed covers and I could feel her cold hands on my leg and the strap to stop me shuffling up the bed was removed.

The doctor and nurse left the room. With difficulty, and not a small amount of pain on my right side, I raised myself into a sitting position and Gerda sat beside me on the bed.

"So Eric, I want some answers," Gerda squeezed my hand as I spoke and I added "please?"

He brought the white chair from across the room and sat beside the bed. He was very serious.

"Marc, we have two options and neither one of them is very palatable."

"Please explain?" I was becoming nervous and I could hear it in my own voice, and again Gerda gently squeezed my hand to try to calm me.

"We believe Mr Dominique is planning something on a much larger scale with far-reaching ramifications. We asked K-P to try and assist us."

"Why involve him? You must have your own henchmen to do your dirty work?"

Eric looked embarrassed and paused before answering "What I am telling you both must stay in this room, because it affects both of you, your families and K-P's family, OK?"

Gerda looked at me and I answered for both of us "Understood Eric."

"We may have a leak, and that's why we asked K-P to assist; plus the person who met with Mr Dominique had to be totally legitimate, to stand any chance of success."

"Has K-P been discovered?"

"I sincerely hope not, otherwise I fear for his well-being." Eric looked worried as he spoke.

"How many people know about K-P?" I asked.

"Only myself and two others, both of whom I can totally vouch for," he continued "but one of them has gone missing. Also the lorry you spoke about."

"Yes!"

"We can find no trace of it," Eric replied.

"It was your people following us on Saturday afternoon, wasn't it?"

"Not exactly my people, but they were from the police" Eric admitted.

"So the man outside the door of this room is from Special Branch?" I suggested.

He nodded.

"And the other has gone missing?"

Again he nodded.

"So there's your leak?"

"I really doubt it because the two men were hand-picked, having no knowledge of my investigations. In fact that was why they were hand-picked. We just do not have enough information yet."

"Well how are you going to sort out this mess?" I asked in a raised voice, and with no accompanying squeeze of the hand from Gerda, she was obviously in agreement with my increasing ire.

"That depends, Marc, on which of the choices you select." The half-smile returned to his lips.

"What do you mean Eric?" My tone was becoming increasingly belligerent.

"The article in the newspaper was deliberately placed to buy us time until you decide which choice you select." He held his hand up to stop me from interrupting. "You can recover from the accident and walk out of here in a few days; however, there is a chance that you and your family's safety might not be guaranteed…"

"Why not?" Gerda asked in a hushed tone.

"Mr Dominique is undoubtedly involved in serious crime, and he is probably aware of your attempts to track down K-P and will be concerned that you might continue, he may even have been behind the lorry that forced you off the road."

"Ah-ah, so you do believe me now?"

"Possibly, possibly not; however, there is a chance that K-P, his family, you and your family might be in danger." Eric stopped for a moment whilst Gerda and I comprehended what he was saying.

"Eric, what is the alternative?" It was Gerda asking in her hushed voice that seemed to carry much more emotion than me shouting.

Eric looked me straight in the eyes. "Officially you are to remain in a coma here……."

"But unofficially?" I interrupted him.

Eric told us his plan.

Eric left Gerda and me alone to make our decision. But before he left, he explained his rationale for announcing for keeping me incapacitated. First and foremost, it would protect our family, only – and he re-emphasised this point over and over again – if we kept this totally secret between ourselves. Gerda could not tell our children, her brother Paul, my parents and my brother or sister. Secondly it might possibly help K-P's situation and protect his family. Lastly – and the most difficult decision for us to take – Eric wanted me to go to Dubai and try and make contact with Mr Dominique. He explained that this would be totally unofficial, and I would have to fund it myself, because he could not trust the leak was from someone in his own department.

"Marc, I don't want you to do it" Gerda said.

I didn't reply.

She continued "We have enough money to last us ten lifetimes. Let us just sell-up and emigrate to- to-"

"South America?" I smiled.

"Yes or a similar land?" Gerda in almost a whisper said what was in my head and my heart. "It's K-P isn't it?"

I nodded "If it wasn't for him, I wouldn't have you, the children, the money, or anything."

It was Gerda's turn to nod.

"He only wants me to try and make contact with Mr Dominique." Even I didn't think I sounded convinced.

Gerda stood up and paced around the room. I knew that it was best not to disturb her, and I surmised that we were being watched, so we would be left alone.

After five minutes or so, Gerda came back to sit on the bed with me.

"It's up to you Marc, but if you say 'yes' we need to plan carefully and make arrangements in case…." she paused "you don't come back to us."

I took her in my arms and held her very tightly. "Of course I will come back to you my darling." I turned my head up to the far corner of the room and nodded my head. Within seconds, Eric had re-entered the room.

The three of us then spent the best part of four hours planning. The biggest sticking point - and the cause of me almost backing out – was that I wanted a way of keeping in touch with Gerda. Any form of mobile, cell or smart phone, was completely out of the question because they could be tracked so easily, as could any other electronic device. Using the public telephone system – especially from abroad – was equally dangerous. I suggested the internet, but again that could be easily hacked. It had to be something totally secure and Eric eventually conceded and said that I needed to go and visit a friend of his in the City, who used to be the quartermaster of a very special regiment in the British Army.

We agreed that a large amount of cash was needed very quickly, and he arranged for a solicitor to visit us the following day, so that a will and power of attorney could be implemented for Gerda to act totally with my authority, whilst I was incapacitated. The plan was for Gerda to put my assets in Goa up for sale. We agreed there was no point in trying to sell the land in Africa because it was essentially worthless. These sales would take time, but the bank should be able to release two hundred thousand pounds from my accounts to Gerda immediately.

I needed to stay in my room until I was to be smuggled out to Eric's own flat in Bermondsey. Being the school holidays, his wife and children were in Scotland with her brother for two weeks, and Eric was to join them at the weekend in three days' time, by which time I should be in Dubai.

Other things which had to be arranged included an identity and a disguise. I favoured disguising myself as an elderly Asian gentleman as I had done some five years previously, but both Eric and Gerda disagreed as it was amateurish. Also it needed to withstand the scrutiny of Mr Dominique. It was decided that I would take on the identity of a South African insurance claims adjuster. My former father-in-law was from Zimbabwe and so I could imitate a Transvaal accent and, particularly with Gerda being Dutch, I also understood a few words of Afrikaans. Eric's quartermaster could fix me up with a passport. We decided to go with flaxen hair including a beard, and Eric would obtain contact lenses to tint my eyes bluer. He would also organise a hand-held sun lamp to give my face a suntanned appearance.

"In the early hours of the morning we will transfer Marc to my flat in London for a couple of days, and there he can work on his disguise. A news release would be given to the media that he had regained consciousness but there were still complications. This would build enough background to the visit by the solicitor tomorrow. Gerda can stay with you here until after the solicitors visit, then we will fly her back to Holland."

"What about the doctor?" I asked.

"Both he and the nurse are totally trustworthy."

I cocked an eye at Eric in view of what he told me earlier about the leak in his department – although he never did say which department he worked in.

In response to my questioning look, he replied "The doctor and the nurse are attached to the Navy."

The morning dragged very slowly in contrast to the night, which passed too quickly with Gerda squeezed in the bed next to me. Even though I was heavily bruised, gently we made love quietly, with an intensity never experienced before, her soft skin yielding to my every touch and caress. In the afternoon the solicitor visited us, I had to give the impression of being of sound mind – to ensure the validity of the Will and Power of Attorney – whilst still appearing poorly following the accident. He was a local solicitor and if he were to be asked by the media he would report that I was on a saline drip with a hacking cough. We had decided this complication after the accident, could lead to pneumonia, because of the fact I had not been found until twelve hours after the accident. We all felt it was a very sound explanation.

Whilst the solicitor was taking instructions, I added a further request, which was that he should form a trust for Jimmy's son, and that Gerda and Jimmy's wife Carla were to be the trustees. The trust would be funded to the tune of two hundred and fifty thousand pounds. When the solicitor returned in the early evening for me to execute the various documents, there were tears in my eyes as I signed the trust.

Eric and I talked about how I would try and reach out to Mr Dominique.

"I think it is something to do with insurance obviously and specifically he was very eager to meet with K-P because of his expertise in Kidnap and Ransom Insurance."

"Special Contingency Insurance" I corrected Eric.

"Yes, of course, Special Contingency Insurance," he smiled "some of our overseas brethren have deemed Kidnap and Ransom Insurance to be illegal."

"So just re-brand it to help the Italians."

"Not just them," Eric added.

"I need a refresher before I meet with Mr Dominique."

"Do you know any underwriters in that market?"

I thought for a moment "Not really – I know a couple by sight and reputation."

"What about Andrew Vervy?" Eric asked.

"No, never met him. Who does he work for?"

"He is the Special Contingency Class of Business Underwriter for Deeks Syndicate in Lloyd's," Eric explained.

Deeks were one of the oldest Lloyd's Syndicates; they were renowned for being very particular about whom they employed – usually only Oxbridge graduates – and they were quite a specialised insurer. They would lead most policies they participated on. In recent years they had formed alliances, first with a successful US Insurer but that ended when they flirted with a Bermudian Reinsurer. Neither of these alliances had lasted the course probably due to Deeks wish to underwrite for profit rather than sheer premium volume. They owned their own Managing Agency, which was privately owned, and thus not publicly quoted on the London Stock Exchange. They prided themselves on their results; however, because they did not underwrite such a broad book of business as other Managing Agents, they were vulnerable if the losses in their chosen markets were worse than the market average. Despite its potential vulnerability the two Deeks Lloyd's syndicates remained in the top quartile of Lloyd's of London results year-after-year. The reason for two Lloyd's syndicates is that the success of Deeks resulted in them still having individual 'names' and not all corporate capital. No matter how hard they tried, the individual 'names' refused to sell out to the corporate capital. Deeks had formed the second corporate capital syndicate so that they could underwrite more business; but Lloyd's of London were very strict, and they would not allow certain risks to be ceded to the individual names' syndicate, and other risks to the corporate capital syndicate. Many years previously there had been a problem, prior to the creation of corporate syndicates, where the seemingly better risks were ceded to 'baby' syndicates. These 'baby' syndicates often had the actual underwriters as the investors, with a larger personal percentage of the 'baby' syndicate, than the main syndicate. There was a scandal and accusations of improper practices. So after the arrival of corporate syndicates, the individual names' rights had to be protected. Lloyd's of London typically would demand that each risk had to be underwritten by both the individual 'names' syndicate, and the corporate syndicate within set parameters. For example, the individual 'names' syndicate might take twenty percent and the corporate syndicate eighty percent of each risk underwritten by the Managing Agency. The percentage underwritten of each risk was usually less than one hundred percent, particularly on the larger and more complex risks. But this was not the case for Special Contingency – or Kidnap and Ransom – Insurance, where the confidentiality of who purchases the insurance is paramount, and favours a single insurer approach. It is the type of business that perfectly suits the private approach by Deeks.

"Good," Eric said. "I will arrange for you to have coffee with him on Friday. He mustn't recognise you as Marcus Edge."

The news of my condition was released to the press at eleven o'clock in the evening of the Wednesday, where it was suggested that a controlled coma may be required, depending upon how I recovered from the previous coma. A substitute occupied my bed, and I was put into a body bag and wheeled out into - as Eric explained - an unmarked van. Once in the van, the body bag was opened by the doctor. He and the nurse were both in the van, but not a word was spoken throughout the hour long, stop-start trip to Eric's flat.

The hardest part was saying goodbye to Gerda, and knowing that she had to deal with the subterfuge, when dealing with our families and friends. She was superb and I was confident that she would be able to cope. I knew that the only way this would end well, was up to me to reach out to Mr Dominique, and hopefully find K-P.

Preparation

Transporting me to Eric's flat in London went without a hitch, and I was installed there just after one o'clock in the morning. From the nature of the journey, I guessed that we had been somewhere in Surrey or Kent, albeit there were no windows in the back of the van.

Eric showed me into the spare room and said that he would see me briefly in the morning. He had changed his plans and decided to travel a couple of days early to Scotland. It took me ages to fall asleep and then it was very fitful. I did not feel rested at all when Eric woke me at seven o'clock.

"Marc, here are the keys to the flat," he passed to me a key ring upon which were three keys "the mortice lock must be engaged every time you leave the flat. The Yale key speaks for itself and the third – smaller – key locks and unlocks the alarm. Please remember to engage it."

I smiled wanly from behind my sleepy façade.

"Here is a phone that I want you to keep turned on at all times."

"Even on an aeroplane?" I questioned.

"Yes, put it into Flight Mode and we'll still be able to track you. All calls will be scrambled, but don't phone any friends, family or work colleagues."

"Is it a satellite phone?" I asked.

"Sort of – if you are out of range of a phone provider it will not work as a phone but you can text, and the tracker will continue to work."

I nodded my head in understanding.

"Now rest for an hour and then you will have a visitor."

"Who's that?"

"Nobby."

"Who?"

He smiled, and said "Good luck," from over his shoulder as he went downstairs. Moments later, I heard the door of the flat close.

I lay back in my bed totally awake with a kaleidoscope of different thoughts running through my mind. I must have dozed off, because I woke with a start to a rapping on the door of the flat, interspersed by the flat bell ringing. I checked my watch, it was exactly eight o'clock.

"Alright, I'm coming!" I shouted as I walked down the stairs to the entrance door "Is that Nobby?" I asked as I reached the door.

"Yes" was the reply from the other side of the closed door.

I hesitated before opening the door "Who are you speaking to?" I asked.

"You're in a coma in the home of a Scotsman."

I opened the door and was met by a caricature of a British Army officer from World War II.

"Hello", he thrust out his left hand and I could see that the right hand had been replaced by a prosthetic. "The name's Colonel Clarke, with an 'e' but please call me Nobby."

He stood over six feet tall, mostly bald with blonde hair at the sides and back. He wore a clipped moustache, which I guess had been bleached by the sun, as his head was a combination of tan and sunburn. He had a long leather coat draped like a cape over his shoulders that looked like it had just been taken from a German Wehrmacht officer. He looked like he was in his sixties, and whilst he had 'filled out', there was more than an underlying hint of a very fit man from his earlier years.

"Well, are you going to let me in?"

"Certainly, please excuse my earlier hesitation."

"Not a problem young man" and he came into the flat with two large suitcases, which he wheeled straight into the kitchen. One was cleverly attached to his artificial hand.

I had hardly shut the door when Nobby called to me. "I want you to take two of these" he held up an unmarked blister pack containing some form of tablets "every four hours starting now - please?"

"What are they?"

"A cheat's way of getting a sun-tan." He smiled as he spoke and his endearing attitude must have made him popular with his troops, but I felt sure just beneath the surface he was as hard as steel, and a mixture of easy charm and resolve probably meant that very few of his orders were ever questioned.

I took the blister pack and dutifully swallowed two with some water, and asked "How quickly do they work?"

"About a week" he replied "but we don't have a week; so I want you stark naked except for your briefs and in front of this sun lamp for twenty minutes twice a day, once first thing in the morning and last thing at night."

"Isn't that dangerous?"

"Not as dangerous as a bullet if you are discovered not to be whom you say you are?"

He had a point, and I went back to my bedroom for some boxer shorts.

When I returned he had set the portable sun lamp on the edge of the kitchen table. He told me to concentrate on my face and upper body, but to try and make sure the rays reached as much of the skin as possible. He left the room and closed the door. I put on the sun goggles and turned on the sun lamp timer for ten minutes. The lamp was about twenty centimetres in diameter, with the front panel opening on a hinge which could be used as a stand. After a bit of adjustment by me standing just over a metre away from the table, the rays were reaching most of my front. The lamp turned itself off after ten minutes, and I reset it for another ten minutes, so I could do the back of my body.

When the sun lamp turned off for the second time, the door opened almost immediately and Nobby walked into the kitchen.

"Good. I will make breakfast and coffee, whilst you have a shower and can you dye your hair and stubble with this?" He held up an unmarked bottle.

"What colour?" I asked.

"Hopefully blonde and you may need two treatments to start with."

I nodded my head.

"Two eggs, or three, in your omelette?" he shouted after me.

"Two – please?" Obviously it was assumed that I liked omelette, which thankfully I did.

"And don't shave" he added.

Fifteen minutes later, I walked back into the kitchen dressed only in the dressing gown from the hospital.

"Where have my clothes gone?" I asked politely.

"Ah," Nobby replied whilst serving the omelettes onto warm plates, which already were laden with tomatoes and mushrooms "gone, my dear fellow." It all looked delicious, and at that moment toast popped up from the toaster. Military efficiency obviously pervaded all parts of Nobby's life as he ushered me to sit down at the table, where the sun lamp was previously.

He let his words sink in, as our teeth sank into the hot breakfast; it tasted absolutely as good as it looked, and we ate in silence. It was the first time I had an appetite since the accident and I ate without feeling queasy. As I finished my second piece of toast, Nobby explained that all my clothes had been disposed of, and I had a new wardrobe contained in one of the suitcases.

"You need to try everything on, and then we need to wash and dry all the clothes a couple of times, so they do not look too new."

"How long ago did you buy the clothes?" I tried to make it sound an idle question but Nobby knew instantly the import of the underlying enquiry.

"Yesterday morning" he smiled.

"Truly?"

"Yes, truly. You can check my passport if you want?"

"What, you bought them yourself?"

He tried to look offended, at which he failed miserably, and said "I am not altogether without a bit of style you know."

"That's not what…."

"I know my boy what you meant. I was already in South Africa when I got the call from Eric."

"Hmm" I replied.

"The fewer the number of people who know about the subterfuge, the better." His voice hardened by more than a modicum.

After clearing the debris from breakfast he emptied the contents of the second suitcase on to the table. I busied myself with the washing up, and when I had finished, I saw there were enough clothes for a fortnight and commented to that effect.

"Hopefully you won't need that long?" It was framed as a question by Nobby but he didn't expect an answer. "Try them all on my lad so we can get them into the washing machine."

About half an hour later, half the clothes were in the washing machine, mostly the shirts and tops which were not dark in colour. The rest including a great pair of moleskins would be for the second load. As well as the moleskins, I really liked the leather jacket Nobby had bought, and as that could not be washed I decided to wear it around the flat, together with a pair of leather loafers to break them in. To complete the wardrobe there was a sports jacket that looked second hand. All of the clothes fitted perfectly, but in the couple of hours of knowing him, it would have been a surprise if Nobby's eye for detail would have let him down.

"Right, that's made a start on the outside," Nobby passed across a bunch of papers "now let's address the inside."

"What's this?" I asked.

"Your new identity" he replied.

I started leafing through the papers. My name was James McMichaels and I was born in the United Kingdom, but moved to Cape Town when I was ten.

"British?" I queried.

"Scottish, it will help with the accent," Nobby explained "also if you want to tell a lie, make it as close to the truth as possible."

"There are two passports here."

"That is not unusual for Brits who emigrated to South Africa twenty years ago, most of the English cricket team was full of South Africans in the seventies and eighties."

"Good point" I remarked.

"I believe your former father-in-law was from Rhodesia, sorry I meant Zimbabwe."

I nodded.

"So you can mimic the accent?" Nobby asked.

"Sort of," I replied sheepishly.

"From now on, try to speak with a South African accent and I will teach you the odd useful phrase – mostly profanity." He smiled.

I carried on reading the legend which had been prepared for me.

Nobby stood up. "I was flying most of the night so I am off for a kip for a couple of hours. I will test you over lunch to establish how much you have learned."

I sat in the comfortable chairs in front of a large television to study the papers Nobby had given me. I didn't get very far because the next thing I knew was the beep from the washing machine. I too had fallen asleep, and to avoid dozing off again I stood up and emptied the washing machine, and then loaded it up with the remaining clothes before Nobby could wake up. I made myself a cup of coffee and resumed reading.

I was unmarried and an insurance surveyor for construction sites, again not straying too far away from my real job, and hopefully I would be able to be convincing, if questioned. Although the saying *you can fool some of the people most of the time, and most of the people some of the time, but you can't fool all of the people all of the time* rang through my mind, and I hoped that the last phrase was not a prophesy of what was to come in Dubai.

The reason for my being in Dubai was to inspect a number of incomplete construction projects, which had been left unfinished when the money ran out in two thousand and eight. Dubai had been hit very hard during the Global Financial Crisis, the property bubble bursting, and a number of extravagant projects remaining idle. Whilst large parts of the world were still suffering and trying to climb out of the economic abyss, Dubai was now forging ahead again. The problem was that the large number of projects that were left unfinished may not now be suitable for completion. Left unprotected and with no maintenance for a number of years, the sensible option for some of the projects would be to tear down what's been built and start again. A lot of contractors were left with large debts, and wound down their operation in Dubai, vowing never to return. One large South African contractor had scaled back their operations, and weathered the storm. My cover was that I had been employed by the Contractors' All Risks' insurers to inspect a number of projects, which a South African contractor was considering for completion. The fire at the Address Hotel also meant that safety standards were under review, which was an excellent additional reason for my visit.

As I looked up from my papers, the washing machine pinged to indicate the second load had been completed. Nobby appeared from his slumber, looking bright as a button.

"Time for lunch I think" he announced.

We worked well in the kitchen together, with Nobby preparing the food and me skivvying for him. I put the first load of washing on for a second wash, not bothering to wait for it to fully dry, and hung up the second load. As we worked Nobby would ask me questions about James McMichaels to see how much I had absorbed; and he caught me out far too often.

"You'll have to do better than that young man." He glared at me over lunch.

I nodded in agreement.

"We need to do some photography straight after lunch, and then back to studying."

Again I just nodded.

The photography was for my two passports, and a South African driving licence.

Before we started, I asked "I thought you wanted me to be unshaven. Won't it look odd if my passport photo does not show me with a beard?"

"Quite the contrary" Nobby remarked, but declined to explain, whilst fiddling with the controls on his camera.

It was much larger that most cameras that are advertised in magazines or on the television. There was also a large flash attachment that was reminiscent of the equipment used by photographers some thirty or forty years ago. And I said as much to Nobby.

"Ah, you are both right and wrong" Nobby looked up from his camera satisfied with the adjustments he had made. "This is a Leica from the late nineteen forties, the flash gun is from nineteen sixties Carnaby Street. The innards of the camera have been gutted and filled with electronic gadgetry." He continued to answer my previous question "Your stubble of two days will hardly show on the passport, but by the time you arrive in Dubai it will be much more pronounced."

I obviously looked confused, because Nobby hardly paused for breath when he explained that a passport photograph which looks too much like the person standing in front of them, will raise more immigration officers' eyebrows than those which don't.

"And if you care to check, those passports are dated as issued two years ago. A beard puts at least five years onto the age of a person."

Nobby took at least a dozen photographs of me in a neutral pose, but he varied the speed of the shutter, the aperture of the lens and lighting. No two photographs were exactly the same, yet there was a very discernible difference between the first and the last. The results were instantaneous as his electronics sent the pictures from his camera to his small laptop computer. He then produced another box, about the size of a cigarette packet – and plugged it into his laptop. Seconds later two passport photographs of me were produced, which he placed immediately into the two passports. He then photographed the results and minutes later they had been sent to the South African High Commission in London, and that would be used to obtain my South African driving licence on the following morning, when I would be required to appear in person.

The rest of the day continued with me studying my legend, having another session in front of the sun lamp and cooking supper with Nobby. By the end of the day – nine o'clock – I was dead on my feet.

"Not bad for a person who has been in a coma for twenty-four hours." Nobby smiled wanly at me as I retired to my bedroom.

I missed Gerda desperately and felt so miserable that my children, parents, family and friends had to cope with my supposed life-threatening condition. But no matter how depressed I felt, I would just think about Jane and K-P. I owed K-P my life, and that was a debt that I hoped I would now be able to repay.

Foolhardy

On Friday morning Nobby enhanced my beard, and he gave me some glasses which were slightly twisted. He explained that they would distract people from the colour of my eyes. By nine o'clock Nobby was packed and ready to leave, at the same time I would start to meet up with the underwriter from Deeks, and visit the South African High Commission.

"I have done my bit my boy," he announced in his genial fashion "the rest is up to you."

I nodded uncertainly.

"Remember to keep that phone on you at all times, and resist the temptation to phone anyone who might know you."

Again I nodded my compliance.

"One last gift for you." He reached inside one of the suitcases, and produced a cardboard cylinder, which he passed to me.

"What is it?" I asked.

"Open it and find out."

I opened the metal lid at one end of the cylinder and removed a panama hat.

"I bought it for myself but I think your need is greater than mine."

I was about to complain when he held up his hand to stop me.

"Until your hair grows, your ears are still a potential giveaway to your identity."

"My ears?" I exclaimed.

"Ears are very difficult to change, when altering a person's identity," Nobby replied "so the best solution is to try and cover them. We don't have enough time, so a hat is the next best thing, plus it will be very hot and sunny in Dubai." With that final remark, he shook my hand firmly, wished me good luck and then he was gone.

The flat seemed empty without Nobby, and so I busied myself with menial household chores, to kill the time before I left for my appointment at the South African High Commission. I knew my legend was watertight, but nevertheless I was nervous about passing myself off as James McMichaels. I had selected a plain cotton twill shirt, the moleskins and the linen jacket for my appointment, which was set for half-past ten at the South African High Commission. A pair of leather loafers completed the ensemble. Luckily it was a bright sunny morning, so the Panama hat and tinted glasses would not seem too incongruous. I left the flat at a quarter to ten, remembering to set the alarm before leaving.

With the pleasant weather I decided to walk to the High Commission. I strolled briskly to London Bridge, where I joined the Thames Path that runs along the river on the south side from the Design Museum, near Tower Bridge, and then to Westminster Bridge. The South African High Commission is in Trafalgar Square. With the sun out the South Bank was already teaming with tourists and street performers that thronged the path, particularly from the Globe Theatre and past the Tate Modern. I headed across the river at Westminster Bridge and then made my way towards Trafalgar Square. I checked my watch and it was already ten fifteen. I quickened my pace and arrived at the High Commission with five minutes to spare.

I went to reception and was directed to another floor of the building. I made myself known to the person in the waiting area who gave me a form to complete. I retreated to a seat where I entered the information that I had committed to memory over the previous days. After fifteen minutes I returned the form and offered my passport. The woman took my form as well as my passport and asked me to sit down again. I picked up a magazine and pretended to read an article, but I could not concentrate as I felt sick; I was sure that my false identity would be blown in an instant. Twenty minutes passed and I was called back to the desk and my passport was returned to me.

"Thank you Mr McMichaels, your new driving licence will be posted to you in two weeks."

This was not what I expected so I gulped audibly and the woman looked up at me. "I am flying to Dubai on business tomorrow and I may need to hire a car."

The receptionist was middle-aged, and cocked her head to one side, indicating that I should have thought about that earlier.

I continued "I'm so sorry but is there anything you are able to do for me?"

She shook her head and then looked through her appointments diary. "A lot of people are on holiday this week, because of the school holidays, so it is very difficult. Come back this afternoon after half past four, and I will see what we can do."

I arrived at St Paul's about an hour ahead of my scheduled appointment with Andrew Vervy from Deeks Syndicate. The rendezvous for the meeting was to be in a café within the square of shops and cafes near the Cathedral, far enough away from the heart of the insurance district. I passed the time by walking down to the Millennium Bridge which crossed the Thames to the old Bankside Power Station now the site of the

Tate Modern Art Gallery. I always liked crossing the Thames to the South Bank, as I enjoyed the panoramic view from here across to St Paul's with the London Eye and the Houses of Parliament to the left, then swinging around past the city to Tower Bridge on my right. I stood there for at least twenty minutes, before returning to the café, where I was to meet Andrew Vervy.

There was a well-dressed middle aged gentleman sitting by himself in the corner of the café. As I approached he lifted his head and asked if I was Mr McMichaels.

"Yes I am." I extended my hand to greet him.

"I understand from Eric Jones that I am not to ask you any questions, but you on the other hand can ask me as many questions as you wish." He paused and gave me half a smile, before he continued. "I will try to answer as many of your questions as possible, so long as it does not revolve around any particular risks that we insure. Special Contingency Insurance is highly confidential, and in some territories certain elements of the cover are illegal."

"Yes, I am aware of that fact," I replied.

We sat talking for over an hour. At first I asked the most basic of questions, so as to try and give the pretence that I was a novice; however, as my questions became more detailed Andrew Vervy hesitated a couple of times before answering, even becoming slightly evasive.

"Are you really a journalist?" he asked at one point.

"Yes, just doing some investigating before starting a new investigative assignment."

"Oh, I see" was his reply, when it was obvious that clearly he didn't understand at all, but Eric's influence in the London Insurance Market carried some weight.

Towards the end of the interview it became clear to me that protecting the identity of those who are insured, and the amount of money they are insured for, are of the highest priority. These aspects are cloaked in absolute secrecy, because in the wrong hands this information could be dynamite, with the result that the people insured could be a bigger target than if they were not insured. I thanked Andrew for his generosity in sparing me his time and wisdom. He wished me good luck and I contrived that he left the café before me.

It was half past twelve, and I had four hours ahead of me, with nothing to do. I walked eastwards, not really having a direction or purpose just turning things over in my mind. Perhaps my sub-conscious was leading me towards Lloyd's and the City of London.

I was brought out of my thoughts when I reached Bank Station; from hereon I was getting close to Lloyd's of London and the centre of the world renowned Insurance Market. Whilst the City of London housed a number of financial services, each are clustered around different areas of the City. The area around Bank Station was dominated by banks and discount houses. At the end of Cornhill was Gracechurch Street the western boundary of the Insurance Market, with Aldgate to the East and the Northern and Southern boundaries being Bishopsgate and Upper Thames Street.

With my panama hat pulled as far forward as possible, so not to look too ridiculous, I walked along Cornhill. I crossed over Gracechurch Street and into Leadenhall Market. It was after one o'clock, and the market was hustling and bustling with a melange of different people, Lloyd's Brokers carrying their slip cases[1], tourists visiting Leadenhall Market and the owners of the street food kiosks. Leadenhall Market was well known long before Lloyd's of London made its home in Lime Street, adjacent to the ancient site. It was originally the site of a Roman Forum, and many years later became the French Poultry Market (the English equivalent being situated at Poultry near Bank Station) and the name Leadenhall Market was the result of the construction of the present structure, being covered by lead slates. The market had a renaissance following the Harry Potter films, as it was the setting for Diagon Alley. The everyday shops had been replaced by up-market boutiques and restaurants. Two public houses survived but even they have been gentrified.

Lunchtime was in full swing and it was Friday with the sun out. Brokers and Underwriters were already out enjoying the early spring weather, so I would probably recognise a number of them. I suddenly realised how foolhardy I had been walking through Leadenhall Market, as someone might see through my disguise. I decided to leave Leadenhall Market and I was just passing The Lamb public house when I stopped in my tracks. When the weather was not too cold, most people would drink outside The Lamb, at the centre of Leadenhall Market, rather than inside. There in front of me was Joshua my brother, within a large group of people, a number of whom I recognised. I don't know what possessed me, but I went inside The Lamb and bought myself a beer. I then stood on the edge of the gathering, and looked away from the group. I

---

[1] A slip-case is a rectangular piece of leather folded in the middle fastened by one slap of leather on the right and another at the bottom. They are used by Lloyd's Brokers to carry 'slips' which are a summary of the risk they are placing.

occasionally glanced at my watch as though I was waiting for somebody, when in fact I was straining as hard as I could to what was being said to or by my brother.

Most of the conversation was unsurprisingly about me. A lot of people were coming up to Joshua, offering their best wishes for my recovery. Initially he seemed OK with what was being said, but after a time I could tell that he was unhappy with the plaudits, and his acknowledgements were becoming shorter and sometimes bordering on the curt. I glanced at him and recognised a face that I had seen throughout my childhood, Joshua was academically far more accomplished than me, but, despite that, he had always been jealous of my luck, and disliked my devil may care attitude.

My sister and mother joined my father when he worked in Singapore. Joshua and I stayed in London, and I had introduced him into Lloyd's, but he was cut from a very different cloth than me. Joshua found underwriting, rather than broking, more to his liking. He soon developed his own circle of friends, very different from my raucous comrades from the Lambers, a group drawn largely from the Lloyd's Rugby Club. When he married his wife - Camila - our relationship became more strained. Camila was the daughter of a colleague of my father, and Camila had been living in Singapore with her parents, but wished to study at a university in England. Joshua was in his last year at university, but when not at university, he would come and stay with me in London. I had no problems with the arrangement because my father helped me with my rent. My father suggested that Joshua and I could show Camila around London in between her university interviews. It was early January when Camila first visited us in London, and from the moment Camila and Joshua met it was love at first sight, for both of them. They had almost everything in common, and they became inseparable. I never went to university because I didn't work hard enough, and I couldn't see the point at the time I started work. I admit that I was quite boorish and my life revolved around work and playing rugby, with the result I would often arrive home, the worse for wear. I resented playing gooseberry in my own flat. My resentment often took the form of poking fun at their blissful relationship, and after goading them once too often, Camila stood up to me. She told me a few home truths, which in hindsight were perfectly valid, but during her tirade she called me the 'blunt-Edge' of the family. Inferring that I was not as sharp, meaning intelligent, as my younger brother. Of course, the truth hurt, so whilst I tried to laugh it off with counter quips, Camila could see that her arrow had pierced my armour. Joshua and Camila married shortly after she graduated from university. Joshua by that time had settled into his underwriting role, and he was progressing quite well as he was good at assessing risks, especially with his propensity for mental arithmetic. Camila's parents gave them a deposit for a house in Bromley, and together they settled down to climbing their respective career greasy poles. My success as a Lloyd's broker was disdainfully referred to as a crafty-market-trader by Camila, who entered one of the big four Accountancy firms. Our paths crossed pretty infrequently and, I heard from a friend of mine who lived in Bromley, that Camila nearly had a fit when she learned of my inheritance after the death of my first wife and her family. I never relished meeting her, and for the sake of keeping the peace in the family, I would keep my comments to myself.

"I'm surprised you are at work today Joshua," one of his group asked him. "I thought you might be with your parents in Norfolk."

"I went to them on Sunday and returned yesterday," Joshua replied.

"Are you going to visit Marc?" the person asked.

"I'm not sure."

"I think you should," the person pressed Joshua "in case he doesn't pull through."

I smiled to myself.

Joshua didn't say anything.

I was so tempted to look at Joshua during this exchange, but I resisted; however, my eye caught someone looking directly at me.

"Shit." I said under my breath, because I recognised the person as an employee of JPG. He was a young bright graduate who had joined our Treaty Reinsurance Department. Time to go, I decided. So as casually as I could, I finished my beer, put my glass on a table and walked across the market into an alley between two shops. I turned right into another alley, and as I did so, I saw in the reflection of the shop window that the JPG employee was walking behind me. Get a hold of yourself Marc; he's probably just walking the same way. I reached the Southern entrance of Leadenhall Market, but instead of walking out along the road, I cut sharply up a narrow alley, which housed a Do-It-Yourself store. At the end of the alley was Gracechurch Street, then at the first opportunity I dashed across the road and entered another alley beside a popular public house, which used to be a banking hall. I was passing a restaurant where the alley opened out into a square and glanced back; he was still walking behind me. I turned right up another narrow alley that led me towards the famous Jamaica Inn - *The Jam Pot* - which was another favourite watering hole for Lloyd's Brokers. I quickened my step and was on the verge of running as I looked first left then right then left again in a series of alleys that led to bespoke tailors, silversmiths and two famous lunchtime restaurants that were tucked away from the main thoroughfare. I did start running as I passed the window of one of the restaurants, from where I could see the plaque on the wall commemorating the place where Charles Dickens frequented for lunch.

I did not look behind me as I was in full flight, breaking cover across Cornhill and I ran straight into the Royal Exchange. I slowed my pace to a respectable walk as I passed the exclusive jewellers and fashion shops. I headed to the far corner where I knew the toilets were located in the basement. I went down the stairs into the cubicle of the Gents toilet and sat down shaking. After fifteen minutes I had composed myself and returned to the ground floor of the Royal Exchange and exited towards Bank Station.

"I thought you were supposed to be in a coma Mr Edge?" It was the young employee from JPG.

"I am sorry but I think you have confused me with someone else." I said in my best South African accent.

"Really?" he replied with a sarcastic tone, "so why did you walk away from your brother's group when you saw me looking at you?"

He paused, but I said nothing so he continued "And then you tried to lose me in Leadenhall Market, and again through the alleys near Simpsons and The George & Vulture. I had to sprint to see you come into the Royal Exchange and I have been waiting for you ever since."

"And why would you want to follow a tourist?" I kept up with the pretence and South African accent.

"Because I knew it was you standing outside The Lamb."

I said nothing.

"I have seen you every day I have been at JPG. I have studied the way you walk, every time you came around the office to talk to people," he started to blush "you're who I want to be when I am successful."

I still said nothing and stared at the young man in front of me. After a moment or two I said "Let's grab a coffee."

We went back into the Royal Exchange and sat at one of the café tables that surrounded a bar in the middle of the ground floor of the Royal Exchange.

I ordered two coffees and waited until they arrived before speaking, during which time I had time to think about what to say to the young employee.

"It's Julian, isn't it?" I kept the South African accent.

He nodded "Julian Webb."

"Yes, I know, you joined our graduate training scheme last September."

"I did and enjoying it very much Mr…"

"McMichaels" I cut in sharply.

He paused for a moment and took a sip from his coffee. "Is Jimmy alive?"

I shook my head and a wave of sadness engulfed me.

"So why are you pretending to still be incapacitated?" A simple question and I didn't know how much to tell him, but it was obvious that he would not be satisfied unless I told him something.

"K-P has gone missing; he may have been kidnapped. Jimmy and I were trying to find him when we were involved in a car accident, which was totally my fault." I paused and drank my coffee in one gulp hoping that it would help me with the unpalatable truth.

"That still does not explain why you are pretending to be unwell in hospital."

"I know, but the authorities believe that K-P may have been taken to Dubai, where they have no jurisdiction and even poking around could have major political ramifications. Whereas I am a free agent."

"Did the people who kidnapped K-P know that you were trying to find him?"

"Julian, it is not certain K-P has been kidnapped," I paused again before replying "but yes, I think they knew that I was taking matters into my own hands."

"Can I do anything to help you?"

I thought about Julian's question for a while before replying.

"I do not want anything that could happen to you to be on my conscience, but I could do with a pair of eyes and ears in the office."

He nodded "To do what?"

"Firstly, I want you to go and buy a cheap pay-as-you-go mobile phone and a sim card, and come back here with it in fifteen minutes." I gave him three fifty pound notes.

Whilst Julian was gone, I contemplated my foolhardiness. It had already killed Jimmy, and my disguise had been seen through by an office boy. The plan was unlikely to succeed unless I took more care. I could have continued to deny my identity but that would not satisfy Julian's curiosity. I could have threatened him but that would only make him resentful, so making him feel wanted was the least bad alternative. I needed to get under cover as soon as possible; however, having Julian as a means of communication may yet prove very useful.

Julian returned in less than ten minutes and I asked him for the phone number.

"Do not use it under any circumstances," I instructed "just leave it turned on and I will text you, do not reply unless I ask you to do so."

He nodded.

"If I do ask you to reply to me, buy another SIM card and include that number in the reply, then destroy the first SIM card."

"Understood" he replied.

"Go to John Eastwood and say that we spoke last Thursday about you working at K-P's desk. He will probably welcome another pair of hands," again I thought about poor Jimmy "and keep your head down until I text you - OK?"

"Yes, but what am I looking for?" He asked.

"Nothing – I will ask you questions."

I stood up and left Julian at the table to pay for the coffees – he had plenty of change from the three fifty pound notes.

I returned to the South African embassy well before half-past four, nervous that firstly the official would not have time to see me, and secondly that they too would see through my disguise. I sat in the waiting area for an hour. As I did so I I again remonstrated with myself for my stupidity earlier in the day. I was also disheartened with the attitude of my brother, and when this episode was over, I would undertake to try and become closer to him and his family.

So I was completely buoyed when I walked out of the South African Embassy at half past four, having seen the official before the appointed time, and within fifteen minutes I had a driving licence. My mood had lifted slightly as I made my way back to Eric's flat, so that I could prepare for my evening flight to Qatar.

Up the Creek

I was travelling to Dubai via Doha, the capital of Qatar, the oil and gas rich state. The reason for not flying direct was to add credence to my cover story. Despite scandals at FIFA, including the ousting of its President Sepp Blatter, and heir apparent Michel Platini, Qatar is due to host the Association Football World Cup Finals in twenty-twenty-two. Accordingly, Qatar has embarked upon an enormous construction programme of infrastructure, and stadia projects, to ensure delivery of the sporting tournament second only to the Olympic Games in worldwide popularity. These projects were underway and to not review their progress might look odd; so the plan was to spend two hours in Doha, before hopping onto a plane for the short flight to Dubai. The diminishing price of oil was starting to take its toll on some of the more hedonistic projects with some being curtailed or truncated, the latest being the major stations aspect of the ambitious Doha Metro project, which would provide additional cover for my reason to visit Doha.

Terminal Two of Heathrow Airport was relatively empty, and the Qatar Airways flight to Doha was uneventful, and I slept for most of the journey. It was a fitful sleep, with dreams and images of K-P and whether I would find him in Dubai. I was also concerned about my family, and that I had been so easily spotted in Leadenhall Market. My eyes closed the moment the plane was aloft, and I only awoke as we started the final descent to Doha.

Getting through the melee at Doha immigration was the first proper time that my South African identity had withstood scrutiny. Whilst waiting for my early morning flight to Dubai I happened to strike up a conversation with an Australian engineer, who was returning to Dubai for the weekend with his family, after spending the week in Doha working on one of the Doha Metro projects. He explained that most of the infrastructure work was subterranean, and the stadia were hardly out of the ground. The Australian was sceptical that all the projects would be completed on time, particularly as the previous year Qatar Rail had terminated the project for major stations, and re-awarded the project to another joint venture. By the time we boarded our flight I was confident that if questioned superficially, I could at least give a plausible sketch of the current construction activity.

The main surprise when I exited Dubai Airport was that it must be at least thirty-five degrees centigrade and it was still before nine o'clock in the morning. I recall a friend of mine speaking about his time in the Middle East, and comparing the climate to that of Chicago.

"What do you mean it's like Chicago? I think the sun has got to you" I told him.

"No Marc think about it; in Chicago you have three months when it is too cold to go outside and people get into their cars in their garage, drive to the underground car parks where they work, shop or dine. The Middle East is no different, but it is in the summer months" he replied.

He had a point until I countered that in Chicago you could dress accordingly and still go outside, but you could not undress sufficiently to cool down in the Middle East. Our conversation finished playing out in my mind as my taxi drew up outside my Hotel in Deira, close to the airport and near the Creek. The Creek is the oldest part of Dubai City and the world famous souks are located beside this waterway.

Before the discovery of oil and gas, fishing was the main source of industry in this Emirati State. Dubai today has a skyline worthy of any major city in the world, with the development of industrial, commercial, retail and residential buildings stretching up to the port of Jebel Ali, before the road heads into the desert and two hours later you reach the big brother of the seven Emirates – Abu Dhabi.

Being the oldest part of Dubai, the hotels in Deira are not as plush and swanky as the newer hotels on the Sheik Zayeed Road or near Jumeirah Beach. The hotel was sufficient for my needs as I wanted to be relatively inconspicuous, leaving me free to search for the ship which was due to dock the following day; eight days after K-P went missing.

Being a Saturday meant it was the weekend in Dubai, and the traffic was lighter than usual. However the Creek was already heaving with tourists as well as immigrant workers, out doing their shopping for the week ahead.

I grabbed a second breakfast on the hoof, and headed out into the Bur Dubai. I wanted to try and familiarise myself with the route to the port, and to check upon the timing of the Masterson Shipping vessels arriving over the next day or so.

I started by going to the Ports and Customs Office in the Bur Dubai at the end of the Jumeirah Road. It was not far from my hotel and in the early morning it was comfortable to walk there. Come the midday and heat of the afternoon, it would be too hot to walk any distance, even in the first few days of April. Friends of mine who live in Dubai have even suffered from Vitamin D deficiency, as they just don't go out in the sun, especially as the summer months' temperatures can at times reach fifty degrees centigrade.

I reached the Ports and Customs Office in twenty minutes, however, being a government office and the weekend, it was closed on a Saturday. I cursed myself when I remembered that I had left my panama hat on the short flight from Dubai. I thought to myself that I needed to buy one later at one of the massive shopping malls in Dubai. I turned back on myself and headed to the nearest metro station, which I established at the hotel was Al Fahidie. As I walked towards the metro station, I recalled the article I read about the Dubai Metro. With a network of seventy-five kilometres it is the largest unmanned metro system in the world, and further expansion to the network was envisaged. The completion of the metro expansion was due to be synchronized with the World twenty-twenty Expo, which had been awarded to Dubai.

As I approached the metro station I fished out a twenty dirham note from my pocket and bought a one-day pass for fourteen dirhams, which at less than three pounds was great value compared to the London Underground. Travelling on the Dubai Metro was like no other metro system I had been on before. Firstly, the stations are air-conditioned as well as the trains themselves. There are carriages reserved for women and their young children. Despite these concessions, very few Emiratis travelled the metro, the main users being tourists and the immigrant workers.

After one stop I changed trains at Bur Juman, switching from the green line to the red line through to its terminus at Jebel Ali. The metro train ran parallel with one of the main thoroughfares in Dubai - the Sheik Zayeed Road. It passed by the current tallest building in the world, the Burj Khalifa, although this could soon be eclipsed by the B2 Observation Tower being contemplated in Saudi Arabia. The journey to Jebel Ali took about an hour and a quarter. Jebel Ali is the industrial heartland of Dubai and at the centre of it is the port. The shipping is dominated by Dubai Ports who a number of years previously acquired P&O, amongst others. Dubai Ports' headquarters were clear for all to see as I exited the metro station at Jebel Ali.

It was mid-morning and the temperature had increased significantly during my journey in the metro. I made my way to the Dubai Ports Authority Free Zone Office, but like the Ports and Customs Offices in Bur Dubai, it was closed. I ruminated as to what to do next, and started walking towards the world's largest man-made harbour. It was like any other large port, quite desolate when not working, plus the industrial buildings on the edge of the desert meant everything seemed so grimy. With no other pedestrian in sight I sauntered along the road running parallel to the port and in a country where transportation was dominated by cars, it was obvious that the planners paid lip-service towards anyone walking, because the pavements in the industrial area were in a poor state of repair. After fifteen minutes I found myself on the junction of Fortieth Street. I had made notes of various places in Dubai when I was in London and Fortieth Street rang a bell. I referred to my scribbled notes and saw that the Dubai Ports Authority Staff Quarters were somewhere along Fortieth Street. I turned right and in a few moments I was in front of the building, with some sign of life as I saw a person leaving the building. I walked over to the entrance and could see a reception desk, which was manned by a uniformed security officer.

"Good morning" I said in my best South African accent.

The security guard looked like he originated from South East Asia, and I conjectured that he might be Filipino, as the Philippines seemed to supply the majority of crew on merchant shipping around the world.

The security guard said nothing.

I continued, "I have been to the Port and Customs Office and the Dubai Ports Authority Office here in Jebel Ali, but they are both closed."

"They are open tomorrow" was his unhelpful reply.

"I am meeting a friend from a ship due to dock tomorrow."

The security guard was inscrutable and didn't acknowledge or deny my question. Not even a shrug of the shoulders.

"Masterson Shipping ship – tomorrow?" I asked in a slightly louder voice.

Still no outward reaction from the security guard, and I was about to walk away when I tried another tack "My friend is Mr Dominique."

At first I thought that the name meant nothing to the security guard, but I saw a slight tick in his right eye. He shook his head; I wondered if he might know more, on the other hand I might just be imagining things. I decided I wasn't going to get anything more out of him so I turned away and walked out of the building. When outside, I looked back at the building and I could see the security guard talking into a telephone.

"Shit" I said to myself. I was concerned that my visit might have been reported, and vowed that I needed to be much more careful, although subtlety was certainly not one of my attributes.

I walked as quickly as possible towards the Jebel Ali metro station, hoping that I might be able to flag down a wayward taxi, but being Saturday there was hardly any traffic around the industrial estate. I was sweating profusely by the time I reached the air conditioning of the metro station. The heat of the day was approaching its zenith and that combined with my quick march to the station had raised my heart rate and I was perspiring profusely.

The station was only sparsely occupied by passengers waiting for the next train, which was due in ten minutes. I placed myself near the entrance so I could dash out if I saw an available taxi. Most of the metro system was built above ground, and I was the only non-immigrant worker in the station, which made me feel conspicuous. The minutes really dragged by and a few more passengers came into the station, but no one seemed to give me a second glance.

The train from Bur Dubai had arrived in the station and although it was an unmanned system, Dubai Metro staff were inspecting the train and cleaning any rubbish before letting us on for the return journey. I was eager to immediately get on the train. A white Hummer with blacked out windows pulled up by the station, but no-one was getting in-or-out of the vehicle. The rear window opened for a few seconds and then closed again. I stared intently at the vehicle, trying to dismiss any thoughts that I might have been discovered as only my own paranoia.

The doors of the metro train closed which signalled that the journey was about to commence. I sat in the middle carriage and watched the Hummer as the train pulled out of the station. I assured myself that I had nothing to fear from the ungainly looking white vehicle, as it remained at the station as we pulled away from the Jebel Ali terminus.

We reached the first station after Jebel Ali and there was no sign of anything untoward; no white Hummer or any other vehicle was waiting at the station. Nevertheless, I felt exposed on the metro. There was nowhere to go if anyone decided to board the train, and with so few people around it would be difficult to lose myself if I disembarked.

At each station on our route I looked for anything suspicious, and as I counted off the nearly twenty stations between Jebel Ali and Bur Dubai, I became calmer. In London I had read that usually the traffic along the Sheik Zayeed Road could be very heavy, but being a Saturday a car could easily keep pace with the train. At that point I spotted a white Hummer, and I tensed only to relax when I noticed its windows were not tinted, then I spotted another white Hummer and realised how popular they were in Dubai.

I decided that I would leave the train at one of the two very large shopping malls on the Red line to Bur Dubai. The first was the Mall of the Emirates and was the next station and I could see that a number of the passengers were getting ready to disembark. I stood up and shuffled behind them as though I was going to join them. As I reached the doors I crouched down as if I was tying my shoe lace, so I was below the bottom of the windows of the train. Also being in the area of the doors I could see if anyone was running to join the train. I could not see anyone. Most of the passengers joining the train carried shopping bags of well-known brands. They made their way past me as I continued to fiddle with my shoes. Only when the doors closed did I stand up, but I didn't return to a seat; I stood by the doors, so that bulkhead might hide me from anyone looking in from the road.

I waited until we were well underway before I dared to peak out of the window. No sign of any white Hummer. I gave an involuntary sigh of relief and sat down again.

We rolled into the next station and I looked out of the doors as they opened, no white Hummer or any other vehicle was stationery at the bottom of the station exit so I left the train at the massive Dubai Mall adjacent to the Burj Khalifa. I positioned myself in the middle of a melee of a group of European tourists as they made their way towards the Dubai Mall. If the rest of Dubai was quiet, the shopping mall was like the souks, absolutely heaving with people and, being lunchtime, all the restaurants were full to bursting. I couldn't see anyone following me.

I walked around the shopping mall looking for a panama hat, and at every possible occasion I would check the reflection in the windows of the shops to see whether anyone was following me. Then I thought to myself that taking precautions within the shopping mall was probably fruitless, because there were only a certain number of exits and if anyone wanted to follow me they could just wait at the exits until I decided to leave the mall. I had no clue what to do when I found myself at the area of the complex that housed the cinemas.

"Kill some time." I said to myself and went to the ticket office and bought a ticket to an action adventure film that was just about to start. I knew it was a long film, and had not received the best of reviews. So I bought myself a burger and nachos, and sat through the film which was totally unmemorable. I found it difficult to concentrate on the film, because although I looked at the screen, I was thinking about the morning's events. I cursed myself for mentioning the name of Mr Dominique. I could not be certain, but I felt that I might have been followed from a distance, although no one had invaded my personal space. Eventually I convinced myself that I was just being paranoid, and the soporific atmosphere of the cinema meant that I could not stop myself from falling asleep.

The lights came on at the end of the film, and I awoke in a shock. The film programme lasted nearly three hours, and I estimated that I had probably watched less than half an hour of the main feature. I left the cinema and I re-entered the main part of the shopping mall; it was still as busy as earlier. I made my way towards the Burj Khalifa and the fountains show that rivals – if not surpasses - the fountain shows in Las Vegas. The heat of the day was passing and the piazzas by the fountains were full of tourists, as well as local residents enjoying their weekend. My spirits lifted as I stopped to marvel at the fountains show, which was accompanied by music. I returned to the Dubai Metro and I took the train back to Bur Dubai.

I made my way from the Bur Dubai station to my hotel and I was not paying much attention to what was around me, as I was thinking how I would establish the docking time and location of the Masterson Shipping vessel. I turned the corner to my hotel and froze. The white Hummer was sitting outside the door of my hotel. I started to turn away but was prevented from doing so by two heavy set Middle Eastern gentlemen dressed in black suits.

The older of the two gentlemen spoke to me in an almost perfect English accent "Mr Dominque wishes to meet you." They escorted me to the white Hummer. As I approached the car, the door swung open, and my escorts ensured that there was no option but to get into the vehicle.

As I climbed into the rear seats, someone grabbed my wrist and in an instant a needle was inserted into my forearm. I briefly looked at the needle and then passed out.

Friends Re-united

When I awoke from my drug induced slumber, I felt that now familiar nausea which had returned, and was accompanied by a discharge of my stomach contents. The act of vomiting was made worse by the fact that my hands were bound behind my back, resulting in most of the spittle and part digested hamburger landing in my lap. My mouth tasted disgusting and my head was thumping with the most horrific headache.

I tried looking at my surroundings, but it was difficult to discern anything as I was in a darkened room with the only light coming from behind a door that was not closed properly, the room was possibly below ground as there were no windows. I was sitting in a chair that had been affixed to the floor. My arms had been pushed through the upright back support of the chair, and then my wrists bound tightly together. There was no way I would be leaving my seat of my own accord.

"Hello?" I called out "Hello?" I tried again, this time I tried shouting but it sounded no louder, and the taste of vomit came back into my mouth.

A few moments later, I heard metal scraping on concrete behind the door, followed by footsteps. The door opened. The light behind the door was so bright that I was temporarily blinded and could not make out my captors. Whoever it was, walked into the room and only did so for a few moments, before walking out again, closing the door behind them.

Darkness returned, more so than before, as this time the door had been closed properly. I did not know what to expect next. I fell into a troubled slumber. I was brought back to consciousness by the door being opened, and once again the brightness of the light blinded me, although the shape of a person was discernible as they walked towards me.

"Where…" I started to speak but was stopped when I was doused with cold water. The shock was almost heart-stopping. I had not expected it and I was just recovering when another load was thrown over me.

"Pig!" Was the only word uttered and then the door was shut firmly again.

The water was obviously not for my benefit but to remove some of the sight and smell of my vomit. I felt that this could only be bad news as whoever captured me intended to return at some point. The cold water had reduced my body temperature dramatically and I started to shiver with cold. I tried stamping my feet but they were bound to the legs of the chair. The chair was not of an ordinary design; it was made of metal and I feared that its purpose was to restrain people. The inability to move my limbs made my shivering worse and I could not stop myself from urinating. I felt terribly sorry for myself, and after what seemed hours I fell asleep. It was a very fitful sleep and had probably been induced by the remains of the drug still within my system.

I was violently awakened by yet another soaking of cold water and I also realised that my head was covered by some kind of sack, which meant I was totally disorientated. If that was not enough, I heard a terrifying animal-like scream from behind me, to be followed by a choking sound, and then whimpering. It was like the sound of a dog which had been badly injured, crying out for help. I heard the door close and was left with the other occupant of the room, whose moans and muffled cries continued for at least an hour or so, and this was interspersed by a choking coughing sound. Eventually the crying died down and the person fell asleep or passed out, because their whimpering was replaced by heavy breathing and a gurgling sound.

The sack over my head heightened the feeling of imprisonment, and there was a faint smell of shoe polish that engulfed every breath I took.

"What the fuck did they give me?" My hoarse whisper was hardly audible.

"Aaagh!" There was a muffled moan behind me.

"Who's that?" Still my voice was no louder than a whisper.

No one answered, and eventually I must have fallen asleep again.

Semi-conscious, I sensed rather than heard the door being opened, and the voices of two men speaking Arabic. "Why are you asking questions about me?" The voice was very well spoken English, although there was a vague hint of a foreign accent.

"Mr Dominique?" I questioned from behind the sack covering my head.

"Yes" came the curt reply. I had no idea how to respond to him without blowing my cover. "I am waiting." His voice had gone up an octave.

I was thinking of what to say when I was soaked again with cold water, the shock slightly less than before, but nevertheless very unpleasant.

"Why were you asking questions about me?" his voice was almost screaming.

"Ok...Ok..., but stop throwing water over me." I remembered the South African accent.

"You stink with piss and vomit, and the water is so I can bring myself to stand in front of you, Mr Edge!"

I was struck dumb.

"Don't think a stupid disguise and a bad South African accent would fool me," his voice had moderated back to the well spoken English accent "so my question remains, why are you asking about me?"

"I am trying to find my friend K-P." I hesitated for a moment before continuing "he has been missing for over a week, and you were the last person he was seen with."

"So why look for him here?" The voice became slightly strained again.

"He left me a clue as to where he was going – I guessed it was on a Masterson Shipping vessel to Dubai due to arrive tomorrow."

"You are wrong Mr Edge; I believe the message was meant for his Special Branch friends. Anyway, the vessel doesn't arrive tomorrow, it docked earlier today."

"But what about K-P?"

"He is behind you."

I tried turning in my seat but it was useless.

"He can't tell you himself because we have performed a partial elinguation." There was a chortle in front of me and I could hear Mr Dominique come closer to me and then he whispered in my ear, "You don't know what elinguation is, do you?"

I shuddered to think and shook my head.

"It is a cruel and unusual punishment for someone who bears false witness. It is the cutting out of the tongue, but we want him to give us information so we did not perform a total elinguation; nevertheless, he is suffering terribly, even though we just removed the tip of his tongue."

I started to retch but my stomach was empty.

"*Now he is in the jungle of sword blades, limbs mangled and hacked, the tongue hauled by hooks, the body beaten and slashed.*" The voice whispered into my ear with real vehemence.

I felt someone fiddle with the underside of my chair, and then it was turned on a spindle so I was facing the opposite direction, at which point the sack hood was removed.

No amount of the most graphic description could have prepared me for the out-and-out barbarism and brutality which met my eyes. A large person was strapped naked to a chair similar to my own, his arms, chest and legs were a matrix of wheals and open wounds, where he had been beaten - but that was not the worst part. His face was almost unrecognisable, cauliflower ears, eyes swollen and closed, scalp and hair covered in oozing blood. The mouth and lips just an open wound, lips swollen and cut, and every time he swallowed, blood flowed freely from his mouth. He had obviously defecated and urinated, because he was subjected to the cold water treatment – but he didn't even flinch.

My voice was barely a whisper "Why?"

Mr Dominique's face was beyond my view as he replied "Because I want information from him. He tried playing spies, and was caught."

Mr Dominique then moved in front of me, and I could see his face. In an instant I recognised him "Aziz – you're Omar Aziz from Masterson Shipping!"

"Correct Marc, but now I go by my real name, Mr Dominique de Silva."

I was dumb-founded "I don't understand."

"Of course you don't; you're a blundering idiot – you always were." He smiled before continuing, and there was a glimpse of that charming young playboy I met a few years ago at Masterson Shipping, only the briefest flash before he retreated behind the psychopathic face he now wore. "Why do you think Masterson tolerated me? I am Philippe de Silva's illegitimate son and Mercédès' young uncle."

It was too much to take in all at once, my head was spinning.

"What you inherited from Philippe de Silva should have come to me."

"Aziz…." I implored.

"Dominique de Silva!" he shouted - his body shaking as he yelled his name.

"Mr de Silva, you didn't have to torture K-P, you could have come to me."

His eyes flared "Don't you patronise me," at which point he calmed down, but what came next was much more frightening. He started laughing louder and louder. The sound bounced off the metal and concrete of the spartan room. "Do you think that's why K-P is here? You are so self-centred Edge, but I couldn't believe my luck when I was sent pictures of you at Jebel Ali Metro Station. What we have in mind for you will far exceed your limited intellect. I almost smiled when I heard that you were in a coma, but your poking around was responsible for the death of your friend Jimmy; such an awful accident. You should take more care when you drive Edge. And now you will see K-P suffer, he might possibly even die here with you. How many people is it this time Marc – three people dead because of your blunderings: It's like history is repeating itself." He paused for a moment and spoke in a moderate tone, "I wish Mercédès had never set eyes on you. You destroyed our family, and now I am going to destroy you."

His eyes dulled to be replaced with dead-like fish eyes, yet the madness remained. I have never feared for my mortality more than I did in the moments as the door shut behind him and we were plunged into darkness.

Darkness in Dubai

After Dominique de Silva left the room, we were visited twice in the next hour by the same person, obviously a servant of some description. I thought he was mute, as he only emitted throaty unintelligible sounds when I tried to communicate with him. I wondered if he had suffered a similar fate as K-P, but a full elinguation, as he showed certain tenderness to K-P in his ministrations. Firstly, he tried pouring a liquid down the semi-conscious K-P's throat, but K-P gagged almost immediately. I couldn't see the liquid but I guessed it was saline or something similar, as it wouldn't do for K-P to die just yet. I had no idea what lay in store for us, but I had no illusions that nothing would be quick as de Silva was obviously going to enjoy seeing me suffer.

After three attempts K-P stopped gagging on the liquid. The servant left our cell, only to return a short while later with water for K-P from which I was allowed a small swig. He released K-P from the chair and laid him on a towel on the floor. I was amazed by the strength of the slight figure. The servant then gently gave K-P a bed bath. K-P's was then dressed in a voluminous dish-dash, and within minutes of the servant leaving, K-P was snoring and sleeping soundly on the floor. I joined him but I could only drift in-and-out of a fitful dream-laden sleep.

When I woke it was because of pains in my stomach as I was hungry, but also my bowels were about to explode. K-P was still unconscious or asleep and, much as I didn't want to rouse him, I needed the toilet badly. I started shouting.

"Hello! Hello! HELLO!!

No response.

"I need the toilet!" I screamed at the top of my voice.

After five minutes of shouting I heard the door open and was faced by a well-built man brandishing a machine-pistol.

"Toilet! Quick! Please?"

He hesitated for a moment then retreated out of the room leaving the door marginally open that cast a weak light around the room.

"Ahhhh" It was K-P, eyes open pointing at his feet.

"What's the matter? Does your foot hurt?" I asked.

I could just about see him shake his head.

"Sh-h-h. Sh-h-h. Sh-h-h."

"You want me to be quiet?" I questioned.

Again the slight shake of the head, whilst pointing to his foot.

"Sh-h-h" I said to myself trying to imitate K-P. "Sh-h-shoe?"

This time, an affirmative nod.

"Your shoe?"

Just a blink this time as if the effort to communicate had been too much for him. I looked around the room and could just about make out something on the floor in the far corner. I had no idea what it was but there was definitely something.

"I think it's in the corner – but I am not sure."

K-P just closed his eyes and at that moment the door was swung fully open by the guard carrying the machine-pistol, and he was accompanied by the servant who carried a bucket and a bowl of water. The guard cocked the pistol; in the concrete and metal room the sound was amplified; the servant undid my bonds and pointed to the same corner where I had espied the objects on the floor.

After a moment when I adjusted to the blood flowing fully through my limbs, I turned away from the guard and servant, and within seconds my bowels opened with an accompanying foul stench. I heard the guard complain and he retreated to just outside the room, but left the door open. Briefly I looked over my shoulder and saw that the armed guard still had his gun trained on me. I motioned to the servant that I needed to clean myself and he brought the bowl of water. I washed myself down-below as well as I could, and then I stood up and re-dressed myself, not before ascertaining that it was a large pair of shoes and a jacket piled in the corner of the room.

The guard jerked the gun towards the chair, and I sat down only to be re-secured, at which point the guard re-entered the room to check that the servant had secured me properly. Thankfully the bucket and bowl were removed leaving us again in the dark cool room.

Once the door was shut, I spoke to K-P, "Yes there are shoes and a jacket in the corner."

He didn't open his eyes but I sensed rather than saw him relax.

I couldn't sleep and strained to hear any noises that would give me a clue as to the time of day or our whereabouts. There was the faintest drone of white noise, which could be traffic, or just air conditioning. More difficult was keeping track of time and despite it seemingly being ages since I had joined K-P, the reality was that only a few hours - possibly one night – had passed. As if on cue I heard faint screams and shouts. I strained my ears as much as I could; I tried to tune-out the white noise drone of the traffic or air-conditioning. The screams and shouts lasted for what I estimated as fifteen minutes, and then stopped as soon as they had started. I tried to isolate the sounds but they were too faint to distinguish, and the snoring of K-P was so soporific, I too fell asleep.

I woke bathed in perspiration and again I could hear the faint screams and shouts. It was much warmer in the room which accounted for the beads of sweat rolling down my face and back. I looked down to the floor and K-P was still asleep. I hoped that the rest would help him recuperate. At that moment I could hear shuffling behind the door as my senses were becoming more attuned to our surroundings, then the key was inserted into the lock. I feared that Dominique de Silva would be back to further torture either myself or K-P. When the door opened it was the servant with two bottles. He gave me a couple of sips of water before leaning over K-P and bringing him up to a sitting position, when he poured liquid from the other bottle into K-P's mouth. K-P coughed but did not gag this time, and although he dribbled some of it over his chin, there was not the accompanying blood. K-P's eyes were open and they looked much clearer and focussed than before. The servant then allowed him to take a deep draught. After settling K-P back on his back I was offered a couple more swigs of the water.

Before the servant departed, I distinguished the screams and shouts, because the door had been left open. They were the screams and shouts of children. I guessed that we were close to a playground or more likely a school, which meant we were probably still in Dubai City. After the door was closed the noise was muffled and the faint screams and shouts continued for another twenty minutes and then stopped, so I guessed that was the end of the lunchtime break.

K-P was asleep again and I tried to rest and soon fell into, for once, a deep sleep. I was literally shaken out of my slumber by K-P. He was on his knees, shaking my own knees. Once awake I found that my eyes had adjusted to their night sight, and the cracks of light from the door were just sufficient for me to make out K-P showing me his right shoe which he had retrieved from the corner of the room. He peeled back the inner sole of the shoe and I could vaguely see that there was a flap, which K-P opened. Once opened there was a button which he pushed and a small green light was illuminated. He closed the flap, replaced the inner sole, and crawled back to the corner where he put the shoe back with its pair.

When he was back on his towel, I spoke "Very James Bond."

He shrugged his shoulders.

"A call for the cavalry?"

He nodded his head.

"I hope they're not too late."

We continued to rest the best we could, K-P much more successfully than me. The time dragged interminably. The servant came back after a few hours, and he gave K-P some broth but only water for me. They obviously wanted K-P alive, which I took to be a positive sign, and hoped that the help K-P had summoned would arrive before Dominique de Silva returned.

I was proved wrong because as soon as the servant left, Dominique de Silva was stood in front of me. He was much calmer than before, the madness no longer in his eyes. The room matched his temperament, as it was much cooler than before; I assumed it was now Monday night. He looked much more like the young Omar Aziz, Masterson Shipping's Middle East Regional Manager, I remembered from five years ago.

"Marc, please try and convince K-P that it is better for him - you and both your families - to give me the information I want quickly."

143

"What information do you want from him?" I asked.

He looked at me as though I was a complete imbecile, then he laughed, "You don't know?"

"No, I don't."

He was laughing more and more, "So you came charging out to the desert to save your friend, and you have no idea - why."

"Perhaps you might like to enlighten me?" I said as calmly as possible. I didn't want his irrational behaviour of the previous day to return.

"I just don't understand why you would risk your life and not know why."

"Because he's my friend."

"It's quite simple really. I want the security details of the World Cup in Russia."

I didn't know whether to laugh and decided against it, because he was obviously unstable, and anyone not acceding to his megalomania would probably suffer. After digesting what he had requested I eventually replied, "There are two problems with what you are asking."

"What?" he replied.

"Firstly, I don't believe K-P has that information."

"Don't try and bullshit me, I know he has arranged the insurance for various football teams already."

I said nothing.

"You didn't know, did you?" Again he was mocking me.

"Any such insurance arrangements have to be kept confidential. We only have code words and numbers on our and the underwriters' records; in case they fall into the wrong hands." I thought about smiling sardonically at him, but decided to keep him in his current humour with a straight face.

"Yes, but K-P knows. I know he knows".

"How?" I asked.

"From information I have received," he replied.

My mind was racing as to how he could have obtained such information: perhaps it was Eric's colleague who went missing? I looked down at K-P whose eyes were closed, and thought he could still be asleep, although I couldn't imagine how.

"The second problem is that it is too far in advance to finalise the security arrangements, and K-P's disappearance may mean there has been a security breach, with the consequence that the security arrangements will likely be changed."

"Exactly," he replied.

"What? So why bother with the information if you know it is useless?"

"I didn't say it was useless, just I know that they will need to change the security arrangements."

"I don't understand."

"You're not meant to understand anything; I just want that information?" he said smugly.

"Security will be even tighter than usual."

"Who said I was concerned about the security?" He framed it as a question, but he wasn't looking for an answer. "What I want is for various people to think I have the information."

I thought about this for a moment. "But if people know K-P has been abducted they may assume he has given you the information already."

"Oh dear Marc, that would mean I can dispose of you both now."

"Exactly. I want to talk to you about a business proposition."

He said nothing and just stared at me. Eventually he said "What is it?"

"I agree I never deserved all of your father's estate. So I had worked out that when you get the information from K-P, we are dispensable. That is why K-P is probably prepared to die, and even let me die too, before divulging the information. So why is the information so important to you."

Dominique de Silva did not like that one bit, I could see him becoming cross and in his anger he said "I am controlled by no-one. I will decide the future; time to turn the tables on certain people." As soon as the words were out of his mouth he regretted it. It showed a possible weakness. He took a moment to regain his earlier composure. "What business proposition do you have in mind?"

"We, K-P and I, need a bargaining chip ourselves and I think I have it."

"What is it?" he sneered.

"I will transfer all of my land and estates in Africa and Goa plus my share in Masterson Shipping to you."

He stood in front of me for a few long seconds, his eyes boring into my eyes, and it was all I could do not to flinch. Then he turned away from me without saying a word and left the room.

And the birds fly away

I sat in the darkness, my eyes trying to adjust after the bright lights outside the room had taken away my night vision. I was totally confused. Dominique de Silva wanted the information from K-P very badly, but yet he knew it was potentially of little value if he – or someone else – wanted to use that information. The more I thought about it, the more I felt he needed the information for blackmail, but I had no clue as to whom he would use the information against.

As my night vision returned, I saw that K-P's eyes were open.

"K-P, did you hear my exchange with Mr Dominique?"

He nodded his head.

"Do you have the information he wants?"

Again a nod of the head.

"Are you going to give it to him?"

No reaction from K-P.

"Is it that you haven't decided yet?"

This time a shake of the head.

I paused for a moment before asking the next question.

"Is it that you are worried about Jane and the girls?"

K-P nodded his head.

"Me too," I added "as well as Gerda and the twins. Do you think my offer will appease him or buy us enough time before help arrives?"

K-P's response was a slight shrug of the shoulders.

I changed tack. "Why did you agree to put yourself in danger?" I knew he couldn't answer me so I asked, "Have you known about Eric Jones's investigation for a long time?"

Again he nodded his head.

"Was it Eric who asked you to assist?"

A nod.

"I think there is something else going on here. Am I correct?"

This time no response.

I sat in silence and in a while K-P was quietly snoring. I too fell asleep.

When I awoke, my mouth was very dry. The servant had not been to visit us. I looked down at K-P, but he wasn't there.

"K-P, K-P?" I called out.

"Sh-h-h" I heard from behind me.

I couldn't turn around sufficiently to be able to see him, but I heard him quietly padding around the room. He had been able to pull himself to his feet. He came up behind me and his fingers probed my bonds. They were tightly tied and K-P was in no position to untie the knots, he could barely stand, and that alone was taking all his strength.

"K-P, is there any water?" I asked "I am so thirsty."

He walked around my chair, using it and me as a crutch, and when in front of me he shook his head. He hobbled over to the door and bent down to the key-hole where the faintest of light shone through; it was the only source of illumination in the room. He peered through the key-hole blocking out the yellow beam and after a minute he crawled back over to the blanket on the floor where he had been lying earlier.

"Is there anyone out there?" I asked.

K-P gave the merest shrug of his shoulders.

I started calling out and yelling, similar to when I wanted to urinate previously. This time there was no reaction, even though I shouted for a good ten minutes.

"K-P, are you able to try the door?" I asked but he had lain down on the floor; obviously the exertions of walking around the room had been too much for him.

I sat thinking about what might happen to K-P and me the next time Mr Dominique returned to our darkened room. I just could not fathom out why he wanted the information from K-P, but also I felt our families would be in danger if K-P did not divulge the information. I hoped that whatever K-P had activated would bring help. The time wore on and the various thoughts kept swirling around in my mind as the hours dragged on. K-P had once again fallen asleep and he was snoring quietly. I believed that many hours had passed, perhaps most of the day with no sign of anyone coming to check on us. Perhaps they were just letting us stew.

I came to the conclusion that we had to do something ourselves; we couldn't wait to be killed, or worse, die of dehydration or starvation.

"K-P," I called out but no reaction. "K-P," a little bit louder; still nothing. "K-P!" I shouted.

A slight murmuring came from his prone body.

"Wake up K-P!" Even louder.

His eyes flickered open.

"K-P, we need to try and get out of here – otherwise we are going to die here."

Initially there was no reaction but, after a few moments, he nodded his head.

"Can you stand up?" I asked.

After some shuffling on the floor he rolled onto his knees.

"K-P, before you get up, can you see if there is anyone outside the door?"

He crawled over to the door and peered through the keyhole again; the room was put into total darkness when he blocked-out the small source of the yellow light. He used the handle of the door to pull himself up and, as he did so, the door opened.

At first, I thought someone had left it completely unlocked, but as K-P pulled at the door it only opened a couple of inches, and then the chain outside the door became taut and the door would not open any further.

"Can you see anything?" I asked.

He shook his head.

"Do you think you can force the door and break the chain?"

Again his body indicated a negative response.

"Are you strong enough to untie my feet please?"

He knelt beside my chair and after much fumbling I felt the rope fastening my right leg to the chair loosen.

"Ahhhh!" I wailed as the blood rushed back into my foot, which I noticed from the increased light from the partially opened door, had swollen.

A few minutes later and my left foot was also free.

He stood up using my chair as a prop, and eventually we were able to turn the chair around so my back was to the door. With the increased light from the doorway, K-P tried again to attack the ropes that bound my hands and arms. He must have tried for half an hour but they wouldn't budge. He was breathing very heavily and I was concerned he might collapse.

"Stop K-P, I have an idea."

I used the increased light to study how the chair in which K-P had sat was attached to the concrete floor. There was a metal cylinder screwed to the floor with a bolt coming from the underside of the chair, screwed into the cylinder.

"K-P, I think I know why they tied our feet." I explained that if we turned the chair anti-clockwise, the chair should become free of the cylinder. I started turning myself around, and I could feel the chair rising so that its legs were off the floor after one complete rotation of the chair. Whilst this was in part good news, unfortunately it also meant that soon I couldn't reach the floor with my feet or toes. K-P was free to help me because of the oversight by the servant in his kindness towards K-P. In a couple of minutes, I felt the chair slew to my right and, were it not for K-P, I would have crashed to the floor. He put the legs of the chair on the floor, and came around to face me, shrugging his shoulders, as if to ask "and now what?"

"Ok. Now we need to try and break off one of the chair legs."

Again K-P shrugged his shoulders.

"Lay the chair on its back, and then use your weight to try and bend one of the legs of the chair." I was counting on the bend in the tubular frame to be weak where it was already bent.

My back was on the floor and I raised my right leg as far as I could. K-P had put his shoes and socks on and come over to the chair. He sat on the leg and with his bulk, the leg bent a little immediately. He stood up and then standing on the back leg, he pulled the leg he had bent slightly, and nearly straightened it. He repeated this process ten times until the leg of the chair sheared off. He had to sit down as the physical exertion had exhausted him. After a while, which I adjudged to be about fifteen minutes, he looked up at me.

"Put me on my side and then see if you can use the jagged end of the leg to prize the knots open?"

I grimaced as he started digging into the rope, fearful that he might slip, and the leg of the chair slash my wrists. A couple of failed attempts but at the third try he got into a knot, I squealed as the ropes tightened further around my wrists to make space for the metal lever. He probed and wriggled it around, before withdrawing and starting again with immediate loosening of one knot, and in no more than another couple of minutes he was unbinding my arms. The same burning sensation I experienced earlier with my feet was simulated when the blood returned to my hands. It took a few moments of massage and finger wiggling to dispel the pins-and-needles in my hands.

"Let's get out of here" I said enthusiastically.

We both leaned against the door but, even with our combined weight, the chain held fast.

"I have another idea." I picked up the leg of the chair and threaded it between the chain and then used it as a lever until the chain was taut. When I couldn't move it any further, K-P took over from me, and was able to make a quarter turn. There was groaning as metal on metal was put under strain. "Hold it there K-P," I said and I picked up the blanket K-P had been laying on. It was torn and frayed in one corner and I tore a strip about two inches wide the length of the blanket. I looped it under the other end of the chair leg and twisted the material, took a firm grip and said to K-P "on the count of three, give it all you have. One, two, three!"

The door flew open as the padlock holding the chain links together broke. We collapsed on the floor on top of each other both panting from the physical exertion. I helped K-P to his feet and we exited our cell. I retrieved the chain and wrapped it around one of my fists as an improvised weapon; K-P kept the metal leg from the chair.

We made our way along the concrete corridor and soon we found the source of the humming white-noise. It was a filtration system. We then came upon a double door which was locked from the outside but we merely opened the bolts at the top and bottom of the doors, and they swung open to reveal a lift and stairs leading upwards. We used the stairs, and it was two floors before we reached ground level, and I then understood why I could hear the sound of children - a swimming pool with slides, as part of a hotel complex.

"Keep to the shadows," I whispered to K-P as we made our way to the hotel building. "We'd better keep out of the hotel in our current state."

We edged around the hotel perimeter and through a service entrance we were able to reach a road behind the hotel. We walked towards the main road, and as we did so a car came racing towards us, with the headlights and additional spotlights on full beam. The car stopped a few meters in front of us, and as I turned I saw another car coming behind us in exactly the same manner. We were trapped and I felt sick as if all our efforts to escape were for nought.

The door of the car in front of us opened and I could vaguely see the figure of a tall man get out of the car "Mr Edge, and K-P as well," it was a much clipped English accent "would you like a ride?" And Nobby stepped into the light. K-P collapsed to the ground, and I felt tears rolling down my cheeks, both of us in our own way reacting to the relief of being found.

Return to Hospital

The following hours were a bit of a blur. The cars that found us in the road behind the hotel turned out to be people carriers, and I was accompanied by Nobby to one, while K-P was attended to by a male nurse in the other. Nobby explained he was sent out to Dubai as soon as I went "off the grid" – in his words.

"Your phone was rendered useless - probably by taking out the battery and sim card," he explained as we drove swiftly along the Sheik Zayeed Road.

"What day is it?" I asked.

Nobby replied "Tuesday."

"Where are we going?" I interrupted his explanation of the last three days – only three days I thought to myself. It felt more like three weeks.

"The airport, old boy – before Mr Dominique realises you have escaped."

I asked him how come he was so close to the hotel. He explained that it was obvious I had been captured, because my hotel room still had all my belongings there awaiting my return."

"Don't worry we have all of them – other than the phone – here in the car, so you can shower and change before we take off."

"Where to?" I asked.

"Southampton," he replied.

"Southampton?"

"Yes, a small airport where we can get you into the country without too much fuss."

"Not Brize Norton?"

"We're not military" was his simple reply when his phone rang and after someone had spoken to him at some length he merely said "Yes, I understand."

When he turned his face to me, it was a mixture of rage and shock. "Did you know what those barbarians did to K-P?"

I nodded my head.

"He is being transferred to an ambulance and will meet us at the airport." He then returned to my original question of how he was in the vicinity of the hotel. "We picked up the faintest trace of the transmitter in K-P's shoe yesterday. We had been monitoring the frequency constantly since you arrived, but it was intermittent and too faint to trace you."

I explained that we had been in a room surrounded by concrete, two floors beneath ground.

"Like a bunker I suppose" Nobby ruminated. "Then about half an hour ago the signal strength increased and we drove to the hotel; we were about to enter the hotel grounds when you came out onto the road behind the hotel."

"What about de Silva - I mean Mr Dominique?"

"What did you call him?"

It was then my turn to explain about Dominique de Silva and how I knew who he was.

Nobby didn't say anything; he just looked at me askance.

"What I don't understand is why Mr Dominique left us there for a whole day without a visit from either himself, or any of his cohorts? One minute he was screaming that he needed the information from K-P, and then he admitted that once he had extracted the details the information might be useless; to me it doesn't add up."

"Best you tell that all to Mr Jones when you see him. I have done my bit, and K-P has been recovered, albeit not quite in one piece."

155

We sat in silence for the rest of the journey. As soon as we pulled to a halt outside the Airport Terminal I realised it was not Dubai International Airport.

"Where are we?" I asked.

"The airport" he replied and held his hand up as if to forbid me from asking further questions. "Please go with the driver. He will show you to the shower room and then please join me for refreshments before our flight."

"What about speaking to our wives…."

He replied before I had finished my sentence. "Eric has spoken to them both whilst we were in the car."

Again I wanted to speak but he cut me short.

"It's not safe to call them from here, walls have ears," quoting British propaganda from World War II.

I followed the driver and saw Nobby typing furiously with one hand on his tablet. I took a long shower and despite drinking water continuously during our journey to the airport, I still felt thirsty. Bathed and clothed in clean clothes I was escorted to a small ante-room where Nobby was drinking what suspiciously looked like a Gin and Tonic; this was indeed the fact when he offered me a G&T.

"No thanks – I think I'd better stick to water."

"Suit yourself. Would you like a sandwich?"

"Yes, please" I replied.

He pulled the cover off a plate to reveal an array of halal sandwiches – they were gorgeous, and I demolished more than my fair share.

"Haven't lost your appetite, I see" Nobby said whilst smiling broadly.

I could only smile back at him with my mouth full of bread, vegetables and chicken.

"K-P will be joining us shortly," he paused for a moment before continuing, "he must have the constitution of an ox."

I nodded and between mouthfuls I explained how we escaped.

"You were lucky and thank God for the servant's mistake," Nobby sighed.

"I think it was deliberate." I explained to Nobby that I thought the servant was trying to help K-P.

"He will be for the high jump" Nobby replied.

We carried on chatting, mainly me filling in the details, and I explained about my offer to Dominique de Silva. I wondered to myself whether that bought us time, or even changed his priorities.

True to Nobby's word, K-P was wheeled into the room a few minutes later. He was sitting up in a wheel-chair, with a saline drip above his head and attached to his right arm. He had been washed and shaved but was wrapped in a hospital gown with blankets tucked into the chair to keep him warm. He looked tired, and despite the swollen face through his beatings, there was definitely a twinkle in his eyes.

"A doctor and the male nurse will accompany us back to Southampton on an air ambulance flight" Nobby seemingly satisfied with the arrangements.

An hour later we were on a small plane. There were seats for thirty or so people, but today there were only five of us, excluding the crew. Very swiftly after boarding, the plane was aloft and within ten minutes of taking-off, K-P was asleep on the flat bed. Nobby was reclined, and with two Gin and Tonics under his belt, he was snoring soundly. The bread from the sandwiches was making me sleepy and I reclined my seat to join them.

I was being shaken gently by the shoulder. It was the male nurse, and as I opened my eyes I saw that everyone else was already awake and strapped into their seats. There was sunshine streaming into the cabin as the pilot gently banked to the left to commence his descent into Southampton Airport. I too strapped myself into my seat as I returned it to the upright position. In less than ten minutes we were on the ground taxiing to a hanger away from the terminal. A few minutes after coming to a halt in the hanger, the door opened, shortly followed by Customs and Immigration officers coming on board, accompanied by Eric Jones who identified K-P and myself. The officers checked us against copies of our passports. They left and then K-P, Nobby and I disembarked. The doctor and nurse exchanged papers with their British counterparts, and we were ushered towards a luxury minibus, where there was a bed for K-P and four armchairs facing each other. Once installed, we were soon underway.

Eric opened the proceedings "Nobby has given me a brief summary of what happened. It sounds as though you were bloody lucky and there was a gross error of judgement on behalf of this Dominique de Silva. I would like a full account please, but first I am sure you want to speak to your wives, yes?"

"Absolutely." I turned in my seat to see that K-P was sitting up in bed. "Should I speak to Jane?"

K-P nodded and smiled for the first time in days.

"Jane first, please?" I said to Eric.

The phone in The Hall was answered on the first ring. I had moved to the bed and put the mobile phone on speaker.

"Hello?" Jane's tense voice bounced around the minibus.

I reduced the volume on the phone and said "Hi Jane, it's Marc, and K-P is sitting beside me. He has an injured tongue so he can't speak but other than that he is fine." K-P gave me an old fashioned look as I described him as 'fine'.

"Tell him that the children and I want him home as soon as possible, and that we love him so much."

I was about to reply when I could hear gently laughing and crying from the other end of the phone.

"I will pass you to Eric Jones who wants to speak to you."

"Thank you Marc, thank you so much and we love you - and Gerda too."

I passed the phone to Eric who spoke to Jane and suggested that she might like to visit K-P in the private hospital - I presumed it was the same hospital where I had been taken after my accident. He instructed her to meet him at Liverpool Street Station in London, and he would drive her to the private hospital where K-P would require some minor surgery.

The phone was then given to me and Gerda likewise answered Paul's phone on the first ring.

"Hello my darling," I said quietly into the mobile cupped in my hand.

"Hello husband" Gerda replied.

I felt my eyes welling up and composed myself, "How are you and the twins?"

"Good, Paul's been fantastic. I was so grumpy since you went away. Worse still when I phoned Eric and he said he lost contact with you three days ago. I love you so much Marc – please promise you won't do anything stupid like that again."

I looked up at K-P and he smiled back at me "I promise." I hoped that I would be able to keep my vow.

"When will we see you?" Gerda asked.

I had been thinking about this during our flight to Southampton. "I hope to drive over to Holland the day after tomorrow?"

"Not tomorrow?" Gerda replied in mock seriousness. "Why so long?"

"I need to buy a car and insure it tomorrow," I replied.

"Ok, but not another Range Rover – that car is bad luck."

"Any suggestions?"

"No - just make sure it has enough space for the children, their toys, and the two of us."

We concluded the call with sweet nothings and I said I would call later in the afternoon.

Our family duty done I swung back towards Eric and Nobby, who had been conversing quietly during my calls to Jane and Gerda.

"Eric, what's going on?"

"What do you mean?" he asked.

"You set K-P up, didn't you?"

At first he said nothing so I interjected "Dominique de Silva said he knew K-P had certain information. You planted that thought, didn't you?"

"Not as such. We know his outfit was being fed detailed information that only a select few people who would have access to," he admitted. "We have had no success from this end so we needed to try a different approach."

"So K-P was set up to flush out Dominique de Silva?" It was more a statement than a question.

"Yes in the first instance, and then we would use some fancy electronics to keep tabs on him, and with patience he would hopefully lead us to the person, or persons who is feeding him the information."

"You must have some idea" I urged.

Eric said nothing, and returned to studying the papers in front of him.

"Information surrounding the security arrangements of the World Cup is significant but not worth the life of anyone." I said.

"And possibly useless which Dominique de Silva concluded" Eric replied.

I said nothing and sat still totally confused.

We all sat in silence for about twenty minutes, as the mini-van made its way towards Winchester, and then on to the private hospital somewhere in South London. I looked over at K-P who was sleeping soundly, at peace with himself. I supposed his innate sense of duty, which drove him to join the Royal Navy, tugged at his conscience. That sense of doing the right-thing was an open door to Eric Jones, when he came knocking on K-P's door.

"Come on Eric, please tell me the full story, what is going on?" I asked, staring him straight in the eyes.

"Marc, you recall the problems five years ago off the Somalian Coast with pirates. The romantic image of pirates is long gone, replaced by well-armed and often desperate men more likely to kidnap and kill a ship's crew than make them walk the plank. Films such as Captain Phillips have raised public understanding of the reality of the problem, but they give little idea of its scale. An industry study put the cost of piracy in seas off Somalia to the global economy at six billion dollars with many hostages taken and six seafarers losing their lives. The figures the previous year were many times higher and a reason for the reduction is the increasing use of armed security personnel on ships sailing through high-risk areas - such as off Africa's East and West coasts - and the UK is at the forefront of training these people. The Lloyd's insurance community worked together with the British Government to create a specific security qualification, Maritime Security Operative. Based on the new international standard for Private Maritime Security Contractors, the qualification is seen as the industry benchmark for the UK shipping businesses and is widely expected to become the global measure. And, on the back of the qualification, insurance accreditation followed. The aim was to train security forces for the protection of vessels on the high seas. I was asked to lead this initiative and it proved to be very successful, although we noticed certain patterns, most notably that it was vessels without the security forces that were being attacked rather than vessels with security forces."

"Well that's obvious," I said completely unimpressed.

"Marc" Eric's voice hardened perceptibly "you're not listening to me. I didn't say successfully attacked – just attacked."

He let what he said sink in, "Ah, someone is tipping off the pirates as to which vessels don't have a security force."

"Nearly" Eric replied "it's subtler than that."

"How so?" I asked.

"The pirates are being told which vessels do have a security force."

"Well that's just good risk management – try and put off the bad guys by telling them certain ships have better security. It's no different from putting your alarm on the outside of your property."

"True, Marc, until we investigated deeper and we found that it was only the voyages protected by members who had qualified with the new security qualification, which were being avoided."

"Sorry, but I still don't understand; you want the security qualification to be a success, don't you?"

"Yes" Eric replied "but the way the information was being leaked was the issue." He paused and took a swig from his ever present water bottle. "By a process of elimination, we determined that the information was coming out of Lloyd's underwriters who had written a scheme, which specifically backed this security qualification."

"So other insurers were being selected against – including Deeks Syndicate."

"No Deeks actually underwrite the scheme, but I am certain that they are not the source of the leak," he replied.

"In the same way that you are certain your own department is not responsible for leaking information to Dominique de Silva's cronies?" Even in the half-light of the mini-bus I could see Eric slightly wince at my words.

He said nothing for a moment and continued "At one stage it was felt that the attacks in Paris and Brussels last year might be a pre-cursor for a similar attack on the Euro 2016 football championship in France last summer. We were trying to use the Kidnap & Ransom policies of the national football teams as a way of establishing the chain of communication to the terrorists, and secondly to stop this confidential information coming out of the Lloyd's market. Appalling enough that one of our own would leak such information to terrorists in the first place for idealogical reasons, but it sickens me that the reason seems to be for financial gain. But there was no such attack on the Euros. The Olympics were not insured, so we needed to focus on the next large sporting event, which is the World Cup in Russia in twenty-eighteen. K-P's objective was to convey certain information regarding the World Cup, that we would then trace both down the line to the terrorists, and up the line to Lloyd's underwriters. The information K-P was to pass on was not the true security details."

"And somehow Dominique de Silva found this out?" I asked.

Eric nodded.

"Then why did he go through with the rendezvous with K-P?"

"I think he was either tipped-off after he had met K-P, or he realised who K-P was and he used him to gain access to you."

"By trying to kill me?" I said in a mocking tone.

"Think about it. With you dead he could miraculously re-appear and claim his inheritance."

"Then what stopped him killing me in Dubai."

"I don't know, perhaps he just hesitated too long......"

"Unless......"

Eric interjected "Unless what?"

"He had second thoughts after I offered him Masterson Shipping, plus the properties in Zimbabwe and Goa."

A few minutes passed and we both remained silent.

"Eric, he let it slip that he wanted the information to turn the tables on someone. What does that mean?"

Eric shrugged his shoulders "The man is crackers. Goodness knows what he meant." There was a slyness to Eric's reply to my question and I felt he was not telling me everything.

"What next?" I asked.

"For you, nothing more; thanks for your help and assistance. K-P should be well enough in a week or two to return to work, and we will continue to look into other trends, where information about comparable risks could have had claims against certain Lloyd's underwriters, and not others."

"Such as?" I questioned.

"Well - Kidnap and Ransom is the most obvious, but also Surety and Specie, and certain fiduciary losses."

"And what has your investigation revealed thus far?" My voice sounded sceptical which Eric picked up on in his response.

"I know it sounds fanciful, but we have identified five Lloyd's Syndicates, three direct Insurers and two Reinsurers who have bettered the odds on these types of risks."

"Are the actual underwriters of these types of risk friends or members of the same masonic lodge?"

Eric frowned at me before answering "That sort of thing is not likely to happen in Lloyd's – otherwise the lodges would not be tolerated. No we believe it is just one person behind the dissemination of the underwriting information."

"Who are the five Lloyd's Syndicates you suspect?"

"I'm afraid I am not at liberty to say."

"I beg your pardon?"

Eric could obviously tell I was getting cross because he said "Calm down," before explaining further. "I am under strict instructions from the Chairman of Lloyd's, and the Serious Fraud Office of the Metropolitan Police not to divulge these names to you."

"Why not?"

"Because you work in the Lloyd's market and, like as not, you would go charging around and undo all the good work we have been doing over the last twelve months."

"Other than nearly getting K-P killed" I shot back at him.

Eric was quiet for a moment or two, as if trying to weigh up what to say next to me and eventually he continued. "We think what started out as bad practice developed into something much more sinister." Again he paused before continuing "The people to whom the information was initially leaked were fairly low level criminals, but as the opportunity was seized on by organised criminals, it wound its way up the food chain to de Silva. The criminal acts became more daring and more serious, as the size of the prize grew ever bigger. We think that once they had started, the Lloyd's Underwriters found they could not stop, and perhaps they are being blackmailed."

"That would fit in with what de Silva said to me."

"Perhaps, but whatever the reason, they are very cunning by surrounding themselves with the same insurers and reinsurers which act as a very effective smoke-screen, and it is possible that one or two of them may be accomplices, innocent or otherwise. As soon as information got into the hands of potential terrorists, this went way above my pay-grade."

"So how was K-P's jaunt going to help?" I asked.

Eric's expression became even graver. "One of the outstanding candidates who applied for the security qualification was formerly a Provost Officer in the Royal Air Force. We tried infiltrating him into the process. Whilst it initially led to your friend Dominique de Silva, it came to an end, when he was killed in an untimely car accident."

"That's a coincidence" I added sarcastically.

"At the time of his death we treated it as just that, an accident, but after your crunch the police are re-investigating the circumstances involving his death."

"Why don't the police just pull the suspects in and grill them?" I was being fairly blunt.

Eric half smiled, "There you go, the typical reckless Marcus Edge approach."

I feigned a hurt expression and Eric's smile was obvious in the darkened vehicle.

"We do not have enough hard evidence; all we have is suspicion, supposition and some inconclusive statistics. We are in danger of frightening them off, while having the death of at least two people on our hands, plus a string of crimes caused by these individuals."

"The question must be what is driving the person? It can't just be better underwriting results" I posed.

"Who knows, and as I just said this latest development has just made the whole issue far more serious. Before we believed that there may be financial rewards being paid by the organised criminals to the person providing the information, this could be part of blackmail against the individual. Perhaps the person is seeking power and control."

"What next?" I asked.

"The matter has been taken out of my hands," another pause for contemplation by Eric before he added "I am pleased that you and K-P are alive. He is strong and he will recover quickly."

"What about Dominique de Silva?" I enquired.

"No idea. He is outside our jurisdiction."

Marcus Edge awakes from his coma

We arrived at the private hospital and the mini-bus had obviously driven into a garage, because I had no clue where we were. I was escorted to a white room, very similar to where I was brought after my car accident. Eric requested that I go to sleep, and refrain from leaving my room. I agreed. I lay down on the bed to rest and was asleep before I could get undressed.

The next morning before I left the hospital, I had to give an interview to the press, saying I had recovered from the induced coma some days ago, but the doctors wished to keep me under close observation. The press consisted of one local reporter, and even he was underwhelmed by a person recovering from a car accident. Eric had prepared a press release and this was passed to the reporter on the understanding that he would have two hours before we sent it down the lines. The interview lasted no more than ten minutes, and most of it was dominated by the death of Jimmy, and whether I had spoken to his wife. With pangs of regret I admitted I had not, and made a mental note to speak to Carla today.

With the interview concluded I went to check on K-P. I was escorted to the next room, and he was sitting-up in bed.

"How are you?" I asked.

He held up a one hand thumb and forefinger creating a circle, in the universal gesture to indicate "OK".

"I am going back to my house this afternoon and hopefully over to Holland tomorrow."

He nodded.

"Where's Jane?" I asked, as I would have liked to talk to Jane.

He mimed a house with his hands.

"Gone back to the children?"

Again he nodded.

"Sorry I missed her, but I was out for the count."

He smiled.

"I am off to buy a car." I went over to K-P and gave him a big hug and left.

Eric had ordered me a chauffeured car, with blacked-out windows, and I was driven through London by an incommunicative driver. In less than an hour I was outside my home. Eric had returned my keys to me before he left the hospital. The house seemed so empty. I retrieved an old pay as you go mobile phone, and topped up the credit. From the house phone I tried calling Paul's home in Holland, but there was no answer. I left a message, giving them my phone number, which I then texted to Gerda. Within a few minutes there was a reply that they had gone to the mainland to watch a film, and that they would not be back to Paul's house until late in the afternoon. I smiled because it would have taken a great deal to persuade Paul to leave his beloved island.

I also sent a text to the pay-as-you-go phone that I asked Julian to buy. The message was a short "I am ok."

I guessed I had a few hours to make the arrangement to purchase a car and insure it within the day. I had already determined that it would have to be a pre-owned vehicle, as a new car would take at least a week to get on the road. I started to work the phones, starting with a Mercédès Benz dealership in East London. They didn't have any 'E' or 'C' class estates available until the weekend.

"Are you dead set on a Merc?" the car salesman asked me.

"Yes because we have two young children and I don't want a four-by-four." I replied.

"That's a shame because we have today taken in an Audi RS6 Sport Avant."

"Is that an estate?" I asked.

"Yes and very quick, but it is four-wheel drive."

"We continued to talk about the car which should have been on its way to an Audi dealer. It had a valid tax disc, and the salesman could have it valeted and ready for collection by six o'clock if I could arrange payment and insurance in time. I assured him that I could, and we agreed on a price that I felt sure had made the salesman's target for the week; but it was a case of demand and supply within the day. I transferred money from a savings account to my current account, and then phoned him back with my debit card details which, following a call from my bank, meant the car was mine. Insurance took fifteen minutes, and by half-past four the salesman called to say he had received a copy of the insurance cover note, and that I could collect the car at six.

"What colour is it?" I asked.

"Why?" the voice of the salesman was nervous, probably fearful that the transaction might not proceed.

"My wife will ask me."

He laughed "It's white."

Inwardly I groaned thinking of the frequent trips to the car wash, but I kept a brave face and said "That's great. See you at six."

Almost immediately the house phone rang. It was Gerda and the children. The twins were full of the film they had been to see, both trying to explain the plot to me at the same time, in a mixture of Dutch and English. Gerda shooed them off the line and at last we had some privacy.

"How are you my darling?" I asked.

Gerda replied "Better now you're safe. Jane phoned me …..."

"She saw K-P earlier" I interrupted.

"Yes, I know. I wouldn't like to be in K-P's shoes when he gets home."

We both laughed simultaneously.

"I love you so much my gorgeous girl" I said to her.

"Show it to me tomorrow" was her inviting reply.

My mind started to race thinking of us in bed together. The conversation then returned to more mundane matters, such as my travel arrangements. I said that I would drive to Folkestone early in the morning and hoped to get an early shuttle, but with the best will in the world I was unlikely to arrive much before dinner time. Gerda promised to try and keep the twins awake for my arrival. We ended the call agreeing that I would call once I had arrived in France.

I ordered a cab to take me to the car salesroom to collect my new car, and with that done I resisted the temptation to go to my office, but instead drove to Jimmy's home in Essex. I should have called ahead to speak to Carla, but I didn't know what to say, and I hoped that when I met Carla face-to-face that the words would come to me. In the event it was a foolish journey because no-one answered the door, and there were no lights on in the house as dusk had transformed into the evening. I scribbled a short note on a scrap of paper, giving Carla my temporary mobile number, asking that she call me. I felt such a coward because I was relieved that Carla was not at home. Her fiery temper and vocabulary of a fish-wife had reduced many men to becoming nervous wrecks – including me. I drove away remembering that when Carla and I were together, it was tempestuous during which time she would swear at me regularly, whether in anger or delight.

Reunion in Texel

It was just after nine o'clock European time – Friday morning - when I drove off the Shuttle at Sangatte, the security arrangements taking longer following Great Britain's decision to leave the European Union, the previous year. I was surprised that I hadn't been stopped for speeding. Driving the Audi was akin to unleashing a monster, difficult to control, but when giving the car its head it took my breath away. The previous evening, I had not realised its potential as the traffic to-and-from Essex was very heavy, but given the clear roads in the early morning going away from London, I understood the power of the car. It was less than three months old with only two thousand miles on the clock. I wondered if the previous owner traded it in for something more sedate, thus giving themselves an even chance of keeping their licence. On a number of occasions as I raced up behind a car in the outside lane of the M20, the speed combined with it being a white car, resulted in the car in front pulling into an inside lane believing me to be police.

The Audi was a four litre V8, weighing nearly two tonnes, but the four-wheel drive could launch the estate car to a – limited – hundred and fifty-five miles an hour. I was amazed at the acceleration and more than once had to ease off the accelerator, as it took me past a hundred and twenty miles an hour in a few short seconds.

I called Gerda and then pointed the car towards Belgium, with the cruise control set at a sensible figure, just on the maximum French speed limit. The weather was a gorgeous early April day and as the long-legged car gobbled up the kilometres, my mind turned to my family, and I knew that the emptiness in my stomach that I had been feeling since flying to Dubai would be soon dispelled when I saw Gerda and the twins.

I stopped for lunch the other side of Antwerp and called Paul's house to tell them of my progress, but there was no answer and I left a message. I assumed they must be taking advantage of the good weather. I was just about to recommence my journey when the telephone rang with no number display.

"Hello?" I said.

"It's Eric."

"How did you get this number?" I asked.

"Don't ask and then I cannot lie to you. We wanted to advise you of a development."

I interrupted "Is K-P OK?"

"Yes, yes, he's OK considering what he has been through. He had a fitful night, probably after being lambasted by his wife."

I laughed.

He continued "But with that all out of their systems, they're all lovey-dovey again, and he is going home today."

"So what's the problem?" I asked.

"Dominique de Silva was seen leaving Dubai Airport headed for London."

"And?" I asked.

"No Dominique de Silva was on any manifest of any plane from Dubai to London, or any point in-between, over the past two days."

"Try the name Omar Aziz" I suggested.

"Thanks, we will search the manifests."

"Why are you concerned?" I asked.

"He was overheard speaking about you, and how he was going to take what was rightfully his." Eric's voice was very solemn.

"How did you come by this information?" I questioned him.

"Special Branch officers are working with Dubai Police and picked up a sad dumb mute..."

"He's the one who helped us when we were locked up."

"Ah, that explains it" Eric said out loud, probably more to himself than to me.

"Explains what?"

"Why he was very eager to help the police."

"I think de Silva performed a full elinguation on the poor man."

"He's a brute, Marc, so keep away from your usual haunts until we find him" Eric warned me.

"He won't find me for at least a week."

"How come?"

I am going to my brother-in-law's house in a remote part of Holland" I explained.

"Who knows you're going there?" Eric asked.

"Only my wife, K-P and now you."

"Keep it to just those people," then, as an afterthought, he added "for your safety and that of your family."

"Of course" I replied.

As I continued my journey towards the Dutch border I found my mind wandering on more than a few occasions, with the result that I was driving well in excess of the Belgian speed limit.

I cruised into Holland heading from Breda, passing by Utrecht and towards Amsterdam, although I would avoid Holland's largest city by skirting around to the west. Once past Amsterdam I headed north, with the motorway ending about fifty kilometres south of Den Helder, when I took the trunk road that led me to the ferry to Texel.

I arrived at the Den Helder ferry port just after half past four, the journey taking me seven and a half hours from when I drove off the Shuttle at Sangatte. I would have to wait until half past five for the next ferry. I was sitting in the car when the phone rang. I recognised the number as Jimmy's home number. I hesitated a moment before answering.

"Hello?" I said tentatively into the phone "Carla is that you?"

Silence from the other end, and then the phone line went dead. I checked my signal which was strong and looked across the grey North Sea towards to where I thought the Essex coast was. I thought about Carla and the private hell she must be going through. I called her number but no answer, and decided that she was not yet in a frame of mind to speak to me yet. I stopped dialling.

The ferry arrived twenty minutes before departure. There were only three cars, two commercial vehicles and a dozen cyclists who disembarked, before the foot passengers were allowed to leave the ferry. I was first to drive on to the ferry, and a long queue had formed behind me, which probably meant that some of them would have to wait for the next ferry. Commuters returning home to Texel for the weekend I guessed.

Texel in the Autumn and Winter is a wild and remote island like the other Wadden Sea Islands which stretch up from Holland towards Denmark. Paul found the solitude helped his recuperation from a bad head injury, which had kept him in an assisted coma for a long period. It also helped him try to forget his own malfeasance when he perpetrated a fraud which nearly cost him his life, and my own. Paul loved the sea and more so the hustle and bustle of ports. So it was a paradox that whilst he lived on an island that was inhospitable for six months of the year, he sought out the most industrial town on all the Wadden Sea Islands. He lived in Oudeschild a working port, which he would stroll around for hours, particularly when the fishermen came to port with their catch. From time-to-time Paul would help them unload their precious cargo, and even fillet fish if they were short-handed.

"Why don't you go out with them?" I once asked.

"Never," he replied firmly "I get terribly sea-sick."

I laughed as I recalled many years previously when Paul had a wonderful home on the island of St. Martten in the Caribbean, unfortunately bought with the proceeds of crime. He loved being around the water, but could not fully experience the exhilaration of the sea.

Texel is the largest of the five Dutch Wadden Sea Islands, part of the Wadden Sea World Heritage Site. Texel is some thirty kilometres long. In the Spring and Summer, it comes into its own with fantastic beaches, beautiful natural scenes, punctuated with thousands of sheep. Texel also boasts a permanent seal population, the Sand Sculpture Festival, a Blues Festival and last but certainly not least the Round Texel Race - the world's largest catamaran race.

My destination was Oudeschild the fourth largest village on Texel and, as well as fishing, the town has a shipyard where welding repairs and construction are performed. Oudeschild is on the eastern side of Texel, at the Wadden Sea Dyke, only twelve kilometres north-east of Den Helder. In the seventeenth century, the Dutch East India Company ships sailing from Amsterdam would wait for favourable winds near Oudeschild.

I arrived at Paul's house just after six o'clock, and before I had turned off the car engine the door swung open, and the twins were shouting "Daddy's here!"

They were being held back by Paul and Gerda both of whom wore very broad smiles across their faces.

I walked over to the twins kissing and hugging them both, at the same time as they tried to climb on me. After a few moments I extricated myself from their limpet grips and gave Paul a bear hug. I noticed that Paul had become much thinner and older than the last time I saw him, almost frail. I hoped he wasn't drinking too heavily.

I then turned to Gerda "Hello my darling." I kissed her.

She pulled away whispering "Later my love."

"I tried phoning earlier, but there was no answer."

"We were returning from Den Helder," Gerda explained "as we needed to stock up on provisions."

Paul interrupted "As Daddy is tired, English is allowed tonight," the twins smiled with delight "but tomorrow back to Dutch."

The twins laughed as they saw my face frown.

It was a wonderful evening with the twins trying to give me a blow-by-blow account of their holiday with Uncle Paul. Luckily they didn't want to know what I had been doing, but I knew that would come later when Gerda and I were in bed. As it happened I was spared the interrogation from Gerda and Paul, because after a plentiful helping of salty Texel lamb and too many glasses of the local spirit – Juttertje – I fell asleep in one of the armchairs. When I awoke, Gerda had gone to bed and I made my apologies to Paul and joined her. She was asleep but, as I climbed in beside her, my cold body stirred her. My hands found her breasts and she turned towards me and we kissed more longingly than earlier, both hungry for each other, and she moaned softly as I gently slid inside her soft and warm thighs. We had always enjoyed a healthy sex life and, following the birth of the twins, time for such was at a premium so our lovemaking developed an urgency and increased physicality. Gerda's slender athletic frame had developed gorgeous curves in all the right places, and she was particularly proud of her enlarged breasts, often wishing to reveal her décolletage. I revelled in her womanly softness, often having to choke back as to prolong her orgasms, but tonight I could not wait and nor could Gerda as we arrived at the point of ecstasy at the same time.

"I love you so much my darling" I said to her as I rolled onto my side to spoon beside her.

"Show me again in the morning." She giggled as she drew my hand onto her breast.

Within minutes we were both fast asleep.

Going out for a long walk

Any thought of reprising the previous evening's seduction was obliterated by both the twins coming into our room shortly after daybreak, and we just had enough time to don night-clothes, before they climbed into our bed.

It was a ritual at the weekends and holidays that they were allowed into our bed to discuss a plan of campaign and Gerda would cook 'Dutch Breakfast', which was basically a fry-up of bacon, chipolatas and fried bread all dipped in chopped tomatoes then cut very small so they could be eaten with fingers from a big bowl.

It was decided that Daddy needed more rest, so Uncle Paul would take the twins out for a long walk, and then after lunch we would all ride bicycles to our favourite beach and fly kites off the dunes.

With the children gone, Gerda and I returned to bed, resuming our lovemaking but with deliberate slowness and tenderness, knowing that we would not be disturbed for at least a couple of hours. As we lay in bed afterwards, I gave a fuller account of what happened in Dubai.

"It doesn't make any sense."

"What doesn't?" I asked.

"That Aziz – or de Silva – just left you there in that room," Gerda paused before continuing "it was as though he wanted you to be found."

"Perhaps he just wanted to think through what I had offered hims"

Gerda turned to me with a questioning look.

"All of it is so bizarre" I hesitated before continuing "the capture of K-P I understand - to teach him a lesson - but I think that Aziz definitely wants control. And what I offered him threw him into turmoil and he needed time to evaluate."

"It still makes no sense" Gerda remarked "but I suggest we keep a low profile here in Texel until he is found."

Gerda was concerned when I told her about what was overheard in Dubai about Aziz reclaiming what he felt was rightfully his.

I showered, shaved and was in Paul's kitchen when my phone rang. 'Unknown number' showed on the display so I let it ring until the voicemail cut in, and a few seconds later the voicemail alert signalled that I had a message waiting for me.

I dialled the voicemail number and accessed the message. It was Eric, "Marc, can you call me urgently, please?"

I dialled his number that was stored in my old phone from five years previously. It was answered on the first ring. "Marc, what is Paul's landline number please?"

I gave it to him.

"I will call you back immediately" Eric said and then he hung up.

Within seconds, Paul's house phone rang.

"What's all this about?" I asked.

"I needed to call you on a secure line and your mobile may have been compromised."

"How?"

"I don't know for certain but we are taking every precaution."

"Why?" I was becoming suspicious.

Eric did not answer immediately. "Jimmy's wife, sorry widow, has gone missing."

"She tried phoning me yesterday."

"Did you actually speak to her?" Eric asked.

"No." I explained how I had tried to visit Carla but she was not at home, so I left my new mobile number and I invited her to call me."

"You idiot!" Eric exclaimed.

"Remove the sim card from your phone immediately, buy yourself another one in Holland, and then send the number to my mobile – only me." He was most insistent.

"What's going on Eric?" I still felt he wasn't telling me everything.

"We can't find Dominique de Silva or Omar Aziz on any passenger lists out of Dubai. Stay in Holland and out of sight until we know more."

"OK."

"And send me your new number by text as soon as you can please?"

Gerda had overheard my conversation with Eric, and wanted me to give her the conversation in full.

I had hardly finished when Gerda said "Let's go and get a sim card before Paul and the twins return."

We went into Oudeschild by car and were back at Paul's house within twenty minutes. Gerda busied herself with the preparation of a light lunch and I did as Eric instructed, receiving an acknowledgement back immediately accompanied by "Keep your head down on Texel." Eric echoed Gerda's earlier thoughts.

Gerda had finished preparing lunch and kept checking her watch. "Paul must have taken them for a very long walk."

"How long have they been gone?" I asked.

"Over three hours", Gerda replied.

"They will be too shattered to go cycling this afternoon."

"Oh no they won't," Gerda retorted "they love it here and they sleep so well."

"Do you think we should move out of London?" I asked.

"Yes" Gerda replied very firmly.

"Ah? So this has been on your mind for a while?"

"Not that long, but seeing them in the wide open spaces of Texel, I think they are ready for a change."

"That's fine by me," I replied.

Gerda's face broke into a broad smile.

We sat chatting about the alternatives, and I mentioned that Jane was unhappy at The Hall.

"I am not surprised," Gerda interrupted "it is a monstrosity and has a bad feeling. Sell it Marc – and give enough money to K-P so he can buy a family home. We can use the rest to buy something in the country, perhaps near K-P and Jane.

"Mmm, you have it all worked out" I said with mock seriousness.

"Yes, I have and I have been looking at houses online not too far from Stansted Airport and the Motorway. Easy for visiting Holland and great commuting links to the City."

"Anything else?" I ventured.

"Why, yes, I have looked at schools in the area as well."

"I love you Gerda Edge." I took her into my arms and kissed her.

"We have no time for that," as Gerda pulled away looking at her watch for the umpteenth time. "Marc I am worried about Paul and the twins; they should have been back ages ago."

"We'll go and look for them, and" I added "just leave them a note to call your mobile if they get back before we meet them."

We started out in relatively good spirits, but after we had covered all of Oudeschild and along each road for at least five kilometres, we became more concerned. We would occasionally stop to ask people if they had seen Paul and the twins but with no success.

Gerda was now very cross with Paul. "What is he playing at? Why doesn't he have a mobile phone?"

After yet another circuit of Oudeschild, which did not take long we returned to Paul's house. As we turned the corner we saw a police car outside. A policeman was about to get into the car and drive away as we pulled up beside him.

Gerda spoke quickly to him in Dutch, he replied and Gerda let out an animal-like wail of despair.

"What's the matter?" I asked.

"Paul's dead!" Gerda's eyes were awash with tears and her cheeks flushed red with anger.

"Oh my God! Where are the twins?"

Gerda turned to me "Nowhere to be seen."

Now it was my turn to cry out.

Gerda spoke again to the policeman, who was speaking on his radio and he held up a hand to Gerda to indicate that he needed a moment.

We were desperate to talk to the policeman, but he was in a detailed conversation with the person at the other end of the radio. From what little Dutch I could speak he was obviously asking about the twins. He finished talking on the radio and turned to Gerda speaking in Dutch, and as he did so, the colour drained from her face.

"Paul was found near the Wadden Sea Dyke."

"Any sign of a struggle?" I asked.

"The police believe the children have been taken. Paul was just alive when he was found by a man walking his dog, but he said nothing before he died."

"Did the man see anything?" I asked.

"We are going to the dyke now to speak with him."

The policeman asked if we wanted to go in his car, but we declined and followed him to the dyke in the Audi.

When we arrived, the police and medical staff were there in droves. I guessed that any crime, let alone a death on Texel, was a very rare event. A makeshift tent had been erected on the ground below the footpath that was some two meters higher than where Paul lay. Even with the people milling around the scene, I could see from the marks on the ground that there had been quite a furore.

Gerda was talking to a tall elderly man, and I was struck by his shock of thick white hair and clear blue eyes, exaggerated by his weather-beaten face. As I walked over to him he looked at me and switched to immaculate English.

"I am so sorry for your loss."

I nodded my head to acknowledge his sentiments.

"Did you see our children as you walked here?" I asked him.

"No, but I did see a black van drive away."

"Did you tell the police this?" My voice rising as I spoke.

He nodded his head and I left him and Gerda to continue to talk as I walked towards the policeman we met at Paul's house. He was talking to a young man dressed in a sports jacket and an open collar shirt.

As I approached him, he offered me his hand. "I am Michiel van Joost, the detective in charge of this" he hesitated for a moment "...situation."

I offered the policeman my hand "Marcus Edge. The man who found Paul said he saw a black van driving away...."

"Yes, and before you ask, we have sent word to the ferry crossing."

"And?"

"No news yet."

"Thank you." I walked back to where Gerda was standing and pulled her aside.

"Gerda, I want to drive to the ferry. I think Aziz – Dominique da Silva – has taken the twins."

"Why?"

"Money I guess… I hope." I was trying to convince myself that de Silva's revenge would not extend to the lives of our children.

"What will you do at the ferry?"

I shrugged my shoulders "Ask questions, I guess."

"Will you go to the mainland?"

"If necessary" I replied.

"I want to come with you."

I was about to protest.

"No arguments!" Gerda said with force and I knew it was not worth arguing with her.

"Sorry, but I overheard your discussion," it was Detective van Joost. I introduced him to Gerda, and as they shook hands he said "there are many details to resolve here before you can leave Texel."

Gerda swung around on Detective van Joost and Gerda gave the detective a piece of her mind, following which his face went pale and then reddened with anger.

"Come on, we're leaving." Gerda took my hand and marched off to the Audi.

I looked back over my shoulder and the detective was speaking animatedly to the first policeman we met. As we sat in the car, I could see the detective running over to an unmarked Golf and prepared to follow us.

"What did you say to him?" I asked as I pulled away.

"I told him that my brother was dead and could wait, the twins required our immediate attention now."

We drove at breakneck speed along the country roads of Texel, and the Detective's Golf became smaller and smaller in my rear view mirror. As we approached the ferry I could see a welcoming party, as two police-cars were parked by the ferry embarkation point. As I came to a stop, I could see the next ferry approaching. We jumped out of the car and a young policeman approached us talking in Dutch. Gerda verbally whipped him and he softened his approach. As he talked to Gerda he pointed to the ferry office, and at that point Detective van Joost's Golf pulled alongside our Audi.

He walked up to me looking very cross "Please tell your wife not to talk to me like that again otherwise I will arrest her...."

"On what charge?"

"I don't know yet, but I am sure I will find something, and you might join her unless you keep your speed down."

All three of them walked over to the ferry offices, and I followed on in their wake. Detective van Joost spoke on his own with the ferry operators. After a few moments he spoke for at least two minutes into his radio before switching to his mobile phone. Five minutes later he returned to us.

"Well it seems a people carrier with dark tinted windows was the last vehicle to join the previous ferry to the mainland," Detective van Joost explained.

"And?" I asked.

"We are getting authority to review the close circuit television records." At that point, his mobile rang "Ja, ja" he said into the phone before walking over to the office again. He handed the phone to the person inside the offices and a moment later he beckoned us into the offices. As the ferry operator busied himself with his computer monitor, Detective van Joost explained that his father was a director of the ferry operator, and that he short circuited the process.

The operator had the close circuit television on screen; he fast forwarded to when the vehicle drove up to pay for the ferry, and I could see Dominique de Silva as clear as daylight, in the left-hand front seat.

"It's Aziz, I am sure of it," I exclaimed, using the name I originally knew him by. "Dominique de Silva is the name he is now using. Can you rewind the tape please?" I spoke to the ferry operator and Gerda spoke to him in Dutch, whereupon he rewound the tape, before playing it again in slow motion.

"Look" I pointed to the screen "it's a British number plate. I think they are going back to Calais."

"That's a big assumption," said Detective van Joost.

"Any better ideas?" I turned to look directly into his eyes as I spoke to him.

His eyes held my stare and he spoke into his radio for a moment. "I have asked that we monitor the traffic cameras from here to Belgium, and to report any sightings of the vehicle."

"I want to follow them," I announced resolutely.

Detective van Joost thought for a moment and then left Gerda and me. He went over to the policeman and handed him his car keys.

Whilst he was speaking to his colleague, I whispered to Gerda "I think I recognise the driver as well."

"Who is it?"

"One of the men who was with de Silva in Dubai."

A moment later Detective van Joost returned to us and agreed that one of us could go across to the mainland, under the exceptional circumstances that our children may have been

188

abducted. But he was insistent that one of us stay on Texel, in case the abductors try to contact us. Also there were a lot of details outstanding surrounding Paul's death that needed answering.

Gerda and I looked at each other, and she nodded her agreement to Detective van Joost. "I will stay to sort Paul's affairs with you Detective."

"No you won't" he replied, "I am going with your husband or he doesn't go to the mainland."

La Chasse

I kissed Gerda goodbye and we promised to keep in touch. The ferry departed on time, and Detective van Joost was busy on his radio, before he lost contact with his control on Texel. Whilst he was not paying too much attention, I switched the dials from kilometres to miles to try and disguise the fact that I would not be keeping to the Dutch speed limit. I also synchronised the new sim card to the Audi's hands free system.

We arrived on the mainland at three o'clock and we had been driving for about thirty minutes when Detective van Joost received a call on his mobile. He spoke quickly and urgently for a few minutes. When he finished his call he turned to me "The traffic cameras on the route to Amsterdam have spotted a black people carrier with a British registration…"

"It's them……." I accelerated a little more – he hadn't said a word about our speed thus far.

"Slow down, both in your conclusions and your speed please."

I pulled a face at him.

He spoke again "We are going to shadow the vehicle from two unmarked police cars."

"Why not just stop them?" I asked.

"We need to be sure it is them and if they have your children we do not want to panic them."

I was about to retort, but I caught myself because it was obviously a sensible approach, to keep the twins safe.

"We are also putting a helicopter on stand-by," Detective van Joost explained "in case we lose contact with them on the ground."

"Thank you Detective."

"We will be travelling for a while together so please call me Michiel." Perhaps it was the fact that he had some positive news, because Detective van Joost's tone was softening a little.

"And you can call me Marc," I replied.

We drove in silence for about another twenty minutes, when I had an idea, and I put it to Michiel "Could you try and slow them down?"

"How can we do that without arousing their suspicions?" Michiel replied.

"A broken-down car on the side of the motorway? I am worried that they will sail past Amsterdam, but we will be caught in the Saturday rush-hour traffic. If we know where the accident is going to be in advance, we can make some time up, or possibly get in front of them."

"Hmm, it will make me very unpopular with my Amsterdam traffic cops, but it would give us an opportunity to verify that it is the people who took the ferry from Texel."

He spoke into his phone for a short time.

"That was quick?" I said.

"Yes I have asked to speak with the Head of Amsterdam's Traffic Police Division."

"And?"

"Apparently he is in a meeting and will contact me very shortly."

I was about to say something when Michiel's phone rang again, an even shorter call.

"Now what?" I asked

Michiel calmly explained that the Commissaris will call me in five minutes, and the two cars are now trailing the vehicle on the A9 motorway, which is about seventy kilometres ahead of us.

"That's a lot to catch up." I must have sounded disheartened.

"Yes, it is," Michiel agreed.

Then my phone rang. It was Gerda asking for news, and I told her what we were planning.

"Be careful," Gerda exclaimed which was amplified throughout the Audi via the stereo system.

"We will," Michiel tried to calm her fears.

I agreed to call her again as soon as we had more news.

Almost immediately after I finished talking with Gerda, Michiel's phone rang. It was a long call as he explained the situation to a superior officer, trying to convince him that a deliberate traffic jam would be a good thing, exactly opposite of what the traffic police want to happen. Michiel was quiet for a few minutes; he covered the phone and whispered to me that the Commissaris is currently checking the traffic situation. Eventually Michiel spoke again into his phone. There were a lot of "Ja's" and "Weg's" and he had a very red face when he stopped talking.

"Is everything organised?" I asked.

"Sort of" he replied "if it goes wrong then it is the end of my promising career."

"It won't be - I am sure."

"Are you always so sure of yourself Marc?" He turned to look at me. I briefly returned his gaze and saw no humour in his face.

"Yes," I said, but did not add that my self-confidence had often got me in a lot of trouble.

We drove along in silence again, and I guessed that Michiel was trying to justify to himself that he was doing the right thing. His phone rang again – and the call was not too long, nor did he say much in the conversation, but he seemed to be in better spirits at the end of the conversation.

"They have agreed to stage a lorry break-down at the beginning of some road works."

"That's good news, where do I go to avoid the traffic jam."

"Well, that's part of the problem" he paused a moment before continuing as he consulted his smart phone, and I could see he was looking at a map. "They won't do anything before Amsterdam, it's the other side of the City…"

"Why?" I asked.

"To lessen the impact of the delay on the City's rush hour."

I knew we could not expect any more, but it was disappointing because I was likely to lose time by being an hour behind them, and I was likely to be snagged in the evening traffic. I increased my speed gently which brought a disapproving stare from Michiel but no verbal admonishment.

I called Gerda and briefly told her of the latest plan. But she was very upset, as she had just been to identify that it was definitely Paul who had been found dead. I sympathised with her and knew it would hit her very hard, as she had no other family alive.

As I finished the call with Gerda, I found Eric's number on my head-up display and called him.

"Hello Marc. What news?"

"Eric, I have some very bad news and we may need some help from you."

"What's happened?" He asked.

"The twins have gone missing. I think Aziz, Dominique da Silva, has taken them…"

"Oh shit." Eric's raised voice was magnified by the Audi's speakers.

"And there's worse - Paul is dead."

"No…. how awful. How's Gerda?"

"Not good. She has just identified his body."

"How was he killed?"

"We don't know, but it seems there might have been a struggle……"

Michiel shrugged his shoulders.

"…..nothing is clear at the moment."

"Are you sure it was Dominique de Silva?"

"Pretty damn sure, yes," I caught Michiel looking at me, questioning the veracity of my statement "also I recognised another person as someone who was with de Silva in Dubai."

Michiel's face reddened with anger, as I had not given him this tit-bit of information.

"How can I help you?" Eric asked.

I explained that an officer of the Dutch Police Force was travelling with me, and that he had two unmarked cars trailing a black people carrier with British number plates; also, that we planned to try and slow the vehicle down without alarming them.

"Detective, you will have to be very careful," Eric was addressing Michiel.

Michiel responded "We will be taking every precaution; we are doing it to predominantly assess the situation in greater detail, before rushing in."

"Very sensible," was Eric's reply.

"Eric, I think they might try to return via Calais."

"And?"

"Can you check all the crossings for the next two days to see where, and when, they may be trying to come back to England?"

"Marc, you know it's the Easter holidays, and the ferries will be heaving."

"Don't forget Dunkirk as well?" I ignored his comments.

"OK, I will call you as soon as we have checked the various manifests and bookings." Eric had resigned himself to the task ahead of him, and he ended the call.

We were now on the A9 motorway, and again I pressed the Audi on above the speed limit, this time with no reaction from the Dutch policeman sitting beside me. He was probably relieved that he no longer had to ensure that we wouldn't crash headlong into an oncoming car while overtaking, due to the fact that the Audi's right hand drive was an impediment when driving on continental Europe's single carriageway roads. Michiel's phone rang after we had just passed Castricum. He was speaking to the Commissaris, although most of the time he was listening rather than talking.

"Well what news?" I asked as soon as the call was completed.

Michiel did not immediately reply to my question.

"Well!" I raised my voice as I suspected something was awry.

"We have lost contact with the vehicle."

"What?" I exclaimed.

"Our cars were trailing them from some distance," he paused "so as not to alert them to the fact they were being followed. A van suffered a blow-out in front of one of the unmarked police cars which collided with the van."

"Oh shit."

"The other car went to their assistance; the driver of the police car in the accident has suffered bad injuries, and has been rushed to hospital."

"Was there anyone else with the driver?" I asked, whilst I kept my foot on the accelerator.

"Yes, but they are just battered and bruised."

"Where did this happen?"

"Just beyond Schiphol Airport on the A4 motorway."

"Will the accident delay us?" I asked.

"Perhaps? The Commissaris is putting a helicopter on the route of the motorway to see if they can spot the people carrier."

"Can you make the delay on the A9 long enough for us to catch them?"

For a moment, I took my eyes from the road to look at him.

"I don't honestly know," he replied, and I saw doubt flicker across his face.

I ploughed on, pushing the Audi faster, and faster. Michiel was on the phone trying to ensure that we would not be held up, at the same time trying to organise a traffic jam between Amsterdam and Rotterdam to slow de Silva. The irony of the situation was not lost on me.

"You know we will not be stopping them, we just want to delay them, and if possible make sure your children are inside the vehicle."

I quizzed him on how the various parts of the operation were going to work. It was cathartic for me, to take my mind off what Jack and Catherine must be feeling. They would take comfort in each other, but they were bound to be petrified by the experience. When I wasn't thinking about the twins, I was trying to establish in my mind the reasoning behind Dominique de Silva's actions. Obviously he wanted to use them as leverage against me, but to what end? I needed to keep my temper under control, because if I saw red and flew at him, I would be endangering my beloved children.

Michiel's phone rang for the umpteenth time, but I could tell by the way he was speaking animatedly that something positive had occurred. Before I had a chance to ask him what he had learned, his phone rang again, and this time a very short call during which he said hardly anything more than "Ja".

"Good news Marc" he then qualified his statement when he added the word "relatively."

"Tell me, please?" I asked him.

"The helicopter has found the vehicle and it appears that they have stopped for fuel and provisions at a service station. We cannot get anyone on the ground to be close to them, but what is good news is that the traffic jam to delay them is arranged to be not far from the service station between the Zoeterwoude and Leidschendam junctions.

"So, we have two opportunities to close the distance on them?"

"Yes, and we will be helped by a police escort to take us through the accident near Schiphol Airport, because as we join the A9 at Badhoevedorp we will be met by a police motorcycle, which we can follow."

The briefest of smiles crossed my lips, as I nodded upon hearing the news.

I checked the clock on the dashboard of the Audi. It was half-past four and the traffic on the motorway had increased discernibly, meaning I was continually having to slow down, and then accelerate. I dialled Gerda's phone and she answered it on the second ring.

"Any news Marc?"

I explained that they were under surveillance from a helicopter and that the police were planning to delay them by a bogus traffic jam.

"I can't just sit here Marc and do nothing?"

For a moment I said nothing.

Gerda spoke again "I have spoken with Paul's lawyer, and I have phoned the funeral company."

"Poor you, having to do all that on your own…….." I tried to console her.

"I want to help you find the twins Marc."

We were talking on the hands-free phone so Michiel heard everything we had discussed.

"Why don't you use my car?" Michiel suggested "I will ask one of my colleagues to drive you to the ferry, and then give you my car keys."

"Thank you." Both Gerda and I spoke simultaneously.

"You will need to refuel when you get to the mainland," Michiel added.

It was about twenty minutes after speaking with Gerda that we joined the A9 motorway, and almost instantly a police motorcycle appeared in front of us, whereupon he switched on his siren and lights - cutting a swathe through the traffic in front of us. What was interesting was the police outrider stayed at a pretty constant speed, just ten kilometres above the speed limit, which initially frustrated me, but after a while of following him I could see that this gave the vehicles enough time to manoeuvre themselves out of the way of our advance. More than once there were strange stares at the fact a Dutch police motorcycle was escorting a car from the United Kingdom; but stare all they like I couldn't give a damn, and I hoped that the police force back home would go to the same lengths, if the roles were reversed.

We were about twenty kilometres beyond Schiphol airport, when Michiel received a call that de Silva's vehicle was in the pre-arranged traffic jam, about four kilometres from the Leidschendam junction. The bottle-neck had been deliberately set, just before the junction, on a stretch of the motorway where there was some nine kilometres between junctions. This meant they should be stuck there for some time. After the call, Michiel explained that we would be exiting the motorway where the vehicle had stopped at the service station – there was an access road we could use – and with the police outriders we should be able to get on the motorway just after the blockage, before they passed that point.

"How will we know if the children are in the car?" I asked.

"We have an infra-red camera in one of our vehicles, and we will be able to detect the heat from any bodies, as they pass us." Michiel further explained that the equipment was very sensitive and that it would be able to determine if the bodies were adults or children.

We continued to make good progress, and I took the opportunity to quickly refuel at the same petrol station where they had stopped. Michiel organised the payment while I was at the petrol pumps. He had been receiving a constant series of calls from the helicopter, which was monitoring their vehicle.

"It will be a close run thing if we manage to get there in time," Michiel relayed after his latest call.

Instantly I regretted refuelling but I had no choice. I wish we could drive quicker, but the conditions would not allow it. We drove down to an access point by the motorway that was constructed for emergency vehicles. I pulled to a stop and turned off the engine. We could not be seen by the oncoming traffic on the motorway, nor could we see the oncoming traffic. We could only see the vehicles just as they passed us. The vehicles appeared to be travelling quite slowly, and only by getting out of the car and walking around the barrier could

I see why. The traffic jam was only twenty metres away, and down to one lane, so as the vehicles passed us they were only just accelerating away from being near stationary for nearly an hour.

Michiel pulled me back behind the barrier. "Careful, they might see you" he warned "they are only ten vehicles from the front of the queue."

I wanted to run to them, and yank open the doors to pull my children to safety.

"Here they come." Michiel's voice was almost a whisper, even though we were twenty metres away. Michiel's phone was an open line and he cursed under his breath.

"What is it?" I pressed him.

"There is only one person in the vehicle…"

"What?" I shouted.

"The camera picked up only the driver."

I pushed past him to look into people carrier as it passed us "That's not the person I saw back in Texel."

"It's the same vehicle" Michiel insisted.

"I think they have switched vehicles."

Michiel was on the phone to the helicopter and spoke for a couple of minutes. When he was finished he spoke to me again. "We have a car near the service station. They are going to review the close circuit television that is used to record the cars, and number plates of the cars, when they were filling up with fuel."

I felt so useless just watching the traffic pass me by, my children could be in any one of the cars or trucks, in front of me.

Michiel went to speak with the Police Officer who had arranged the traffic jam, and within less than five minutes the traffic was passing much quicker. Michiel returned and told me that the traffic jam had been cleared.

"What now?" I asked.

"Wait for the news from the service station, I guess."

Michiel's voice had lost its earlier conviction.

I returned to the car and called Eric. "Hello?"

"Hello Eric, it's not good news I am afraid, it looks like they switched vehicles."

"Well, that's not surprising because we couldn't find anything booked on the ferries or Eurotunnel in the next day or two."

"Shit." I swore more to myself than at Eric.

"But I think I might have something else."

"What's that?" I asked.

"There are two Masterson Shipping vessels which have just asked to dock in continental ports at short notice; one at Antwerp, and the other at Le Havre."

"Antwerp's just about an hour's drive from where I am now."

"Hmm" Eric replied "and that's why I would suggest he is going to Le Havre."

"I am going to call the Operations Director at Masterson..."

Before I could finish, Eric interrupted me "No! He obviously has friends within Masterson Shipping and you would alert him."

"So I should just stay put? I don't think so," I answered my own question.

"Nor me," Eric agreed "ask the Dutch Police to go to Antwerp in case I am wrong, and you go to Le Havre. If you drive quickly you should be there by midnight. The ship will not be able to sail until the morning tide. Let me know what you decide."

I went in search of Michiel and found him walking towards me on his phone. He finished his call as he reached me. "We have no proof, because they were obscured by a large lorry, but we think they transferred to a van."

"How do you come to that conclusion?"

"The cashier felt sure the person who drove the van into the service station, was the person who then drove the people carrier out of the petrol station."

"What type of van? What markings?"

Michiel paused "It is just a plain white van and I have just been informed that it is driving on false number plates."

"Have they driven past here?" I asked.

Michiel gave me a wan smile to indicate he didn't know.

I then explained what I had learned from Eric.

Michiel nodded and said "Interesting; can you phone your wife and tell her to divert to Antwerp. I presume you will drive to Le Havre?"

"Yes," I replied.

"I will call the Belgian and French police to expect you," he smiled before adding "and ask them not to stop you for speeding."

"Thank you."

"I will let you have one of the motor cyclists as far as the Belgium border."

It was my turn to smile and I shook his hand before returning to the Audi.

I drove as fast as the police outrider would let me. Although my speed was only ten kilometres above the speed limit, I made good progress; the police outrider waved me past him, accompanied by a thumbs-up, just before I drove into Belgium. I was barely a kilometre over the border when a police car with lights flashing was following me. I slowed down marginally to let him pass me. As he drew up beside me, my phone rang "Hello?" I spoke in response to the 'unknown' caller on my hand-free screen.

"Suivons-nous, si vous plait?" The Belgian-French voice echoed over the hands free system.

I looked across to the police car and the officer in the passenger seat smiled at me and pointed forwards.

I replied. "Tout la journée à France."

"Oui."

The Belgian police car drove faster than the Dutch motor cyclist, and I felt sure that I would soon pass their plain white van, but there was nothing. I started to regret taking Eric's advice; I wished I was going to Antwerp. As I left the scene of the traffic jam I had phoned Gerda who was on the mainland, and relayed instructions to head towards Antwerp. The conversation was brief because Gerda was obviously upset that the traffic jam ruse had not worked.

I wished I had taken the opportunity to go to the toilet, when I stopped to refuel in Holland. I flashed my lights a couple of times and the phone rang a few seconds later "Problem Monsieur?" The French-Belgian voice once again filled the car.

"Est-ce que possible arrêt pour une pissette?"

No immediate answer.

I repeated my request.

"Oui, nous comprends; attends une petite moment." After a few more seconds the voice returned to the Audi "Nous arrêtons en trente kilometres?"

"Ok, mais pas encore," I answered hesitantly.

We pulled over at a service station, and night had fallen. I went to the toilet, and then bought a sandwich plus a bottle of water. In less than five minutes, our strange little convoy was on the road again. I had not been paying too much attention to which route we were taking as I was just following the Belgian police car, but when I was inside the service station I noticed from the map on the wall that we were much further south than I expected.

Just at that moment Gerda phoned. "Hi, my darling," I said.

"Hello Marc, how are you doing?"

"Still in Belgium; what about you?"

"I have met up with Michiel, and he is driving now, but too slowly."

"But within the speed limit," I heard Michiel say in the background.

"Gerda, can you ask Michiel why the Belgian police are not taking me the most direct route to Calais?"

I hear Gerda ask the question which was followed by a muffled exchange "Two reasons, apparently. Firstly, the quickest route to Le Havre is not via Calais, and secondly you are not likely to pass the van on this route. They – the police – wish to monitor the van on its journey without interference from you or me."

"Huh?" was my reply.

"Interpol have now taken command of the situation," Gerda relayed the conversation with Michiel.

"Any sign of them?" I asked.

Again muffled voices as Gerda spoke with Michiel.

"Yes, the Belgian police have it under surveillance;" Gerda paused "hang on, Michiel's taking a call."

My car was filled with the sound of Dutch voices from Michiel's hands free, and I heard Gerda gasp.

"What's the matter?" I called out, but no reply other than the Dutch voices talking to each other, and the cadences rose and rose until the end of the call.

"Hello, hello," I called out.

"Marc, I think they have found the van and the twins…….." Gerda's voice was shaky.

"Where?"

"At a lay-by on the AutoRoute to Calais."

"Damn it, I am heading in the wrong direction."

"Wait Marc, before doing anything."

"Why?" I asked.

"Because we are going to drive towards them, and they want you to be on the road in front of them. Your escort will change direction shortly to put you on the French AutoRoute between Calais and Le Havre; you will probably go through Rouen and then head north."

"How did they find the van?"

"The people carrier led them straight to the van" Gerda paused "and, when it stopped, the helicopter picked up two smaller bodies being taken to the facilities then put into the van."

"They probably thought that by changing vehicles they would shake off anyone following them."

"Marc, I hope they're alright?" Gerda's voice was very strained again.

"Dominique de Silva wants them for bargaining," I answered her, "and they will be safe, as long as we don't do anything stupid."

"That's what Michiel says as well," her voice sounding steadier.

"Good."

"Marc?"

"Yes?"

"Michiel also says that we should expect a call from Dominique de Silva."

"Really?"

"Yes. He thinks that as soon as Dominique de Silva feels he is safe he may try and contact us."

"Hmm, how will he do that?" I asked.

"If he phones Paul's home number, any call will be forwarded to my mobile" Gerda explained.

"He may call me on my old mobile phone number," I said.

"Did you forward calls to the number of the new sim card we bought in Texel?"

"I did," I replied. "I find it strange that he may have killed your brother, abducted our children, and then he may just call us?"

"I don't know what to think, but we must do everything to protect Jack and Catherine. Let's speak again in an hour, please?" Gerda said.

"Yes my darling."

During the conversation with Gerda the police car had exited the AutoRoute, swung around and re-joined the AutoRoute travelling back the way we had come towards Ghent. As the traffic started to thin out they increased their speed. I was surprised how long-legged the Audi was at these high speeds. I was not feeling the weariness that used to accompany driving the Range Rover, and I guessed it was due to the overall balance and sports suspension of the Audi R6. Shortly we took an exit off the AutoRoute that brought us on to trunk roads, even though the police car's lights and sirens were flashing and wailing continuously we had to slow down. We passed around Merelbeke and then joined another motorway towards Lille, and I felt more relaxed that whoever was controlling events knew what they were doing.

After about ten minutes, my phone rang and I recognised Eric's number.

"Hello, you're burning the midnight oil."

"Not yet, but I am sure I will be, before this latest Edge family escapade is over," was Eric's *sotto voce* reply.

"How so?" I asked.

"Interpol are now running the show."

"So I gather," I replied.

"What you don't know is that Interpol have passed us the decision making."

"Who exactly is 'us'?" I asked.

"You know I can't tell you that Marc. But what I can assure you is that the safety of your family is paramount."

"And the capture of de Silva, and all the perpetrators of the fraud in Lloyd's, is put on hold?"

"Don't be so cynical, Marc," Eric scolded me.

"Gerda said that Interpol – you – expect him to call her."

"Yes, if he feels safe and in control; he will probably want to tell you and Gerda his demands, for the return of all four captives."

"Four?" I asked.

"Yes" Eric replied "we are pretty sure they have Jimmy's wife – Carla - and child as well…."

"To add guilt to the leverage."

"Exactly Marc."

I was quiet as the pain of Jimmy's death attacked my senses and I could not stop the tears running from the corner of each of my eyes.

"Marc?"

"Yes, I am here."

"Please be calm, and follow our directions."

"Of course I will……." I snapped back at Eric.

"Marc, following instructions hasn't always been your strong suit."

"I promise," I added superfluously.

"Good. I want you to drive to the French border where the French police will take over and take you to a service area called Baie de Somme."

"OK, and then what?" I asked.

"Try to get some food and rest. I am guessing the lorry will be about thirty minutes behind you."

"And then what?"

"You must keep out of view, because we want to create the illusion that you and Gerda are still in Texel. If they see that Audi of yours, it will undoubtedly give the game away. They may have people behind them to see if anyone is following…."

"Hence the two vehicles" I interjected.

"Exactly. They will probably play leap-frog with each other, with another car further behind, but they're unlikely to have one in front of them."

"I see; but you will get me on the road in good time before they pass me?"

"I would have preferred you and Gerda had stayed in Texel, but I know how headstrong you are, and that was very unlikely."

"They took our children," I was on the verge of shouting "and what about Paul - there needs to be atonement."

"You're overwrought, you don't know for certain how Paul died; it could have been an accident," Eric paused "plus Paul was badly weakened from his accident and coma six years ago."

I said nothing as the veracity of Eric's words sank in, and recalled how Paul seemed frail when I saw him in Texel.

"Marc, I hope that de Silva's motives are driven by money and power rather than a vendetta."

"Yes - I hope you are right." I felt sick as I said the words and images of my twins filled my head.

"And you probably gave him the idea when you were negotiating in Dubai."

"Yes – that's a point. Quite frankly I would be more than happy to give him the whole lot to get our children back safely."

"Would you?" Eric sounded sceptical.

"Certainly I would. The responsibility of managing all the assets is almost a full-time job in itself."

"Are you sure?" Eric asked.

"Yes, yes and yes."

"Well I suggest you tell that to Gerda before – if – he tries to speak to her."

"OK, I will do so now. Bye for now."

I was near Waregem, and the distance to Lille was less than seventy kilometres. We were now averaging a hundred and forty kilometres an hour and I felt sure that the French border could not be far away, so I certainly should be in France in less than half an hour. I was about to phone Gerda when I noticed my mobile battery was very low.

"Gerda, my mobile battery is nearly exhausted so I will be very brief. Eric is running the show for Interpol. He thinks de Silva wants money. I have told him that I will give him half of all we have as – if – he is Philip de Silva's son. Do you agree?"

"For our children, I would give him everything," Gerda replied.

"Let's hope it does not come to that."

"What about Paul's death?" Gerda asked.

"Eric said that will depend upon how Paul died," I explained.

"Why? How? I don't understand."

"What if it was an accidental blow and Paul's skull was still susceptible after his accident six years ago?"

"I – I – I don't know......" Gerda was wavering "....and what about K-P?"

I felt very guilty but pushed on. "For the moment we need to keep de Silva on-side, and have him believe we will truly give him what he asks."

"OK my darling. Anything for the children."

"And Gerda, they probably have Carla and her son."

"Oh my God!" Gerda exclaimed.

Pas de Calais

The French police car escorted me from Lille to the services at Baie de Somme in less than two hours, as the French Police seemed to outdo their Belgian counterparts in terms of speed. It was eleven thirty by the time I rolled into Baie de Somme and the French Police car flashed his headlights briefly, before they accelerated out of the service station back to Lille, their escort duties fulfilled.

I had just pulled up outside the entrance of the services at Baie de Somme when there was a short sharp rapping on my window. I was shocked to see a tall fair-haired man dressed in a black bomber jacket. I wound down the window.

"Get this car out of sight please?"

It wasn't a question but a command from someone I seemed to recognise but couldn't quite place.

He then continued "Mr Jones was quite explicit wasn't he?"

There was only one reply. "Yes," I replied tentatively.

"So please drive it to the end of the parking," he pointed to my right "and there you will see two black mini-vans."

I nodded.

"Park in between them, and I will meet you there, shortly."

I drove to where the fair-haired man indicated and parked between the two vans. As I got out of my car, someone walked out of the shadows and threw a cover over my car. They were taking every precaution to ensure I was not spotted.

"Do you need the toilet?" the fair-haired man spoke from behind me. He must be wearing rubber soled shoes because I never heard him approach me.

"Umm... yes...please?" I replied uncertainly.

"Well you need to use the toilet block near where the lorries are parked. On no account are you to go inside the service station. Is that clear?"

"Y-y-yes," I replied, the vibrato in my voice making it obvious that he was making me feel very uncomfortable.

"Come on then." He marched me over to the toilets.

He had the good grace to wait outside the toilet block otherwise I was not sure I could have emptied my bladder.

When I returned from the toilet block I spoke to the fair-haired man.

"What's your name?" I asked.

"That's no concern of yours," he replied testily.

"So what should I call you?"

"Simon will do."

"You were watching for K-P and Mr Dominique at the Grange Hotel by Tower Hill."

He shot me a sideways glance "Very good Mr Edge; perhaps you aren't a total buffoon after all."

If ever a back-handed compliment could stop a conversation, that was it. Nevertheless, I had the fortitude of a Lloyd's Broker and continued "Buffoon or not, I still managed to lose you on the drive to Southampton."

Ouch, that stung him. Even in the dim immenseness of the car park lighting, I could see him colour up. But he just allowed himself a small smile and replied – appropriately in French – "Touché".

As we approached the two mini-vans and my covered car, Simon motioned me towards the van on the left – it was the furthest of the three vehicles from the service station. I opened the door and inside sitting at a camp table was Nobby.

"Hello Marcus," he said very jovially "excuse me for not standing up, but it's a bit low for my bonce?"

"Hello Nobby," I replied "mind telling me how you and…" I paused very briefly "Simon just happened to be here?"

He hesitated for an instant; he looked at Simon who merely shrugged his shoulders, as if to say it's your decision if you want to tell him.

"Come and have a glass of wine and a plate of steak frites and I will tell you Marcus." Nobby pointed to the chair opposite him and he was pouring a gorgeous looking red wine into a glass. As if he was reading my mind he spoke again "Don't worry you won't be driving again until morning."

"How do you know?" I asked.

"Dominique de Silva has stopped at a service station with a hotel near Calais, and the twins are safely tucked up in bed."

"Again, please tell me how you know all this?"

"Sit down, eat and drink then sleep – if you can – because tomorrow is likely to be a very long day." He held his glass up to toast me, and his smile persuaded me to acquiesce.

I emptied the glass with one deep swig and tore ravenously into the steak and chips.

"These two vehicles have been loaned to us by Interpol, and were driven up from Rouen about an hour ago." He put his hand up to stop me from talking. "Eric sent laughing boy, and me, over by helicopter shortly after he spoke to you this evening."

I nodded.

"This van is for eating – and sleeping" he pointed to a hammock over his shoulder "and the other is a communications centre."

Again I nodded as I chewed through the gorgeous entrecôte and thought to myself how different the English and French were measured by the quality of their service station fayre.

Nobby continued to give me all the details I could have wanted about the two vans. He topped up my glass with wine and then proceeded to polish off the remains himself.

"Why can't we just pick him up?"

"Marcus, my boy, you know that just isn't feasible."

"Jimmy's wife and son Johnny?"

Nobby nodded.

I ruminated for a few moments before asking "So what now?"

"I suggest you get some sleep," was Nobby's practical advice.

I thought about fighting the urge to sleep, but that only made me feel wearier. I climbed into the hammock in the van and within seconds I was asleep.

I slept fitfully which was unsurprising given the fact my children had been kidnapped, and I had hardly any time to digest my steak before sleeping. I dreamt of Paul and Gerda, eventually waking to the sound of Gerda's voice.

"Marc, wake up, it's me."

"Gerda…. Gerda?" I opened my eyes and my wife was standing over me. Slightly dishevelled but still looking as gorgeous as ever.

"Hello, my darling." Gerda's soft voice sounded like liquid velvet.

"Hello, my darling," I replied and gently stroked the side of Gerda's face "any news?"

"Not yet but Michiel is with an Englishman, I think he might be a policeman of sorts…"

"Of sorts is right. He goes by the name of Simon, but I think that is just a name he made up. I think he is Special Branch."

"And a very strange older military man."

"He is English as well, and he is Nobby." I smiled when I thought of Nobby being described as a strange old man.

"Ah, the one who prepared you for Dubai."

"The very same; what time is it?"

"Just after five o'clock."

"Have you slept?" I asked.

"I dozed a bit in the car," Gerda continued, "Michiel is a very considerate driver."

"You mean slow?"

"Yes." At which point we both smiled.

"Ok, why don't you try and get some rest now? Give me your phone and I will wake you as soon as I hear anything."

Gerda tried to say she felt fine but I persuaded her that we might need to share the driving. We switched places, and I waited until I could hear the slow rhythmic sound of her breathing to indicate that she was asleep, and then I left the van to go to the other van. I opened the door to see Simon listening on the headphones in front of six monitors, four or which were active. Nobby and Michiel were drinking coffee at a table the other end of the van.

"Good morning Marc," Nobby greeted me "did you get any sleep?"

"Better than I could have expected." I turned to Michiel, "Thank you for bringing Gerda, she's sleeping now."

Michiel merely nodded his head to acknowledge my gratitude.

I continued "Nobby, can you charge my phone please?"

"Certainly, Simon can you assist Marcus please?"

Simon held out his hand and I passed the handset to him.

"Any chance of some coffee and breakfast?"

"Coffee we can do but the service station does not open for food until six o'clock." Nobby offered me a mug of black coffee.

"What now?" I enquired.

"We wait…which I guess is not what you want to hear, but it is up to de Silva to make the first move."

"Gerda and I have decided that we'll pay him anything to get the children back unharmed, as well as Carla and her son."

Michiel spoke "He has to answer for Paul's death…"

"Plus K-P's abduction and his part in the Lloyd's fraud, and anything associated with the passing on of confidential information to people who might want to create terror and havoc," Nobby added.

"Say he turns Queen's evidence on the fraud, and Paul's death was an accident…"

"Two very big assumptions," Simon joined the conversation.

"I know, but if that were so, could he go free?"

"That's not our decision?" was Nobby's non-committal reply. "Now let me explain what Simon is listening, and looking, for." Nobby continued talking for another fifteen minutes giving me details about the surveillance equipment. Two of the monitors were relays from close circuit televisions at the service station where de Silva had stopped for the night. One showed the car park, and despite the fact that dawn had yet to break in Northern France, I could just make out the silhouettes of a lorry and a people carrier parked next to each other. The other was the Acceuil of the hotel, which would remain unmanned until six o'clock, like that at the Baie de Somme. Simon's headphones were part of a listening device that could pick up voices through walls if necessary, and the other two monitors were able to pick up details of any numbers dialled by any mobile telephone. There was also a separate open line to Eric in London.

"Anything he tries to do or say, we will know about it instantly." Nobby words were reassuring.

I drank my coffee slowly, even though it was no longer hot. The four of us sat without speaking, the silence only being broken by the static of the radio. The minutes ticked by slowly and I must have fallen asleep, because I was startled awake by the sound of Gerda's phone ringing. I looked at Simon but he only shrugged his shoulders shaking his head.

I picked up the mobile and greeted the caller with a very English "Hello."

"Edge?"

"Yes."

"It's Dominique de Silva."

"Where are my children?" I shouted into the phone.

"Safe," was his monotone response. He continued "Where are you?"

"In Texel."

"I don't believe you."

"It's true."

"No it isn't," he insisted.

"Yes, it is. Why do you think differently?" I asked, but I was fearful he already knew the answer.

"This call has been switched from the Texel telephone number I called."

"Yes, to Gerda's mobile."

"Where is she?"

"Next door asleep." I wasn't lying.

"I will call back in fifteen minutes. I want to speak to you and Gerda together, as well as someone else who can prove you are still in Texel."

"Will the Chief of Police do?"

"He will." He seemed less agitated and hung up.

I swung around to Simon who was looking at Nobby "Nothing on the mobile monitors and just muffled sounds through the listening device."

"How can he not be traced?" I asked.

"Mmm…." Nobby was thinking "perhaps he has your satellite phone we gave you, and he has re-programmed it."

"I will check other band widths to see if I get a reading, but they are damn difficult to trace, especially if he has changed the frequency," said Simon without much confidence.

I hurried to the other van and woke Gerda from her sleep. In less than five minutes Gerda, Michiel and I were huddled around Gerda's phone. It was nearly another twenty minutes until the phone rang and Gerda answered it immediately on speaker.

"Hello."

"Mrs Edge, I am so pleased to speak to you; your children are lovely."

"I want them back now!" Gerda's eyes were welling up with tears.

"They will be returned safely but not to you I am afraid, as I am a long way from Texel, and you are still there?" It was a statement but it seemed to demand a reply.

"Yes I am," Gerda replied testily.

"Prove it please."

"I have the Texel Chief of Police beside me."

Michiel leant over the phone to speak to de Silva. After a moment or two, de Silva was satisfied that he was a Dutch policeman, and that he was convinced we were in Texel.

"Marc, listen carefully. You spoke in Dubai of giving me what is rightfully mine."

"I did; but you didn't have to take our children to force me to do it." I paused for a moment, "If you are who you say you are I will give you half willingly."

There was silence from de Silva.

"What happened to Paul?" I asked.

"We were looking for you, and by coincidence we met with Paul, and your children. Paul recognised who I was and he tried to take Jack and Catherine away, but he collapsed after he slipped and fell. No-one touched him, and the children will tell you that their uncle Paul just fell over."

"Then why take them?" Gerda's voice was raised.

"I saw an opportunity to leverage the situation."

"What about Jimmy's wife and son?" I tried to keep my voice even. "Another leverage opportunity?"

"I don't know what you are talking about Marc."

I looked at Nobby and he just shrugged his shoulders.

"So what about our children?" I asked.

"Marc I want you to stay in Texel, and make arrangements to transfer a number of assets to me. Once that has been completed, the children and you will be reunited."

"How can I trust you?"

"You will have to cross your fingers and hope. I want Mrs Edge to meet me in Normandy tonight, so she can comfort the children and show them they have nothing to fear from their 'Uncle Aziz', especially as I was related by marriage to their father. Very nearly family you could say." He laughed and I could hear echoes of his demented behaviour in Dubai.

"If we agree, then all we have done is to increase your bargaining position."

"Correct," he replied.

"Call back again in ten minutes please?" I didn't give him a chance to reply and I ended the call.

"Do we have a different option?" I asked the assembled company and no-one in particular.

"Of course we do Marc," Nobby was first to reply "but you won't like it because it is a high risk strategy."

"What is it?"

"Try to immobilise de Silva and his team whilst he is in France."

No one responded.

"There are too many variables in my opinion to make that work safely." Simon said.

"I don't want to risk the children," said Gerda and I nodded my head in agreement.

"We can't sweat it out, because he will get agitated, and the children will become distressed." This time it was Nobby who spoke.

"If I agree to what he suggests, what will you do?" I directed the question towards Michiel.

"If what he says about Paul is confirmed by post mortem and the evidence of the children, then he is still guilty of abduction of the children and extortion. The other matters are a case for Interpol to decide."

"But not if Gerda and I say that he was only looking after the children."

"I heard what he said……." Michiel was trying to take a firm stance.

"We were already going to give him what is rightfully his anyway." I was starting to become angry.

"Let's not forget his part in the Lloyd's fraud, the mutilation of K-P, and your own kidnapping," Nobby interjected.

"I have an idea how to deal with those issues," I replied, just as Gerda's phone rang.

"de Silva – I agree, but there are conditions of our own."

"I don't negotiate, Edge!" he shouted down the phone.

"Really? How are you going to avoid arrest for abduction and extortion? You have just confessed such to a Senior Dutch Policeman. Furthermore, I am not giving you cash, I am giving you control of a large corporation that trades around the world not in the shadows of the Dubai Creek."

There was silence at the end of the phone.

"You will have to make your own peace with K-P, which may prove to be costly, but I want you to deliver to me the person who is behind the fraudulent trading in Lloyd's."

"I don't know who it is," he replied.

"But I am sure you can help me flush them out?"

"I am listening. I am not agreeing just listening."

"The Dutch Police can fly both of us to a service station in Normandy called Baie de Somme."

"I said…"

"You said you were listening so please listen," I cut across him firmly. "We will be joined by my father who is about to take the Eurotunnel from Folkestone, and I will ask him to come to the service station as well. The children will travel in my father's car with Gerda, and one of your associates; I will travel with you."

"You are mad if you think I would agree to your suggestion."

"What if I were to tell you that, if you don't agree, you will never leave your motel room either alive or in handcuffs?"

"You're bluffing Edge?" A hint of malice accompanied the uncertainty in his voice.

"Simon will you indicate your presence please?" I turned to the bewildered faces in the van.

Simon flicked a switch and spoke into a radio for a few seconds. Moments later I heard the officer of the Gendarmes outside de Silva's motel speak into a megaphone. "Monsieur de Silva, nous avons le motel couvert par vingt officiers de gendarmerie."

The officer's voice echoed through Gerda's phone a second after the radio in the van.

"I will kill your children."

"No, you will not, because if you touch a hair on their head I will make sure you will die a very painful death in prison. I would spend every penny I have to make it happen, or do it myself and damn the consequences."

"You don't have the guts."

"Try me? I am offering you a way out, and I promise on my children's lives that I will keep my word, and transfer what I promised to you."

Silence – whilst he thought about the proposition.

"Also, where are Jimmy's wife and child?"

"I told you I don't know." He shot back so convincingly that I was inclined to believe him.

"So do you agree?" I asked.

"I need to think about it."

"You don't have long because the captain of the gendarmerie has been outside your motel for most of the night and he and his officers are hungry, cold and he is burning through his overtime allowance. You have five minutes." Again I didn't let him reply and I ended the call.

Immediately after the call I asked Simon to turn up the volume on his listening device. Simon turned some dials and flicked a switch but there was only an increase in the static. I hoped de Silva was thinking through the alternatives. It was a calculated risk, because I had shown him that he had been located and surrounded, I had also given him an escape.

Four minutes had elapsed. "Simon can you give him a nudge, please?"

Simon spoke into the radio and a moment later I heard the voice of the Captain of the Gendarmerie through the listening device, "trente, vingt-neuf, vingt-huit…"

The phone rang "Marc, I have someone who wants to speak to you" the phone went quiet for a moment and then I heard Jack's voice "Daddy, Uncle Aziz says we are going to meet you, Mummy and Granddad today."

I breathed a sigh of relief "Yes, Jack. Be a good boy and make sure you and your sister have a good breakfast because we are going home today. Can you pass me back to Uncle Aziz please?"

"So what now?" de Silva asked.

"It's nearly six o'clock; we can be at the Baie de Somme shortly after half-past nine. Please meet us there and, to make sure you have no problems on the road, you will have your own private police escort. OK?"

"OK," was his reply and he hung up.

"Mmm? That was a bit ballsy Marc." Nobby was the first to speak.

"Not really – he is desperate for wealth, always has been, and I offered him a way out." I was lying through my teeth so my hands were wringing with sweat.

Gerda looked at me and just nodded her head in affirmation that she agreed with me.

Michiel asked the obvious question "Your father is about to board Eurotunnel?"

"Ah, that was a bit of improvising"

"Sorry I don't understand?" Michiel asked.

"de Silva has never met my father, and as far as we are concerned he is now sitting in this van." I looked at Nobby.

"He is not stupid," Nobby said "and he knows he will have to atone in some way."

"Perhaps?" I replied "Or maybe he is just focused on the money. He didn't seem stable in Dubai."

"That's why we must do everything to get our children back quickly," Gerda said and no-one was going to disagree with her.

The convoy to Calais

Gerda and I tried to eat something for breakfast but we were both too nervous and could only manage coffee. We walked up the observation tower that looks over the marshlands of Baie de Somme. Dominated by a large modern wind turbine, the flat panorama means that from the top of the tower, one can see for many kilometres. The mist of the morning was being slowly burned off by the sunshine.

We had hardly spoken a word over our attempt at eating breakfast.

Gerda broke the silence "Poor Paul, he was not very lucky, was he?"

"No he wasn't," I agreed.

"The injury to his head when he fell in Rotterdam years ago that put him in a coma must have weakened him greatly."

I nodded my head.

"I will keep Paul's house for the children," tears were running down her cheeks and I took her into my arms and held her tightly "please tell me the children will be alright?"

"I promise they will be, and don't underestimate Nobby, he will keep you safe."

"And what about you?" Gerda asked.

"I will be fine. Simon will be shadowing me from a safe distance, listening to every word de Silva and I say to each other, through microphones on me."

"So what will Nobby be driving? It can't be our car; de Silva will suspect something."

"'Simon has arranged for a British registration people carrier to be made available to us."

"How?"

"I am not quite sure. I think he has commandeered one from a British tourist returning to the UK."

"You're joking?"

"No. I am not," I replied "they are driving the Audi back to England in return for the loan of their people carrier for a couple of days."

Gerda turned away from me and looked across the flatlands towards the AutoRoute, willing our children towards us.

"After our talk in Texel I have decided to sell The Hall," I murmured abstractedly.

Gerda nodded her agreement.

"Whatever I sell it for I will give half to K-P, and the other half we will use to buy that house you have been looking at."

Gerda smiled.

"I hope K-P will accept my offer – he's such a proud man".

"Leave him to me," Gerda said confidently "I will get Jane to work on him."

I smiled thinking of how Jane could wrap K-P around her little finger.

"What are you going to give 'him'?"

"You mean Dominique de Silva, I presume?"

Gerda nodded.

"I will give him the shipping company and the land in both Africa and Goa."

"Will you be OK with that?" Gerda turned to me.

"The house in London, plus a new one in the country, together with JPG is more than sufficient for us. I was finding the shipping company a burden, and it distracted me from JPG."

"Don't forget Paul's house in Texel?"

"I won't but they are yours, and for Jack and Catherine, so they never forget their Dutch roots."

Gerda slipped her arm through mine and pulled me close so we could both look for the arrival of our twins.

Simon came and found us at about eleven o'clock. "Time to get wired-up Marc."

We followed him down to the car park and found that our area had been cordoned off from the rest of the parking area and there was much police presence in evidence.

As if he was reading my mind, Simon assured me that before de Silva arrived, the police would be out of sight and the cordon lifted at the last moment.

Gerda made her excuses and headed towards the toilet block.

Simon and I went towards one of the French mini-vans. After we climbed inside he asked me to take my shirt off. He taped one microphone to my chest, and another he hid under my left cuff so it couldn't be seen from the right-hand driver's side of the car.

Nobby had dressed down so he did not have his usual smart natty appearance.

"Hello Dad," I smiled as I spoke to the slightly shabby looking man.

"Less of that insolence my boy." Nobby was definitely in character.

Simon passed to me a black electronic device which at first glance looked like an electric razor.

"What's this?" I asked.

"It's a small hand-held taser," Simon explained, "and before you ask, it will not seriously harm an adult, but a blast from that for a few seconds can gain you a brief advantage. But beware" Simon continued "the taser will only deliver one good blast. There might be enough charge remaining to give a second milder shock, but don't count on it."

I was in two minds whether to accept the gadget, and decided Gerda would probably feel more relaxed knowing I had it with me.

Simon said that the best place to keep it was just inside my left ankle.

"Why?" I asked.

"That way you can access it easily with your right hand and the left ankle is obscured to anyone in the driver's seat of de Silva's right-hand drive vehicle."

"The biggest risk we have is that the twins spill the beans that Nobby is not their Granddad." I was talking to all the assembled company with Dominique de Silva expected within thirty minutes.

"For Nobby's cover we have fixed a knob to the steering wheel to help him steer the borrowed people carrier," Simon said.

"And I have obtained a handicapped sticker," Nobby chipped in "but I also am very concerned that the children are our weakest link."

Gerda spoke "I will tell them it is a game and they must pretend that Nobby is their Granddad."

We had only ten minutes warning of de Silva's arrival. There was a flurry of activity and within three minutes the cordon disappeared. Michiel drove his car to the other end of the car park. Simon parked one of the French mini-vans by the gonflate, seemingly checking the tyres of his vehicle. Once he was assured the transfer had gone according to plan, he would head off first up the A16 towards Sangatte, keeping about a kilometre ahead of the rest of us with Michiel in the back of the mini-van monitoring and recording anything that was said between de Silva and me. They also had a feed from the people carrier that Nobby would be driving.

de Silva's vehicle swung into view, being driven by the same person I saw in Dubai. Behind him was a van being driven by another Middle Eastern man, and a girl was in the passenger seat that seemed vaguely familiar. The police escort of one car and two motorcycles remained a discrete thirty metres behind de Silva's vehicles. They drew to a slow stop parking beside the borrowed people carrier. Gerda, Nobby and I were standing by the vehicles ready to greet Jack and Catherine.

Dominique de Silva opened the door slowly and got out "Just you three?" He was his urbane self, looking very much like the playboy I met at St Catherine's dock at the headquarters of Masterson Shipping nearly six years previously "I expected more – no police?"

"Only those who arrived with you," I lied fluently. "Where are the twins?"

"Asleep in the back" he smiled "their 'uncle' has taken good care of them."

"Thank you," I said but the words came out a croak.

Gerda walked towards the people carrier and opened the side door and smiled to me with tears of happiness running down her cheeks.

"Let's get them into my father's car, so we can get going…"

"Whoa – hold on," de Silva put his hand up "they stay with me."

"Trust me" I stretched my hand around the car park "there are no police – I will stick to the bargain we struck."

"Is that right?" de Silva's urbane facade slipped, and for a second his face changed and a glimpse of the man I saw in Dubai returned.

"So what are you going to give me?"

"That's why I thought we would travel alone in your car to get into the weeds and discuss what I propose in detail."

He said nothing but his body language seemed to relax so I continued, "Jack and Catherine can travel with Gerda and my father. If you want, one of your colleagues can travel with them - perhaps the girl?"

Dominique de Silva smiled "Do you recognise her?"

I was searching her face intently and a ghost of the past was looking out at me. "She looks like Mercédès?"

"Very good" he mocked me "she is Krishna and is the cousin of Mercédès on her mother's side, and the closest person I have as a living relative. We may marry one day."

I said nothing.

"She is not a first cousin so I see no reason not to."

"She's very pretty."

"Yes she is, isn't she?"

He was smiling as he tried to rile me, but I wasn't rising to the bait.

"OK, Krishna will ride with the children. I will lead, and then your father and my other men will follow in the van."

"As you wish," I agreed.

It took about fifteen minutes to organise everyone, as well as allow time for de Silva, Krishna and his colleagues to go to the toilets in relay. At no time were we left alone with the children. Nobby kept in the background only saying "hello" softly to de Silva when he was introduced.

Gerda and I transferred the children to the British people carrier, during which time neither of them awoke. Simon had contacted London earlier and Eric had booked a Eurotunnel reservation for five o'clock. I saw him pull away from the service station just as the rest of us were starting to get into our various forms of transport. Dominique de Silva led off with me beside him; then Nobby with Gerda, and the twins accompanied by Mercédès' cousin. Bringing up the rear was the van with de Silva's two henchmen.

We had been travelling for less than twenty minutes with not a word spoken between us – when de Silva's phone rang. It was the satellite phone that Nobby had given to me, which de Silva had taken from me, when I was held captive in Dubai.

"We have to stop," de Silva said to me.

"Why?" I asked.

"The van is no longer following us."

"There is a rest stop just up ahead; you can stop there. It is too dangerous to pull over on the side of a French AutoRoute."

It was about a kilometre ahead and, when he pulled into the parking area, I espied a black mini-van at the other end of the parking, pulling out slowly towards the exit route. I felt sure that Simon and Michiel would stop just out of sight from the parking area.

de Silva was talking quickly into his phone in Arabic. He then tried phoning another number with no success, which I guessed to be one of the two men in the van. He jumped out and walked over to Nobby's vehicle to talk with Krishna, who had got out to meet him.

I looked at Nobby and raised my eyebrows, as if to ask Nobby what had happened. He replied with a shrug of his shoulders. I opened the side door and I could see that Jack and Catherine were awake and Gerda was cuddling them both face on. I joined them in a team hug, and I could hear Gerda whispering to them very quietly that they were to pretend that the man driving the car was their Granddad. Both of them nodded, and then all four of us managed a kiss at the same time.

I walked over to de Silva and Krishna, who was still trying to call his men in the van "What's going on Edge?"

"Search me," I replied honestly, "no-one went near your van when you met us at Baie de Somme."

He nodded, knowing what I said to be correct.

"We will go to the next junction and go back to Baie de Somme to see what happened."

I walked towards Nobby and Gerda, who were just returning from the toilets with Jack and Catherine, Jack holding Nobby's good hand. Even I thought he looked a doting Granddad. I explained to them we were going to retrace our steps.

As soon as we re-joined the AutoRoute, de Silva accelerated hard and we were speeding well above a hundred and forty kilometres an hour, and where possible exceeded two hundred kilometres an hour. We passed Simon and Michiel in less than three minutes, and in twenty minutes we came off the AutoRoute, and drive down the other carriageway back towards Baie de Somme. As we drove, de Silva scoured the opposite carriageway for a sign of the van. About five minutes after passing the 'Aire' where we stopped, we saw the van on its side some way off the carriageway, and emergency vehicles in attendance. de Silva said nothing and continued driving as fast as possible to the Baie de Somme and upon reaching the services he immediately swung round to head back north on the A16.

Ten minutes later, he slowed and we pulled up behind the accident. Police were controlling the traffic flow and an officer came up to the right-hand driver's side of the car. Dominique de Silva opened the window and spoke perfect French to the policeman, who replied quite politely.

"We continue?" I asked.

He nodded and then dialled a number on the satellite phone and spoke briefly in Arabic.

He re-joined the AutoRoute driving at our original speed.

"What happened?" I asked.

"Apparently it was a puncture in one of the rear tyres. They are both injured and have been taken to hospital. One is hurt more seriously than the other, who is suffering from dizziness, and has passed out. When we get to England I will send someone out to the hospital."

We soon returned to the 'Aire' where Nobby, Gerda, Krishna and the twins were waiting. We didn't stop, and Nobby followed us out on to the AutoRoute. It took about fifteen minutes before I caught sight of the black mini-van of Simon and Michiel in the distance. They had remained with de Silva and me, and had not followed us into the parking area the second time, but they continued sedately on the AutoRoute. Having seen us I felt they would accelerate to maintain the distance ahead of the two British people carriers behind them.

We were not far from Boulogne when I decided to start exploring the details of what I planned to transfer to de Silva. It took me about ten minutes to go through my ideas. He was silent throughout the time I spoke. When I finished he said "So you and K-P keep The Hall?"

"Yes," I replied "I have no interest in Masterson Shipping – I never did."

He was silent for a few moments and then asked "And the assets in Goa and Zimbabwe?"

"Goa is of some interest but everything in Zimbabwe is worthless until Mugabe goes," I replied.

de Silva retorted "Land is land and I want as much of it as possible."

I then confirmed, "When we get to London, I will call my solicitor to start preparing the papers – but nothing can be validated until you prove who you are. And if you are to stand any chance of walking free you need to deliver to the authorities the names of the perpetrators of the Lloyd's fraud."

"I do not know who they are." He was consistent with his story from before.

"How do they contact you?" I asked.

"They phone my office in Dubai every Thursday at twelve noon local time."

"What do they sound like?"

"It's always the voice of a woman."

"An English voice?" I enquired.

"Yes I think so."

"What does she sound like?"

"She just sounds normal to me."

"What happens when you are not in Dubai?"

"I route it through to my mobile." He held up the satellite handset "This is very good you know".

"Pleased I could be of service," I replied sarcastically. "Have you ever tried to trace the call?"

"No. I was told that any attempt by me to make contact with them would bring our arrangement to an end".

"So how are you rewarded for your information and actions?"

He hesitated before answering "Sometimes it's nothing."

I frowned at him.

He held up his hands. "I enjoyed it just for the thrill of playing the system, I felt empowered."

"But not always philanthropically?"

"No – sometimes a gift would be left at the Dubai office."

"What sort of gift?"

"Gold, jewellery, silver, but mainly gold. Once we even received bit-coins." I had heard of the phrase bit-coins and knew them only to be a cyber currency.

"Did you know the information related to insurance fraud?"

"Not initially – but when I thought about the gifts, I thought there must be a connection."

"Why?" I asked.

"One gift was recognizably part of a theft that was widely publicised and a payment was made by Lloyd's underwriters. With such a recognisable piece, I was being implicated so I guessed it was due to the theft itself."

"That's a big supposition." It sounded like he was bull-shitting.

"That was not the only clue. When the details of the Lloyd's policy payment were disclosed, an intermediary in Dubai was mentioned as well as the Lloyd's broker."

"Who was the Lloyd's broker?"

He turned to my face to reply. "Why, JPG of course."

He laughed and swerved partially into the next lane of the A16.

As we continued I thought about what he had told me. It sounded very plausible but I had the feeling he was telling me what I wanted to hear. I felt sure he was either not telling the truth, or holding something back from me. I decided to leave it for the rest of the journey, and let Eric know my misgivings.

We remained silent for the rest of the journey and arrived at the Channel Tunnel just before two thirty in the afternoon. He drove up to a manned kiosk. I could see the black mini-van pulled over to the side of the road just beyond the manned check-in point.

"Hello, I believe that a reservation for the five o'clock crossing has been made in the name of Edge?" I addressed the woman sitting in the kiosk.

"Oui, two cars and one van."

"We are just two cars now," I explained.

"OK," she tapped away on her keyboard looking occasionally at the two vehicles, "I can offer you places on the next shuttle that leaves in twenty minutes."

I looked at de Silva and he nodded his agreement.

"Yes please," I answered and as soon as I hung the letter of the shuttle on the rear view mirror, the black mini-van shot off and we pulled over to wait for Nobby.

"I need to get my passport from Krishna." de Silva got out of the car to wait for Nobby to drive through the check-in and when Nobby drew up I could see that Krishna's head was lolled down on her chest. de Silva opened her door and was talking quite loudly to her, having to shake her arm to wake her up. She lifted her head and I heard the word passport mentioned a couple of times, and she went into a briefcase that was by her feet. She brought out passports, gave one to de Silva.

I walked around to the door where Gerda was sitting. The twins were asleep and she opened the window so I could speak to her. "All OK?" I asked.

"Yes. Your father is a very considerate driver; all the passengers snoozed for most of the journey." She gave me the slightest wink that would have been imperceptible to anyone else.

Krishna got out of the car and de Silva spoke to me. "Krishna and I need the toilet."

"So do I," Nobby said.

As the three of them walked to the toilets Gerda spoke to me.

"Nobby was able to slip something into Krishna's water and she fell asleep. His left arm extends and he was able to lift the briefcase up and I took it to look through the papers and passports. We took lots of photos on my mobile phone, before putting the briefcase back by Krishna's feet. You were right, he is very resourceful."

I also wondered if the van accident had in fact been planned.

Crossing the Channel

The two vehicles were ushered through customs, both French and UK, and we were directed to the front of an empty lane alongside a number of other lanes full of cars on our left and coaches to our right. The black mini-van was just two vehicles in front of us.

All the other lanes were cleared before we were directed towards the shuttle running from Sangatte to Folkestone due for departure at three-thirty. We followed the directions and we entered a carriage with a high-ceiling usually reserved for coaches. The only other vehicle was the black mini-van that Simon and Michiel drove ahead of the convoy. No other vehicle entered the carriage and the doors were shut almost immediately we stopped. Within five minutes, we were underway, and being towards the back of the shuttle, toilets were behind us and we would have no cause to go forwards to the other part of the train. Krishna and de Silva decided to travel outside the vehicles, standing in the space behind the car Nobby had driven on to the train, and they were talking quietly to each other. Nobby had reclined his seat appearing to sleep, but I could see no rhythmical rise and fall of his chest, and I assumed he was feigning. Gerda and I played with the children, who had woken up before we drove onto the train. There was no movement from the black mini-van at the front of the carriage. The journey passed off without incident.

Thirty-five minutes later, we were out of the tunnel, the British sunshine shining brightly into the carriage at just after three o'clock British time. The shuttle pulled to a stop and we all went back into our vehicles waiting for the doors of the carriage to open. The doors of all the other carriages opened and the vehicles drove off, but ours remained resolutely shut.

"Would the passengers in the last carriage please remain in their vehicles whilst we resolve a small technical issue?" was the announcement over the tannoy, which was then repeated in French.

We waited for ten minutes during which time de Silva was becoming more and more agitated, until he opened the car door and strode towards the doors at the front of the carriage.

He was about a metre away from the black mini-van when both doors opened simultaneously. Simon and Michiel blocked his passageway. He turned around and ran towards the back of the carriage, but Nobby was out of his people carrier blocking his exit. At that moment the back doors of the carriage were opened, and we were greeted by six heavily armed policemen, which brought de Silva to a standstill.

"What's going on Edge?" he shouted.

I climbed out of the other people carrier and replied honestly "I don't know."

"Liar!" he shouted and started to advance upon me.

I had already retrieved the taser which I held in my hand hidden from his view, but he was stopped by an authoritative voice coming from the front of the carriage.

"He's not lying de Silva." It was Eric Jones flanked by another six armed policemen "and before you ask, yes, you do have a deal when a few facts are checked out and verified by us."

Dominique de Silva's face looked like it might explode as he glared at me.

I merely shrugged my shoulders.

"What facts?" de Silva spat at Eric.

"Confirmation that Paul's death was an accident," Eric looked at Michiel. "When will the post-mortem be completed?"

"It was being conducted today, with preliminary findings hopefully available tomorrow," Michiel replied.

De Silva's head turned towards Michiel. "You, I presume, are the Dutch Policeman I spoke to?"

Michiel nodded his head.

"And what else?" de Silva asked.

"To help us lure out the person or persons at the centre of the Lloyd's fraud" Eric responded.

"How do you propose I should do that?" de Silva had turned to face Eric.

"By saying that Marc suspects who the perpetrators of the fraud are. You will do this when the person calls you on Thursday."

"And then what?"

"Nothing."

"Nothing?"

"We will let events unfold from there," said Eric.

"So I am to be a tethered goat?" I asked.

"Sort of?" Eric replied with a half-smile.

"Thanks," I replied sarcastically.

"And me?" de Silva asked.

"You and Krishna will be kept at a special facility," Eric continued, "for the safety of both of you."

"And then?"

"Assuming K-P does not wish to press charges, assuming all goes well in Holland and in Lloyd's, you will be a free man and woman. Marc, I presume you still intend to make good your promises?"

"Absolutely."

"Good, then shall we get you and Krishna safe." Eric's arm directed de Silva towards the back of the carriage."

"I knew nothing of this," I said to de Silva.

"I believe you – just make sure you live to fulfil your promises to me."

After de Silva and Krishna had left the carriage I walked over to Eric "Why?" I asked.

"Did we not tell you that we were going to pick him up?"

"Yes."

"We did it like this because you wear your heart on your sleeve, and you would not have acted the way you did when you rendezvous-ed with him on the journey to here."

"The van?"

"Ah!" Eric hesitated "a bit of a miscalculation on the part of our French colleagues. They were supposed to engineer a slow puncture but instead the tyre burst."

"The driver and his passenger?"

"The driver is unconscious, but stable. The passenger is fine, just proving to be a bit of a handful. I need to ask de Silva to tell him to calm down."

"Have you heard the discussion I had with de Silva on the way to Sangatte?"

"Yes" Eric replied.

"So you heard about the telephone calls on Thursday morning?" I asked.

He nodded.

"I think there's more to it than that."

Eric nodded "Possibly, but we have to start somewhere."

My questions answered "And what now?"

"Go home. Go to work as normal. We will be watching you and, if you don't mind, please continue to wear the wire when you're out of your house."

"One last question?" I asked.

"Yes."

"Did you know de Silva was following me to Texel?"

"Yes, but too late to do anything about it."

"Why? You were following another lead?" I enquired.

"Yes," Eric looked uncomfortable.

"What was it?"

He paused before answering "The disappearance of Carla and her child."

I was disappointed, but did not know why.

PART III

JPG

It was early Thursday morning and I was sitting in my office at JPG. I had my desktop computer switched on, but I was failing to concentrate on the thousand plus unread emails that adorned my Inbox since I returned from my car accident. Over two hundred were *Get well soon* or similar. This was the third day I had been in my office. Each day was the same. I was determined to get back into the swing of things, but my resolve crumbled as soon as I sat in my chair opposite the ever demanding blue-screened monster, which was my personal computer.

Monday only consisted of two hours in the office as most of the day was spent with Gerda and the twins. The reality of Paul's death – accident or not – was starting to sink in, especially when the stress of the twins' abduction subsided. I felt I should spend more time at home, and Gerda's way of dealing with the situation was to focus on the possibility of moving to the Essex countryside.

Monday evening, I went to The Hall. K-P had been released from hospital but was undergoing speech therapy before attempting to return to work. I met with him and Jane in the kitchen – we all agreed it was the least gloomy room in the house. I held my breath as I outlined what Gerda and I had discussed in France. I needn't have done so because Jane was smiling before I had finished speaking, and spoke for both of them. "Marc, you are being incredibly generous…."

"No I'm not," I interrupted "I would be dead, and have nothing if it were not for K-P."

I swear he was blushing, but it was hard to tell.

Jane spoke next "This house is not a happy place with too many ghosts. The children love the garden and grounds."

"I know, and so do the twins when they come and visit here. It will be a shame but…"

"But nothing" Jane said firmly "you say that Gerda wants to move into this area, so why don't you sell The Hall but with only part of the land?"

"And then…?" I questioned Jane.

"We build two houses either side of the remaining land, giving the children a field in-between to play in; and perhaps a shared swimming pool too?"

"Hmmm, it could work. We could have access through the field gates on the back road. Let me talk to Gerda when I get home tonight."

Gerda was all for Jane's idea. Tuesday was spent with my solicitor, during which I outlined what we wanted to do with The Hall, Masterson Shipping, as well as my assets in Goa and Africa. He spent most of the morning trying to dissuade me from my plans, citing tax reasons and a general foolhardiness. The exception was the setting up of a trust for Carla and Jimmy's son, which he totally agreed was appropriate. In the afternoon I returned home and spoke to my accountant, which resulted in more sucking of teeth. Later I contacted a firm of Estate Agents who could handle the disposal of The Hall, and they were able to recommend a firm of Architects-Land Planners in Cambridge, for the partitioning of The Hall grounds plus the design of two new houses. I was tired but nevertheless found the process cathartic, as though a burden had been lifted off my shoulders.

Wednesday morning, I went to the offices of Masterson Shipping and told the Managing Director that I would be resigning as Chairman and transferring my shareholding to Philippe de Silva's son.

The Managing Director was fairly ambivalent after I finished speaking. "Well Marc, I can see that you have made your mind up, and I only hope that de Silva's son leaves us alone as you have done."

"Like an absentee landlord?" I interjected.

"Perhaps?" he smiled "but your share dividend has been quite substantial over the last five years. I will make arrangements for it to be paid to you as soon as your resignation has been accepted by the Board."

"Thank you, I would have normally foregone it but I will have a lot of legal and accountancy fees to pay, so it will help me."

I stood up and the Managing Director gave me a hearty handshake with a very genuine "Good luck Marc, to you and your family."

It was Wednesday afternoon when I sat at my desk to make a start on my emails, but I was restless and decided to walk to Lloyd's with Julian the junior broker in JPG who spotted me when I was in a poor disguise before I went to Dubai.

As we walked towards Lloyd's, Julian turned to me and said "Mr Edge, what do you want me to do with the mobile phone I bought," then he added "with your money."

"Keep it in the office – you never know if it might come in handy one day."

We carried on walking and then I asked him how things had been in the office whilst I was away.

"A very sombre mood particularly with Jimmy no longer with us and K-P missing. While I knew you were not in a coma, I couldn't tell anyone, and it was very disconcerting for everyone. John Eastwood was great, and he said that everything would work itself out in the end."

I smiled and turned to Julian nodding that he would make a good broker. "John was right and I appreciate your discretion."

John Eastwood was my mentor and had been incredibly loyal to JPG and me, even though five years previously I had been falsely accused of his son's murder. I had retained John as Deputy Chairman and it was one of the best decisions I ever made. He was only supposed to work ten days a month, but frequently he would be in the office more than the required days. A great sounding board and a font of wisdom, who I was looking forward to meet for lunch on Thursday, as we had much to discuss.

Upon arriving at Lloyd's, Julian and I went our separate ways. I took the north east lifts up to the first floor and wandered around the underwriting floor. I passed the Deeks Syndicate and saw Andrew Vervy whom I met prior to going to Dubai. He lifted his head as I walked past. I saw only the faintest nod of acknowledgement, which meant he too had seen through my poor disguise, when we met for coffee prior to Dubai.

I walked past another syndicate's underwriting box and jumped out of my skin when a very familiar voice spoke from behind me, "so the prodigal son returns." I turned slowly to see the smirking face of my brother. "I didn't know you knew Andrew Vervy at Deeks?"

To deny my acquaintance with Andrew Vervy would have been futile, "Hello Joshua, are you spying on me?"

Joshua's face flushed.

I continued, "I met him after a lunchtime seminar in the Old Lloyd's Library. He was introduced to me by a mutual friend."

"Who? I actually know Andrew Vervy quite well." Joshua was definitely fishing for information but I was not going to satisfy his interest.

I paused for a moment to accentuate the fact that I was trying to remember who introduced me ...... I shook my head. "Sorry it must be the coma, because for the life of me I can't remember who it was."

Joshua pulled a face. Perhaps he knew when I was lying, which I most definitely was, but he did not have the gumption to call me out.

"So you are back from a near-death car accident? You must have nearly used up all your nine lives," he smirked.

"Yes it was very hairy."

"And how was the hospital?"

"Don't know. I was in a coma for most of the time."

"Pa and Ma were out of their wits. No one gave them any information in Australia."

"I am sorry." I was genuinely sorry.

"I was in the Middle East phoning numerous hospitals to try and find out where they were treating you."

I said nothing.

"And your wife wasn't much help either. She didn't return one of my voice messages."

"She was in Holland – her brother died." I turned to face him "Did you hear about that?"

Again Joshua seemed uncomfortable and his faced flushed, although he was prone to that with his fair skin colouring. "I only found out yesterday from Ma."

I detested Joshua referring to my mother and father as 'Ma and Pa', it was so falsely snobby. But that was Joshua all over, trying to be something he wasn't and throughout our lives he had been intensely critical of me. He felt I was reckless, not considerate enough that my actions might upset our parents. He might have had a point, but his continuous whining and admonishment of my life, had only served to emphasise how different we were from each other.

"Paul was lucky to get another five years after he recovered from his accident." Joshua's negativity was another trait I disliked in him, but perhaps that was why he was a successful underwriter. I, on the other hand, was forever the optimist, forever the broker.

"I don't think Gerda and the twins see it that way," I replied.

That remark brought a full deep red faced grimace from Joshua.

I tried to lighten the mood. "We are going to Norfolk at the end of the month for Mum's birthday, and to hear all about their trip to Australia."

"Yes, Ma asked us to come for dinner."

"Will you be staying the night?"

"Yes, but we will probably go to a hotel and make a long weekend of it, as it's the Bank Holiday."

"Of course – I had forgotten." Which I had. It wasn't the first time that my memory was playing tricks on me. Perhaps the car accident had shaken my brain. Then for some unaccountable reason I told Joshua about my decision to sell The Hall, and also to give away my shareholding in Masterson Shipping. I stopped short of telling Joshua to whom I was giving the shares to.

His reaction was very different to everyone else. "They weren't yours in the first place, so easy come easy go, I suppose. Anyway, I must go now, I can't afford to saunter around the market like you good-for-nothing brokers." He tried to make it sound like a joke but he didn't carry it off; because he was honestly of the belief that brokers were an encumbrance that the underwriters had to endure.

"See you in Norfolk," I said to the back of his head.

I continued around the Lloyd's underwriting floor, saying hello to a number of people, brokers and underwriters alike. All, without exception, seemed pleased to see me and wished me well, so Joshua's pettiness became inconsequential and I pushed it to the back of my mind. As I walked back to JPG, I felt invigorated and rejuvenated to make a start on my backlog of emails.

So here I was on Thursday sitting at my desk, my mind wandering, as I had a fitful night's sleep. I had been woken by one of the twins who had a nightmare that also woke Gerda. After settling Jack back to sleep, we lay talking about our future plans, not falling asleep until the early hours exhausted after making love. I looked at my screen and yawned; another dozen or so emails had dropped into my Inbox in the last fifteen minutes. I decided I needed some fresh air and coffee. I walked out of my office and unconsciously walked towards K-P's and Jimmy's desks. Both were empty and someone had cleared Jimmy's personal effects which brought a twinge to my chest – plus there was no news about Carla or her son. I wanted to talk to her to tell her about the provisions I would make for them both.

As I left the office and walked towards the new Australian barista coffee shop, I called Eric Jones. He answered it on the second ring.

"Good morning Marc. I thought you might call."

"Yes, anything to report from the phone call?" I asked.

"Yes and no," he replied.

"What do you mean?"

"The call came through exactly on time. But the voice at the other end just said 'Nothing to report' and hung up."

"So what next?"

"We quizzed de Silva and he said that this happens now and again." "How is de Silva behaving?"

"Ok, but very moody. One moment, quite quiet and morose, and the next very cocky and almost hysterical. Are you out of the office?"

"Yes - damn – I left the wire on my desk."

Eric said nothing.

"I will promise to wear it whenever I am out and about."

"Alright," Eric replied.

"I have put certain things into motion, including the transfer of my shareholding in Masterson Shipping and overseas assets to de Silva."

"Yes we heard when you were discussing your plans with your solicitor. I only hope you don't subsequently regret your decision Marc."

"He has a right to them," I replied "perhaps more than me"

"Maybe, but his instability could drive a fine shipping company onto the rocks, if you'll pardon the pun."

"The Board are very experienced and should keep him in check."

"I hope you are right, but have you considered either transferring the shares over a period of years, or at least keeping a golden share?"

"No."

"Think about it Marc, as a favour to me, please?"

"I will consider it" I said very unconvincingly. "Before I go, any sign of Carla?"

"Nothing, I regret." Eric replied.

I returned to the office with my coffee and focussed once again on my Inbox. I forced myself to read, and answer where necessary, the plethora of messages. I decided to start with the most recent and work backwards. I was about an hour into my task when I read something that jogged my sluggish memory. It was a report I received of all large claims JPG had settled in the last month, and I recalled de Silva's comments that one item he received was part of a stolen haul, for which JPG apparently arranged the insurance. I filed the report and then looked at the historical reports and after a few minutes I found the claim; it was on the bordereau some four months previously. There were only brief details, so I made a note of the Date of Loss (three months before the claim was settled which was quite usual for such claims), the claim number and I also wrote down the Policy Number, as I wanted to know who actually placed the risk.

I took the information and went to JPG's head of claims Ben McDonald. Ben was a bright graduate who joined JPG at the same time as me. I thought him initially to be my competition but Ben was drawn to the claims side of the broking operation. Normally insurance brokers treat claims as a backwater, failing to resource them properly. Many times I witnessed fierce debates between Sir Hugh and John Eastwood about the necessity to keep claims well resourced. Sir Hugh saw claims as an overhead that needed reducing to maintain profitability, whereas John Eastwood would insist that claims needed our brightest technical staff as the settlement of claims was JPG's shop window. Thankfully John prevailed, and on a large number of occasions our claims department's service had stopped a client from moving to another insurance broker. Instead of his name plate on his desk, Ben sported a banner proclaiming his area as *JPG's shop window*. I continued to resource claims well and Ben was one of our highest paid employees, sitting on our Executive Committee.

"Good morning Ben," I greeted him as his head was buried in his iPad.

He looked up and smiled "Hello boss."

"Ben, what do you know about this claim please?" I passed to him the claim details scribbled on a post-it note.

"Hmm, nothing jumps out at me, I will look into it and come back to you shortly."

"Before lunch if possible with a full copy of the placing slip please?"

"Okey, dokey," Ben replied with a thick Scottish brogue and a broad smile.

I returned to my office and continued with my emails. After about three quarters of an hour, Ben came into my office with a number of sheets of paper he had recently printed as they were still warm.

He observed "Nothing seems to be out of the ordinary. Gold bullion and jewellery theft, somewhere en route from India, Calcutta, to Dubai. The owner was a rich Indian businessman who was going to use the proceeds in a major property transaction."

I nodded and commented that with the end of the Global Financial Crisis, Dubai was once again building profusely after being quiet for a number of years.

"Apparently the proposed property development was for low-cost housing for the migrant workers, mostly coming in from the Indian sub-continent."

"What? In Dubai itself?" I questioned Ben.

"No, Sharjah."

"That makes more sense," I nodded in understanding and asked who the broker was.

Ben paused for a moment as he looked at the papers. "Jimmy" he replied.

"Jimmy!" I looked up surprised. "Why was he handling a Surety and Specie risk?"

Ben merely shrugged his shoulders.

I looked at the copy Placing Slip that was in the papers Ben had passed to me. Although it was essentially a Transit risk, because the subject matter was precious metals, the risk was placed in the Surety and Specie market.

"Ben could you please check out if the panel of insurers are typical for these risks?"

He took back the Placing Slip and turned to the pages where the underwriters had stamped the Placing Slip, indicating their acceptance of the risk and the proportion of the risk they were prepared to accept.

"Yes, pretty much as I would expect, Deeks Syndicate are the leaders, taking fifty percent. Even your brother has a small line." He pointed to the initial beside the last underwriter who only underwrote five percent.

"So he does." I smiled thinking Joshua would have been upset at underwriting a risk with a claim.

"Who was the producer of the risk?" I asked.

Once again Ben checked his papers "One of our regular producers in Dubai."

"Hmm" I said more to myself than to Ben.

"Anything else?" Ben checked his watch and I automatically did the same. It was five to one and John Eastwood was about to appear for our luncheon appointment.

"No, that's all thanks Ben."

He turned and was about to leave the room when I asked him for some more claims information. "Ben, sorry, but could you run a report of all claims on risks over the last year where Jimmy was the broker and all claims for risks produced by the producer in Dubai."

Ben frowned at me.

"Idle curiosity" I retorted "ask young Julian to help you if you need more resource."

As Ben left I could see that John Eastwood was waiting patiently outside my office. I stood up and put my jacket on, remembering the wire.

"Come on John, I am starving."

We walked briskly out of the building and headed towards a quiet Italian Restaurant nestled in a small alleyway near Spitalfields. We exchanged pleasantries as we walked, but did not start any detailed discussions until we were sat at the table. We both had ordered the pasta special of the day and a large bottle of sparkling water.

John gave me a rundown of the business whilst I had been out of the office. It was particularly difficult when it came to Jimmy and K-P. John had drafted in a couple of young guys, including Julian, whom he was supervising - but he wished to return to his normal part-time role rather than being in the office full time.

"I expect it will take wild horses to keep K-P from returning next week."

John nodded in agreement. "What about Jimmy's replacement?"

"I thought Carla might want to come back to JPG rather than moping around the house. I want to see the family right. I am putting some money in trust for Jimmy's son, but they will need a monthly income."

"On top of the life insurance pay-out which will be quite generous."

"I know Carla, and she needs to be kept busy," I remarked.

"Have you spoken to her about this?" John asked as our food arrived.

I shook my head as I took a mouthful of linguine wrapped around my fork. "I haven't been able to reach her since I returned from Dubai."

John said that perhaps she wanted to go to ground to deal with the grief of losing Jimmy.

"Yes, that's probably it" I nodded my head as I twirled more pasta onto my fork "but I have asked Eric Jones to have a word with his shadowy friends."

John said nothing in reply as he negotiated his pasta, trying to avoid spilling the sauce onto his shirt and tie.

"John, I came across a Surety and Specie risk placed by Jimmy."

"And?"

"Isn't that unusual?"

"No, Jimmy would often help out anyone who was busy."

"I suppose that's right" I agreed with John's explanation.

We continued lunch and I moved the conversation to my plans, and John was all in favour of my decision to sell The Hall.

"A gloomy old place," was John's description.

He also thought the idea of building two houses in the grounds for my and K-P's families was a sound idea. But, when I told him about Masterson Shipping, he was shocked.

"Have you gone mad?" John asked me. "de Silva abducts the twins and then you give him Masterson Shipping..."

"And the land in Zimbabwe and Goa," I added.

"You're completely certifiable."

"They weren't mine in the first place."

"Nor were they his either." John certainly had the bit between his teeth.

"Eric suggested I should do it in stages and hold on to a golden-share."

"He's absolutely right."

"I will think about it. Coffee, John?"

We both had double espressos, to keep us awake after the pasta, and we returned to the office. John said he wouldn't come into the office for ten days, as he wanted to take his wife on a short break, especially as he had worked full time during my time out of the office.

When I returned to my desk, there was a pile of papers lying on my blotter, with a yellow post-it note on top. 'Give me a call when you have read these please'. I looked at the first page with six lines of data; it was a claims report of risks emanating from the Dubai producer, and most of them fairly small, three personal accident claims, the largest by a country mile being the gold and jewellery loss. I then picked up the next claims report which consisted of two pages, with claims running over the first page and halfway down the next. I counted the claims and there were more than thirty.

· "Wow!" I said to myself. I looked more closely and ten were closed with no claim payment; nothing out of the ordinary. Twenty plus were settled claims, and most amounts were way over fifty thousand pounds. Some Kidnap and Ransom risks, which Jimmy would work on with K-P, were less than half of the paid claims. The rest were a myriad of different risks. Most involved loss of property with theft being a high proportion of the cause of the loss. I put the claims report down and started to feel sick. A horrible thought went through my mind. Was Jimmy feeding information to Dominique de Silva?

"No, not Jimmy." I sat at my desk looking into the middle distance. I couldn't – didn't – want to believe it. Jimmy was one of my loyalist employees, and alongside K-P and John Eastwood, I would trust Jimmy with my life. My mind wandered back to the accident when Jimmy was killed, and I wondered if Jimmy had told someone about where we were heading on that ill-fated night; because I felt sure the lorry, with the lights blazing, was bearing down on my car causing me to swerve and crash the Range Rover.

My day-dreaming was interrupted by my mobile phone. I glanced at the screen – it was Eric. "Hello Eric."

"Marc, de Silva is threatening to not cooperate unless he sees some proof that what you promised him comes to fruition, soon."

"I am going to honour my word," I told Eric.

"I know you will, but don't give it to him all at once, please?"

"Why?"

"It should make him more compliant. We need to keep him onside, until they contact him with firm instructions."

"I will come and talk to him if you think that will help."

"Yes please," Eric accepted my offer "and are you available tomorrow?"

"I am free in the afternoon."

"Good. We will pick you up at two o'clock from your office."

I walked over to Ben's desk, but he was not there. His computer was switched off. I spoke to one of his team and they told me that he had left for the night, but as per his note to me, he wanted me to call him. I went back to my office and duly rang his mobile number which he answered on the second ring.

"Hello, this is Ben McDonald speaking." Ben's Scottish brogue was much more noticeable on the phone.

"It's Marc."

"Thanks for calling. Did you look at the claims reports on your desk?"

"Yes I did. It makes for interesting reading." I paused for a moment. "Jimmy's risks are certainly got good value for the insurers."

"Hmm…" was Ben's response "you suspected this, didn't you?" It was framed as a question but it felt like an accusation.

"No, I was just curious."

"Well I ran some comparison reports for each Account Director and Broker."

I went quiet as I was fearful of what he was going to tell me.

"Hello Marc. Can you hear me? Do you want to know what I found?"

"I suppose you are going to tell me anyway."

"Yes, I am."

He explained that Jimmy's risks over the last eighteen months had five times more claims that the average of anyone else and twice that of the next highest Account Executive or Broker.

I groaned.

"I did a bit more digging and over seventy-five percent had Deeks Syndicate as the major, if not the lead, insurer."

"Oh really," I said but sounded unconvincing.

"Marc, you know something, don't you?"

"Well," I paused "I may do, but I need you to keep it completely to yourself please?"

"I thought so" Ben said triumphantly. "I was going to have a quiet word with the claims manager at Deeks."

"Before you do so, I want you and me – only – to do some more investigation first."

"OK, you're the boss."

"Can you be in early tomorrow morning? I will explain more and we can do some more digging."

"Is eight o'clock early enough?"

"Sure," I said and wished him a good evening, and without prompting he explained that he had a claims forum meeting, and that is why he had left the office early.

I returned to my emails and made a determined effort to clear as many as possible as Friday was now filling up quickly with appointments with Ben and a meeting with Eric and de Silva.

Violated

Sleep did not come easily Thursday night. Upon arriving home, I gave Gerda an account of my day, and she knew how sad I would be, if Jimmy was supplying information to enable the thefts and abductions to take place. Gerda herself had her own sad news; Paul's body was ready for his funeral; the pathologists had completed their tests. The results were inconclusive, and from what de Silva said – which the twins corroborated to an extent – it seems he slipped and fell on his head. It appeared that the previous injury, which made Paul comatose for over a year, was a weak point and another bang on his head – however minor - was likely to prove fatal. We didn't want to upset the twins further, so we agreed to accept the verdict, and make arrangements to collect Paul from the morgue. Gerda and I would return to Holland the following week, with the twins staying with my parents in Norfolk for the last week of their Easter holidays. It was my mother's birthday at the end of that week, and we should be back from Holland in good time to join the celebrations, and then bring the twins back to London on the Sunday. Gerda had made the arrangements and she would fly out on Saturday whilst I took the twins to Norfolk. I would join her on Wednesday, allowing Gerda enough time to make the necessary arrangements for the funeral and crematorium.

When I did fall asleep, it was dream-filled and fitful. The lorry's lights coming towards me, followed by Carla's face contorted and shouting at me "Why Marc? Why? Why? Why?" I woke bathed in sweat and Gerda trying to comfort me by gently stroking my hair with her hand.

I was in the office before seven o'clock, and started to do some preparation before Ben arrived. The lack of sleep had perversely sharpened my thoughts, and I created a spreadsheet onto which I entered certain risk details from the policy that was the subject of the theft of the gold and jewellery. I included the percentage of each insurer and recorded the individual underwriter, where I recognised their initials from the placing slip. Where the risk was finalised electronically I would need someone else to enter that information, as well as those underwriters whose initials I didn't recognise.

I had just completed entering the information I could glean from the risk details I had on that one particular risk when I heard Ben's voice at my door.

"Morning boss, couldn't you sleep?" he asked jovially.

"Not brilliantly. Have a look at this, please?" I beckoned Ben around to my side of the desk so he could look at my screen.

"I am guessing you want the same information for all the other risks we identified yesterday?"

"Yes please, and then I will ask Julian to fill in the gaps," Ben frowned at me "for the identity of the individual underwriters."

Still Ben frowned at me.

"I can trust him. I will not give him the whole spreadsheet or the context."

"OK, send me what you have completed thus far and give me an hour and I should be able to populate the spreadsheet with most of the other information."

"That quickly?" I sounded surprised.

"Possibly less if Gupta is in early."

It was just under the hour at a quarter to nine that Ben and Gupta walked back into my office.

"Check your email, boss," Ben said.

I dutifully did as commanded and there in my Inbox was an email from Gupta. I opened up the attachment and most of the boxes were completed, the only gaps were the actual underwriters at each insurer. The evidence was damning. The insurer profile for more than three quarters of the risks was almost identical. If the risks were the same class of insurance, then it would make more sense but it was a myriad of different types of insurance.

Ben could see the look on my face "Boss, something's a bit awry here."

It was as clear as the nose on my face, but I didn't want to believe it. Jimmy had placed these risks with certain markets and then fed information to someone who organised losses on those policies.

Ben continued "What is odd is that some of these risks are where Jimmy was only the broker and not the Account Executive."

I felt that was almost more damning "Which means what?" I asked.

"He might not be aware of the claims happening on those risks, unless he was also the Account Executive. We also looked at a number of other risks Jimmy placed with no claims and most of the schedules of Insurers are very similar."

"So someone at Deeks Syndicate should have been suspicious?"

"Not necessarily" replied Ben because they are a large syndicate, they have different Line of Business managers and different claims managers."

"So identifying the actual underwriters is now even more important?"

Ben replied "Yes, and another thing we should do is identify the Insurers and underwriters on the risks without claims that Jimmy placed."

"Why?" I asked.

"It may be a coincidence, but there are a group of four or five smaller Insurers, who appear regularly on all Jimmy's risks; however, they either don't insure the risks which have claims, or they have much smaller lines." Ben was watching me closely for a reaction.

I thought for a moment and then thanked Gupta for his assistance this morning but asked Ben to stay behind for a moment.

"Ben would you please close the door?" He did so and then sat in the seat opposite me.

"K-P's disappearance was part of a play to try to flush out people behind a fraud ring at Lloyd's."

Ben showed no reaction.

"Lloyd's are investigating and they think they are getting close."

"Who at Lloyd's is investigating?" Ben asked.

"Eric Jones has been retained by Lloyd's, but that is secret Ben."

"Hmm?" I knew that Ben and Eric were not best buddies, as they had sparred more than once on large claims, with Ben usually coming second best.

"Eric Jones and I think that there is a possibility my car was forced off the road the night Jimmy died."

"Could it be that Jimmy was the target?"

My head was spinning. My self-centredness presumed it was me who they were trying to stop. Only now the spectre of Jimmy being involved potentially changed my opinion. I said nothing for a moment.

Ben could see that I was in turmoil. "Why don't you speak to K-P?"

My mind was unfocussed, images of Jimmy, the accident, K-P in Dubai, Carla, all flashed in front of my eyes.

"K-P?" I mouthed in a faint whisper as I came back to Ben in the room "Yes, yes, that's a good idea."

"Does Deeks Syndicate know about this issue?" Ben asked.

I nodded in the affirmative. "They were the ones who brought it to Lloyd's of London's attention. Why do you ask?"

"I am very close to one of their claims managers," Ben explained.

"Margaret Browne?"

"Yes," Ben confirmed but did not elaborate on the nature of the relationship. I knew he was unmarried but Ben kept himself to himself.

"What are you proposing?" I asked.

"That I would share with Margaret what we have determined. I am seeing her over the weekend."

Ben probably divulged more that he would do normally about his private life.

"Possibly?" I replied tentatively. "I am seeing Eric this afternoon, and I will ask him then."

"OK, boss. Just let me know." Ben left my office.

I manipulated the spreadsheet Gupta had sent me, leaving just the policy numbers, the Insurers and the partially completed underwriter field. I saved the edited document as a new file, and sent it to Julian. I then went in search of Julian. He was sitting at his desk enjoying his morning coffee.

"Hi Julian, how are you?" I greeted him.

"Very good Mr Edge."

"Please call me Marc," I invited him.

"Ah, yes, Marc," he replied nervously.

"Can you do a task urgently for me, please?"

"Sure."

"Aren't you going to ask me what it is before agreeing?" I smiled to try and relax him.

"Sure – of course – yes. What is the task?"

I explained about the attachment to the email I had sent him, and that I wanted him to complete the underwriter field as best he could and then send it back to me before two o'clock.

It was nearly ten o'clock and I was tired from the lack of sleep and the mental and emotional stress of the morning's discoveries. I decided a cup of coffee was in order, and I put my jacket on to go to my Australian barista. As I left the office, I had the feeling that someone was watching me, but when I turned to look for such a person I didn't see anything out of the ordinary.

"Marc!" Someone called from behind me, and when I turned around I could see Gupta trying to catch up with me.

I stopped as he walked quickly to my side.

"Yes Gupta?"

"Can we have a chat please?"

"Ok, let me buy you a coffee Gupta."

We walked for a few paces before Gupta spoke.

"Marc, you looked very upset when you looked at the information we compiled this morning."

I said nothing.

"You are already upset because of Jimmy dying in your car, and now you think he may have done something wrong, no?"

Still I said nothing.

"Jimmy and I were very good friends. He worshipped you Marc, and he adored K-P. He wouldn't have done anything to harm you or JPG's reputation."

I slowed my walk and turned towards Gupta. "That's what I thought, but look at the evidence?"

"What if Jimmy was the source of the information but he gave it unwittingly?"

"What do you mean?"

"An IT leak."

I bought Gupta and me our coffees and we took a seat on a makeshift bench outside the barista's shop.

"Marc, I have a number of friends who I met at university who are involved in IT security and what they tell me is absolutely astounding. The year before last, global cyber-attacks rose by forty eight percent with the actual number of incidents being nearly forty three million at an average of nearly a hundred and twenty thousand per day."

He then gave me a piece of paper which explained at a very high level the different forms of cyber-attacks, and their protagonists.

Hacktivism: cyber terrorism where criminals remain ahead of their victims on innovation with cyber-criminal tactics evolved at exponential rate. Some of the biggest and most costly cyber events in history occurred in 2014. The costliest cyber event of that year with 750,000 customers' bitcoins were lost and an additional 100,000 bitcoins belonging to the company involved had disappeared, for a total loss of more than USD500 million worth of bitcoins.

Internal staff errors – data leaks.
Third party failures.
Staff Data Theft.
Disgruntled employees.

Gupta took a sip of his coffee and continued, "Cyber criminals are becoming cleverer and cleverer. No security system is absolutely secure, and when a security breach is detected a patch is put in place and then the cyber criminals have their own programmes to find another way into the system. It is relentless, and with more cyber criminals at work – some of whom are state sponsored by unfriendly foreign governments – the pressure is increasing day by day."

"Why do they do it? Is it just to steal credit card details?"

"Yes and no" Gupta replied "a lot of times it is to undermine, distract and destabilise. Private individuals often do it just for fun, they treat it as a sport, but there is a significant element of organised crime that is systematically attacking industrial, financial institutions and other high profile targets such as retail and healthcare to obtain money by fraud and deception."

"So how do we as individuals and the corporate world defend ourselves?" I asked.

Gupta paused for a moment collecting his thoughts. "Marc, no system is totally safe and secure, and one way that cyber criminals obtain access to a system is by attacking it from many sources and devices from different parts of the world, and, whilst it is being peppered by attacks, it can fail and its defences close down which then lets the cyber criminals into the system. Do you recall the North Sea floods in the nineteen fifties?"

"Not personally, but we studied them when I was at school, but that's a long time ago."

"Well, as a result of the floods, the UK government decided to build coastal defences down the East Coast, but recently there has been a change of approach. The reason is that the sea-defences push the seawater to another part of the coast, until it finds a gap in the sea-defences. Therefore, a new idea is being considered that involves identifying low lying land, which will have no defence, and will act as a flood plain. The land might become a saltmarsh and is ecologically beneficial, as it becomes a haven for wildlife, and that in turn is good for the animals and tourism."

"Yes, I know about this, because one is being proposed near my parents in Norfolk."

"The defence to a cyber-attack is similar, where a company may have a number of servers sitting idle, and when an attack is detected all the messages are deflected to these idle servers."

"Clever," I retorted.

"Yes, but our system has not been attacked in such a way."

I pulled a face.

Gupta had a wan smile on his face "Unfortunately the other way cyber criminals get into a system is via individuals being careless or not vigilant with their passwords. People have so many, that they write them down somewhere – and possibly pop them into their wallet or purse?"

I blushed because that is exactly what I do.

Gupta continued. "I met a friend for a drink recently. He works for GCHQ in Cheltenham, and he brought a colleague along, who was quite quiet and fiddled with his phone whilst my friend and I chatted. After twenty minutes my friend's colleague showed me that he had got into my iPhone – which had been sitting on the table – turned it on, taken a photo of the ceiling and sent it back to him on his phone."

"You're joking!"

He shook his head. "There is a rumour that the Russian Secret Service have reverted to typewriters – without using carbon paper obviously."

I sat quietly for a few minutes whilst I digested what Gupta had told me.

"So someone could be in our system now?" I asked.

"Yes," Gupta replied.

"How can you tell?"

"I will need to close down the whole system and undertake some forensics work."

"How long will that take?"

"A whole weekend."

Again I sat thinking before responding.

"OK, don't do anything for the moment, but send around an email to everyone to say that we are going to conduct a routine Disaster Recovery test from early tomorrow morning.

Explain that the systems will be down from two o'clock until noon."

Gupta and I stood to walk back to the office. During our return he explained that as a minimum we should change our password protocols, as well as increase the security on how we access the firm's IT system remotely. I thought about his request before replying.

"You are probably right, but don't do anything until I agree to the changes, please?" I was formulating an idea that I wanted to discuss with Eric that afternoon.

When I returned to the office I was barely in my seat when Julian appeared at my door.

"Yes Julian?"

"Marc, I am making good progress, but some of the syndicates are unfamiliar to me, so I am not recognising the individual underwriter's scratches. Should I speak to other people to help me with the underwriter identification?"

I hesitated a moment before answering Julian "No, not just for the moment. Give me what you have for my meeting at two o'clock, and I will let you know after then." Julian turned and I called after him asking if he would kindly close the door.

I picked up the office phone to call The Hall, but, halfway through dialling the number, I hung up. I had been spooked by what Gupta had told me. I went out of my office and went to Julian's desk.

"Julian, excuse me, but can I borrow that mobile phone, please?"

He reached into his desk drawers and passed it to me with the charging lead.

"Thanks. You haven't given anyone this number?"

"No, Marc."

"Good. I will let you have it back before I leave the office later".

Back in my office with the door closed, I called The Hall on the mobile phone.

"Hello?" It was K-P who answered in whispered tones.

"It's Marc, how are you doing?"

"Much better thank you. I hope to be in the office on Monday for a half day and then ease back in." K-P's speech was less muffled than when I saw him and Jane earlier in the week.

"It will be good to have you with me here."

"Is there a problem?" K-P asked.

"Yes, I think there is." I then explained to K-P that I was calling from a new mobile phone and the reasons why. It took me ten minutes to give him the full picture, and K-P's naval intelligence training was invaluable. He probed and challenged my thinking and assumptions. After half an hour's conversation, he agreed with me on what I was proposing. The only area he disagreed with was my assertion that Jimmy had been careless with his access protocols to JPG's systems.

"He was maniacally careful with his passwords," K-P said as firmly as his condition would allow.

"So that's where my theory goes to pot."

Tethering the Goat

I was outside at just before two o'clock, with a print-out of Julian's work product. He had not progressed much farther forward than when he asked me for assistance. I told him that what he had done in the time available was excellent, and returned the mobile phone to him, not before making a note of the number. Dead on two o'clock, a mini-van with blacked-out windows pulled up, and out jumped Simon.

"Hello Marc. Will you join us, please?"

I could see Eric Jones sitting inside the mini-van and, as I climbed in, he extended his arm to shake hands. "Afternoon Marc."

I clasped his hand and answered with "I think I have some interesting news for you."

No sooner had I sat down that we sped off. The darkened glass made the drive disorientating, and I commented to that effect.

"That's part of the reason for using this vehicle. I am afraid I can't have you knowing all our secrets."

I just shrugged my shoulders.

"Now what is your news Marc?"

"Before I tell you, I want to ask you a question. Are you having me watched?"

"Not by us. Why do you ask?"

"It's just a nagging feeling I have been experiencing for the last couple of days, particularly when I am at the office."

"It could be one of de Silva's goons. We will keep a discreet eye on you if you want?"

"Leave it for now, and if I think there's anything more suspicious I will let you know."

"So tell me your news, Marc?"

I explained about de Silva's reference to the gold bullion robbery that was insured by JPG. I also told Eric that I had discovered Jimmy was involved in the placement. I passed Eric the printout of the spreadsheet I had started, which Julian had worked on during the morning, and I walked Eric through the document.

"I was devastated Eric, as Jimmy was one of my loyalist employees, and a good friend."

Eric nodded saying nothing as he studied the spreadsheet. At one point he took out a pen and annotated something, before passing the papers to Simon.

"That's not all," I added.

Eric looked away from his iPad where he had been making notes with the stylus end of his pen.

"Our IT manager believes we could have been hacked."

I had Eric's full attention.

"We have sent a note around to say we are losing the systems over the weekend for a routine IT Disaster Recovery test."

"And then what?" Simon asked.

"Gupta, my IT manager, said he will run a number of protocols," I replied.

"And then what?" Eric asked the next question.

"I am not sure. Probably ask everyone to change passwords and massively increase security."

"What you are suggesting is very sensible," Eric observed "but I would like you to do nothing, for now."

"Not even run the test tomorrow?" I questioned.

"Yes, please run the test, and we will lend you one of Simon's colleagues, or perhaps even Simon himself?" Eric smiled at Simon.

"To do what?" I asked.

"Just observe and offer assistance, if required."

"Do you know something I don't?"

"No, but if you are right, we might have an advantage knowing they are accessing your systems."

"Gupta told me that once in through a back-door, hackers could gain access to everything, including personal mobile phones."

Eric and Simon just nodded their heads in agreement.

"How does the spreadsheet compare to your investigation?" I asked.

Eric looked at Simon and Simon just raised his eyebrows. "I must admit there are certain similarities," Eric conceded.

"Even I can see a pattern."

"It's not that simple Marc," Eric paused "we need to know who the actual fraudsters are, as opposed to those underwriters who are merely following a known leading underwriter on a certain risk. If we are to assume – which I think we should – that the placing brokers are not part of the fraud, how do the fraudsters ensure they are shown the risks in the first place. The network must be very subtle, otherwise someone would have suspected this much earlier. So there is a good chance that the risks were written first, and that the underwriting information was shared by the leading insurers with the rest of the fraudulent insurers, and somehow they were able to underwrite the risk, adjusting their proportion accordingly.

So more of a problem for the following insurers who were part of the fraud to make sure they wrote the better risks. Avoiding a bad risk would be relatively straight-forward; they would just call each other and decline that risk. Alternatively, an underwriter who has seen the risk declines it, or deliberately quotes a high premium, or even more subtle – they write the risk with a smaller participation or they reinsure the risk. Some innocent underwriters would undoubtedly be part of the schedule of insurers on the good risks, because they are known by the brokers to underwrite certain types of risks. This would even help the fraudulent insurers keep below the radar, because I expect the fraudulent insurers are keeping a record somewhere of the 'good' and 'bad' risks."

"You said at the start you didn't believe that the placing brokers were involved. Surely what I have discovered about the risks that Jimmy placed, you must now change your hypothesis?"

"No, not yet. I want you to check your IT system first, because I do not believe that Jimmy would have betrayed you. I did some research on Jimmy after the accident, and he is without doubt one of your most loyal employees. For the time being the underwriters are the focus of my investigation."

"Can we flush them out, or at least put pressure on certain of the underwriters?" I asked.

"Possibly, but what we do need is de Silva on-side, so please focus on that this afternoon Marc?"

I nodded my head in agreement. I was guessing that we were still in South East London but where, I had no clue, other than we went through the Rotherhithe tunnel, which I could discern by the echoes off the other vehicles, together with the low speed we were travelling and the smell of exhaust fumes.

About thirty minutes after exiting the Rotherhithe Tunnel, we slowed to a stop, and I heard the doors being closed. It was a large warehouse type building, with white walls all around, which were accentuated by very bright fluorescent lighting. There was nothing against any wall and a clear three metre gap before three-metre-high fencing that was topped by a further metre of barbed wire, angled inward at forty-five degrees. Within the fencing there were four pre-fabricated structures inter-connected with each other. Eric and I approached a door in one of the structures, and rang the bell on the outside. I glanced up and saw that there was very fine netting that stretched all across the compound, attached to the top of the barbed wire.

Krishna came to the door and managed a half smile to me, but scowled at Eric.

"Come into our prison," Krishna said and led us into a large room that had been comfortably furnished as a living room, with an office area at one end; de Silva was sitting at a desk, tapping on a computer.

"It's not in real time," Eric whispered "everything is monitored – in and out – on a nine second delay."

"Just like radio stations," I commented.

"Correct."

Upon hearing my voice, de Silva had stopped typing, swung around in his chair and lit one of his favourite foul smelling French cigarettes. He said nothing; he just sat in his seat inhaling deeply before exhaling, blowing smoke rings towards the ceiling as he did so.

"We have had to amend the settings for the air conditioning so that the number of air changes per hour in these rooms increases, in case Mr de Silva smokes himself to death before the end of the month."

de Silva laughed but still said nothing.

"Let me give you the tour," Eric led me into the next room which was a well-appointed kitchen. "We offer our guests the choice of served food or self-catering. After a few days almost all opt for the latter."

"To kill the boredom I guess."

Eric nodded in the affirmative.

"Alcohol?"

"Limited. de Silva enjoys a bottle of wine a night plus a glass of brandy."

I nodded. Old habits die hard, and years ago when he and I went out partying, he rarely drank more than that.

"Krishna?"

"Very enigmatic that one." Eric made sure she was out of earshot. "If anything she is proving more difficult than de Silva."

"How so?"

"One minute happy and gaily talking along with anyone, and the next sullen and morose. At that point she tends to wind-up de Silva."

I said nothing but recalled Mercédès, who exhibited exactly the same traits, when she couldn't get her own way. Nature once again triumphs over nurture.

"She is however a magnificent cook, and when the mood suits her she will gladly prepare wonderful three course meals for everyone on site."

"So they know exactly how many people are here?"

Eric didn't like my little dig; he ignored me and walked into the next room. An en-suite bedroom, de Silva's I surmised by the clothes and other items strewn across the room, and then via an interconnecting door was Krishna's bedroom – immaculately tidy by comparison.

"Not sharing?" I queried with Eric.

"Sometimes yes and sometimes no." Eric replied with no emotion.

We returned to the living room and de Silva was now sitting on the sofa with Krishna leaning against him, and in other circumstances it could be seen as a loving blissful scene. He had half an eye on the television screen and he nodded to the armchair next to him, inviting me to sit down. He waited until the end of the news bulletin he was watching, and after it finished he turned the television off.

"Krishna, please make our guests some tea." As Krishna stood up, he asked me "Earl Grey, no milk?"

"Yes, please" I answered.

He looked at Eric "Just water for me please?"

"How are you de Silva?" I asked.

He didn't reply immediately, his eyes bored into Eric, and then turned his gaze to me. He lit another cigarette and smoked it halfway before he spoke "I am very well, but unsure what the future holds for myself .... and Krishna." He added her name almost as an afterthought.

I hadn't a clue how to answer him. I turned to Eric for help.

"It depends on how well disposed you are to helping us uncover the perpetrators of the fraud in Lloyd's. We need to be successful, very successful, if we are going to persuade the authorities to overlook your criminal activities."

"I said I would not press charges with respect to the twins," I interrupted.

"I am not talking about the twins, but Mr de Silva's previous involvement in a number of kidnaps, and kidnapping attempts off the coast of Ethiopia."

I looked at de Silva and he appeared very calm. He shrugged his shoulders in a 'what me?' expression.

"I have some good news for you." I began to explain.

He changed and his demeanour became much more alert, sitting up straighter and his eyes wide open in expectancy.

"I have instructed my lawyer to prepare the transfer of the property and land in Goa and Zimbabwe to you..."

"Not me, all that must go to Krishna; and more importantly, what about Masterson Shipping?"

"That too is proceeding, but more slowly..."

"Why?"

"I was coming to that, if you let me finish? We need to involve accountants and tax advisers. It looks like the most efficient way is to transfer my ownership to you in tranches. I will still draw up a binding agreement saying that all my shares will ultimately be transferred to you over the course of eighteen months."

His face didn't change, as he turned this news over in his mind. I was holding my breath as I changed my mind, heeding the advice given to me over the last few days.

"Also, it will mean the other shareholders and employees of Masterson's will be less skittish, as they get used to you."

He nodded.

Eric smiled.

I felt relieved, but uneasy.

"We just have to wait until Thursday for my next phone call from those idiots" de Silva blurted out.

"What do you mean?"

"Nothing, it's just annoying that today's call was unproductive" he was back-tracking but he lacked sincerity.

"Are you able to manage all your operations from here?" I waved my hand to the desk at which de Silva had been working when I entered the room.

"Yes" he said reaching for another cigarette even though the previous one still lay smoking in the ash tray.

As he lit the tobacco, I could see the lines that had been etched into those boyish good looks, and I recalled the dashing looks of Philippe de Silva dancing around his face.

"What happens if next Thursday's call is another dead-duck?" he asked.

"Then we wait for the following week, or the week after that, and so on," Eric answered in a matter-of-fact voice.

"No problem" de Silva nodded.

"I have been doing some checking and cross-referencing, and it seems that JPG's clients seemed to fair worse than other brokers" I commented.

Eric tried to keep absolutely calm, but I could discern a slight tightening of his expression, as I started to go off-piste.

"Unlucky I guess," was de Silva's off hand riposte.

"I don't think so?" I pushed harder.

He said nothing.

"Perhaps we have a mole in JPG?" I ventured.

"Don't be ridiculous Marc," he laughed heartily.

"Perhaps it's not a person but an electronic mole." The laughing continued; however, I felt it was less genuine, and perhaps I had touched a nerve. "Thank-you, you have just confirmed what we suspected. JPG's systems have been breached. Your associates are screening our every email aren't they?"

He had stopped laughing. He lit yet another cigarette, the lines on his face etching deeper into his skin, as my discovery had weakened his bargaining position.

Krishna stood up abruptly and walked out of the room. I was sure I could see tears in her eyes.

"Maybe?" de Silva eventually replied.

"So we might be able to flush them out with a nice juicy risk, mightn't we?" I asked.

He merely shrugged his shoulders.

"So you knew their focus was on JPG?" I asked.

"Yes," he conceded with a smirk on his face.

"Why?"

"Don't be so naive, you must know. You only have to put two and two together." de Silva was smiling again as he thought his knowledge gave him the upper hand. He bent down to stub out his cigarette in the now overflowing ash tray.

As he did so, I saw a movement out of the corner of my eye. Krishna ran running out of the kitchen, screaming at de Silva and then she plunged a knife into his chest. The scene in the room seemed to freeze, silence fell and in slow motion, Dominique de Silva's wide eyed stare didn't change as he removed the knife from his chest. His hands fell by his side, and in the next instant he thrust his right hand upwards and buried the knife into Krishna's stomach. Still turning the blade in the thin girl's torso, it eventually hit an artery or her heart, because blood then spewed from her mouth. She fell and her killer fell on top of her. For what seemed like an eternity took place in less than five seconds, or the time that it took for Eric to get out of his seat and cross the room to where de Silva had been standing. The couple lay at his feet motionless.

"Shit!!" Eric shouted and then he stared at me.

Simon burst into the room taking each of the body's wrists in turn. He looked up "de Silva is still alive."

I took myself into the kitchen to let the first aiders and then the paramedics do their thing. There was an ambulance at the building within five minutes, and it resembled the vehicle that rescued me from the accident when Jimmy died. I presumed he would be taken to the same private establishment where I was housed to recover.

After he had gone I went over to Eric. He still looked furious.

"Will he live?" I asked.

"Unlikely," was his reply "his right lung has collapsed. Coupled with the shock, I would guess he has less than twenty-four hours. If he gets through that, then maybe he has a fifty percent chance of surviving. He will need to be sedated into an induced coma." Eric walked away.

"I am…."

"Sorry?"

"Yes," I answered.

"What for?"

"For trying to force the issue."

"Hmmm," he said non-committally.

"I don't know what made her flip? Why would my saying a breach of JPG's computer systems cause such a reaction?"

"You are an oaf sometimes Marc. It was not what you said but what I said," Eric replied.

"What do you mean?" I queried.

Eric stared at me "Really can't you guess?"

I thought for a moment while I replayed the conversation in the living room before Krishna went to the kitchen.

Eric could not wait for my memory to recall what was said. "I said that this could go on for many weeks."

"So?"

"Krishna was already becoming stir-crazy, and I thought de Silva could appease her."

"She just flipped?" I asked.

"Possibly? I think it goes deeper than that. She was essentially his concubine."

"A sex slave?"

"Something like that. There was certainly an uneasy tension between the two of them."

"They were cousins once removed; in some countries a relationship between two people so close is considered incest" I ventured.

"What do we do next?"

Eric was silent for a minute "You return home and do nothing please, until you hear from me, and that includes anything to do with JPG's IT system."

I nodded and as Eric made to leave the kitchen, I called after him "What do you think he meant when he said I should know why the focus was on JPG?"

"Oh, probably just that he had a score to settle with you." Eric said in an off-hand manner and he turned on his heel and left the room.

Baiting the trap

Nightmares again plagued my Friday night's sleep with visions of Jimmy, Eric, de Silva and Krishna appearing through the revolving door at Lloyd's. I then was in a court of law being accused of their deaths. Gerda was my defence counsel. Eric, John, Carla, K-P, Jane, Julian, Ben, Brian, Joshua, my sister, mother and father were the jury.

I woke up in a sweat to find that Gerda was already awake, dressed and packing her clothes.

"I let you sleep," she said to me "you were exhausted last night, and fell asleep without turning the television off."

I smiled at her. I was grateful I woke before my nightmare reached its conclusion.

"Come on; get up, you promised to take me to the airport on your way to Norfolk," Gerda chided me.

I had a sense of *deja-vu* after dropping Gerda at Stansted airport, because it was the same time in the morning as when I took Gerda and the twins to start their Easter holidays in Holland, and it was as I left the airport that Jane called me just over three weeks previously to say K-P had gone missing. This time there was no phone call as I exited the airport and we headed north towards Norfolk. The twins were excited about seeing their grandparents. They had not seen them for some little while, as my parents had been away for a few months, visiting my sister in Australia. The twins loved the wide sandy beaches of the North Norfolk coastline, as did I. I knew that I would be getting the third degree from my mother about my escapades, as well as Paul dying in Holland. In fact the twins were so preoccupied by the thought of a week by the seaside that they hardly paid any attention to the fact that their mother was travelling to Holland. We kept Paul's funeral out of the conversation, and I would ask my parents to do the same.

We reached the outskirts of Thetford Chase on the A11, one of the ancient forests of England, in less than an hour. Here I turned off the dual carriageway using the two-way trunk roads heading towards the north west of the county. We first passed Grimes Graves, the site of a Neolithic flint mine in the heart of Breckland in West Norfolk. The going was quite slow as we encountered caravans on their way to the coast for the weekend. Popular with families and bird-watchers, the towns by the coast had become much sought after, and one of the most desirable – Brancaster – had been given the nickname 'Chelsea-by-the-Sea'.

I was about ten miles from my parents when I called them from the hands-free phone in the car, alerting them to our arrival in half-an-hour. When I finished the call I saw that there were two voice messages waiting for me. The first was from Gerda saying that she had landed and was on her way to Texel in a hire-car, and she would call again when she arrived. The second was from Eric asking me to call him as soon as possible.

"Hello Marc, thanks for returning my call…"

"Eric, I am on hands-free in the car with the twins," I interrupted him.

"OK… call me back when you are alone please."

"I should be free in about an hour."

"Sooner, if possible, please?" he requested.

It was sunny, but breezy as I manoeuvred my car next to my father's short wheelbase Land Rover. I don't think it had been washed once since he bought it. The house was on a road that frequently seemed to be under water, and his vehicle was far more practical than my newly acquired Audi. Hot chocolate and biscuits were already prepared, awaiting our arrival. Both my parents looked the picture of health, only recently returning from Christmas and subsequent three months in New South Wales. My father's hair was bleached white, and his face a mahogany brown from the southern hemisphere sun. My mother by contrast was much fairer but even her face radiated the glow of their holiday. After the chocolate, and showing the twins and me to our respective bedrooms, I made my excuses to make a couple of phone calls. The reception was always sporadic so I walked into the garden to gain a better signal, which afforded me some privacy.

Eric answered on the first ring. "Hello Marc, are you alone?"

"Yes."

"Good. We have an idea but we need your help over the forthcoming weekend."

I groaned "I am at my parents in Norfolk."

"When are you back in London?"

"Probably after nine o'clock on Sunday night," I replied.

"OK, we can talk then but in the meantime, can you do one thing for me please?"

"What is it?" I tried to sound conciliatory.

"Can you ask your IT manager to send a general email to all staff saying that the disaster recovery test will be postponed until after the end of the month?"

"And what should he give as the reason?" I asked.

"You do not wish to interfere with any month-end processes?"

"But isn't that the point of a disaster recovery test?"

"Please don't be awkward Marc." Eric sounded a bit testy so I agreed.

"Good. I will call you after nine tomorrow evening." Eric ended the call without indicating what awaited me when I had returned from Norfolk.

I sent the email Eric requested to Gupta. The rest of the day was delightful, spending time with my parents, and the twins. The only dark cloud was when Gerda phoned from Texel. She was in tears after seeing Paul's body at the undertakers. I offered to go over to Holland on Monday, if she wished, but Gerda said for me to stick to Wednesday, as previously arranged. Gerda cheered up when she heard how much fun the twins were having, and that my parents had planned a full week of activities.

I slept the sleep of the dead and awoke to the smell of bacon wafting through the house. Breakfast was followed by a walk to fetch the Sunday papers. It was sunny one moment and rainy the next, but the twins loved it. My father had borrowed a dog from one of the neighbours, and the children were having a great time taking turns in holding the dog's lead, splashing through the puddles in their wellington boots. A big Sunday roast lunch required more walking and this time we went to the beach, picking up shells and unusual coloured stones that would be given to my mother and Gerda. By the time we returned from the beach, I could see the twins were tired, so I decided to have a cup of tea and then head back to London. As I drove away from my parents, I was more convinced than ever that we should move out of London, and even consider buying a dog.

The traffic from Norfolk to London was interminably slow, even though the Easter holiday had another week to run. It was quarter-to-nine by the time I got home, and I was putting a pre-cooked meal into the microwave, when my telephone rang.

"Hello Marc." It was Eric phoning at exactly nine o'clock.

"Yes Eric, how can I help?"

Eric then spent the next twenty minutes explaining his plan. I listened as I ate my supper, grunting occasionally to affirm what Eric had planned could work. After I finished eating my food, I attempted to summarise the plan back to him.

"So you are going to get one of our usual producers to send an email about an urgent and valuable shipment from Rome to Dubai that will act as bait. We then have to run around the market to get it placed in double quick time, providing extensive information about the shipment, with full disclosure about the security arrangements."

"Correct, and make sure you see all the usual insurers. We will make sure the request for a quotation states that the client wants a minimum of three options from different insurers," Eric augmented.

"You are then hoping someone will contact de Silva and you will use a recording of his voice to simulate de Silva."

"Yes, thankfully he was quite garrulous when he was staying with us."

"Will he survive?" I asked.

"He is still unconscious," Eric replied.

"How are you going to draw them into the open?" I asked.

"I am not. You are." Eric replied.

"Me?"

"Yes. On Friday, you are going to speak to all the insurers who have quoted the risk and say that you suspect a theft of the shipment is about to be committed."

"What then?"

"Nothing."

"Nothing?"

"Nothing, because all the potential suspects will be under very close surveillance, and sooner or later one, or more of them, will make a mistake."

"Just one thing. I am going to Holland on Wednesday for Paul's funeral on Thursday."

"When will you be back?" Eric asked.

"Friday, and then Gerda and I are going to go back to Norfolk to collect the twins and celebrate my mother's birthday."

"It should still work as long as you have the contact numbers with you to call all the insurers early on Friday morning."

"Gerda won't be pleased."

"I am sorry Marc, but we really need your help on this please?" Eric sounded genuinely apologetic.

"I will speak to Gerda in the morning and come back to you if there are any problems."

With no children or Gerda at home, every noise and creek seemed to be magnified. With the result that I awoke early, and was at my desk in JPG by half past seven, although, just before I walked through the doors of JPG, Eric called me.

"Morning Eric …..."

Before I could finish my greeting, Eric interrupted me "Dominique de Silva is dead."

"Shit."

"Shit indeed; and I am up a creek full of the stuff. Have you spoken to Gerda?"

"Not yet. I am about to call her after I have checked on the twins and my parents."

"Please call me back as soon as you have spoken to her, either way? And for goodness sake keep de Silva's death a secret." Eric was obviously under a great deal of pressure.

I asked if I could inform K-P and he confirmed that was OK as long as there were no more than him and Gerda. I said I would not tell anyone else.

I spoke with my mother who was in the process of cooking eggy bread for the twins. They had slept well and were looking forward to a trip to the Norfolk Broads for two days, including an overnight stay on a Broads' cruiser. I was reminded about the poor phone reception on the Broads but was told not to worry if I couldn't speak to them until the evening of the following day. No sooner had I spoken to my mother than my phone rang again. It was Gerda.

"Hello my darling," I said.

"Hello. I have been trying to call you for a while."

I told her about the twins first and then I broke the news of de Silva's death.

"I can't say that I am upset," Gerda responded.

"We must keep it hush hush for the time being."

"Why?"

I then explained what Eric had in mind.

"Oh Marc!" Gerda sounded exasperated.

"I know my darling, but whoever is conducting this fraud has infiltrated JPG. Before Krishna stabbed him, de Silva said something. He inferred that I am missing something."

"What did he say?" Gerda asked.

"He said I was naïve if I didn't know why JPG had been targeted."

"Have you any ideas?" Gerda asked.

"None whatsoever, I can only think it is something personal against me."

"Marc, yes that is the obvious conclusion, now try to think of some non-obvious reasons."

"I will try, but I need to call Eric to say whether I will go along with his plan; but really it's your decision."

Gerda sighed "I don't really have a choice."

"Thank you my darling. I love you so much."

"And me you too. That's the only reason why I am agreeing. Plus, I want you to protect yourself."

"What do you mean?" I asked.

"Can Eric give you a gun?"

"Probably not," I replied.

"Well ask him anyway, please?"

"Let's talk this evening."

"Not too late Marc as I didn't sleep well last night."

"Me neither my darling. I missed you beside me."

I phoned Eric. "We're on, Gerda's agreed."

"Great. An email will be coming through from one of your regular producing brokers in the Middle East."

"Who will it be addressed to?" I queried.

"Probably Jimmy and copied to K-P."

"Really?"

"Have you sent out a note to all your producing brokers about Jimmy?" Eric asked probably already knowing the answer.

"No. There is just an Out-of-Office message saying Jimmy no longer works at JPG, with all enquiries being directed to K-P, and a young broker here called Julian."

"And K-P?"

"Yes, he is due to start back in the office today for a couple of hours."

"Excellent."

"I will take K-P into my confidence."

"Fine," Eric agreed.

"Julian helped me prepare the spreadsheet I shared with you last week."

"What have you told him?" Eric sounded anxious.

"Just that I am suspicious of the high loss ratios of business we are placing with certain insurers."

"I presume he is no fool, so we shouldn't treat him as one. I propose you say to him that this enquiry is being carefully monitored, but it should be treated in all respects as a normal piece of business. Who else knows about our suspicions?"

"As I told you already, my IT Manager, and Ben McKenzie."

"I trust Ben to keep quiet. What about the IT Manager?"

"I am pretty certain he will be secure but I will get K-P to have a word with him."

"Good idea. The email will be with JPG by ten o'clock…"

"Before you hang up, Gerda has asked that you afford me some protection."

"What does she mean?"

"Can you give me a firearm?" I asked.

Eric laughed "You are joking I hope. With your past record of action first and thinking second. I could imagine bodies strewn across the south-east of England. You are being totally melodramatic and you probably have spooked Gerda."

"Possibly, but she is very nervous." I replied knowing that Eric needed to keep Gerda and myself on-board.

After a few moments silence, Eric replied "I will send over a Kevlar torso protector. You can buy yourself something like Farb Gel Spray, which will disorientate someone, and colour them red. The colour won't immediately rub off and also, if rubbed, it will irritate the eyes more than if left alone."

"Is that all?" I questioned.

"Anything else is not legal in the United Kingdom."

"Alright, I will order some on-line."

"I will send you one small canister with the Kevlar."

"Thanks Eric."

"Let's talk again this afternoon please?" With that Eric hung up.

Julian was at his desk at nine o'clock and I quickly briefed him about the email that would be bounced on to him when they received the Out-of-Office message from Jimmy's now defunct mailbox. He asked me how I knew. I lied fluently saying the producing broker phoned earlier, and as I was the only person in the office, I picked up the call. Julian seemed to accept my untruth; I added that I was concerned about this enquiry and that, until K-P came into the office, could Julian keep me posted. He agreed to do so.

I decided to go and get a coffee from my regular barista, then took a detour to the closest bank on Bishopsgate. It was just opening and I went to the counter and asked for one pound in pennies. When the cashier passed it to me I weighed the plastic bag in my hand. I asked for another hundred pennies. The cashier gave me a very old-fashioned look which I ignored and then gave her a two-pound coin. Coffee in hand, I returned to JPG. On my return I had the similar feeling to that of the previous week and I felt the hairs on the back of my neck standing on end. I was sure I was being watched. I resisted the urge to turn around, but once in the JPG building I went directly to the top floor. There were no offices at this level; the floor was devoted to the air conditioning systems, cold water tanks and the boilers. Although it was shared leasehold, as the anchor tenant I had the keys to a door on this floor, which when opened revealed a staircase that led to the roof. I walked up to the roof, careful not to stand too close to the wall, so not to be spotted from the ground. Crouching down I crept around the perimeter of the roof. The weather was similar to that in Norfolk over the weekend, blustery with a mix of sunshine and showers. Fairly typical weather for a spring day in England. I couldn't spot anything untoward; no-one seemed to be hanging around. Eric was right. I was being melodramatic.

When I went downstairs to my office I was greeted by a cacophony of noise that heralded K-P's return to the office. K-P himself wasn't speaking much, if anything at all. The entire hubbub was coming from his colleagues, and unsurprisingly mostly from the female staff. I don't think Jane would have approved of the number of hugs and kisses he was receiving. I nodded to him and he made his excuses and came into my office.

"Close the door, please?" I asked him. "Thank you so much for coming back today".

K-P could sense something was amiss and cocked an eye at me.

"I will tell you all in a minute, but first how are you?"

K-P nodded and held up his left hand with his forefinger pressed to his thumb and the other fingers raised in the universal sign of 'OK'.

"Good, but please do not stay in the office beyond one o'clock."

He raised his eyebrows.

"Two reasons. Firstly, I don't want you to tire yourself, I need you back full time as soon as possible. Secondly Dominic de Silva and Krishna are dead."

"What" K-P exclaimed.

I explained what happened.

"What's going to happen now?"

"Eric is running a scam to try to flush out the fraudulent insurers."

I then explained what was going to be tried.

K-P spoke for the first time since he had sat in the office. "It's a bullshit idea," his voice lisping and croaky.

"Thanks for your support," I said ironically.

K-P just smiled revealing his white teeth.

"Julian is going to run the broking and I want you to run point-of-contact from the office. Is your laptop working?"

He shook his head.

I reached into my drawer and pulled mine out. "Use mine, and ask Gupta to set it up for you this morning so you can use it from home later today, after Lloyd's has closed. I will get Julian to run everything past you."

K-P nodded.

"Julian knows we are following the enquiry closely because of the high loss ratios but he does not know about the fraud investigation. Gupta and Ben McKenzie do and so does John Eastwood. Eric knows that you Gupta and Ben know but not John."

K-P cocked his head on one side.

"I forgot to tell him," I replied to his unspoken question.

K-P left my office and I saw him going over to Julian. A few minutes later Julian was sitting next to K-P in Jimmy's old desk. K-P was absolutely adamant that Jimmy was not the mole, nor would he have breached our security protocols. I really wanted to believe K-P, but the evidence against Jimmy was growing, nothing conclusive though. I was very distressed, made all the more frustrating by de Silva's words that I should know why JPG had been targeted. My head was spinning and I decided to take another walk and buy myself some thick sports socks, so I could fashion a cosh with the pennies, similar to that favoured by Indian Thuggees of the mid-nineteenth century.

I decided to use the back entrance of the office and took a circuitous route to get to Liverpool Street. I no longer felt as though I was being watched, and I occasionally stopped in front of a shop window to check if anyone was behind me. There was no-one, nor any quick movements from anyone. I told myself to relax. After making my purchases, I picked up another coffee, plus one for K-P and sauntered back through the front entrance of the office. Neither Julian nor K-P were around, so I left the coffee on K-P's desk and returned to my emails. After half an hour, K-P returned to his desk with my laptop in hand.

I wandered over to him "Your coffee is probably cold by now."

He shrugged his shoulders, drank it in one gulp, which was probably a welcome change from the bottle of mouthwash he had on his desk.

"Is Julian in the market?"

K-P nodded.

"Does he know who he needs to see today?"

K-P just stared at me.

"Sorry. I am being an old woman."

K-P nodded.

"When are you going home?" I asked.

K-P held up one finger.

"After Julian comes back from the market for lunch?"

Again K-P nodded.

"Can you blind copy me into your emails, please?"

This time K-P gave the thumbs up to signify his agreement.

"I am going to see my solicitor this afternoon."

K-P shot a questioning look at me.

"I will tell him that I am having second thoughts with regard to Masterson Shipping and the land in Goa and Zimbabwe. However, I want him to concentrate on The Hall.

The twins loved it in Norfolk and always enjoy Texel, so the sooner we are able to move out of London the better. Ideally I would like them to start in new schools the next academic year. I know the new houses will not be built, but we can easily rent something in the area."

In a hoarse whisper K-P said, "No, you won't." Upon hearing K-P's voice a couple of people turned their heads in our direction "you will stay with us."

I knew that when K-P made his mind up that only Jane could persuade him of a different point of view, and I suspected that on this subject she would probably agree with him.

"Thank you."

At that point one of our young administrative assistants came up to me. The young man said that there was a package at reception that required my personal signature before the courier would deliver the parcel. I went to reception, showed the lady courier my Lloyd's pass bearing my name and photograph, and she gave me the parcel after I had signed three documents. I took the package back to my desk and started to open the items that were individually wrapped in brown paper. The largest was the Kevlar jacket, thin and sleeveless, designed to be worn under a shirt. I was pleased I did not favour the slim fitting shirts, which was the fashion of my younger members of staff. The smallest item was a canister of Farb Gel. The last item weighed a few pounds and was in a case. When I opened the case, my eyes couldn't believe what I saw. Inside was a German Issue World War II automatic Luger pistol, the magazine was separate, as were twenty rounds of nine-millimetre ammunition. There was also a handwritten envelope addressed to me. As I opened the envelope I wondered what had transpired to make Eric relent to my request. Upon reading the note I realised that he hadn't. *'Marc, it is an antique but still works fine. I used it at the range last week. Hopefully you will only need to wave it around, try not to shoot anyone, including yourself. Instructions enclosed. N'*

"Nobby," I said out loud, and surmised that Eric could not give me anything, but he may have mentioned something to Nobby. I quickly put the three items in my briefcase and then returned to my emails.

The Mole Revealed

After being early in the office, I felt no guilt returning home before five o'clock, following the visit to my solicitor. My parents had sent a text to say they and the twins were fine. They were cruising out from Wroxham towards Potter Heigham and would moor there overnight. I returned the text acknowledging theirs and said that I was glad the children were having a great time. I checked my emails on my iPad, and saw that K-P had provided an initial quotation from a number of insurers, whom he listed, and said that they would see the remaining insurers tomorrow. He suggested that the risk should be bound on Thursday morning because of the start of the weekend in Dubai, as the shipment was due to commence on Sunday.

I then phoned Paul's house phone in Texel and Gerda picked up on the second ring.

"Hello my darling, how are you?" I asked.

"Exhausted." Despite what she said, she sounded much brighter than the previous day.

"How so?"

"I have spent hours going through Paul's clothes, possessions and his papers."

"Why today? I could have helped you when I joined you."

"It was cathartic for me, and I didn't want to sit around doing nothing," Gerda replied. "Anyway, it's done now, and tomorrow a house clearance person is coming to take almost everything away."

"Hmmm" I mused. I felt something was coming, "Yes, and why is that?"

"Well, when we move to the country we will need new furniture, won't we?"

"Yes I suppose so - will we be keeping the London flat?"

"Of course we will" Gerda said firmly "but I want to sell my flat in Amsterdam. So I thought I would move some of my things from there to here, and it might by cheaper to buy two of certain things, one for the country house in England…"

"And one for the country house in Texel" I finished her thought processes.

"Exactly and why don't you sell the property and land you were going to give to de Silva?"

"Why?" I asked.

"It's not worth much and it's a distraction you could do without."

"You seem to have it all worked out," I laughed.

"I have a clear view in my head," Gerda replied.

"And what shall we spend the money on?" I asked.

"Nothing, we will donate half to a charity in Zimbabwe and half to a charity in Goa. God knows charities are crying out for the cash."

"I was with our solicitor today and told him nothing about de Silva's death. I asked him to slow down on the transfer of the shares in Masterson Shipping and the sale of the land, but to hurry up with the documents on The Hall, so we can put that on the market."

"Good," Gerda replied.

"K-P was back at work for a few hours today."

"How is he?"

"Not bad……. not speaking much but looking stronger. All the girls in the office made a fuss of him."

Gerda laughed.

"He's working on this enquiry that Eric has orchestrated."

"Did you ask Eric for protection?" Gerda asked.

"I have in my possession a Kevlar jacket, pepper spray and an old automatic pistol, with bullets."

"Good," Gerda sounded relieved.

"K-P insisted that we stay at The Hall whilst the houses are being built, if we want the twins to start at a new school after the summer holidays."

"Yes, that would be lovely." Gerda obviously liked that idea.

I hoped that K-P wouldn't regret the offer when we descended upon them for more than just an overnight stay.

"So what does tomorrow hold for you my love?" I asked Gerda.

"After the house clearance man, I have a meeting with Paul's solicitor. He is coming from Rotterdam, and then after that I need to make arrangements for food and drinks after Paul's funeral."

"I hadn't thought of that. How many people are you expecting?" I asked.

"I have no idea, but I have answered the door at least six times, with neighbours offering their condolences."

"I would say aim for twenty to twenty-five," I suggested.

"That sounds about right. How are the twins?" Gerda asked.

"They're having a great time. I received a text from my parents earlier and not to expect a call until later, if at all."

"Ok my darling. I think I might have a bath, supper and then an early night."

"I wish I was there, and then we definitely would have an early night, possibly skipping food and bathing," I suggested.

"Stop it Marc, I will get all flustered and blush," Gerda replied in mock seriousness. "Go take a cold shower and calm down."

"Thanks!"

"Not at all."

"Love you loads, my darling, and speak in the morning. Sleep tight."

"You too." Gerda blew me a kiss down the phone before hanging up.

I yawned. The thought of Gerda going to bed had made me feel tired. I went into the kitchen, boiled a kettle and then made myself a big bowl of pasta. Whilst I was cooking, I opened a bottle of wine and drank at the same time as checking my personal emails. I seemed to receive as many personal emails as I did into my JPG address. Keeping on top of them both was sometimes a cottage industry in itself.

Before I knew it I had drunk half a bottle. I served myself the pasta with a stir-in sauce. As the pasta finished so did the wine. Unsurprisingly I felt tired so I turned in for the night. No television, no iPad, just cleaned my teeth and lights out.

Soon fast asleep, I dreamt of Gerda climbing in beside me, her warm body gently snuggling against me. She stroked my abdomen and ran her fingers down the inside of my thighs, using just the ends of her nails against my skin as her hand moved towards my groin. I could feel myself becoming aroused, and then felt Gerda gently blowing on the end of my nether regions. My hands went in search of her body to pull her onto me; they found her breasts fulsome, too fulsome, something was wrong. It wasn't Gerda beside me; I awoke abruptly from my dream.

"Take me Marc" the female voice whispered into my ear "I know you want me."

It was very dark and I couldn't see who was beside me but I recognised the voice. Its harshness and edge was unmistakeable, even when making love which we had done many years ago.

"Carla!" I cried out.

I swung around and tried to turn on the light beside my bed.

"No you don't." Carla's hand slapped me hard across the face and as I recoiled she brought her knee hard into my groin.

I tried to shout but I was gasping for air. She hit me again across the face shouting "You bastard. You will not deny me again. I will take everything from you."

I covered my face with my hands, crossed my legs to protect my groin, but Carla was still beating me as hard as she cold. Her attack now focused on my arms and stomach. My night vision was starting to come to me, and through my fingers I could see her face snarling, teeth bared and her large breasts swinging wildly as she threw each punch. Then gradually her punches started to lose their intensity as she tired. She now sat astride me and I slowly uncrossed my legs beneath her and brought my heels closer to my haunches.

She felt the movement beneath her and she cried out triumphantly "I knew you couldn't resist me." Her punches stopped for a second. In that instant I pushed my pelvis upward as hard and quickly as possible, my backside coming clear off the bed. Carla was propelled forward, totally not expecting my manoeuvre, her head hit the wall above the bed, and then she fell off me and the bed. In an instant, I jumped out of bed, flicking on the light I reached for earlier. She was groggy and there was a large bump on her forehead. I stood up and put on my boxer shorts that I had left lying by the bed. I fetched my dressing gown, which I put over Carla's naked body, not before removing the cord.

Carla was starting to come around, and I quickly bound her hands together. She was sobbing quietly with her eyes closed. I left her lying on the floor while I continued to put on some more clothes.

"Untie me Marc. Please?" she whimpered.

I said nothing.

"I won't try to hit you."

Still I kept quiet, debating what to do.

"I promise." She said through the tears running down her face.

I leaned down and loosened the cord so she could slip her hands out of the knots.

"Put the dressing gown on and then sit on the bed" I commanded "Do you want a hand?"

"Yes please." She smiled weakly at me.

When she was sitting on the bed I sat in a chair, which I positioned a couple of metres away in case she flew at me again.

"What the heck was that all about?" I asked.

"I love you and I want you to love me Marc." She hesitated for a few seconds and then continued "like we used to, before you met that bitch Mercédès."

I was astonished and didn't know what to say. I decided to quickly change the subject.

"How did you get here?" I asked.

"I have a key" Carla smirked at me.

"How?"

"I took an impression from your keys." Her smile became wider but at the same time there was a cruelness in her visage.

"When?" My one word questions seemed to be eliciting the right results so I continued.

"Two months ago. You always leave them on your desk at JPG, it was easy." Her smile broader than ever.

"Why? To spy on me?"

Before she answered I said "Did Jimmy know?"

"Of course not, he idolised you, he would have been mortified." Carla's voice sounded sad at the mention of Jimmy's voice.

303

"So you were prepared when you came to the office?"

Carla nodded.

A thought came to me - I confronted Carla with my suspicions. "You gave someone Jimmy's JPG login and password?"

She nodded.

"Who was it?"

She said nothing.

"Was it someone called Aziz, or de Silva or a Mr Dominique?" I asked.

Carla blushed as though she had been caught red handed with her hand in the cookie jar. "It wasn't him."

"But you know who he is, don't you?"

"Y-y-yes." She admitted.

"Did you tell de Silva about Jimmy and me going to Southampton?"

Again all she could do was nod her head.

"It killed Jimmy."

"No, *you* did," she shouted at me.

"Why betray Jimmy? OK, I jilted you, but that was years ago. You married Jimmy."

She said nothing.

"Didn't you love him?" I asked.

She bowed her head again, this time slowly shaking it.

"Then why marry him? To have children?" I questioned.

"To be close to you. My son was an accident."

I sat quietly for a few moments. "Then why give de Silva this information? Was it for money?"

She shook her head.

"Why for God's sake Carla?"

"He said that he would destroy you financially, you would lose all you've inherited."

"And then what? I am married and have children myself."

"Gerda would leave you if you had nothing, she would go back to Holland taking your precious twins." The spite was pouring out of her mouth. "You would not have your airs and graces and you would be mine again." She laughed and then in an instant started crying again.

"And, you passed him my phone message to you when I went to Holland."

She said nothing.

"Get dressed Carla, let me take you home."

"No. I don't live there anymore." She shot back at me.

"Why?" I asked.

"Dominic de Silva threatened me. I needed to disappear."

"Where are you living?"

"In a flat across the road from JPG. I can see right into your office Marc."

A shiver ran through me, but at least I knew that the feeling I had of being watched was not without foundation.

"Where's your son?"

"He's with my mother in Frinton" Carla replied.

The Haunted

I hardly slept for the rest of the night. I called a taxi for Carla and she left just before midnight. If any of the neighbours saw her leave, knowing that Gerda was away, they could have a field day at my expense.

Eventually I dozed off and then woke with a start at the sound of my phone ringing, it was six o'clock and it was Eric calling. After Carla had left, I sent Eric a text saying I had some important news. So whilst I expected a call from him, I didn't expect it so early.

"What news?" he asked without any preamble.

"Good morning Eric," I replied.

"Don't be sarcastic. My arse is hanging out there at the moment and I need some good news."

"Well I don't know if this is good news, but it certainly helps to clear the mist."

"What is it?" Eric was becoming impatient.

I explained that Carla had a key and got into my flat and that she attacked me. I told Eric about Carla passing on Jimmy's JPG login and password to de Silva, and that she was the one who told de Silva about Jimmy and I going to Southampton, plus my departure to Holland. I left out the part about her wanting me to make love to her, although I would tell Gerda but only when we were together.

"Why would she do that?" Eric asked.

I told him that Carla still held a light for me and she hoped to destroy me financially in the hope that Gerda would leave me taking the twins back to Holland.

"'Hell hath no fury like a woman scorned,'" Eric quoted down the phone.

"Thanks," I replied.

"Where is she now?" he asked.

"She lives in a flat next to JPG's offices. Apparently she can see into my office."

"That's more than a bit weird" Eric observed "and uncomfortable for you."

"You're not kidding. I am going to move out of my office and convert it into a client meeting room with a cocktail cabinet, sofa and chairs."

"Very decadent," Eric mocked me.

"I have been thinking about moving out onto the floor with the rest of the team. It's becoming the 'done-thing' in London. InterContinental have recently moved to agile-working and apparently it has been a big success."

"I apologise" Eric retorted "how very politically correct."

"I thought so too."

"When are you leaving for Holland?"

"Tonight."

"And during the day you're in the office?"

"This morning certainly, but this afternoon I have some private matters to deal with".

"Has K-P everything under control?"

"Yes, and he will be relieved to learn of Jimmy's innocence."

"Please ask him not to tell anyone else yet."

"Understood Eric." Upon which I ended the phone call.

I didn't want to fall asleep but after unburdening myself to Eric I relaxed and fatigue enveloped me. I woke with a shock to my phone ringing. It was Gerda. We spoke briefly and I told her about Carla breaking into the flat and that she was the person who had given information to de Silva.

"Why?"

"She was jealous."

"Have all the locks changed" Gerda was very firm "and organise to have an alarm fitted."

"I am taking the afternoon off work to do just that and go and see our solicitors again."

"Good."

Gerda asked me to do some shopping for her and requested that I bring some other of her clothes with me.

The phone rang almost immediately and this time it was my parents. They said they had decided to go to Great Yarmouth for the day. The boat would be left at Potter Heigham and they would take a bus. The twins were very excited, because they had been promised a trip to the fun fair and candy floss.

I showered and took myself to the office but falling back to sleep meant I was pretty much the last person on the floor by the time I arrived. I felt uncomfortable as soon as I entered my office, trying to close the blind which was proving difficult as I can never remember them being closed.

K-P wasn't at this desk, but I had seen Julian and caught his eye, motioning him to come into my office.

"Good morning Marc," he greeted me.

I smiled in reply to his politeness "Good morning to you too. What plans have you for the day?"

"Well I am going to scoot up to Lloyd's shortly and try and see more underwriters on this bullion enquiry."

"It's a bit early isn't it?"

As he replied, his chest puffed out slightly "I e-mailed some people who I couldn't see yesterday and I have arranged appointments in……" he looked at his watch "fifteen minutes' time."

"OK. Before you go, can you please send me your market sheet?"

"Sure," he replied.

"Does it have all the names of the individuals you broked the risk to?"

"Not yet, but I can populate those details at lunchtime."

"OK, but please make sure I have it completed – including the declinatures – before you go into the market this afternoon, as long as you will have seen all the underwriters who could possibly write this risk."

"I should be done by then because I sent lots of emails yesterday, and a number of underwriters have declined the risk already."

"Did they give a reason as to why they declined?"

"Yes, do you want the reason entered on the spreadsheet" Julian hesitated because, whilst it was good practice to enter the reason, most brokers found it a laborious task.

I replied "The reason for the declinatures is very important for this enquiry, which I am monitoring carefully to be able to judge our trading relationship with the market." It was not a complete fabrication because JPG had been the focus of someone's unwelcome attention. K-P was standing at the door of my office as I finished talking to Julian.

"Morning K-P, please come in. Julian, would you be kind enough to close the door on your way out, please?"

Julian left and then I recounted Carla's visit. At first K-P was bemused about Carla attacking me, but when I told him that she was the source by which de Silva gained access to JPG, putting himself and Jimmy in harm's way, he became very cross. And when I told him her aim was to destroy my family he was furious. He stood up, walked over to the window, opened the blind and stared at all of the buildings overlooking my office, presumably to try to spot the flat where she was living. Luckily for Carla he could not discern where she was living. As he turned back towards me the anger had turned to tears.

"Poor Jimmy," he whispered quietly, and sat down again opposite me.

I stood up and closed the blinds again. "We need to trap them K-P. I want you to look at Julian's market sheet, which he said he would complete at lunchtime, and see if there are any anomalies. Particularly underwriters declining the risk who you would normally expect to participate on this type of risk. Check other similar risks and use your instinct. Anyone who has declined or quoted a premium higher than normal, I would like you to e-mail them and gently challenge them."

He nodded in reply.

"Then tomorrow I want us to give an order to the market at a premium that has been quoted by a respectable leading underwriter – say Deeks – where you would expect most insurers would participate. Increase the sum insured substantially to give a reason why we need full market support and Julian needs to push them hard for their capacity. Once we have done that we need to reassess which insurers have not given their usual capacity. Then on Friday we are going to cancel the risk because we became aware that it was going to be the subject of a heist. We are going to say that the information on the potential robbery had been leaked from the London insurance market, and that Lloyd's, the FCA, Italian and British Police Forces were investigating. I am then going to phone the most senior person I can at each insurer who declined the risks and say we are co-operating with the various authorities as we think we have been at the centre of fraudulent behaviour by a number of individual underwriters."

"Does Eric agree to this?" K-P said softly and I could tell that his voice was recovering from the trauma in Dubai.

"It was his idea. They think they know the protagonists. And they are monitoring them closely, hoping this will panic some of them. Some might even break ranks and come forward."

"It not, then what?" K-P asked.

"Then they will call for Lloyd's and the FCA to suspend those underwriters, of whom they are suspicious, whilst they investigate the slow methodical way by pouring over the risks they wrote – or didn't – and cross referencing to the claims into the market over the past five years."

K-P mouthed the word 'Wow'.

"Eric's in a tough spot by losing de Silva and is fearful his investigation will be pulled, possibly even him losing his position."

"So Marcus Edge to the rescue?" K-P whispered sarcastically.

"Well it wouldn't be out of character for me to stir things up would it?"

K-P just pulled a face.

"You know I am leaving for Holland this afternoon, and not back until Tuesday? Paul's funeral and then my Mother's birthday."

He nodded.

"Can you run things when I am away?"

Again he nodded.

I spent the rest of the morning catching up on other work, and met with JPG's Chief Financial Officer and Chief Operations Officer for our regular monthly update. The final figures for the first quarter were showing a good start to the year as the world economies continued to recover from the Global Financial Crisis and the United Kingdom's decision to leave the European Union had little effect this far. With that information I asked that they prepare proposals for the next formal Board Meeting for an office refurbishment taking me onto the trading floor, as well as anyone else who had offices. Also, I asked if they could cost an upgrade to our IT system with improved security, and put feelers out regarding the salary for a Chief Security Officer. I hoped Gupta would apply, when the post was advertised, but I wanted to see other options. They were both pleased to see me loosening the purse strings, and, seizing on an opening, they suggested that we should consider investing in new teams, as the major brokers consolidation was presenting opportunities.

The whole insurance market was in a state of flux following a number of high profile mergers. Lloyd's themselves had challenged the community to think about how efficiencies could be made, through their Target Operating Model process, so that London did not lose its position in the worldwide insurance market. The uncertainty around Brexit meant there was a general review by insurers and brokers alike.

I went out to get myself a coffee and pick up a sandwich. On my way back Carla was standing on the corner of the street next to JPG's offices. She had a big bruise on her forehead, and she was wearing a big pair of sunglasses. When I approached her I could see that she had two black eyes. I was preparing for her wrath, but she was unexpectedly calm, and asked if I had reported her visit to my flat to the police.

"No," I replied, which was correct because Eric didn't actually work for the police.

"But if I were you I would make myself scarce."

"Why?" Carla questioned.

"K-P was furious with you, and it was all I could do to stop him searching all the properties overlooking my office."

Carla was already looking pale, but she blanched further when she heard K-P was on the rampage, because the fearsome Jane would not be too far behind.

"Carla, you never indicated you were upset when I married Mercédès, and even when I was estranged from Mercédès you didn't say anything."

Carla didn't say anything; a tear ran from behind the big panda sunglasses then another ran down the other cheek. She didn't want to take off the sunglasses to wipe her eyes. She searched in her bag, and when she couldn't find anything, I offered her my clean handkerchief. She blew her nose loudly, and sniffed, then offered me my handkerchief back but I motioned for her to keep it.

"Well?" I wanted to know more.

"I was cross with you; in fact, I have always been an angry person." She paused for a moment and then she started sobbing, tears cascading down both cheeks.

Even I felt for her, and I held her in my arms. She buried her head into my neck.

"Jimmy and my child stopped me being angry for the first time in my life."

"But I thought you said you didn't love Jimmy?"

"Of course I did. Not like I love you but yes, Jimmy's kindness and fidelity was lovely. Just I didn't fancy him like I lust for you and your power."

"Believe me power is not an aphrodisiac, quite the opposite actually."

"But I would like to find out for myself," Carla was almost shouting.

I said nothing to calm her down.

After almost a minute I asked to whom she gave the JPG log-in and password.

"I don't know her name. She just called me one day and asked me if I would help taking you down a peg or two. To stop you wearing that smug look on your face. It sounded a good idea at the time. She sent me a letter asking for certain information which I gathered over time."

"When was this?" I asked.

"About two and half years ago, just before I fell pregnant."

"How did you communicate with her?"

"She gave me half a dozen envelopes with a Post Office Box Number, and I sent the details she wanted in these."

"Do you have any of these envelopes left?"

She shook her head.

"Can you remember the Post Office Box Number."

Again a shake of the head.

"How did you meet de Silva?"

"He bumped into me in the supermarket one day after Johnny was born. He said he wanted me to supply information directly to him so I could ensure my son's future. I agreed and initially he was charming but he felt that things were not moving quickly enough, and wanted one big pay-day and then get out."

I said nothing.

"You met up with him in France, didn't you?"

"You are remarkably well informed."

"He was keeping in touch with me throughout. He was really pleased when you agreed to give him Masterson Shipping."

I thought hard before saying what I did. "He's dead." I was hoping to shock her and it had the desired effect, because the redness in her cheeks from crying disappeared instantly.

"How?"

"Stabbed; it took him two days to die." I was deliberately trying to put her ill at ease, and it was working, so I added "It was by Krishna."

Carla stared at me, possibly because I was scaring her. Whatever, it had the desired effect.

"Marc, what I do know is that JPG was not picked at random as the intermediary to front this scheme. Dominique de Silva had a personal vendetta against you, but the other people involved, within Lloyd's, wanted to bring you down.

314

And for you personally to be blamed for leaking underwriting information to criminals. I wouldn't say that the primary focus of the operation was an elaborate set-up of JPG, but it certainly was an important secondary aim."

I was surprised by Carla's vocabulary, certainly not what I was used to, but I was also surprised by what she said. "Why?"

"I don't know that…..." after a moment she added "sorry Marc."

I didn't know if she was apologizing for not knowing the identity of who else was involved, or whether it was remorsefulness for what she had done.

"I am going to heed your warning and disappear for a while Marc. Please tell K-P that I didn't mean for him and Jimmy to get wrapped up in this…..." she searched for the right word "situation." She kissed me on the cheek, turned around towards Liverpool Street Station, and walked away at a brisk pace.

I watched her until she turned the corner. She did not look back. I felt a great sadness, as I had thought of Carla as a friend and ally. Had I really been that cruel and insensitive to her, so that she wanted to hurt me?

I returned to the office and spoke to K-P to make sure he didn't overdo things. I cleared my desk as I wouldn't be coming back until the following Tuesday and I left the offices of JPG vowing that when I returned I would make some serious changes. I was haunted by what Carla said to me, so before I left the office I dropped a note to John Eastwood asking him for a whole morning's strategy meeting for the following Tuesday when I would return from Holland. Six days would allow me to marshal and clarify my thoughts.

I drove home with Carla's words ringing in my ears. I was home only a few minutes when the doorbell rang. It was the locksmith. I explained what was required and he agreed to temporarily change the locks on the exterior doors today, but the alarm, window locks and new exterior doors would take longer. I explained that I would be away until Monday evening. After a bit of pressure, as well as agreeing to pay him triple time overtime rates for the weekend, he confirmed the work would be completed before we returned.

About another half-hour elapsed and then there was another ring at my door. It was Chris Worcester, our family solicitor for personal matters. I invited him into the kitchen and offered him tea which he accepted.

"So what was so important that we couldn't discuss at my offices?" Chris said in a half mocking tone.

We had known each other from rugby playing days and whilst he might not have a particular specialism, he had a good all round legal knowledge, which had been invaluable to me when requiring advice on matrimonial, corporate, property, trustee and even criminal matters. Most importantly I trusted him and he was very discrete.

"I have some confidential and difficult matters to discuss with you, plus I am having the locks changed this afternoon."

He looked up surprised "Are you and Gerda…...?"

I interrupted him and assured him that all was good in that direction, but I did explain about the episode with Carla the previous evening.

"Do you still want to proceed with the trust for Carla and Jimmy's child?"

I nodded. "The transfer of Masterson Shipping to de Silva is now not required, but the sale of the land in Goa and Zimbabwe is now back on."

"Why?"

"He's dead. Krishna stabbed him and he then killed her."

"Wow."

I passed across to him a sheet of paper on which I had scribbled the following tasks: -

'Sell The Hall after portioning enough land for two houses to be built for K-P's family and ourselves.

Apply for planning permission for the two new houses, together with road access.

Convert Masterson Shipping into a Limited Liability Partnership with a view to the current management and employees buying out my shareholding completely in five to ten years.

Convert JPG into a Limited Liability Partnership with a view to the current management and employees buying out seventy-four percent of my shareholding within five to ten years.

Dispose of the land in Zimbabwe and Goa and the proceeds to be donated to Oxfam and Save the Children in equal amounts, for exclusive use in those countries.

Sell Gerda's flat in Amsterdam.

Create trust for Carla and Jimmy's child Johnny, with Carla as sole trustee, amount to be finalised.

Create trusts for Jack and Catherine with access when the twins reach the age of thirty-five, or earlier if both Gerda and I predecease prior to them being thirty-five.'

"Is that all?" he asked sardonically.

"For the moment," I smiled as I replied.

"I presume Gerda is happy with all of this?"

"All, except the shareholding in Masterson and JPG. I am flying to Holland tonight for Paul's funeral tomorrow, and I don't expect any problems, particularly with respect to Masterson Shipping."

"And JPG?"

"I will still retain a golden share so I can prevent it being sold if I disagree."

He looked down the list once more and asked how much would be put into the twins' trusts.

"I will ask Gerda but my idea is to split the payments from Masterson and JPG between the four of us each year, depending upon what we require for their education needs, holidays, etc."

We then spent another hour going over each of the tasks. As we reached the conclusion he asked what priority he should apply to each task.

"As I listed them, please" I replied.

Goodbye to Paul

After Chris left I threw some clothes into an overnight bag, and phoned Gerda to see whether she wanted anything from London. She said no but reminded me that she wished me to pick up some items from her flat in Amsterdam. I drove to Stansted Airport, caught the flight to Schiphol. Once at Schiphol, I hired a small car, made a detour to Gerda's flat and then headed towards Texel, hoping I would make the last ferry of the day. I arrived at the Den Helder port at quarter past nine so I made the last ferry with only fifteen minutes to spare. An hour later, I was lying in bed with Gerda slowing caressing her, and after all that had happened over the last couple of days, words were not needed and we devoured each other, falling asleep from exhaustion.

We woke early and I brought her coffee and we caught up on my meeting with Chris and Gerda agreed with all my instructions to him. The previous night's exertions had made us both weary and we drifted back to sleep, but thankfully our slumber was broken by my parents calling to wish Gerda courage for the day ahead, as well as giving us the opportunity to speak with the twins now they were back at my parents' house. They had spent a wonderful time on the rivers and broads of Norfolk and both asked if we could do a holiday with them on a boat. Both Gerda and I assured them that we probably would do so and soon. I wanted to spend as much time with my children as possible, and that was part of my thinking about the disposal of a lot of my assets, together with a disproportionate amount of responsibility. I had enjoyed a lot of my parents love and devotion whilst growing up, and I wanted to do the same with my children.

Gerda and I attacked the chores of the day with gusto and mostly in silence. I wished to give her support but also let her be alone with her thoughts.

The hearse arrived at Paul's house at quarter to twelve. We didn't want a mourners' car and we followed the hearse in the small car I had hired. The church was only a few minutes away and after the service we would be driving across the island to the crematorium. We were expecting a few of Paul's neighbours, but not many more as Paul had kept himself to himself since moving to Texel. We were therefore astounded to find the church packed, with some people standing at the back. I looked around and most people seemed to be dressed locals, but over half were in lounge suits. I recognised some from Paul's old shipping company, but even more surprising was the number of people from England. I saw K-P with Jane, John Eastwood, Eric, Simon, Brian Smithson, as well as half-a-dozen members of the Lambers, of which Paul became a member after visiting the UK on a number of occasions to watch the Lloyd's Rugby Team in London and on tour.

The service was short, even though the pastor spoke firstly in Dutch and then reprised his sermon and key prayers in English. Gerda spoke for some length in both Dutch and English. She held back the tears, and on more than one occasion brought coughs and smiles from the congregation.

Gerda and I followed the coffin out of the church and saw it loaded into the hearse. I then turned to find K-P and Jane standing beside Gerda. Jane was speaking to Gerda whilst giving her a hug.

"This is a surprise," I said to K-P.

He smiled.

Jane returned to K-P's side. "We were going to come anyway and Eric Jones called K-P yesterday to say he had organised a plane from Stansted, the old terminal, to the airport at Den Helder."

"Wow," I exclaimed.

"I think Eric is hoping that he can persuade you and Gerda to return with us tonight," Jane said.

"Why?"

K-P whispered "So that you are with him when you call the senior people at the insurers who have agreed to underwrite the gold transit risk."

Anticipating my questions K-P passed me a piece of paper. *'The order to bind the risk and to increase the sum insured was given today. Julian is out placing and pushing underwriters for bigger participation, and I am emailing those who have declined so far.'*

"I have rented a car that I need to return to Schiphol…"

K-P pointed to Brian Smithson, indicating that he had been detailed to drive it.

K-P could see I was starting to get cross.

"Don't blame Brian. He offered when Eric learnt you had hired a car." The croakiness in K-P's voice was worsening.

"I think I need to have a word with Eric." I was still smarting.

Jane was Eric's unexpected defender. "Marc, Eric's arse is in a sling on this whole investigation. It's been ongoing for over two years, his main lead and witness to turn Queen's Evidence died in his custody. Millions of pounds and Eric's career are about to disappear in a puff of smoke."

"I don't like being taken for granted."

"I know, and the timing with Paul's funeral stinks, but that is how it is," Jane said quite firmly.

"Gerda may not be ready to return today."

Jane nodded. "Perhaps Brian could be persuaded to stay on for a day."

"Hmm, I suppose so, but I don't fancy telling Gerda that Eric wants me back in London."

"Let's do it together" Jane offered and she and K-P walked over to Gerda before I could stop her.

Gerda embraced K-P and he wrapped his enormous arms around her, almost obliterating her from my view.

Jane was speaking to Gerda as I joined them. "Eric flew us all out here to pay our respects to Paul, and he wondered whether in return you and Marc could accompany us home today?"

Gerda looked at me but I just shrugged my shoulders.

Gerda asked why.

Jane explained that the plane was only chartered for one day and it would be extremely helpful if Marc and K-P were in London early tomorrow morning.

I could see that Gerda was not happy. And she said she would think about it later.

Other mourners paid their respects to Gerda and me. When Eric came up to Gerda I saw her slightly stiffen when he spoke to her.

After fifteen minutes from exiting the church we were following the hearse to the crematorium.

"What did Eric say to you?" I asked.

"He said that you will not be safe until the perpetrators of this fraud are caught."

"That's emotional blackmail." I felt my face reddening.

"Yes, but he is right Marc......" she paused for a moment "you should return with them on the proviso they stay close to you. I will come back tomorrow as planned."

"Brian has offered to drive the car to Schiphol."

"That's very sweet of him. I don't want to be alone tonight. I will ask him if he will stay."

"I love you my darling," I said.

"And I you Marc, and" she put her left hand on my leg as I drove "I think I'm pregnant."

The Snare

Gerda's organisation of Paul's final departure was meticulous. The short service committing Paul's coffin to the furnace at the crematorium was accompanied by the hymn Jerusalem and then we sang Abide with me, with some of the Dutch mourners shedding more than a tear or two due to the poignancy of the hymn they sang for the first time. We then returned to Paul's house for the wake which was quite an uplifting affair as the fun side of his life was remembered by people. His neighbours on Texel said how much he doted on our children, and he looked forward to seeing them when they visited. Everyone agreed that the time Paul had after waking from his coma was a bonus for him, as his life could have ended without ever meeting the twins. I kept to myself the fact he would not be meeting their new brother or sister and now, with the possibility Gerda was pregnant, I could see she was carrying herself differently and wondered how long it would be until others noticed.

About four o'clock, Eric came over to me and said we needed to start to make tracks. I looked around the room and saw that it was largely the British contingent left. I took Gerda into the bedroom to say my goodbyes in private.

"I have agreed with Eric that I will come and pick you up on Friday at Stansted and that we will be going directly to Norfolk."

"Good," Gerda replied.

"We will have done our part, and it is up to him to finish everything."

"Protect yourself Marc. Keep wearing the Kevlar vest and carry that pistol with you."

"I will my darling."

We kissed our farewells, and as soon as I returned to the sitting room Eric whisked the London party away, and I turned to see Brian at Gerda's side. I hoped that Eric's planning would mean this situation would soon be at an end.

A mini-bus took us to the airport via the ferry and in less than an hour from leaving Paul's we were airborne. Another forty minutes and we were on the ground at Stansted Airport, albeit I needed to make my way to the main terminal so I could collect my car from the mid-term stay car park.

"Marc, I will pick you up at seven o'clock tomorrow morning," Eric said.

"Eric, K-P's going to stay with me tonight."

"OK it's both of you I will see in the morning."

K-P and I had a lovely evening. K-P chose a meal from his favourite Indian restaurant, which I ordered and had delivered. The food was marvellous, together with a full stomach and a bottle of red wine from my wine rack, I was ready for bed by ten o'clock. I slept deeply until my phone rang at six o'clock. It was Gerda wishing me luck for the day ahead. Brian was still sleeping, but when awake he had agreed to help her continue to clear Paul's house. I finished my call with Gerda and made my way to the bathroom. As I left the bathroom I was met by a fully dressed K-P brandishing a mug of tea and butter soaked toast.

"Leave in fifteen minutes?" I asked.

He nodded in reply.

The Kevlar vest was hanging on the chair by my bed and, to appease Gerda I put it on, but left the pistol in the bottom of my wardrobe.

Predictably Eric was punctual and he had Simon beside him in the black mini-van. I began to wonder if it was in fact his own personal vehicle. We drove south and then through the Rotherhithe Tunnel and towards Lewisham where we arrived at the building where de Silva and Krishna had been held. The inside looked very different, with the pre-fabricated living quarters now replaced by a communications centre in the middle of the warehouse, and a few glass booths which I guessed were for quiet conversations. There were already a dozen people sat at their workstations which comprised at least three computer screens. The workstations were arranged in two crescents one behind another and about five metres in front of the nearest crescent was a bank of twelve television screens. I guessed that each television screen was related to each workstation, and by the changing pictures I further guessed that Eric's colleagues were switching the television screen feed between their three screens.

"This is impressive," I commented.

"We have over thirty people under surveillance and the visual feeds are all from close circuit cameras near where we think the suspects are at the moment."

"Did you put the cameras in place?" I asked.

"Goodness, no, these are all there already."

I raised my eyebrows.

"London has more close circuit cameras than anywhere else in the world."

Eric escorted me and K-P to one of the booths. "OK Marc, the key is the scheduled call this morning to de Silva without which this whole operation, and possibly my future, is in tatters." If Eric was nervous, he was hiding it well.

Simon joined us and then proceeded to play a series of phrases and sentences, which he had configured from recordings of when de Silva had been held in the facility.

There were over fifty vignettes of de Silva speaking, and Simon had them all numbered, so that in an instant he could press a button to play the relevant recording, dependent upon what was being said at the other end of the phone. It took nearly forty-five minutes to play through all the recordings and it appeared to me that most eventualities had been covered. Most were short responses from one word to six words, very few were longer that six words. Simon explained that longer phrases were more difficult to stitch together, because of the voice inflection.

When they finished I said "Equally impressive."

"The bait is out there and K-P chivvied the insurers again yesterday and we now have a completed placement for the increased limit. When can we have the placing slip?" Simon asked.

"Julian will be in the office at nine o'clock and I have already asked him to send it across as soon as he is in the office," I replied.

"OK Marc, we have prepared a script for you." Whereupon Eric passed me a sheet of A4, both sides covered with detailed instructions.

"Have you got the necessary telephone numbers?" Eric asked me and I pointed to my iPad that I had brought with me. "Good. I want you to say to each person the same story, please don't deviate from the script, otherwise it could affect our success when bringing a prosecution."

I read the paper Eric had given me. Essentially I was to explain that as part of an ongoing investigation by Lloyd's of London and the Financial Conduct Authority, they have become aware that a transit risk placed this week by JPG was the subject of a potential robbery. It was apparent that the risk information had been provided to the potential thieves from the underwriters in London. Accordingly, the transit and the associated policy had been cancelled. Furthermore, it is believed that this risk is not an isolated incident, and that there were a number of other risks placed by JPG under investigation. K-P would be contacting the individual underwriters by email, who underwrote the risk together with a list of the other risks that are being investigated, and that a team from Lloyd's internal investigations team will arrive at noon. The Lloyd's team will collect any papers with regard to these risks, as well as the personal computers of the underwriters, who underwrote the risks. If the underwriters are not available today, I was to ask that they nominate someone to assist with the collection of the papers and computers today.

"Anything else I should know?" I enquired.

"If they say that we need a warrant, you are to explain that - if need be - one could be obtained but that you would hope that they would wish to co-operate with their regulators in an investigation into fraudulent activities."

I nodded. "What happens after I speak to them?"

"At the end of each call we will have a quick debrief, and then K-P will email the underwriter of that insurer you have just spoken to. I expect that we will get to the underwriter first, because the person you speak to may call his own superior - or his legal team - before contacting the underwriter."

"Are you monitoring the phones of all the underwriters?" I asked.

"Yes. Those we know about. If they have personal 'pay-as-you-go' mobiles we don't have those details," Eric replied.

"But I guess if they don't use their phones you are monitoring, then that could place them under suspicion?"

"Possibly," Eric said.

Eric left K-P and I to continue to swot up on our scripts.

"Do you think this will work?" I asked K-P.

K-P just shrugged his shoulders and raised his eyebrows.

We both continued reading and then the mobile phone Julian bought rang.

"Hello."

"It's Julian." And his voice filled the room as I switched to speaker mode.

"Hi Julian, I have K-P here with me. How are you getting on?"

"Not bad, I am in the office." I checked my watch and it was only half past seven. Julian was keen and I recognised a lot of myself in him.

"Have you the completed placing slip?"

"Yes," Julian replied.

"Can you scan the whole document and then send it to me and K-P together with the market sheet, showing all those who wrote the risk and those who declined please?"

"OK, and then what?" He was obviously curious.

"Nothing for the moment. K-P and I will be back about lunchtime. Thanks Julian," I called out and then I ended the conversation.

Eric returned at eight o'clock brandishing a hot bacon roll for me plus n egg and melted cheese roll for K-P.

"Any news from Julian?" He asked.

"Yes, the placing slip and market sheet just came through on my laptop." K-P passed the computer to Eric so he could see.

"Great, if I could borrow your laptop?" He looked at me. I nodded.

"I'll have it back to you in ten minutes."

"Wouldn't it be easier for me to just e-mail it to you?" I asked.

Both K-P and Eric looked at me as though I was an idiot. They said nothing until the stupidity of what I said sunk in.

"Ah!" It finally dawned on me that the hackers were probably monitoring JPG's e-mails.

Eric smiled as though indulging an errant child. "Can you go through the market sheet and indicate what the insurers' maximum and usual capacity would be for a risk like this."

"And the same script to everyone you speak to, whether they underwrote the risk or not," Eric said as he exited the glass booth.

We worked on the market sheet which helped to pass the time before de Silva's scheduled Thursday call. I could see that Eric's earlier composure had evaporated and he was taut with nerves. He and Simon came into the booth some ten minutes before nine. "We need you to try to identify the voice," Simon said.

The minutes ticked by and no call at nine. Another five minutes passed and Eric was becoming more agitated.

"Damn it!" Eric brought his fist down heavily on the table. "Are you sure you haven't told anyone about de Silva's death?"

The phone rang at that very instant, the old fashioned peel was being amplified throughout the building. Eric closed the door to the booth and nodded to Simon. Simon moved the cursor on his screen and the ringing stopped.

"Hello." It was Dominique de Silva's voice greeting the caller.

"Are you aware of a large bullion shipment from Rome to Dubai?" The voice was heavily disguised as though it had been passed through a synthesizer.

"No," came de Silva's reply.

"On Friday a shipment will be leaving Rome on an Alitalia cargo flight bound for Dubai." The vocabulary definitely placed the speaker as English and well educated in my opinion.

"OK," was the response.

"It will land at Dubai Airport very early Saturday morning. A number of armoured security vans will be used to transport the gold. The security guards will be armed, ex-military, and will not know which van is carrying the bullion. The gold will be in the second and third vans…."

"Time is very short," de Silva's voice was quiet with each consonant clearly enunciated, and the melodious cadences were very noticeable, as they were being amplified through the digital telephone network.

"This is the last time I will call you, so you can leave if you want." There was a pause "Well!" The metallic voice was slightly louder and obviously impatient for an answer.

"I am thinking." Simon was playing a dangerous game and Eric stared at him hard. "Ok," de Silva's voice eventually replied.

"Good, the details of the shipment are as follows…" the metallic voice was on a much more even keel and then proceeded to provide the exact timings and route of the convoy "… you will need to intercept the convoy on the open road, because once at the vault the opportunity will be gone."

"OK." Simon finished the call and then the line went dead.

No-one said anything for at least two minutes after the call.

It was K-P whose whispered voice broke the silence. "I have no idea who it was."

"Me neither," I said but there was something nagging in the back of my head.

Eric stood up and paced the booth.

"It's shit or bust," Simon said.

Eric nodded to me and left the room. That was the signal for me to start phoning.

All in all there were over fifty insurers to call, and I started at the top of the Placing Slip working my way down. The biggest problem was tracking down the senior person at each firm, and over half had to call me back. Some were dragged out of meetings once they realised the importance of the call. Some were definitely dodging me and so I would ask to speak with the head of compliance and magically that seemed to open the door. As soon as I spoke to the senior person I would cross them off my list and then K-P would email the actual underwriters and, even though we were heading towards a Bank Holiday weekend, most people were in the office.

We worked quickly without a break but it was nearly noon by the time I had finished speaking with the insurers who write the risk, and then I started with those who declined the risk. The declining insurers were split evenly as to those who were understanding and those who thought it was a hassle and not their problem. Almost all of the insurers who wrote the risk were more than accommodating, but that was unsurprising given we had saved them from an almost total loss; even though the whole transit was fictitious in the first place.

I finished at a quarter to three and my voice was very strained. The last dozen calls were very easy, because word had spread around the market like wild bushfire, and underwriters were expecting the call.

Eric came into the booth when I had made the final call. He looked tired, his face etched with worry lines.

"Well it's done; all we can do is wait to see if the tangled web starts to break."

"Any unusual activity from any of the suspects?" I asked.

"Even if there was I couldn't – wouldn't – tell you Marc."

I pulled a mock frown in his direction. Not even a flicker of a smile. He was very serious.

"You can go back to JPG and of course continue as normal. We will be impounding your files on this and the other placements we identified. Over the weekend, can you plan to run your Disaster Recovery exercise please? We will be providing your IT manager – Gupta – with some assistance to collect evidence."

"When might we know what the outcome is?" K-P asked quietly.

"A much more sensible question K-P," Eric replied "but I am afraid it will only be after our investigations are complete, and those could take as long as six months."

As we were driven back to JPG's offices, I felt deflated. All the adrenalin had pumped through my veins and I felt both physically and mentally exhausted. K-P was asleep before we entered the Rotherhithe Tunnel, and we spent only a short time in the office. I spoke to Julian and told him the bullion transit risk had been compromised, and it had to be cancelled. Julian was obviously suspicious, but he kept a straight face and he said he would get the lines on the placing slips marked as not-taken-up. I spoke to Gupta and asked if he could conduct the Disaster Recovery protocol this weekend as it was a Bank Holiday.

I called Gerda, she and Brian were in the midst of returning the two cars to the car rental at Schiphol Airport. I told her it all went well and that I would pick her up at Stansted Airport, when we would go direct to Norfolk for the long Bank Holiday weekend. Gerda asked me to pack certain clothes for my mother's birthday on Sunday. I went in search of K-P to offer him a lift home, only to find he had already left the office.

I took the bus to go home and it was full of children enjoying the final days of their Easter Holiday. The chatter was incessant and I looked forward to seeing Jack and Catherine. They would be back at school the following week as they had longer holidays than the children on the bus. I smiled to myself as I thought that the more we paid for education the less time the children spent at school. When I challenged the twins' school on this point they replied that the school day was longer than most schools, and they needed time for the boarders to return home – often overseas – during the holidays.

To keep awake I showered and then made myself a large cup of coffee, and drank it as I packed my and Gerda's clothes for the long weekend. As I was about to leave our bedroom I saw the Kevlar vest that I wore earlier hanging on a chair. I was going to leave it there but the thought of Gerda being nervous upset me, and I threw it in the overnight bag. The luger, however, remained buried under my sweater on a shelf above my suits.

I arrived just before six o'clock at Stansted Airport. Gerda's plane had arrived, but she and Brian had not come through customs. I rang The Hall and Jane answered "Hello."

"It's Marc, how's K-P?"

"In bed. His mouth is sore and he is very tired. I don't want to wake him." Jane's voice was resolute.

"Tell him not to come in until Tuesday when I return from Norfolk."

"He wasn't going to anyway; we're taking the children away for the weekend to Paris."

"Lovely, have a great time," I replied. "Tell him I will see him when he is next in the office."

It was another fifteen minutes before Gerda and Brian made an appearance through arrivals. Brian headed toward the rail station, but not before I thanked him profusely, and Gerda gave him a hug accompanied by a peck on his check.

Gerda's mood seemed lighter. With Paul's funeral behind her, and my part in the Lloyd's investigation over, we chatted about future plans as we drove to Norfolk. Gerda was excited about the building of the houses in the grounds of The Hall, and she was delighted with Jane's offer to stay there, to allow the twins to start new schools in the Autumn. Even discussing the selling of her flat in Amsterdam, and how we would modify and adapt Paul's house on Texel, Gerda was positive. We were both greatly looking forward to seeing the twins, as well as celebrating my Mother's birthday over a sunny weekend in Norfolk. "What's not to like?" we chorused together. A chapter closed.

Big skies in Norfolk

We were woken by the twins jumping on the bed at seven o'clock. They were overjoyed to see us and wanted us to get up straightaway, to be followed by taking the dog for a walk. It was the neighbours' dog that my father had borrowed for the time whilst Jack and Catherine stayed, and in that time they had become avid dog walkers. It was an English spaniel which obediently responded to their commands. What then transpired was obviously a well-orchestrated episode, with Jack holding Gerda's hand and Catherine holding mine, whilst the spaniel roamed freely on the path towards the beach. Almost in unison they asked whether they could have a dog of their own. They explained in detail how they would look after the dog, and they had worked out an exercise programme, which they said would be good for the whole family. Gerda and I couldn't help but laugh. Gerda said yes, when we move to the country. Their faces fell as they thought it to be delaying tactics on our part, and then Gerda explained to the twins our plans. They were delighted at the thought of having a dog, living in the country; sharing a swimming pool with neighbours Jane and K-P's children, was the icing on the top of the cake. We didn't tell them that they might have a baby brother or sister to look after as well.

By the time we returned to my parents it was nearly nine o'clock, and my father had breakfast prepared for us. Names of their own dog were fiercely debated over the breakfast table, and the decision was made that an English spaniel was the breed of choice, with my father agreeing to investigate where their neighbour had bought their dog. As a birthday treat

Gerda had planned a girlie day for her and my mother with a trip to Norwich, shopping in the morning, lunch and then relaxation at a spa in the afternoon. My father had volunteered to drive them to Norwich so they could enjoy a drink over lunch. There was a new Disney film that had just opened and he was going to take the twins. He asked if I wanted to join them but I declined as I wanted to go for a long run. Age and sitting behind a desk far too long was taking its toll, and one of the benefits of moving into the country was to try and reverse the onset of middle age spread. Today was going to be the start of my new regime.

After I was alone in the house I checked my e-mails, but there was very little of any consequence. A lot of people had taken advantage of the long weekend and decided to have the Friday as a holiday. Gupta sent out warning e-mails that JPG's systems would be unavailable from Friday evening – eight o'clock – until six o'clock Tuesday morning while the Disaster Recovery test was run. Obviously Eric wished to have the maximum time available for his team to investigate the breach into JPG's systems. Even though it was the weekend I fired off a couple of e-mails from my personal account, one to my lawyer and the other to my estate agent, asking how plans with The Hall had progressed in the last week. I didn't want any delays now we had told the twins.

I decided to drive to Holkham, near Sandringham House, where I could park the car and have an enjoyable long run through the woods onto the beach and back again. Holkham beach is one of a few on the North Norfolk coast where the tide goes out a very long way. If you are caught when the tide turns there can be disastrous consequences and it is not unusual for people to tragically lose their lives by drowning. I made sure that the tide was going to still be going out when I estimated I would arrive at the beach. The weather had changed from the day before; it was cloudy and there was a breeze blowing. I really disliked running in the wind. I didn't mind the rain – up to a point – but the wind was unforgiving. I thought that I might be sharing Holkham beach with people for whom the wind was welcome. Many years previously Prince Charles in his youth had sailed a land yacht on Holkham beach. Nowadays land yachts had been replaced by long-boards and kites.

It was just after eleven when I parked the Audi. I jogged through the woods and felt really good, bouncing along unaffected by the elements. As soon as I left the shelter of the woods however the wind hit me in the face. The breeze of earlier had freshened and it was now quite stiff. Undeterred I ploughed on and, as I ran along the solid sand towards the water's edge, the wind hindered my progress. The weather had obviously put off the fair weather walkers, as I passed far fewer than I was expecting, most of them scuttling away from the water back to their cars. There were only a couple of long-boarders with kites, and they too were struggling with the windy conditions. Onwards I ran and when I turned to run parallel with the foam there was only slight relief. I convinced myself that my return journey would be a lot easier, with the wind behind me. I had been running for well over half an hour by the time I turned for the return journey. I couldn't see anyone else on the beach as I retraced my steps in the opposite direction. The wind was definitely stronger and I had difficulty keeping my balance when it was blowing from left to right. Halfway along the water's edge I conceded defeat and turned away from the water to run a diagonal line to where I joined the beach. Whilst the wind was not directly behind me, the difference was immediate and my stride lengthened.

With the struggle against the wind won, I relaxed and started to turn the events of the previous month over in my mind. Why had JPG been targeted? I didn't even know about Dominic de Silva's heritage, so how had he linked up with the underwriters in Lloyd's who were perpetrating this fraudulent activity? Had I really been so obnoxious that someone would single me out. I couldn't think of anyone, but it obviously was the case as Carla held a major grudge against me. Also the violence associated with the criminal activity didn't seem to fit with people operating in the shadows in the London Insurance Market. If anything they would want everything kept quiet.

Before I knew it, I had reached the woods, and the effects of the wind diminished palpably. I decided to run a loop of the woods before returning to my car, and in the quietness of the woods a thought came to me that perhaps de Silva had started out as the vassel of the Lloyd's underwriters, but overtime the tables turned and he became the driving force behind the robberies and abductions. I thought about the scene in the warehouse when Krishna flipped; we had thought it was because of her incarceration, but de Sliva was very confident. Perhaps he was about to divulge some information and Krishna wanted to stop him.

I was cutting across from one path to another, dodging the trees as I did so. I was just making such a manoeuvre when I heard something behind me and as I turned my head......

"Marc! Marc, wake up." It was a man's voice. It sounded vaguely familiar but I could not place it.

I moaned, my head was splitting.

"Don't move Marc." The voice was reassuring, commanding, but still I couldn't recognise it.

I felt cold water being poured over my head and left eye. "Ow!" I yelled, not from the shock of the cold water but from the pain in my head when I recoiled from the water.

"Sorry, I am trying to clean up the blood from the back of your head which has also run into your eyes."

"Who are you?" I asked.

"Simon," was his reply.

"Simon, what are you doing here?"

"Keeping an eye on you, but not very successfully."

"Why?"

"I will tell you later." He continued to pour water over my head and face.

"I think I must have run into a branch".

"Hmm," was the non-committal reply from Simon "can you open your eyes now?"

After a bit of a struggle I opened my eyelids. I looked at my watch to try and focus and when I did so I saw that it was after two o'clock. "I have been out for a couple for hours."

"Yes," Simon agreed with me.

I shivered, I was very cold.

Simon took off his padded jacket and put it over me. I tried to sit up but he put his hand on my shoulder. "Stay there until the ambulance arrives."

"What?"

"I called an ambulance as soon as I found you, about twenty minutes ago. After I checked you were alive I decided to leave you unconscious until you started to stir. I think we need to check that you do not have a fractured skull."

"Can I have some of that water?" I was very thirsty.

"I saw you come back into the woods but when you didn't make a reappearance at your car, I started to look for you. It was only luck that I saw you. I had been around the woods twice. I just happened to go off the path as there is a rise over there" he pointed into the distance but as I was not allowed to move it meant little to me "and then I saw your legs."

I said nothing as all the questions crowded into my head.

"And here is the branch you ran into." He picked up a branch as thick as my forearm and about the same length. It had not been attached to a tree when I hit it; or more precisely when it hit me.

Another twenty minutes elapsed and I could hear the sound of sirens wailing. Simon's phone rang and he was told to keep on the line as the medic made his way towards us. A couple of minutes later I heard a motorcycle close by. Its engine cut and a paramedic joined us. He gently felt my head, asked me a number of inane questions, and then asked me to slowly sit up. My head was swimming and I felt sick but I did not pass out.

"Marc, you are very lucky, you were struck with great force on the back of the head. Had it been a couple of inches to the left you might not have woken up," Simon explained.

Gradually they lifted me to my feet and after a couple of ungainly steps I was able to stand and walk without assistance.

The paramedic gave me some pain-killers and dressed my wound. He then gave Simon and me a lecture about what to do after concussion. I wouldn't be able to drive for a few days, I shouldn't watch television for twenty-four hours and no work for three days; very limited exercise, and if the headaches don't clear I should go to hospital. He explained that this was the normal procedure for concussion in sports injuries. Neither Simon nor I enlightened him on the fact that I had been attacked. He followed us on his motorcycle to the car park, and I saw the ubiquitous black mini-van parked next to my Audi. Once alone in my car I asked him why he was watching me.

He thought for a moment before speaking. "Two of the underwriters who were under suspicion were found dead at the bottom of Beachy Head."

"When?"

"Friday evening. They had both left work at lunchtime on Friday, apparently for a business meeting. Both live near to the South Downs".

I said nothing.

"Eric and I are worried that someone is trying to cover their tracks. He sent me here and Nobby is shadowing K-P."

"K-P's abroad."

"Yes, we know."

"How?"

"It's not only hacktivists who can spy on people." Simon explained that they had been tracking our mobile phones since Thursday, and now Nobby is enjoying a few days in France.

I wasn't altogether comfortable with that thought but it probably saved my life, and I smiled at the thought of Nobby trying to be discrete at Euro Disney.

"Why didn't whoever hit me not finish me off?" I asked.

"Good question. Your blood had been wiped off the branch I showed you, and some smeared on the trunk of a tree next to where you lay, but it was all wrong. Very amateurish as there was no flesh on the tree, I looked while I waited for the ambulance. They wanted to portray it as an accident."

"Simon, what is your real name?" I asked.

"Simon," he replied.

Mum's birthday

Simon returned me to my parents in my car. I called him a taxi, so he could collect his own car. Afterwards he would drive back to a local hotel where he was already staying, and frequented by bird watchers in Titchwell. Before leaving me to explain my bump, he advised me to wear my Kevlar vest at all times when out of the house, here and in London.

I managed to bathe myself without getting my dressing wet, and shortly afterwards the house was filled with females who had enjoyed a good lunch and noisy children who were full of the film they had seen. I played down my bump on the head until I was with Gerda in bed, when I told her what had really happened, and that Simon was staying not far away. Gerda was no fool and had already worked out that my injury was more serious that I had been saying.

"Is Simon certain you didn't just run into a tree?" she asked.

I explained about the blood but no flesh on the tree trunk.

"I thought this was behind us. I allowed myself a small drink over lunch."

"Did you tell Mum that you think you might be pregnant?"

Gerda nodded "I thought it would be a nice birthday present for her. She was very happy for me, especially after losing Paul."

I smiled, at which point Gerda laid her head on my chest. I switched off the light and closed my eyes. The pain-killers were wearing off but I didn't want to disturb Gerda as her breathing gradually deepened. I lay in the dark playing over today's events, what was worrying was being watched by two people who I didn't see, but more importantly they didn't see each other. That was strange and a disturbing thought crossed my mind. Was there just one person? Was it Simon who knocked me unconscious? But for what purpose? To frighten me and then tell me to wear the Kevlar jacket to keep me on edge? Gerda was asleep and I gently placed her head on the pillow as I slipped quietly from under the covers. I went to the bathroom to fill my glass with water, and reached into the pocket of the hoodie I wore earlier, for the pain-killers the medic provided.

My hand also brought out my phone and I saw there was a message from Eric. 'Hope you are OK? Simon will be close by; his number is ...' I knew Eric well and could not believe he would wish me any harm.

I sent a text back to him 'Thx. Any idea who hit me?'

Almost immediately he replied 'No, but they must know the area well.'

I returned to bed and waited for the painkillers to take effect. I lay awake for another hour no clearer as to what exactly happened and eventually I drifted off to sleep.

I could smell bacon being cooked. I slowly opened my eyes. The curtains were still drawn but I could see that it was a sunny day. I reached across to my phone and saw that the time was after nine o'clock. There was no sign of Gerda and her side of the bed was no longer warm, which meant she had arisen quite some time before. I figured it was to keep the twins away from me so I could continue to sleep. I turned over and prepared to huddle down under the covers when I was aware the light on my phone was illuminated. I pulled it towards me and saw it was a message from an unfamiliar number.

'How R U? S.'

'OK.' I replied.

'I am outside watching the house.'

I was unsure whether the thought of Simon with binoculars trained on our every move filled me with comfort or trepidation. Whatever, it certainly meant I would not be able to go back to sleep.

I sat up in bed and put Gerda's pillow on top of mine and slouched back against them. The noise increased with the ring of the house phone, amplified by the fact an extension was in the guest bedroom, in which we were sleeping. I was tempted to answer it myself as the noise was aiding my headache's return. It stopped as someone picked up the handset downstairs. There was lots of hub-bub, and I deduced it was my sister in Australia wishing my mother happy birthday. Then it went very quiet, and a few minutes later, the door of the bedroom opened gradually and it was my daughter and Gerda who poked their heads around the door to see if I was awake.

"I can see you," I called out and the door swung back fully to reveal Gerda carrying a tray with breakfast.

"Open the curtains please?" Gerda asked Catherine.

"Where's Jack?" I asked.

"He's taken the dog for a walk with your father."

Gerda settled the tray on my lap and my senses were correct, bacon sandwich and coffee.

"Yummy," I said.

"How's your head Daddy?"

"A bit sore, poppet."

Gerda proffered two tablets in her fist. I took them, put them in my mouth and swigged the coffee.

"What's my Mum doing?"

"She has gone to see a friend who's preparing the food for lunch today. It's a lovely day and I think we will be able to take our food outside if we wish."

"Great. What time is lunch?" I asked.

"Champagne at noon, and then food at half-past twelve." Gerda replied.

"Any sign of my brother and his family?"

"They are staying in a hotel close by. I think he was a bit upset that we are staying here."

"How so?"

"I was talking to your father and he apparently overheard Joshua's wife say 'Marc's got more money than us, he should be paying for the hotel rooms'."

"Camila's chip-on-her-shoulder that Joshua is brighter than me always comes out at family occasions."

Gerda nodded "I know."

"Why does Aunty Camila have chips on her shoulder?" Catherine asked.

Both Gerda and I laughed.

"It is an expression," I explained to Catherine.

"What does it mean?" she asked.

"Come on Catherine," Gerda interjected "Daddy needs a lot of time to get ready."

I smiled at Gerda in acknowledgement that she had dug me out of a sticky situation of explaining my sister-in-law's jealousy to my daughter.

As I shaved and showered, I felt relieved that Gerda and Camila jogged along quite well, but even so Camila and Joshua's children - Freddie and George - were very much like their mother. They would eye our children's presents with envious green eyes, even though they were older than Catherine and Jack. We now made a point of not opening our presents at family gatherings.

I grimaced when I touched the back of my head, and I felt sure that Camila would be pleased about my discomfort.

I finished dressing and I made an appearance downstairs just after half-past ten, and almost immediately Jack, my mother and father all returned to the house at the same time. The noise level increased to an extent that, after saying good morning to everyone and wishing my mother happy birthday, I had to go into the garden. It was very sunny and warm and looked as though it was set to remain so for the rest of the day. Gerda came to find me.

"How are you feeling?" she asked.

I didn't reply and just pointed to my head.

"When can you next take some pills?"

"Lunchtime," I said.

"No drinking," Gerda chided me.

"I will just have a small glass to toast my Mother's birthday."

Gerda frowned "Why don't you go for a walk? It might help to clear your head."

"You sure that'll be alright?" I was worried I might offend my mother.

"Don't worry I will cover for you." Gerda smiled and went back into the house.

I went to our car and picked up a light blouson jacket that I left on the back seat the previous day, and then walked down to the end of the garden, heading towards the coastal path. I hadn't been walking for more than five minutes before I was aware that someone was following me. I turned and saw Simon dressed in a thick parka jacket, favoured by bird-spotters, jogging after me. I stopped to let him catch up with me.

"What are you doing?" Simon remonstrated with me.

"Going for a walk to try and get rid of my headache."

"Huh!" he grunted.

"Care to join me?"

"I have broken my cover, so I might as well," he conceded.

We walked together another five minutes before either of us spoke.

"Any news from Eric?" It was me who broke the silence.

"Possibly," Simon replied enigmatically.

"Well?" I retorted.

"I can't say anything but the net may be closing in on the ringmaster."

"How so?" I asked.

"I told you I couldn't say anything, so please don't ask me again."

We walked on for a further ten minutes and reached the end of the path. Where my parents lived the coast was muddy marshland, with thickets of trees interspersed with wetland fields. Ideal for bird-spotters to sit in their hides for hours on end. The birds were obviously protected, yet every now and again we could hear the noise of bird-scarers, where the farmers were trying to keep the birds from eating their spring shoots. We stood for a few minutes at the end of the path.

I said to Simon, "Shall we go back?"

The noise of a bird-scarer was much closer. I turned back to Simon and saw him lying on the ground motionless with blood running from his head. Instinctively I dropped to the ground. I was in the open and a sitting duck. I jumped up and ran for the nearest thicket. I was about five metres away when I was thrown to the ground by shotgun pellets. I scrambled to the thicket and was surprised that I wasn't hit by a second volley. My left arm hung limply by my side, but luckily the Kevlar vest had prevented a worse injury. I saw that I had also been hit in the side of my leg and I was bleeding. I looked over to Simon but he was just a pile of clothes. My mind was working frantically. The time between shots probably meant it was a single shotgun, and the fact I was not more injured led me to believe it was not a twelve bore but a lighter gauge gun. My suspicions were confirmed when two figures both wearing black ski masks, and one carrying a four-ten shotgun emerged from a thicket on the path, from where we had walked. They had obviously followed us and the figure was dithering, perhaps shocked at the fact they had shot two people.

I recognised my father's gun, and from the stature and indecision of the figure, I knew it was my brother who had fired the shots.

"It's over Joshua. I have my phone with me and I am calling the police."

He raised the gun and shot at where I had called out to him but I had moved. As soon as he fired, I ran towards him before he could reload. I shoulder barged him to the ground with my good shoulder. He dropped the gun. I picked it up with my right hand and threw it into the salt water by the path. Joshua was about to stand up when I kicked his legs from under him, and he fell to the ground. I jumped on top of him and pulled the ski mask to reveal his face. His face was red with rage and he struggled to get up, but my knees were pinning his arms to the floor.

"Get off him," came a woman's voice from behind me "or I will finish the job from yesterday, and cave your head in."

As I stood up slowly, I turned to see Camila standing on the path with a branch, very similar to that lying by me the previous day.

I nodded and spoke at the same time. "Joshua wouldn't have the balls. I should have realised it would need someone with your twisted mentality."

Her mouth became a gash when she shouted to me to shut up. Joshua walked over to where she was standing "What shall we do?"

349

"I don't know," Camila replied.

"Surely two minds the size of planets must have thought this through?" I mocked them. "Only an idiot like me would go charging in with no thought to the consequences."

I walked over to Simon's body and bent down to check his breathing. As I did so he whispered "Keep them talking."

I stood up "Unless I call an ambulance you'll have his death on your hands as well as Jimmy's, and your conspirators at the bottom of Beachy Head."

At the mention of Beachy Head, they stopped talking to each other and looked at me.

"That was a mistake. You frightened others who were involved and our little charade earlier this week has started to flush out the birds from their hiding and they're singing… well, like birds."

"It's over." Joshua turned to Camila.

"Shut up you fool. Say nothing."

"That's right. Don't say anything to incriminate yourselves. It's too late anyway. Dominique de Silva has told us everything."

"He's a liar," Camila said.

"Really, both him and Krishna?"

"He'll say anything to save his own skin," Joshua reasoned.

"Maybe, but someone who knew he had a grudge against me, as well as knowing Carla's feelings for me, had to be someone close to me. I just didn't think you had the guts for it Joshua. It must be that money-grabbing wife of yours. Her jealousy must have eaten away at her like a cancer to a point that you would even contemplate such a venture. You're both intelligent people, and that intelligence meant that you were almost undetected, but you couldn't resist only focussing on JPG risks. That was your undoing because even an idiotic lucky market trader worked it out. Your jealousy and envy was your blind spot, and what's more I recognised your voice as the one who called de Silva each week." I was guessing but the last statement seemed to hit the spot.

"I told you we should have been more careful!" Joshua shouted at Camila.

Camila swung the branch at Joshua and caught him full in the face. He fell to the floor and Camila dropped the branch shouting "Oh my darling what have I done?" and wept over his prone body.

I ran over to him and saw he was still alive.

A voice behind me was speaking rapidly "Please send police and two ambulances to this location to treat gunshot wounds and a concussion. I will leave my phone on." Simon stood shakily and walked over to Camila. "Mrs Edge, you will be arrested for assault and actual bodily harm to your husband, and he will be charged for the attempted murder of myself and Marc. I suggest you sit down and think very carefully about both of your precarious situations. Whilst you are in police custody they will also be questioning you about defrauding Lloyd's names, and passing on sensitive information to known criminals for the intention of robbery."

She sank to her knees stroking Joshua's face as he started to regain consciousness.

Simon walked away from Camila and I joined him "I feared when you first hit the ground that you were dead."

He looked over to where Camila and Joshua were sitting "Don't tell them, but it is quite difficult to kill a human at distance with a four-ten shotgun, especially when I am wearing a full Kevlar jacket." He opened his parka coat to show me.

"I saw you bleeding".

"The force of the shot knocked me to the ground where my head hit a branch. I passed out momentarily and when I came to I heard you knock your brother to the ground."

"You were expecting trouble," I nodded towards his Kevlar clothes.

Simon nodded back.

"Did you know it was Joshua?" I asked.

"We had our suspicions, and when you were attacked yesterday, Eric and I felt there could be little doubt. The person had to know the area well."

"What will happen now?"

"They will be arrested and Joshua checked over at King's Lynn Hospital, before being charged locally. We will be taken to hospital and, by the looks of your arm you will need to have some surgery, to stop it becoming infected."

"My poor Mother's birthday."

Epilogue

Lloyd's of London -
Three months later

I was sitting in the ante-room on the eleventh floor of the Lloyd's of London building, outside the opulent Adam Room that also served as the Committee Room where matters of state are discussed. And today was such a day. The fraudulent behaviour of certain underwriters was under the microscope, and I was due to be called to give my account of events. During the preceding six weeks, since I had come back to work after three operations on my arm, I had little contact with Eric and Simon. Relations had cooled significantly since I was paying for Camila and Joshua's defence to the criminal charges and the concurrent civil action.

As Simon had said, Camila and Joshua were arrested and bail was posted at five hundred thousand pounds for the two of them. There was no way they could afford to pay it as their house was mortgaged to the hilt. After the shock of the day's events, my Mother and Father recovered quickly to take care of Freddie and George. But the boys needed to go back to school, which meant my parents would need to stay in Camila and Joshua's house in Bromley. I felt somehow responsible, because it was my good fortune that had led to the resultant malfeasance of Camila and Joshua. I put up the bail and paid for the best lawyers that money could buy. I had also put The Hall up for sale, and pushed on with getting the planning permission for the two houses, one for us and one for K-P and his family, in the grounds of The Hall. The summer holidays were about to commence and I had decided to take a month off work, partially to recuperate, but also to move some furniture from our London flat and all the furniture from Gerda's flat in Amsterdam to Paul's old house in Texel. It would be quite a job for me as Gerda was now heavily pregnant. The children would spend the rest of the summer with Gerda in Holland, during which time she would organise the sale of her flat and obtain permissions and quotations for the building work to make the alterations to Paul's house. We decided to keep the flat in London, but treat it as a pied-a-terre rather than as the family home.

I sold the land in Zimbabwe and Goa, and donated all the proceeds to Save the Children and Oxfam, in particular for projects in India and Zimbabwe. I had all of these changes in mind before my Mother's birthday earlier in the year; however, after the events of that day, changed my mind with regard to Masterson Shipping and offered all my shares to the current management. I also introduced a share-save scheme at JPG, so the current staff could purchase most of my shares, leaving me with just twenty-six percent of the firm. With the majority of the proceeds from the sale of Masterson Shipping and JPG, I created a family trust for our three children, as Gerda was due to give birth to our third child in October. I also included Joshua and Camila's boys, and my sister's three children. If any more children were born to me or my siblings, they would also get an equal share. Hey presto, the cause of Camila and Joshua's jealousy had gone away. I also persuaded the Norfolk Police to reduce the charges of attempted murder to grievous bodily harm, but Simon declined to follow suit because I was supporting Camila and Joshua's defence. The remaining proceeds I used to set up a trust for Jimmy and Carla's son.

The door to the ante-room swung open and Eric walked in.

"Good morning Marc," Eric's tone was quite formal.

"Hello Eric," I replied.

We sat in an awkward silence for about a minute until Eric asked "How's Gerda."

"Very well thank you, and in the full bloom of pregnancy."

He smiled and then said "And how's your arm?"

"The physiotherapist has given me lots of exercises to do over the summer whilst we are in Holland."

Eric nodded.

"They think I will regain most of my movement, but the nerve damage means it will probably always feel a bit numb."

"Joshua did that to you, yet you are paying for all his legal costs and bail. I get that blood is thicker than water, but aren't you angry with him?"

"If there is anyone for me to be angry with, it is myself. My selfishness caused the rift, and after Joshua and Camila have paid their dues, the family will still be there, so I have to make amends."

Eric slowly nodded his head.

"How's the fraud investigation going?" I asked.

"Not good," Eric replied.

"How so?"

"A lot of the evidence is circumstantial, and Joshua's lawyer is very good," he shot me a hard stare "no thanks to you."

"Oh," was all I could think to say.

"Any civil action will be even more difficult to prove," Eric confirmed.

"But you have the passing on of information to criminals?"

"That's the circumstantial evidence, we can't prove who actually did it, and with de Silva dead it makes that possibility even more unlikely. Joshua's fancy lawyer has suggested our exercise is inadmissible as it was tantamount to a honey-trap."

I couldn't help but smile and tried to keep it hidden from Eric by coughing.

"Off the record what do you think happened?" I asked.

Eric paused for a number of seconds before replying "Oh well it will all come out I guess in court, and for my sake I would appreciate you keeping this to yourself until then?"

I nodded my agreement.

"It all started with a chance meeting between de Silva and Joshua in Dubai. Joshua was there ironically promoting the new insurance scheme backing the security qualification for Maritime Security Operatives. We think that de Silva had already been involved with some ship-hijackings. When he learned who Joshua was, we believe he stoked the antipathy he and your sister-in-law had for you, and put the idea into Joshua's mind that the information he had as an underwriter could be used against other insurers. We suspect it started slowly and then de Silva obtained enough evidence against Joshua, whereby he blackmailed them to divulge more and more information, so that major robberies could be committed."

"So de Silva was pulling the strings at the end."

"Yes, but we didn't realise this until after he had taken your children" Eric admitted.

"And Carla?"

"Yes, Carla. That was definitely Joshua's doing. He remembered her from when you were younger, and he introduced Carla to de Silva. It was de Silva's idea to infiltrate JPG's IT system."

"Did Carla tell you this?" I asked.

He nodded his head. "de Silva threatened Carla, to obtain the message you left for Carla, and that's when she took Johnny to his grandmother's."

Silence returned for a moment.

"How's Simon?" I asked.

"Fine. He's gone to Russia for a few weeks. We want to make sure that none of de Silva's hair-brained schemes to kidnap any competitors gets any traction."

"What's happened to de Silva's accomplices detained by the French police?"

"Still there, they're using their extensive Anti-Terrorism powers to keep them locked up," Eric replied.

"Forever?" I questioned.

"I think the French Authorities are going to make them an offer to return to Dubai, on the proviso that they pass any interesting information back to France."

"What about you Eric?"

He thought for a moment and was about to reply when the door from the ante-room into the Adam Room opened and one of the Lloyd's waiters asked me to join the Committee. I stood up and looked over my shoulder at Eric.

"That would be telling: How about you?" He smiled at me.

"After I am finished giving my statement today I am going to give this very expensive bottle of champagne to the concierge of the Grange Hotel." I picked up the package by my feet and walked into the Adam Room.

The Players

Marcus ('Marc') Edge .... *Managing Director of Lloyd's insurance brokers JPG*

Gerda Edge .... *Marc's wife*

Sgt Brian Smithson .... *Former Policeman*

Jack & Katherine Edge .... *Twin son and daughter of Marc and Gerda*

Knapp-Pahl Sethia ('K-P' .... *Friend of Marc and Lloyd's insurance broker*

Jane Sethia .... *K-P's wife*

Omar Aziz/Dominique de Silva .... *Former employee of Masterson Shipping*

Eric Jones .... *Claims manager at Neptune Re*

Jimmy Black .... *Lloyd's insurance broker at JPG*

Carla Black .... *Jimmy's wife*

Johnny Black .... *Son of Jimmy and Carla*

John Eastwood .... *Chairman of Lloyd's insurance broker JPG*

Paul van de Kohl .... *Gerda's brother*

Nobby Clarke .... *Former British Army Officer*

Andrew Vervy .... *Underwriter for Deeks Syndicate in Lloyd's*

Gupta .... *IT Manager at Lloyd's insurance broker JPG*

Julian Webb .... *Junior broker at Lloyd's insurance broker JPG*

Ben McKenzie .... *Claims Manager at Lloyd's insurance broker JPG*

Chris Worcester .... *Marc and Gerda Edge's solicitor*

Michiel van Joost .... *Dutch Policeman*

Joshua Edge .... *Marc Edge's brother*

Camila Edge .... *Joshua's wife*

Simon .... *Special Branch Officer*

Krishna .... *Cousin of Marc's former (deceased) wife*

First Bromley Coughlan novel

Scorpion's Tale by Bromley Coughlan
(ISBN: 9781449055974)

First novel that has been
burning a hole in the author's
head for a number of years

After a number of false starts this novel has taken five years to complete, written mainly on holidays or transatlantic plane journeys. Bromley Coughlan is a pen-name for the author, who has worked in the insurance industry - particularly Lloyd's of London - for over thirty years. Insurance is seen by many as a 'dry' and boring subject, and probably the reason why few novels have been written about the subject. However, the author has used the back-drop of the insurance market location and the people for his inaugural novel. Born in East Anglia, this region of the United Kingdom also features heavily throughout.

Set at the end of 2009, the book follows a tumultuous two-week period in the life of Marcus Edge. An insurance broker unjustly banned by Lloyd's of London, who is barely scratching a living as an insurance claims investigator. He is framed for murder of his arch-rival, and then goes on the run. Marcus Edge has to fathom the business intrigues of Sir Hugh Masterson, nicknamed 'The Scorpion', a wealthy shipping magnate, owner of a Lloyd's Insurance Broking firm and Marcus Edge's father-in-law. The story is a helter skelter ride of high's and low's, during which Edge has to unravel a number of mysteries to save his life and reputation.

Manufactured by Amazon.ca
Bolton, ON